# *AUDACITY*
## Privateer
## Out of Portsmouth

## Other Books by J. E. Fender

*Easy Victories* (Houghton Mifflin, 1973)
　Under the pseudonym of James Trowbridge

*The Private Revolution of Geoffrey Frost* (UPNE, 2002),
　Book 1 of the Frost Saga

## Hardscrabble Books—Fiction of New England

Laurie Alberts, *Lost Daughters*

Laurie Alberts, *The Price of Land in Shelby*

Thomas Bailey Aldrich, *The Story of a Bad Boy*

Robert J. Begiebing, *The Adventures of Allegra Fullerton: Or, A Memoir of Startling and Amusing Episodes from Itinerant Life*

Robert J. Begiebing, *Rebecca Wentworth's Distraction*

Anne Bernays, *Professor Romeo*

Chris Bohjalian, *Water Witches*

Dona Brown, ed., *A Tourist's New England: Travel Fiction, 1820–1920*

Joseph Bruchac, *The Waters Between: A Novel of the Dawn Land*

Joseph A. Citro, *The Gore*

Joseph A. Citro, *Guardian Angels*

Joseph A. Citro, *Shadow Child*

Sean Connolly, *A Great Place to Die*

J. E. Fender, *The Frost Saga*
   *The Private Revolution of Geoffrey Frost: Being an Account of the Life and Times of Geoffrey Frost, Mariner, of Portsmouth, in New Hampshire, as Faithfully Translated from the Ming Tsun Chronicles, and Diligently Compared with Other Contemporary Histories*

   Audacity, *Privateer Out of Portsmouth: Continuing the Account of the Life and Times of Geoffrey Frost, Mariner, of Portsmouth, in New Hampshire, as Faithfully Translated from the Ming Tsun Chronicles, and Diligently Compared with Other Contemporary Histories*

Dorothy Canfield Fisher (Mark J. Madigan, ed.), *Seasoned Timber*

Dorothy Canfield Fisher, *Understood Betsy*

Joseph Freda, *Suburban Guerrillas*

Castle Freeman, Jr., *Judgment Hill*

Frank Gaspar, *Leaving Pico*

Robert Harnum, *Exile in the Kingdom*

Ernest Hebert, *The Dogs of March*

Ernest Hebert, *Live Free or Die*

Ernest Hebert, *The Old American*

Sarah Orne Jewett (Sarah Way Sherman, ed.), *The Country of the Pointed Firs and Other Stories*

Lisa MacFarlane, ed., *This World Is Not Conclusion: Faith in Nineteenth-Century New England Fiction*

G. F. Michelsen, *Hard Bottom*

Anne Whitney Pierce, *Rain Line*

Kit Reed, *J. Eden*

Rowland E. Robinson (David Budbill, ed.), *Danvis Tales: Selected Stories*

Roxana Robinson, *Summer Light*

Rebecca Rule, *The Best Revenge: Short Stories*

Catharine Maria Sedgwick (Maria Karafilis, ed.), *The Linwoods: or, "Sixty Years Since" in America*

R. D. Skillings, *How Many Die*

R. D. Skillings, *Where the Time Goes*

Lynn Stegner, *Pipers at the Gates of Dawn: A Triptych*

Theodore Weesner, *Novemberfest*

W. D. Wetherell, *The Wisest Man in America*

Edith Wharton (Barbara A. White, ed.), *Wharton's New England: Seven Stories and* Ethan Frome

Thomas Williams, *The Hair of Harold Roux*

Suzi Wizowaty, *The Round Barn*

# *AUDACITY*

## Privateer Out of Portsmouth

Continuing the Account of the *Life and Times*
of Geoffrey Frost, Mariner, of Portsmouth,
in New Hampshire, as *Faithfully Translated*
from the Ming Tsun Chronicles, and
*Diligently Compared* with Other
Contemporary Histories

*J. E. FENDER*

University Press of New England
HANOVER AND LONDON

University Press of New England, 37 Lafayette St., Lebanon, NH 03766

© 2003 by J. E. Fender

Printed in the United States of America

5  4  3  2  1


Library of Congress Cataloging-in-Publication Data

Fender, J. E.

Audacity, privateer out of Portsmouth : continuing the account
of the life and times of Geoffrey Frost, mariner, of Portsmouth,
in New Hampshire, as faithfully translated from the
Ming Tsun chronicles, and diligently compared
with other contemporary histories / J.E. Fender.

p.    cm. — (Hardscrabble books)

ISBN 1–58465–316–7 (cloth : alk. paper)

1. United States — History — Revolution, 1775–1783 — Fiction.

2. New Hampshire — History — Revolution, 1775–1783 — Fiction.

3. Portsmouth (N.H.) — Fiction.  4. Privateering — Fiction.

5. Sailors — Fiction.  I. Title.  II. Series.

PS3606.E53A95  2003

813'.6—dc21      2003002729

To All Who Were—

And Are—

Involved in the Pursuit

of American Independence

and Freedoms

# *AUDACITY*
## Privateer
## Out of Portsmouth

## I

**G**EOFFREY FROST ASCENDED TO HIS QUARTERDECK IN A FAIR STATE OF CHOLER. THE ANGLE OF THE SUN'S SLANTING THROUGH HIS CABIN'S larboard quarter badge announced a time of the day closer to noon than the dawn, and no one of his crew had troubled to awaken him. His displeasure increased as he lifted one foot ahead of the other up the companionway leading from cabin to quarterdeck. Frost realized that he had slept the entire night in and had not awakened of his own volition a minimum of one hour prior to sunrise, as had been his wont virtually every day of the nigh on to fifteen years he had spent at sea. He studiously ignored the fact that his muscles were crank, and every joint in his body ached and complained with each step.

But Frost's nascent vexation cooled immediately he saw Marcus Whipple. His brother-in-law was seated in a hammock-chair suspended from the driver boom, a towel wound around his loins and another over his shoulders, while the half-Indian shaman-healer Ishmael Hymsinger knelt before Marcus and gently massaged oil into Marcus' withered, wasted feet. The chill westerly wind had raised gooseflesh on Marcus' hollow chest, though the gooseflesh did not conceal the fleabites scarring his hideously pale torso.

"Geoffrey!" Marcus cried in a thin, tired voice, "you've no idea how this sun strikes with such glory on my body and my soul. I remember not when last I felt the sun so."

Frost glanced skyward at the blackish-silver clouds gathered like a shoal of mackerel, reveling in the sun and the triumph of having freed Marcus and other New Hampshire men, a few Massachusetts men also, a total of forty-seven including Marcus, from their foul confinement in the British gaol at Louisbourg. The placid scene aboard ex-HM *Jaguar*, temporarily named "the cat" until he could think of a better name for her, could almost be an illusion. Frost could scarcely comprehend that barely thirty-six hours earlier he had taken a hesitant, frightened, and sketchily trained cram of farmers, petty shopkeepers, blacksmiths, cobblers, and coastal fishermen past the cannons on Battery Island into Louisbourg Harbor at the end of Cape Breton. Almost as incomprehensible had been his successful, although temporary, subjugation of the fortress's garrison and the destruction of the Royal Navy's sixth-rate man-o-war *Scimitar*, which had purchased the precious time necessary to bring the prisoners away.

Now ex-HM *Jaguar* and her freight of freed souls was safely offshore and south of Nova Scotia. For a few moments he could not trust himself to speak.

"The marvelous oyl that friend Ishmael anoints my feet—it is fragrant and soothing—what is this wonderous lotion?"

"Spermaceti oyl, Marcus, from the head cask of the sperm whale," Frost answered finally. "It is what the Wise Men should have brought the Infant Jesus rather than frankincense and myrrh."

Hymsinger was working the oil into Marcus' lacerated knees. The mute, horribly scarred Chinese mandarin, Ming Tsun, far more than Frost's body servant, sole confidant, and dearest friend in life, appeared with a pair of Frost's heaviest woolen stockings. Frost's eyes narrowed as he glanced down at the scabs, shot through with the reddish tendrils of past infection, surrounding Marcus' crudely severed Achilles' tendons at the backs of his heels. Marcus' tendons had been cut by that brute of a prison keeper, Whip Loring, as punishment for his attempting to escape the Louisbourg fortress. The method of the prison keeper's death had not been painful enough by half.

Marcus glanced down at his shrunken chest, scarred with fleabites. "I well appreciate your having caused all of us borne away from that heinous gaol to be bathed 'ere we were brought aboard. I ken these tiny animals that inflicted so much misery on us would likewise do the same to your crew."

Frost crossed first to the binnacles to check the cat's course: southwest by west and lying well into a larboard tack, with the wind coming almost directly out of the west. The notation chalked on the slate gave the last toss of the log as a comfortable six and a half knots. One point abaft the starboard beam and half a mile away, brig number 49 was steady on the same course, and holding company with her over an arc of slightly more than a mile were brig 27 and snows 52 and 71. Dios and the Golden Buddha, hold this wind fair and the cat and its flotilla of prize vessels would raise the Isles of Shoals and be well into the Piscataqua in five days. Five days in which anything could happen.

Frost minutely scrutinized the sail plan that Herbert Collingwood—his newly rated bosun now that the cat's regular bosun, Slocum Plaisted, commanded brig number 49 with a small prize crew—had stretched. Courses and top sails, and jib and fore staysail, though the cat was taut on a larboard tack with all sails drawing fully. The satisfaction of a rattle of spray thrown up and blown sternward as the cat confidently shouldered its way through a rogue wave confirmed that the cat was as well managed as he could have ordered himself.

"This breeze may be too frigid for your temperament, Marcus—perhaps the enclosure of the cabin with its more moderate temperatures would be more beneficial . . ."

"Dear Geoffrey," Marcus Whipple demurred, "please speak not of enclosures. My colleagues and I have emerged from a lengthy nightmare of dank, cold enclosures. This glorious sun draws out all the ill humors, pleurisies, agues, and arthritics percolated into our bodies in airless, crowded hulks and wet, moldy stone. Ming Tsun has indicated that he shall presently shave me, and earlier I drank a complete pot of your excellent tea, with wonderful bread freshly baked by your cook, more competent with one hand than sea cooks in the possession of both limbs and helpers I've shipped. Butter, fresh butter, from I know not where, and a hearty molasses! Topped off with more excellent tea! If I might have a blanket around my shoulders I shall want nothing else." Marcus paused. "I could want the company of some others shut up with us in Halifax. One in particular was that stout patriot, Ethan Allen, he who with a chap named Arnold took Fort Ticonderoga. But alas, he was to be transported to Britain, to be tried there, I believe, for treason."

Marcus smiled wistfully. "Others there were, too, who had been conveyed to Sydney, there to work the coal mines. Word reached us in Louisbourg gaol that all sent there found the work so dangerous and detestable that all our fellows enlisted in the British Navy. The greater sorrow to the British, since the mines were no longer worked."

"Being without coal was the reason the commandant of the garrison dispatched the wood-gathering and foraging parties that so aggrieved poor Caleb," Frost said. "I misdoubt that any coal or firewood was shared out to you."

"What little combustibles may have been intended for those of us in gaol was intercepted by Mister Loring for his own use and comfort," Marcus said, with just a hint of bitterness in his voice.

Hannibal Bowditch from Salem, Massachusetts, one of the three sous-officers or ship's gentlemen, appeared with a wood and canvas three-legged stool. "Perhaps you may wish to sit and gam with Captain Whipple," Hannibal shrilled in his absurdly childish voice.

"Quite right, Mister Bowditch," Frost acknowledged, taking the seat. "I would be obliged if you could promote another pot of tea for Captain Whipple and me to share. If by chance Cook Barnes has a heel of freshly baked bread remaining, I would not turn aside a well-buttered piece."

Frost read Ming Tsun's quick signing. "Ah, lay below to the galley, Mister Bowditch. Ming Tsun informs me that Cook Barnes has a tray reserved for me keeping warm on the galley stove." He took Marcus Whipple's emaciated left hand in both of his and squeezed it gently. "You and your colleagues shall respond admirably to all the ministrations of your mates aboard this cat, who desire only to know how to contribute better to your well-being."

Marcus Whipple answered with a barely perceptible squeeze of Frost's hands. "Faith, Geoffrey, everyone aboard this marvelous vessel has been far too solicitous and concerned about our welfare—well above our station, I assure you. We wish no special consideration. Being freed of the brutish treatment in that pestilential Louisbourg gaol is tonic enough, that and being Portsmouth bound to be reunited with our families." Marcus raptly surveyed the decks and sails of the cat. "Geoffrey, I understand from conversations with your fellows that in some wise you subdued this cat, as you style her—but candidly, I cannot fathom how you were so favored as to win her." Marcus winced as Ming Tsun began to wrap his ankles in strips of soft linen, crisscross fashion.

Frost twisted on his stool, nostrils twitching at the aroma he detected. Hannibal Bowditch was at his elbow, a tray held at arm's length. "Cook Barnes' compliments, Captain, sir, and here be your breakfast, with some manner of greenish leaf Cook says you particularly savor. A heel of well-buttered bread, and a pot of tea."

"Fiddlehead ferns!" Frost exclaimed. "Fresh fiddlehead ferns! They were being served out by Hymsinger and the woods-cruizers as anti-scorbutic for our lads released from Whip Loring's gaol! I had thought such long consumed!" He balanced the tray on his lap, picked up the chopsticks and selected a fern from the bowl. He chewed it with delight. "Elegant! Cook Barnes is to be congratulated for steaming the ferns rather than boiling them. The nutlike savor is much more delicate and there is a firmness to the fern that boiling would otherwise destroy!"

"Cook Barnes used some type of wooden contraption that Mister Ming Tsun instructed him in its use," Hannibal said. "It involved some sort of large pan of boiling water, these ferns, as you call them, being suspended like over the boiling water."

"An estimable way of preparing vegetables for the table, Mister Bowditch—a method of steaming invented centuries afore by the Chinese. I had forgot that Ming Tsun possessed such a device."

"Yes, sir," Hannibal said, rather doubtfully.

"Do you collect where aboard this vessel of ours there be slates stowed, Mister Bowditch?" Frost asked, restraining himself from devouring the fiddlehead ferns in one glorious paean to the palate of the epicure.

"Beg pardon, sir?"

"Slates, Mister Bowditch. And chalk. You will recall having used such to learn your letters and cyphers with a schoolmaster. Similar to the very materials upon which we periodically scribe the course and speed of this vessel."

"I have never remarked such," Hannibal said doubtfully. Then he brightened, "But I shall ask Nathaniel. What Nathaniel does not know about this vessel ain't worth the knowing."

"Pray proceed, Mister Bowditch, to query Mister Dance on the whereabouts of the slates used in the instruction of midshipmen aboard this vessel. And when you fetch the slates, fetch also Mister Dance, since he figures prominently in my request. And fetch also Mister Langdon."

"Mister Langdon, sir?"

"You may know him less formally as Darius, Mister Bowditch, but his true name be Darius Langdon. I trust I shall see the three of you on this quarterdeck within five minutes, equipped with slates, chalks and a thirst for knowledge."

As Hannibal Bowditch scampered away, Geoffrey Frost crunched several more fiddlehead ferns and luxuriated in the taste of the crusty, freshly baked bread, well buttered. "It is a marvel, Marcus!" he said. "Most naval vessels and privateers put to sea with hard biscuit only. And certainly we have a bread room so filled. But thankfully Cook Barnes is able to refresh us with newly baked bread! It is a marvel and an unutterable joy!"

"Yes, Geoffrey," Marcus Whipple agreed, "but you have yet to tell me how your captured this noble vessel."

Frost chewed the crusty bread introspectively and thought about the myriad mistakes and blunders he had committed in the course of the attempt to win the Piscataqua approaches scarce the month before. When he found HM *Jaguar* athwart the approaches, he should immediately have sheered off for New London and sought refuge with Esek Hopkins' fleet. He should never have jettisoned the cannon John Langdon so desperately needed for the *Raleigh*. He should have taken in sail immediately upon descrying the intensity of the storm from the south. He should never have sent Ming Tsun to the powder magazine. There were numerous other examples of his grievous errors in judgment, but these came first to mind.

"I made one fewer mistake than that very able naval officer Hugh Stuart, who commanded *Jaguar*," he said shortly and in a tone that clearly told Marcus Geoffrey Frost did not care to discuss the matter further.

"Stuart, did you say?" Marcus queried. "There was a British officer named Stuart at Breed's Hill. Geoffrey, my crew was with Reed's New Hampshire men at the rail fence to the left flank of the redoubt. Oh! If only reinforcement had come from Bunker's Hill! Our arms would have carried the day! This Stuart fellow, I collect him well, for he treated us captives with kindness. He ordered one of the soldiers under his command to give us water from his canteen, and insured our wounds were tended. I overheard him speaking to another officer; this Stuart called us a shrewd people. He called us artful and cunning as well. I believe he spoke with grudging admiration. Would these two Stuarts be related, do you think?"

Frost did not answer, for Nathaniel Dance, Hannibal Bowditch, and Darius Langdon appeared, hesitantly, at the top of the companionway leading onto the quarterdeck. Frost took a sip of his tea. It was altogether too cool for his liking. "Gentlemen, welcome all! Please gather 'round. Mister Dance, I am most pleased that you twigged the location of the midshipmen's slates."

"Please, sir," Nathaniel asked tremulously, "why do ye require us to attend with slates and chalk?"

Frost smiled: "Because we are here to observe able-bodied seamen matching the gulls wingbeat for wingbeat, Mister Dance, as we observed before Louisbourg. I fail this vessel and all embarked in her if I do not nurture into sous-officers those who have distinguished themselves in the vessel's service." He took another swallow of the cold tea and grimaced. But the fiddlehead ferns had been manna from heaven! And fresh bread betimes!

"Please, sir," Darius moaned, "I be ill-suited for this company . . ."

"Nor me, Captain Frost, sir," Nathaniel interrupted. "I be suited only for a powder monkey . . ."

"On the contrary, Mister Langdon, and Mister Dance," Frost said. "You have displayed great ingenuity, and daring, though fortunately well tempered with caution. Powder monkeys can be had in abundance, but proper sous-officers are an exceedingly rare commodity. I mark the three of you for merit, but advancement must come through application. And with application we begin. Mister Bowditch, you have the advantage of some years of pedagogy, so I shall of necessity depend upon you as a tutor for your colleagues."

"Please, sir," Darius interjected again, haltingly, "I be not fit for such preference . . ."

"Mister Langdon," Frost thundered, tossing off the last of the cold, cold tea. "Your actions, not my preferences, have singled out you and your colleagues as ship's gentlemen, appropriate for advancement upon the attainment of educations and experiences appropriate for your increased stations. It is not a matter of the stations being conferred gratuitously. Merit calls out for recognition." Frost smiled with his eyes and mouth and raised his hand to the ugly bruise on his left cheekbone. "Your triple-charged musket visited such devastation upon His Majesty's sixth-rate vessel *Scimitar* that, fearing greater injuries, her crew yielded to us."

"I think it was not triple-charged, sir, more like two . . ." Darius protested, though timorously.

"Whatever the charge, 'twas sufficient to shatter a sturdy musket stock built to withstand all the brutality inflicted by a British soldier." Frost winked solemnly at Darius to draw the sting from his words. "But Mister Langdon, you and Mister Dance and Mister Bowditch, I marked the three of you—and more, whom I have already advanced—as displaying initiatives. Your initiatives were of the reasoned sort, not foolhardy born." Frost handed each of the youths a slate and nugget of chalk. "Each of you bears the stamp of men who may someday command at sea. You three also have the makings of traders— we shall need traders after the Peace. Whether you shall or no is beyond my ken. But I know you shall not unless the three of you possess as tools certain rudiments of knowledge. Hence this schooling . . ."

"Oh, Darius!" Hannibal Bowditch interrupted, "Schooling be ever so much fun! Just wait until you see the beauty of the mathematics . . ." His voice trailed off as he realized Frost was scowling at him. Then he colored most furiously.

"The correct form of address is 'Mister Langdon,' Mister Bowditch, as you of course realize." Frost cleared his throat, arched an eyebrow, and glanced around at the assembled youths. "We shall begin with the apprehension of the alphabet and the numbers through ten . . ."

"Captain Frost," Marcus Whipple said in his weak, pain-wracked voice, "if you will but place the feet of these ship's gentlemen upon the path of learning, I shall be happy to take your place as schoolmaster. I must tell you that only by exercising my mind was I able to retain my sanity in that miserable dungeon under the afflictions of prison keeper Whip Loring."

"Verily true, Captain Frost," Ishmael Hymsinger interjected. "I misdoubt the number of times Captain Whipple and I cast square roots of the most obscure principal numbers, or engaged in the grand comfort of discussing Descartes . . ."

"Mister Hymsinger!" Frost raised his voice. But Marcus Whipple had grasped Hymsinger by the sleeve and pulled him urgently down to whisper in his ear that nautical convention generally forbade addressing a vessel's commanding officer or master until given leave. Frost began meticulously to form the letters of the alphabet upon the slate he held.

"Deck, sail ho!" the lookout in the mainmast crosstrees shouted down.

"Where away?" Herbert Collingwood roared.

"One point abaft the larboard beam," the lookout shouted down, "'n' there be more ahind 'em! A passel more!"

Frost continued to form the letters of the alphabet. He was only up to "M." "Mister Collingwood, pray maintain present course. Ensure that the captains of our flotilla are apprised of the sails to our south. But I shall be exceedingly busy for the next hour. Captain Whipple, I would be grateful if you would complete this alphabet for me. I collect that a few of these noble fiddlehead ferns still reside in this bowl, and faith, I have not enjoyed their like for more years than I care to remember."

**F**ROST SUSPENDED HIS PEDAGOGY FIF-
TEEN MINUTES BEFORE THE TIME HE
RECKONED THE NOON SIGHT WAS DUE.
"ENOUGH FOR THIS MORNING, GEN-
tlemen," he said briskly. He glanced at Nathaniel Dance,
whose slate bore scratches in chalk no wise resembling the
Latin alphabet. "Congratulations, Mister Dance, I believe you
have struck upon the runic alphabet of the Norsemen who
plied these waters hundreds of years betimes. I suspect the keel
of a Viking longship plowed these waters we now traverse centuries before the Spanish, the Portuguese, and the French happened hither. But the runic alphabet, though derived from
both the Latin and the Greek, bears little relationship to the
alphabet we study. Captain Whipple has graciously offered to
provide you three ship's gentlemen with additional instruction." Frost cocked an eyebrow at all three youths, dwelling
significantly upon Hannibal Bowditch. "This is a generous
offer that even one who previously benefited from attendance
at a private writing school would be loath to forego.

"Mister Langdon, I would take it as a great kindness if you
would fetch my sextant case from my cabin. After which you
and Mister Dance may, if you wish, take a telescope to the
mainmast crosstrees, then report to me the sails you descry.
Mister Bowditch, I know your inclination would be to join
your fellow ship's gentlemen, but I would prefer your assistance with recording my noon observations."

"Capital, yes, Captain Frost, simply capital," Hannibal Bowditch enthused, "I would indeed join my mates in the crosstrees, but I am bewitched by the sums we conjure from the sun!"

"Best shape a sharper point on your chalk, then, Mister Bowditch, for we must know our position intimately in these dangerous waters off New Scotland." Frost turned to his brother-in-law: "I thank you for all the instruction you can provide in the week before I land you in our dear Portsmouth, Marcus. These are likely lads all, and reflecting upon them in our old age will allow us vicarious lives."

Frost looked steadily at Ishmael Hymsinger, who was holding the pan of hot water as Ming Tsun plied a razor in the final stages of scraping away Marcus' beard. "I greatly enjoyed the bait of fiddlehead greens provided by your generosity, Mister Hymsinger, though I collect those I have consumed were all you were able to bear away from Louisbourg."

Hymsinger nodded warily. "I was able to secret only a small amount in a fold of sailcloth, sir, before we transported the infirm from the courtyard where we bathed and deloused them. I marked your liking for the ostrich fern but desired the bulk be devoted to the vitalization of the weak and infirm."

"Quite right, Mister Hymsinger. The taste of fern you preserved for me served as a gentle reminder of all the Lord's bounties. For that I thank you."

Frost turned to meet Darius Langdon as he hurried up with the sextant case. Frost threw back the lid and removed the sextant, instantly noting the ladybug gleaming like a bright gem against the dark wood encasing the sextant. He hastily closed the lid. "Mister Langdon, you will immediately return to my cabin. There you will carefully open this sextant case. You will espy therein a marvelously small insect known as a ladybug. You will carefully propel the ladybug into flight. You may use your breath, or the tip of a feather pen. In no wise shall you move the ladybug to flight by other means. The best place for this insect's repose is my night cabin. Do you ken?"

"Aye, sir," Darius said, not daring to wonder at the strange order of his captain. "Your night cabin the place of repose for this rare creature inside."

"A creature of exceeding good fortune, Mister Langdon. You have but to ask Caleb Mansfield. He will gladly attest to the virtues of this mild insect. I charge you never to harm any of its tribe."

"Oh, no sir, never in life!" Darius swore quickly. He wrapped the sextant case in his arms and beat a swift retreat down the companionway to Frost's cabin beneath the quarter-deck on which they stood. Nathaniel Dance was already standing by the starboard mainmast shrouds, a cased telescope looped over his shoulder, anxious to be aloft.

Frost cleared every thought from his mind save the care and meticulousness with which he performed the ritual of capturing the sun's reflection in the sextant's mirrors and magically fetching it down to touch the sea's horizon. He called out the numbers to Hannibal, who transcribed them in his small, neat hand. "We'll work our position in my cabin, Mister Bowditch, and measure out the distance from the nearest land by reference to the chart of these latitudes." Then to Herbert Collingwood: "Mister Collingwood, in five minutes' time please summon the two ship's gentlemen now aloft and bid them report their discoveries to me."

"Aye, sir," Collingwood said tautly, eyes moving involuntarily to the southern horizon.

Frost looked at his brother-in-law. Ming Tsun and Ishmael Hymsinger had transferred Marcus from the hammock-chair to a pallet. Securely wrapped in two blankets, his pallor shaded against the unaccustomed sun by a rectangle of sailcloth expertly rigged above the pallet, Marcus Whipple slept, his features composed in a beatific smile of incredulous peacefulness. Frost scowled. He did not know what the sails to the southward portended, but Dios, Insh'allah, and the Great Buddha, he would see Marcus and his fellow former prisoners safely delivered to Portsmouth. If he had to forfeit his life, he would do so willingly.

Frost and Hannibal had calculated the cat's position and

were measuring off the distance to the Nova Scotia coast when the polite tap on the cabin door that Frost had been expecting came. Frost nodded approval at Hannibal's casting of the reduction sums. There was far less than 1 percent variance between their independently reckoned positions, and while Frost would accept his own calculations as the more accurate, Hannibal's mathematics represented a most impressive achievement. Indeed, Frost would have accepted Hannibal Bowditch's calculations in preference to those of Struan Ferguson, his first mate who now commanded a prize crew in the accompanying brig number 27. "Please usher in your colleagues, Mister Bowditch," Frost said without looking up from the chart. In a moment the three youths were standing respectfully in front of his desk.

"Gentlemen, you shall henceforth sling your hammocks in the gun room, as befits your new stations as aspiring sous-officers. Mister Dance, I believe you have accurately counted all sails visible to our south. Think how much more valuable you will be to your mates when you can communicate that number in writing." Frost permitted himself a slight smile at Nathaniel's discomfiture.

"Darius"—Nathaniel corrected himself swiftly—"Mister Langdon and I counted fifteen sail, sir."

Frost scrawled the corresponding number in bold numerals on the reverse of the scrap of paper containing his reduction calculations. Both Nathaniel and Darius nodded unconsciously, their apprehension of the written number's significance dawning on both their faces simultaneously. "Have you a conclusion as to the identities of the vessels spreading those sails?"

"Brigs, snows, and various of merchantmen, sir," Nathaniel opined.

"My conclusion also," Frost said slowly. "I believe we have come by chance upon the convoy of victuallers from which our prize vessels were earlier separated." He cocked an eyebrow at both Darius and Nathaniel and indicated the chart spread on his desk. "Would either of you gentlemen care to postulate the position of our vessel?"

Both youths looked at the chart with consternation and, mercifully, a touch of chagrin. "I trust you see now the necessity of some modicum of educational attainment," Frost said dryly. "Celestial navigation, gentlemen, is the science of coordinating the trigonometry of a sphere to solve for distance, and time to solve for longitude. Regarded together, the correlated solution equals position. Mister Bowditch has reduced our noon sight . . ." He glanced sharply at Hannibal. "I took the azimuth, though Mister Bowditch was perfectly capable of manipulating the sextant, and I have confirmed his cyphers. His computations place our vessel at forty-four degrees and fifty minutes north of the equator circling our globe's middle, and sixty-one degrees and ten minutes west of a meridian bisecting Greenwich, England." Frost tapped the chart with the dividers. "That reading, which I confirm as most reliable, places us due south of the town of Canso, in Nova Scotia, just below the horizon to our north. So . . ." Frost paused for effect, "thanks to Mister Bowditch, we know our position relative to known navigational hazards. Without his mathematical and astronomical abilities, we would not know if our vessel were heading into the Bay of Rocks off the Isle Madame, or perhaps trending onto Tilbury Rock, where the unfortunate HM *Tilbury* met its demise during the last war. Gentlemen, before this cruize pays off in Portsmouth some five months hence, I expect you both to be capable of the same deductions."

Frost examined both Darius and Nathaniel shrewdly: "I take it that neither of you young gentlemen fault our derived position?"

"No, sir," Nathaniel blurted out, one hand darting out to the chart, " 'lest we know where off we lie to a certainty, we be laid 'cross the breakers sure. It be a prodigious task ye have set for us, but Mister Langdon and I, never fear, sir, we'll learn our cyphers 'n' make ye proud of us, sir, never ye doubt. We do ask yere understandin' 'n' all, whilst we learn."

"Thank you, Mister Dance," Frost said formally, "I've no doubt all three of you young gentlemen will apply yourselves with the greatest dexterity. May I suggest that we refresh ourselves with a turn on my quarterdeck? Mister Bowditch, I'll trouble you to fetch the code book Mister Collingwood so thoughtfully retrieved from HM *Scimitar*. We shall study it presently, for I am convinced a shepherd there be to this flock of victuallers, and such shepherd shall be flying a red, blue or white ensign and armed with cannons cast at an English foundry." Frost consulted the Kendall chronometer for the exact time. One hour past noon. It bid fair to be a lengthy afternoon.

As soon as Frost appeared on his quarterdeck, the woods-cruiser Caleb Mansfield, who had been aloft studying the sails on the horizon with his telescope, which had belonged to Frost's illustrious uncle, William Pepperrell, descended the lee main shrouds with all the care and both-handed caution expected of a person who would never reach an accommodation with the sway and lurch of a tall mast. But Frost mightily appreciated the effort Caleb had made to glean what information he could about the convoy into which the cat had sailed.

"I ain't never seed so many ships," Caleb said dourly when he joined Frost on his quarterdeck. "Whole ocean's covered wit' 'em," his jaws twitched, " 'n there be one 'mong 'em that be a warship fer sure. She be twice over our size. I reckon we'se got ourselves smack in the middle of the hull British Navy."

"More prizes for us to escort back to Portsmouth, Caleb," Frost responded with feigned lightness. "We are saved the tortuous necessity of seeking them out."

"I just as wise we never raised 'em," Caleb said. "No good'll come of it, I warrant."

"Poorly spoken by the conqueror of Louisbourg," Frost said, attempting to banter Caleb out of his funk. "For the nonce we appear as but five of their number. I ken this lot is standing in for Halifax, some one hundred and fifty sea miles to our west. We'll sail along as peaceable members of their convoy. Shortly before dusk we'll coalesce our flotilla and in the darkness bear away south and southwest."

Marcus Whipple suddenly thrashed violently on his pallet, threw off a blanket, and moaned, a low, lugubrious moan that ended abruptly as his body was wracked with great spasms. The moan was as despairing as any Frost had ever heard, alarming him greatly as he knelt quickly by his brother-in-law. He succeeded in restraining Marcus on the pallet, but Marcus continued to writhe uncontrollably in his sleep.

"Bring Hymsinger directly here," Frost ordered Caleb, deducing that Hymsinger would be better acquainted with his brother-in-law's malady than Surgeon Ezrah Green.

Frost experienced an eternity before Hymsinger arrived on the quarterdeck, though it took Caleb no more than a minute to locate and summon the shaman. Hymsinger quickly sat down cross-legged on the deck, withdrew a pipe from the deerskin bag he had brought with him, and placed one end in his mouth. No, it was not a pipe, it was a flute! Hymsinger blew steadily into the mouthpiece and moved his fingers up and down the flute's shaft, covering and uncovering the simple instrument's six holes. A sweet, clear, mellow tone emerged, lilting and soothing. Marcus continued to struggle in his sleep.

Then Ming Tsun was seated beside Hymsinger, bringing a *sheng*, a Chinese mouth organ, to his lips. Frost had heard the *sheng* only rarely, though he knew that Ming Tsun played the instrument for his own pleasure and sometimes at the request of the hands, when a cheerful hornpipe relieved the tedium and drudgery of work such as weighing anchor. Without hesitation Ming Tsun picked up Hymsinger's flute's simple melody, blended into it, and then amplified it, taking the lead from Hymsinger, who followed instinctively. The music of the flute and *sheng* was the only sound on the ship; all the crew had fallen silent. Marcus still moaned and struggled, but not as violently. Frost did not know if his brother-in-law's struggling was lessening from some influence of the music or because Marcus' frail reserve of strength had been spent.

And here was Nathaniel Dance on the quarterdeck, standing behind Ming Tsun and Ishmael Hymsinger. He hummed a low tune and looked inquiringly to both men. First Ming Tsun and then Hymsinger nodded, and Nathaniel began to sing in a low, tremulous, boyish soprano.

"Alas, my love, ye do me wrong—to cast me off so discourteously . . ." Nathaniel slurred the pronunciation of the unfamiliar word, but continued, "And I have loved ye for so long—delighting in yere pleasant company."

Herbert Collingwood cleared his throat as he quietly stepped to Nathaniel's side and joined the youth in the chorus, Hymsinger's flute and Ming Tsun's mouth organ carrying the ancient melody, though Frost considered it unlikely in the extreme that either Hymsinger or Ming Tsun had ever heard the melody before.

"Greensleeves was all my one true joy—Greensleeves was my delight. Greensleeves was my heart o' gold—and who but my Lady Greensleeves."

Frost regarded Marcus Whipple anxiously, but his brother-in-law had stopped struggling; he lay quietly on the pallet, his face no longer contorted, his breathing low and regular. Nathaniel and Collingwood continued through several verses of the "Dittye of the Lady Greensleeves"—though Frost thought that their last verse was the result of much extemporization—before they paused for breath. Ming Tsun and Ishmael Hymsinger immediately transitioned to another melody, Hymsinger once again in the lead, point, then counterpoint, exchanging the melody with amazing virtuosity. The music slowly tapered off and then stopped as both men acknowledged Marcus Whipple's deep sleep. The last fluid notes floated hauntingly over the cat's quarterdeck while they laid down their simple instruments.

"I believe you may remove my brother-in-law to my night cabin without disturbing his repose," Frost said quietly, loathe to break the music's spell, awestruck that such beguiling tones could have come from Ming Tsun's tortured throat, or that two antipodal cultures, so alien to each other, could breed men with the incredible gift of communication and understanding through music.

"I believe Captain Whipple's disquietude will lessen as our

voyage progresses, Captain Frost," Hymsinger said, equally quietly. "All of the prisoners suffered from evil phantasms and hallucinations, their minds driven there by the horrors of their gaol, especially the disintegration of their fellow captives, daily, before their eyes. Fortunately, this Montagnais Flute of cherry wood would offer solace, for it was the only specific we possessed against the troubled spirits pressed around us."

"A flute voluntary well played," Frost said, and then to Nathaniel Dance, "and well sung. Who taught you that dittye? Do you ken the words?"

"My mate, Townsend, sir. He taught me several tunes. We would sing them together for the diversion of our mess. Some liked it, some didn't. I fail the words, but the tune be most pleasin'."

Frost did not tell Nathaniel that the lyrics were not some innocuous swain's song of unrequited love but a plea to the bored mistress of some jaded late-sixteenth-century cavalier. Nathaniel would learn soon enough on his own that there were myriad lyrics to the tune, from the ribald to the sublime, but the tune itself was indeed exceedingly pleasing and given to improvisation. "A most meaningful entertainment, Mister Dance. It fed the soul as well as delighted the ear. Now I must ask you to ascend again to the main top and focus all your powers of discernment upon the ship-rigged vessel that has grown ominously larger three points abaft the larboard beam."

Frost had marked the approach of the vessel with grudging admiration. Instead of rounding up into the wind and tacking directly toward the cat, the vessel had broadened the reach of its current tack to point up by the thirty or so degrees necessary for the courses of the two vessels to converge sometime within the next two hours. The captain at her con was a right mariner. He concentrated on the code book in an effort to deduce a signal that would allay the suspicions of the vessel to the south, a vessel Frost had already marked with great certainty as a man-o-war, a sixth-rate at the very least. While he was studying the code book, Frost ordered Herbert Collingwood to broaden the cat's reach to starboard—not by too much, no more than three spokes of the wheel—not enough to be perceived as turning away from the southward vessel but sufficient to extend the leg of the hypotenuse Frost was mentally calculating, and to delay the convergence of the two vessels for another fifteen minutes, at least.

The sea shepherd to the south would undoubtedly be familiar with the sail plan and appearance of HM *Scimitar*, another escort of the victuallers, so Frost ruled out posing as the *Scimitar*. He consulted his brother Jonathan's watch and calculated that the southerly vessel would be hull up in forty-five minutes, within hailing distance by half-three at the minimum. And the days were long in these latitudes in the late spring. He sent for Roderick Rawbone, his taciturn master matross or cannons master.

"Mister Rawbone, if the warship to our south twigs our true nature we shall have a scrap for sure. Please ensure all cannons are properly charged and won't be found wanting if we need to call upon them. Congregate the crews, but slowly. Outwardly we must appear placid—no one must perceive us as a threat."

Frost felt anything but placid, but he kept his countenance inscrutable as he dispatched Rawbone on his task. He consulted the code book again. The code book contained a five page addendum, well thumbed, a table of Royal Navy commissioned ships and their cruising stations that was dated 1 April 1776, somewhat water spoiled in places and therefore difficult to read. He had noted at first review that the name of HM *Jaguar*, 18, had been annotated in the margin in a neat, precise pen: "ordered to join Vice Admiral of the Red, Gayton, on the Jamaica Station, with dispatches." The capture of the cat had been known to the anchor watch of the brig in Louisbourg Harbor. How had that man known? Had that knowledge come from St. Johns or Halifax and been current in Louisbourg when the small flotilla of four vessels had sought refuge from the North Atlantic storm? Did the fact that the list taken from HM *Scimitar* did not mark the *Jaguar* as taken mean that the convoy's sea shepherd was unaware of the *Jag-*

*uar*'s fate? Could Frost continue to impersonate the *Jaguar*? He was sorely tempted. The battle off the Isles of Shoals had taken place Easter week, scarce a month ago. Word could have reached Halifax from a spy in Portsmouth within a fortnight. Could word of the *Jaguar*'s capture then have reached Great Britain within a month? Frost computed that the sea shepherd's convoy would have been at sea since mid-April at least.

Frost shook his head in irritation: he had promised himself to interrogate Nathaniel Dance about the *Jaguar* and her captain but had not done so. Ordered to join Vice Admiral Gayton in Jamaica . . . While at the Jamaica Station word could have been received of the amphibious assault on New Providence Island. The Dear knew Hopkins had dwelt there long enough! So, gleaning the destination of the cannons taken from Fort Montagu, it would have been an easy enough assumption to plot the cannon for the Piscataqua and the *Raleigh*. And Hugh Stuart and his smart new sloop-o-war, flying the red ensign of his admiral, had been dispatched to intercept the old *Salmon* in the Piscataqua approaches.

Most unlikely word could have reached Great Britain. But how had the anchor watch known *Jaguar* had been taken? Could a tender have already touched at Halifax or St. Johns and communicated to the sea shepherd the intelligence of the *Jaguar*'s capture? Frost considered but quickly rejected all the vessels listed as being assigned to the North American station. Their collective identities would all be well known to their respective captains on the North American venue. He mused over a small group of five vessels listed as being commissioned for unknown destinations, and momentarily thought of selecting HM *Camilla*, 20, as being closest in size to the cat.

Frost shook his head and dispatched Ming Tsun to collect the portfolio of signal flags and the Royal Navy red ensign that had within the month draped the coffin of Hugh Stuart. Captain Hugh Stuart had left him no code book, but at least the code book taken from HM *Scimitar* listed the *Jaguar*'s number. With the assistance of Ming Tsun and Hannibal Bowditch, he laid out the signals in what he hoped was the correct order. He spared a glance over his right shoulder at the four prize vessels keeping station on the cat. How Frost wished for some quick and efficacious way of communicating with his charges! He had to outline at least the rudiments of his plan to his sub-captains Struan Ferguson, Slocum Plaisted, Jack Lacey and Daniel O'Buck. Though had he a plan or only a desperate gamble?

"No!" Frost commanded sharply, as the giant Newfoundland dog feared mightily by all the American prisoners in Louisbourg gaol but actually of gentle temperament once taken away from the cruelty of Whip Loring attempted to purloin one of the signal flags. The dog desisted and threw himself down beside a cannon. He rested his massive head on his equally massive paws, eyes rolled up to regard Frost quizzically. Frost scratched the dog's ears affectionately, then moved one flag above another on the quarterdeck. "I believe this grouping of signals to be hoisted first reads 'senior officer on board,' and this set of flags reads 'reporting Halifax from St. John.'" With the toe of his shoe Frost indicated the third cluster of signal flags. "And this is the number of HM *Jaguar*."

Ming Tsun signed, "An idea most brazen. Is there not among these British some special signal of recognition?"

Frost replied aloud for Hannibal's benefit. "Yes, I know there is a secret recognition code for use between British Navy ships to confirm identities, but it exists not in the signals text. Belike, the secret code was possessed solely by Captain Mortimer and Captain Stuart, and they are unlikely to share the secret." Frost shrugged. "If all appears normal when the British warship approaches near enough to challenge, we hopefully shall not require that knowledge. Mister Bowditch, I must ask you to undertake an extremely hazardous duty."

Hannibal Bowditch brightened perceptibly. "Yours to command, sir," he said simply.

"In five minutes I intend to fall off as we lay our ship momentarily on a larboard tack. Then resume the starboard tack. Select such men as you require to sway the gig overside to starboard, and properly crewed. Then pull for the brig, number twenty-seven, Captain Ferguson commands. Deliver this order first to Captain Ferguson, and sequentially to the other three captains. The last vessel you speak shall take the gig in tow and deliver you back to me."

"The order, Captain Frost?" Hannibal said enthusiastically.

"If the British warship to our south smokes our true identities, I shall draw her away. Captain Ferguson as senior is to hold our prizes together, cut south-southwest through the British convoy, and proceed directly to Portsmouth with all possible speed."

"Yes sir, Captain Ferguson to cut south-southwest through the British convoy, and proceed directly to Portsmouth with our prizes should you be compelled to draw away the British," Hannibal repeated.

"With all possible speed, Mister Bowditch," Frost emphasized again.

"Yes sir," Hannibal nodded soberly.

"Tell off the men you'll require, Mister Bowditch. I'll warrant you wish men with strong arms who shan't flag in their rowing."

Frost was loathe to send the youth on such a dangerous mission; the sea was deceptively calm, but he knew a spell of weather was brewing, and the hour before nightfall would likely see a shift in wind and, in all likelihood, a mini-gale. "Mister Collingwood," he addressed the acting bosun, "please send forward to inquire of Cook Barnes if he would be kind enough to lay on an hearty repast for our evening meal. I fancy we shall be in need of it."

## ❧ III ❧

⁂⁂⁂⁂⁂ HE SEA SHEPHERD WAS CLOSE ENOUGH ⁂ T ⁂ BY FOUR O'CLOCK IN THE AFTERNOON, ⁂ ⁂ WELL HULL UP, THAT HER SIGNALS ⁂⁂⁂⁂⁂ WOULD BE UNMISTAKABLE. AS THE convoy escort and largest warship, her commander had the right to challenge any unidentified vessel. Brightly colored buntings rose smartly up her signal halyard against the weather mizzenmast peak brail and snapped in the breeze from the east. The sea shepherd had a taut commander, Frost conceded grimly. Through his telescope he read the signals streaming from the halyard and then compared his reading with the groupings of flags in the code book. The topmost group was a vessel number: HM *Lark*, 32. A light frigate. The remainder of the message was terse: identify yourself.

Frost ordered the red ensign raised on the ensign staff and the composed flags, preceded by the number of HM *Jaguar*, raised on the signal halyard. "In for a penny, in for a pound," Frost told himself. "Senior officer aboard for Halifax." He mentally composed the response to the challenge he antici-pated from the commander of HM *Lark*. "Down signals," Frost ordered Nathaniel Dance and Cato Calite as soon as he saw the serried flags start down *Lark*'s signal halyard. He was tempted to order Nathaniel to drumble and respond slowly in a delaying effort but reckoned it better to appear as taut in his ship handling as any Royal Navy commander.

"Captain repair aboard" was the next signal raised by HM

*Lark*. Frost had expected it. He handed Ming Tsun the scrap of paper with the next order of flags to be bent on the cat's signal halyard. Ming Tsun strung the code together to spell out "Unable to comply—senior officer and dispatches for Halifax" as efficiently as any Royal Navy signals lieutenant. And Nathaniel Dance raised the halyard as smartly as any Royal Navy hand, which of course he had been.

The flags aboard *Lark* dipped and were smartly replaced by a single flag. Frost searched among the bunting laid on the quarterdeck for a similar flag and spied it. "Bend on that flag and raise it," he signed to Ming Tsun. Then, to his acting bosun, "Mister Collingwood, please be ready to order top-men aloft to spread canvas, though we shall do so leisurely." The single flag on the *Lark*'s signal halyard was a preemptory demand for the *Jaguar*'s secret recognition code.

"Down flag and repeat the last signal," Frost commanded Ming Tsun. "Mister Collingwood, stand by fore topgallant sail, lay aloft topgallant yardmen. Lay out and loose!"

Frost watched the fore topgallant and then the main top-gallant unfurl and slant with wind. The cat began to draw away from HM *Lark*, deliberately but slowly and, Frost hoped, arrogantly. He was gambling that the boldness of the move would perplex *Lark*'s commander enough that he would consider the cat's failure to respond with the secret recognition signal, and its continuation on course, to be dictated by a sufficiently high-ranking officer who superciliously wished not to be delayed by an inferior officer detailed to the unglamorous and ungrateful work of convoying a fleet of victuallers. Or, alternately, make the man suspicious enough of the cat to take up the chase, with Frost supremely confident in the speed of his vessel to outdistance the British warship handily. But Frost conceded that there was a third alternative, and the *Lark*'s commander chose it. HM *Lark* turned toward the four prize vessels.

"He would have marked the absence of those four vessels from the victuallers fleet," Frost mused to himself, "and quite rightly questions their return." Frost turned to his acting bosun. "Mister Collingwood, prepare to come about! Mister Dance! My compliments to Surgeon Green, and desire him to superintend the removal of our passengers from Louisbourg to a place of safety below our waterline. After Captain Whipple is removed from my cabin, please wrap our ship's chronometer in the mattress and sequester it in my wardrobe. As you pass our chief gunnery officer, please advise that if he can spare a moment to consult with me I shall be extremely grateful."

Immediately apprehending that Frost was readying the cat for battle, Nathaniel asked hesitantly: "Shall sand be spread on the decks so the gun crews can keep their footin' better if there be blood 'n' all, sir?"

"I don't collect we shipped such article, Mister Dance. I am aware of the convention, and it mayhap be efficacious on a large man-o-war preparing a protracted engagement. Such is not my intention. The trussed-up hammocks atop our bulwarks are as far toward naval convention as we can accommodate."

"Aye, sir," Nathaniel replied and turned to speed away, almost bowling over Darius.

"Mister Langdon, I would be obliged if you would inquire of Cook Barnes if he has immediate access to any pickled beef barrels. I would appreciate the loan of at least four such tuns."

Darius stood for a second, then bobbed his head affirmatively and sped away, almost bowling over Roderick Rawbone.

"Mister Collingwood, we are going to wear short a-round. Stations for wearing ship! Helm up and back the foreyards immediately. Helmsman! Being on a starboard tack, expect the bows to fall off to larboard, so meet her! Main clewgarnets and buntlines! Spanker brails! Lee crossjack braces! Haul taut!" Frost waited anxiously as his orders were executed. He knew what great strains were being placed on the cat's stays and spars as canvas was thrown flat aback, but he had to reverse direction in the smallest circumference possible. He waited, all in a lather, until his orders were being carried out, before turning to Rawbone.

"Mister Rawbone, a bag of nails atop every charge, langrage, chain-shot such as we have. We must concentrate our fire on the British warship's rigging and sails. We must wound her sorely there, or else she will maul us most severely between wind and water."

"Shall I order the cannons run out now, sir?" Rawbone asked anxiously. Despite the chill of the afternoon, he was perspiring copiously from his exertions.

"We shall keep our appearance as unwarlike as possible for a few minutes longer, Mister Rawbone," Frost said as the cat heeled over in her turn to starboard. He lifted his telescope for a brief observation of HM *Lark*, putting himself in the place of *Lark*'s commander, doing his best to think as a taut Royal Navy officer would think. The prospect of engaging *Lark* was daunting, more daunting even that the engagement with HM *Jaguar*. With *Jaguar* Frost had known he could not fight the ship, so he had determined to fight the ship's crew, and his plan, born of desperation and surprise, had succeeded, even though *Jaguar*'s crew had been a trained fighting force greatly exceeding his own.

But now Frost would have to fight the *Lark*. He had to preserve his vessel and the newly freed prisoners now sheltered in the scant safety of the cat's holds, and preserve his men on the prizes. So Geoffrey Frost was preparing to engage a light frigate mounting thirty-two cannons with his own paltry twenty cannons. He mentally calculated the *Lark*'s armaments. A Royal Navy light frigate typically would be armed with twelve 18-pounders, fourteen 12-pounders, and six 9-pounders on a main gun deck and the quarterdeck. Those combined cannons could throw a total weight of four hundred and thirty-eight pounds of metal. A full broadside would be half that, say two hundred and nineteen pounds of round shot. There might be a slight reduction in that metal if the *Lark*'s commander had two cannons mounted in his cabin as sternchasers. Frost reminded himself to avoid crossing the *Lark*'s stern. But any way Frost looked at it, the cat would have to endure the ferocity of at least fifteen cannons.

A full broadside of the cat's nine 6-pounders and one 9-pounder would be a mere sixty-three pounds. Frost was confronting a warship that could easily discharge almost three and a half times the cat's weight of metal. The *Lark*'s battery of seven 12-pounders alone could throw twenty pounds more iron than a full broadside from the cat.

Now that the cat had reversed course, Frost calculated the distance between HM *Lark* and his vessel as just on one sea mile. The breeze from the west was freshening, and with the wind coming directly behind, Frost judged the cat's speed at a few fathoms above eight knots. He would be well within effective broadside range of HM *Lark* in eight minutes or less.

"Mister Collingwood, for better visibility we'll need to brail up the main course, but not overly much." Then to the helmsman, a taciturn cobbler from Durham named Amiable Grossett: "Hold fair for yonder vessel's cutwater!" This business of fighting ship-to-ship did not appeal to Frost. He had to assume the British warship's commander now considered the cat a hostile vessel, but the cat held the weather gage and, approaching bows-on, the *Lark*'s commander could only guess down which side of his ship the cat would pass.

Darius, with a small gang of men with barrels suspended from their shoulders on poles and scissors, arrived at the break of the waist. "Mister Langdon, you and the barrels of pickled beef arrive at a propitious time. Capital! Please ask if Mister Rawbone can spare me a moment of his valuable time. Then I would thank you and Ming Tsun to display our rattlesnake flag. The British commander has long smoked who we are, and the sight of our flag will only confirm his knowledge."

"Ah, Mister Rawbone," Frost said when his master gunner appeared. "Staple some slow match to the head of each barrel, enough to smolder for at least ten minutes. You," Frost indicated the largest of the men in the gang holding the barrels, "Cronin Abernathy, while our master gunner is securing sufficient slow match, sling two of those barrels to the foremast brace pendants and raise one on either side to the fore yard. Rig the other two barrels likewise to the main yard brace pendants." A second later Joseph, Geoffrey Frost's youngest brother, who had deduced Frost's private revolution to free the American prisoners in Louisbourg under the guise of a privateering expedition and smuggled himself aboard the cat in a coffin, appeared out of the mass of men in the waist. Joseph held a tub of slow match in his arms. Frost's stomach knotted. Rawbone was quite rightly striding along his iron charges, exhorting the gun crews to finish loading the nails, langrage and chain into the barrels. Gathering up the slow match was a task properly delegated to his mate, a task, with his knowledge gained assisting Henry Knox in the gargantuan task of bringing cannon from Fort Ticonderoga, properly assigned to Joseph—another life particularly dear to him freighted on this vessel, now in mortal risk. Insh'allah. Joss. Dios.

"Geoff, what on earth . . ." Joseph began to his brother.

"Why, landsman, we are hoisting aloft two hundred-pound barrels of pickled beef with fuses to be lighted," Frost replied curtly. He hastened to salve the hurt he saw rising in Joseph's eyes and wished he had not spoken so sharply. "We know them to be beef barrels, Joseph, but mayhap the commander of yonder British warship will ken them to be combustible infernal devices, or fire carcasses as they are sometimes known," Frost said more kindly.

Joseph brightened. "A rap stratagem, right smart."

Frost winked. "A tactic, not a stratagem, Joseph, now be off with you to do your duty." He did not say how desperate a tactic he considered it. Frost raised his telescope and sought first the four prize vessels, finding them and noting with satisfaction that Struan Ferguson's brig number 27 was on a sharp tack across the wind in a southerly direction, the other brig and the two snows closely following. The flotilla of prize vessels was a sea mile astern HM *Lark*. He focused his glass on the British warship as the barrels of pickled beef and the rattlesnake flag rose on riggings and ensign staff. Frost sent Nathaniel Dance to summon his master gunner.

"Mister Rawbone," Frost said when the master gunner, face aflame with exertion, stood beside him on the quarterdeck, taking pains to include acting bosun Collingwood in the conversation, "the plan is a simple one. We shall stay course directly at the frigate. She can no more bring a cannon to bear than can we as we rush together so. One of us must presently turn aside for the other. It must be the Britisher. I expect she'll veer off to her starboard to lose way, thereby granting us the slight advantage of a mark slower than our own, and we must engage her, larboard cannons to larboard cannons. If she veers off to her larboard, then starboard cannons to starboard cannons. The Britisher will be firing into our hull, of that we may be sure. I do not know when he will choose to fire, but we must fire first—directly into his masts and riggings. We must deliver our full broadside first. We cannot risque having any of our cannons put out of action by the Britisher's first discharge. Whatever side we engage, immediately must our broadside be delivered. Mister Collingwood shall then bring us about and we shall engage with our other battery. Again, our fire directed against our enemy's masts and riggings."

Roderick Rawbone nodded his understanding. "A broadside it must be, since the Britisher will answer in kind and firing in rapid sequence risques the unfired cannons." Rawbone knew he was dismissed and hastened back to his station.

Frost studied his sail plan and computed the angles of convergence with HM *Lark*. Dios and the Golden Buddha, but he was going to demand a lot of this cat that was serving him so well. The strain on hull, masts, riggings and sails demanded by the maneuvers he envisioned would be severe. Would some crucial component yield under the stress? Would damage to a mast or yard cause a failure that would prevent a rapid course reversal into the wind?

"Two spokes more to starboard," Frost crisply instructed the helmsman. "Do not deviate directly from the Britisher's bowsprit." Again he calculated the closure rate: HM *Lark* was pointed as close into the wind as a ship-rig could possibly lie, and the cat was charging directly downwind at the frigate at a good eight knots. Assume a speed over the bottom of six knots for the frigate, and the two vessels were closing at the rate of some five hundred yards per minute. At this rate they would close the half a sea mile between them in slightly more than two minutes. Forward at the mainmast Caleb and half his *coureuse des bois*, woods-cruisers, were carefully ascending the ratlines to their fighting positions in the main top, while the remaining woods-cruisers were ascending to the foretop.

"And which way will you veer, my beauty?" Frost asked himself. HM *Lark* was holding firm on a starboard tack, and Frost thought the frigate would go broad on that tack. Without benefit of telescope, he could see the barbaric slate gray sea peeling away cleanly to either side of the *Lark*'s bows as precisely, mathematically divided by the vessel's fore foot. He identified the *Lark*'s figurehead: a crowned lion.

"All cannons out, Mister Rawbone! You may fire as you bear!" Frost shouted through his speaking trumpet and was rewarded with the satisfying thumps of gunports springing up as gunport tackle halyards were pulled taut in disciplined unison. The cannons' trucks squealed like piglets struggling to gain a place at a sow's teat. At their combined closure rates the cat and the frigate would smash into each other in thirty seconds. Frost glanced aloft at the beef barrels streaming satisfying tendrils of smoke from smoldering slow match. Now, which way would the frigate turn? For several dismaying seconds he thought *Lark* would not veer, and Frost composed himself for the shock of the two vessels' collision. Joss. But then the frigate pivoted ponderously around her rudder—to starboard! The cat's bows drew even with the *Lark*'s bows at a distance of fifty yards, just as *Lark* lost a slight turn of speed.

The nine larboard 6-pounders sputtered into a sullen broadside with slightly more than one second separating the first cannon to fire and the last. Frost heard the sharp crack-crack of the woods-cruisers' long rifles from the tops, and then the cat was racing alongside the frigate, Frost keenly conscious that Ming Tsun was standing in front of him, arrow nocked on bowstring. Then the larboard cannons of the frigate grumbled and a half-second later the devastating broadside pummeled the cat with the weight of some two hundred twenty pounds of iron lashing the cat's main deck. The air immediately filled with the despairing shrieks and terrified cries of wounded men, and Frost saw a cannon overturned, its crew thrown aside like so many child's dolls, and most of the larboard planksheer of his quarterdeck dissolved in a deadly cloud of flying splinters and saw-edged baulks of wood, one of which tore a large irregular hole in the spanker sail.

The swivel guns along the larboard rail and in the tops were coughing; lacking a target, Ming Tsun husbanded his arrows, though the distance of fifty yards between the two vessels would have rendered accuracy problematic. Then the cat's stern had passed the frigate's stern, and Frost shouted, "Ready about! Ease down the helm—helm a-weather!" Frost had determined to wear his ship rather than boxhauling in order to spare the strain borne by stays and spars when the cat's canvas was thrown aback. Frost's intent was to describe the smallest possible circle. "Brace in the afteryards! Lay the headyards square!"

The cat was coming about, not laboriously but agilely, and Frost exulted! "Brace up headyards!" The cat was pivoting on her rudder and coming bows on into the wind, and Frost spared a glance at the frigate. By the Great Buddha! The frigate's foremast was tottering, and the larboard mainmast shrouds had been severed! The cat was now close-hauled on a larboard tack and coming up behind the *Lark*. "Ease off," Frost commanded Helmsman Grossett, who had remained remarkably calm though a splinter had transfixed his upper right arm and blood dripped down the shoulder of his tunic and fell in bright scarlet droplets on the quarterdeck's planking. "Jib sheets, haul aft!" The frigate's larboard counter was looming up, and the crack-crack of the long rifles continued.

"Ready as your cannons bear, Mister Rawbone!" Frost shouted into his speaking trumpet. The cat was crowding the frigate, a smaller dog yapping at the heels of a much larger cur. The cat's starboard battery fired simultaneously, and the acrid, suffocating fog of sulphurous smoke engulfed the cat and Frost. Through a rent in the smoke cloud Frost saw the frigate's mainmast begin to sway as the deadly swarm of chain and nails clawed at sails and riggings. He instructed the helmsman to point two spokes higher, and the topsails flattened as the wind took them aback. The swivels on the starboard rail coughed, joined by the sporadic crack-crack of the long rifles. The cat was drawing ahead of the frigate as the cat emerged from the cloud of its own smoke to reveal the frigate coasting to a dead stop in the water, foremast and its sails collapsed forward, bowsprit broken and grotesquely askew. The main topgallant mast had already fallen, trailing over the larboard beam in a welter of canvas and cordage, and the rest of the mainmast was tottering, tottering.

Now Frost had to disengage before the *Lark*'s larboard cannons could be reloaded. "Ready about! Stations for stays! Ready! Ease down the helm! Let go the fore sheet and headsheets!" The sail trimmers were working frantically to bring the cat through the wind and onto a starboard tack to draw away from *Lark* as rapidly as possible. Frost added his strength to the helmsman's. "As soon as we're steady on the starboard tack, lay below to the surgeon to see about that splinter."

"Reckon they'll be plenty ahead of me, Captain," Grossett responded quietly. Strain came off the rudder as the fore course was thrown aback and the yards were braced up. The canvas filled nicely as the cat settled onto a starboard tack and accelerated away from the British light frigate. Frost spared a glance astern, fearful of seeing the glower of grayish-black smoke marking the discharge of one or more cannons. But *Lark*'s commander was evidently concentrating on saving his vessel's mainmast and must need every hand to reeve and splice.

Frost stepped to the breast rail, the first opportunity to survey the damage inflicted upon his vessel. The sight of the carnage struck him a physical blow. Dios, the Senhor, the Great Buddha, how could men have lived through the scything of the frigate's broadside that the cat had endured? Frost feared that many had not. He anxiously sought for his brother among the tumbled forms, some still, others faintly stirring, thrown about the main deck like dolls scattered in a child's tantrum. There was Joseph! He and Cronin Abernathy were assisting

Ming Tsun and Roderick Rawbone in taking wounded men below for Surgeon Green's ministrations. Insh'allah. One less worry to know that Joseph was alive and well.

Now where were the prize vessels? A sweep of the horizon to the south revealed several sails, but he could not make out which might be the two snows and two brigs of his small flotilla. Frost seized a telescope from its beckets by the Judas binnacle: "Steady on this course," he ordered Helmsman Grossett, then sought out Herbert Collingwood. "Locate the carpenter and lay below to learn the nature of damage to our vessel. Dispatch someone to retrieve those beef barrels; I believe their fuses have long consumed themselves." Frost made his way through the brief engagement's debris: gouts of wood and splinters and two overturned cannons, some cordage, deadeyes and blocks, to the mainmast weather shrouds. How long had the engagement lasted from the time the cat's first broadside fired, through the course reversal, the second broadside, and now the cat's speeding away on this starboard tack? Fifteen minutes at best.

He ascended the ratlines to the main top. All of the woodscruisers except Caleb, who was gingerly easing his way down the lee shrouds, had already left. Then upward to the main topmast crosstrees, where he seated himself and unslung the telescope.

Yes! Frost captured the four prize vessels in the ellipse of his telescope. The four were some three miles to the southwest, efficiently shepherded by Struan Ferguson's brig. He brought the glass to the Royal Navy frigate now well behind and out of effective cannon shot. The mainmast of HM *Lark*, less its topgallant mast and shorn of all its yards, was suspended at a forty-five degree angle to the ship's starboard, but it had not fallen. In its weakened condition the frigate posed no danger to the cat, and Frost reckoned a hard two days of work would be required to piece together a jury rig sufficient to get the frigate underweigh. He continued the sweep the horizon and stopped when he discovered the sails of a schooner coming directly out of the east.

The schooner was still hull down but evidently had the frigate well in sight, for the schooner was heading directly toward HM *Lark*. Frost did not doubt in the least that the schooner was a British warship, and after speaking the wounded *Lark* would be a bloodhound on his trail.

## IV

ROST PAUSED HIS CREW IN THEIR FEVERISH REPAIRS TO THE CAT AND LAY-TO IN A SULLEN, BUILDING SEA LONG ENOUGH TO COMMIT HIS DEAD to the mercies of their maker and the harsh Atlantic: Robert Badger, cordage maker of Kittery, Morris Chenowith, farmer from Newmarket, Thomas Garrigan, tailor from Newburyport, and George Pettus, carpenter from Portsmouth, all from one gun crew killed instantly in *Lark*'s broadside, and Timothy Gerrish, fisherman and farmer from Kittery, who had bled to death just as he had been lifted onto the canvas-covered table secured to the heads of two heavy casks that was Surgeon Ezrah Green's operating table. Another five men who had walked through the wall between life and death for Geoffrey Frost. Two men remained in the surgery below the waterline where Ezrah Green, Ishmael Hymsinger and Ming Tsun, now that Frost could spare him, labored equally feverishly to bring them back from the edge of death upon which they teetered so precariously following radical amputations. Another six men wounded severely enough that convalescence would be lengthy, and fourteen men with minor wounds such as the long splinter Ishmael Hymsinger had extracted from the shoulder of Amiable Grossett.

The butcher's bill had been extensive, and Frost soberly reflected that had *Lark* been able to fire a second broadside the butcher's bill would have been far heavier. He had directed the use of the best canvas from the sail locker to be sewn as shrouds, with two 9-pounder cannon balls neatly stitched without haste into a pouch at the feet of each corpse. He ordered the rattlesnake flag flown at half-staff on the ensign staff, and Acting Bosun Herbert Collingwood marshaled the crew into rough, though respectful, ranks. Frost read the same service he had delivered two weeks earlier over the body of Hugh Stuart, late commander of ex-HM *Jaguar*. Frost solemnly called off each man's name as the grating was tipped at the larboard waist entry and the canvas shrouded bodies of men who had been alive two hours before disappeared into the angry slate-gray sea.

Frost was gratified that no man raised his eyes to the eastern horizon, where the sails of the British schooner were visible in the fast ebbing light, until after the service had been read. He handed his Bible to Hannibal Bowditch, who, given Ming Tsun's service in the operating theater, had been entrusted to write down the names, occupations and home towns of the men who had died in his service. "Please dismiss the men, Mister Collingwood," he said to his acting bosun, "and bid them return to their duties." Then to Hannibal: "Deliver the Bible to my cabin, and place the list of the men who have performed their supreme duty for their shipmates atop the ship's log. Immediately afterwards, you and Mister Langdon please see to the striking of the rattlesnake flag and the lighting of our stern lantern."

Several of the crew within earshot glanced at him quickly, but Frost had never seen the need to draw men into his confidence unless he had ample reason and chose to do so. He knew from the reports of the lookout in the main topmast crosstrees that Struan Ferguson and the four prizes taken from Louisbourg Harbor had vanished over the horizon to the southwest an hour earlier. But this following schooner was a concern. It was small, agile and fast, and with its fore-and-aft rig could point much higher into the wind than a ship-rigged vessel; it would be well nigh impossible to run down in a chase directly into the wind. A vessel ideally suited for courier duties, peering into harbors, all forms of intelligence gathering. Yes, spying out and following a quarry, then stealthily slipping away to divulge its intelligence to those best able to capitalize upon it.

Frost did a turn around his main deck, admiring the skill with which Cato Calite employed an adze to shape and scarf a piece of seasoned oak into a section of bulwark sundered by the ferocity of the *Lark*'s broadside. He complimented Cato on his carpentry skills, meaning the compliment sincerely, eliciting a smile of gratitude from the man, and thought that, despite its innocuous namesake, HM *Lark* had sung a song of death and destruction to equal that of any harpy. The cat's main deck was a shambles, and Frost considered it a miracle that his butcher's bill had been only the five men—though another two lives might well be added to the reckoning ere long. But the overturned cannons could be righted and their carriages repaired, likewise the bulwarks and the scored decks. The *Lark*'s gunnery had been well planned and executed, concentrated on his main deck and a few balls into his hull, though well above the waterline, already deftly plugged by the industrious and efficient Chips. *Lark*'s commander was a veritable tartar, and Geoffrey Frost was heartily glad that his losses had not been far, far heavier.

"Mister Ming Tsun's compliments, sir," Hannibal Bowditch said, interposing himself in front of Frost, "but Mister Ming Tsun came away from the lazarette long enough to instruct Cook Barnes in your dinner. It waits now in your cabin."

Frost reflected that he had indeed earlier directed Cook Barnes to "lay on a hearty repast for the evening meal." There were now substantially fewer crew of the cat to enjoy it. "Thank you, Mister Bowditch, it seems that I, alone of all this ship's company, have no task to occupy my hand or mind." Frost made one more turn of his main deck, noting how the sea was beginning to increase as the wind rose and a fine spate of rain began to lash from the eastward. He noted that the stern lantern had been lighted and upon gaining his quarterdeck glanced once at both binnacles, the cat's own and the one taken out of his dear old *Salmon*, to confirm the vessel's course.

"Mister Collingwood, I pray you keep our vessel upon our present course. I ken you have long been about your duties, and I believe Tilling Pickerel is fit to relieve you on the hour. You may sup at your position at the helm, or later, after you have been relieved."

"I savor the freshness of the evening, Captain Frost," Herbert Collingwood said, with a smile that was all but unseen in the darkness. "A plate of beans and salt pork washed down with cider as I continue our course will constitute a feast indeed."

"Hold yourself so," Frost replied. "Do you think you can retain the deck until midnight?"

"I'll hold it lightly, Captain, so long as your orders are to maintain easy sail, this course, and permit our men to carry out the emergent repairs so desperately needed."

"Reefs in the fore and main topgallants, and one tuck in the main course just now, Mister Bosun," Frost said. "Repairs on deck to cease with darkness, though repairs may continue below. I shall relieve you at midnight." Frost went below to his cabin, where Hannibal Bowditch helped him out of his wet coat. A brisk fire in the coal stove sent welcome heat into the small cabin. The Newfoundland dog followed Nathaniel Dance into the cabin as he brought in a tray of food. Frost snapped his fingers, and the giant dog lay down contentedly at the foot of his desk.

Nathaniel pulled the napkin off the tray and said in a tone of great disappointment, for he was still far more accustomed to servings of salt pork, pease, and hardtack, "Cook Barnes knows your diet as well as Mister Ming Tsun. He prepared a chowder—he called it a bisque—made from lobster he took from a trap in Louisbourg Harbor. The last of the bread, freshly baked, and a pot of the chocolate."

Frost went first to his night cabin, where he washed his hands and face, then sat down at his desk. He was immensely tired and pumped. "Thank you, Mister Dance. I need not remind you that when this bread was freshly baked, our number included five men who now slumber perpetually many fathoms down on North Atlantic sands, and a dozen others who have become intimately acquainted with pain of vast excruciation."

"Yes sir, one of whom includes yere brother, if ye don't mind my saying so, sir. Yere brother took a terrible concussion to the head when his cannon wus overturned, but he was on his feet helpin' others immediately, with no thought for his own well-being."

"As I would expect of any member of this crew," Frost said shortly, "and which you demonstrate admirably. I must sleep soon, but you are charged to awaken me thirty minutes prior to midnight. Then you shall oversee the return to my night cabin of my brother-in-law." He shook his head in disbelief. Little more than twenty-four hours earlier he had been sleeping soundly, with the great Newfoundland dog as his bunkmate, on the sole of this cabin. The world had altered considerably in those twenty-four hours, and men had died on his behalf. Frost consciously put those thoughts aside and poked a spoon into the bisque. It was exquisite. So was the heel of buttered freshly baked bread. And the chocolate was refreshingly hot and invigorating. He felt a nagging guilt about enjoying the food so. Dios, and Joseph and Mary, and the Prophet, but what he would not give to have Joseph, Marcus Whipple and the former prisoners in his charge safely delivered to his company's wharf on Portsmouth's Christian Shore!

Frost relieved Herbert Collingwood exactly at midnight in a heavy rain. He ordered all sheets eased and the stern lantern extinguished. Then he sent Darius about the ship to maintain light discipline, then to report on the condition of the men in Surgeon Green's lazarette.

"Surgeon Green sends joy for no deaths, and all wounds attended," Darius reported. "He prepares to sleep now, while Mister Ming Tsun and Mister Hymsinger stand watch in the lazarette."

"Thank you, Mister Langdon. Sleep should be your lot also,

after one further survey of our vessel to ensure we have no lights showing." Frost was left with his thoughts and the helmsman aboard his darkened ship, which was beginning to pitch and roll now that he had taken way off her. He mentally calculated the derived speed of the pursuing schooner from his last observation of her. He had estimated the schooner's speed at eight knots to his seven and doubted the schooner's commander would reduce sail after nightfall. Once he half fancied he saw a glimmer of light ever so briefly a sea mile or so off his larboard beam, though he considered it unlikely, given the heavy rain. Frost mentally summoned the chart of these waters, factoring in his knowledge of the currents and tides. The tidal ranges off the Nova Scotia and New Brunswick coasts were far greater than further south, and he had to keep that fact ever in mind. Frost mentally calculated the tide table for the waters east and south of the Bay of Fundy.

During the morning hours the helm was relieved every two hours. The false dawn found Tilling Pickerel as helmsman. Frost took a glass and very carefully made his way to the mainmast crosstrees, where he waited patiently for the thin, watery dawn to break and went over his calculations of drift, tide and wind. The horizon was limited by the rain, and Frost deliberately swept the glass first sternward, and then to starboard. Nothing crafted by human hands was visible. Then he shifted his scan to the larboard beam and continued moving carefully along the horizon to the southwest, pausing frequently to wipe the telescope's forward lens of rain. He saw the sail two points off the larboard bow at two sea miles distance. He judged the wind as coming directly from the west, and the schooner lay hard over on a starboard tack.

Frost was calling out orders as he descended the lee mainmast shrouds as fast as ever he could. "Mister Collingwood! Stand by to make sail! Set topgallants and flying jib! Lay aloft topgallant men! Lay out and loose!" Frost gained his main deck, then his quarterdeck, where Herbert Collingwood, hair all askew, stood alternately knuckling sleep from his eyes and shouting orders to the cat's topmen and sail trimmers.

"Man the topgallant halyards and sheets! Weather topgallant braces! Haul taut!"

Frost took station by the helmsman, hands clasped behind his back, watching Collingwood intently but trusting his acting bosun to order the precise maneuvers in the correct sequence. "Let go topgallant clewlines, lee braces, jib downhaul!"

Satisfied with Collingwood's performance, Frost turned to accept a cup of hot tea sweetened with honey from Ming Tsun. If Ming Tsun was fatigued from his long labors in the lazarette, or his lack of sleep, it did not show either in his face or his demeanor. Nathaniel Dance stood anxiously by, waiting to be noticed. Frost inclined his head once in Nathaniel's direction.

"Orders for me, sir? Shall I order out Mister Rawbone and the matrosses?"

"In good time, Mister Dance. For the nonce you may take possession of this glass, being mindful to keep it as dry as possible in this wet, and take care in cleaning the lens that you use only a soft cloth. Aloft to the mainmast crosstrees and there observe the schooner two sea miles away off our larboard bow." Frost peered closely at Nathaniel Dance. "You do have a proper kerchief, do you not, Mister Dance? A clean one, I trust?"

"No, sir," Nathaniel said, more than a little abashed. "It is an article I have always sadly lacked."

"Proper kerchiefs, clean kerchiefs, are ever the mark of a ship's gentleman, a sous-officer, Mister Dance," Frost said severely. "Please accept this kerchief of mine. But mark, you have prize money owing you more than sufficient to outfit yourself with a ship's gentleman's appropriate wardrobe."

"Where may I purchase such at this latitude, Capt'n, sir?" Nathaniel said, a touch defensively.

"Point well taken, Mister Dance. I ken there are no tailors, much less ship's chandlers, on the Isle of Sable. Until we fetch a port where we may take our ease, please send your fellow sous-officers to Ming Tsun. He will be pleased to advance one kerchief to each from my wardrobe." Frost looked down at the lad. By the Great Buddha, but he had neglected the lad in his relentless drive to get the cat ready for sea and away to Louisbourg. He gleaned that Mrs. Rutherford had purchased Nathaniel a decent pair of trousers, shirt and tunic from a neighbor whose son was serving with His Excellency, General Washington, as a musketeer. But Nathaniel stood in dire need of a pair of proper shoes and other clothes.

"The Isle of Sable, sir?" Nathaniel said.

"The Isle of Sable, Mister Dance, lies just below the horizon off our larboard bow. By noon we shall have smoked the identity of this schooner ahead, and if she be British, as I suspect, we shall check her career thereafter."

The cat was shouldering her way serenely through the swells, with courses, topsails, topgallants, jibs and fore topmast staysail completely sated and filled with air. Gradually Frost worked the cat around onto a starboard tack and began coaxing every fathom of speed he could from his nimble vessel.

The schooner was not aware that she had passed the cat during the night, and the bloodhound was being pursued by its quarry. Now that it was full light, the crew, driven by the fastidious carpenter John Brandon, known to all as Chips, was hard at work mending ship. Frost was munching on a piece of cold cornbread when Roderick Rawbone arrived at his summons. "Mister Rawbone, the odds are so overwhelming that yonder schooner is a British warship that I would fain take no money from anyone who thought otherwise. Please send to Doctor Green and ascertain if his patients will be unduly discomfited if we fire off a cannon ever now and again, and continue certain carpentry tasks." Frost finished the cornbread and began on a morsel of cheese to complete his breakfast. Or it would be once he had another cup of tea.

Rawbone went himself immediately to Ezrah Green and subsequently reported that Doctor Green, given the choice, would prefer not to discomfit his patients with cannon fire, but Captain Frost knew far more about these matters than he. "Mister Rawbone, clear away the first three cannon of the larboard battery. Please to skip a few balls in the schooner's direction whenever you feel a salutary result may ensue, though of course the range be long." The cat had narrowed the chase to one sea mile, and Frost did not want to dwell upon the devastation visited upon his faithful old *Salmon* by a cannon fired from HM *Jaguar*, perhaps the very cannon that would fire first at the schooner.

Frost watched Rawbone lay the first cannon himself. The driving rain had fallen off to a light mist, but the wind had increased somewhat, and the seas had quickened to three-foot crests. The schooner was well hull-up now, and Rawbone took his time adjusting for the roll, twist and plunge of the cat. Rawbone fired as the cat poised momentarily on a wave crest. Frost heard the shot and quickly seized a telescope to mark the shot. He did not manage to get the glass completely in focus, but he was able to mark the shot as short, and several hundred yards behind the schooner. Frost knew Rawbone had marked the shot as well as he, and he was content with the gunnery. He motioned for Darius, who was standing by waiting to run orders.

"Mister Langdon, I'll thank you to convey my regrets to Captain Whipple that I cannot wait upon him as yet, but please to inquire if there is aught he requires . . . And Mister Langdon," Frost added quietly as Darius prepared to scuttle off, "I would take it very kindly if you would inquire as to the health of my brother. I understand that he was concussed in yesterday's engagement."

"Aye, Capt'n Frost," Darius acknowledged and leaped down the companionway to the waist. Rawbone essayed another shot when he judged the moment opportune, and Frost marked the shot as still short, but less than a hundred yards behind the schooner.

"Deck there!" Nathaniel Dance called from the mainmast crosstrees.

"Deck, aye!" Herbert Collingwood replied.

"Land one point off the larboard bow, a low island most like."

Frost consulted the watch his mother had given Jonathan.

Later, if time permitted, he would check and reset it against the Kendall chronometer in his cabin. Nine o'clock. The morning was advancing. He referred to his mental table of tides and concluded the tide was just at its height.

"If I be not mistook, Captain, that land be the Isle of Sable," Herbert Collingwood said.

"Quite right you are, Mister Collingwood," he said, pleased at his acting bosun's deduction. Frost had always considered Collingwood to be a right mariner, and now that he had been given a position far more responsible than that of a helmsman, the man was confirming his beliefs. "The Isle of Sable is quite low, I do not believe more than seventy-five feet above the sea at any point, and long, lying as you know mostly east to west, with her shoals extending far out."

Herbert Collingwood sucked a tooth reflectively. "I ken a schooner such as before us would have a draught between seven and eight feet."

"If she has accompanied the British convoy all the way from the British Isles, running hither and yon as a tender and dispatch vessel, and eaten deeply into her stores, her draught would be nearer seven feet," Frost replied.

"Pardon me, Capt'n Frost, but I have not the advantage of knowing our draught exact, though I ken it be greater than twelve feet."

"Marvelous exact, Mister Collingwood. Laden as we are, we draw eleven feet, five inches afore, and twelve feet, five inches abaft."

A cannon from the larboard forward battery boomed again. The sun came out momentarily. Frost paced his quarterdeck, reached the weather mizzen shrouds, threw himself upward to grasp the ratlines as high as he could reach, and hauled himself up and down half a dozen times to exercise and stretch himself. Like a cat. "Mister Collingwood, please bring us a point off the wind. Close until we are half a mile from the schooner, but mind, no closer. We must not let her come onto a larboard tack. With her rig she can point higher into the wind and perhaps escape us can she but tack. I expect our master gunner to exert every effort to dissuade yonder schooner from any thought of laying about on a larboard tack. Her commander can do so, but for several minutes he will be completely exposed to our broadside." Frost was gratified at the bark of a cannon but continued to luxuriate in the pleasure of exercise, the warmth flowing into his muscles, the joints loosening and complaining less, and he took no notice of the fall of the shot.

## V

T HE SCHOONER STRUCK THE FIRST SHOAL AT THIRTY MINUTES PAST TWELVE, SHORTLY AFTER FROST HAD TAKEN ADVANTAGE OF A FEW MO-ments of sunshine exactly at noon to shoot the sun and fix his position, again checking Hannibal Bowditch's computations against his derivations. All the while Chips and his mates, bemoaning the fact they had gone through the scant reserves of seasoned wood, had carried on with minor repairs to the cat's battle damages. Ming Tsun and Cook Barnes used the time to bring up for sunshine and air the shallow, wooden, dirt-filled trays of just-sprouting vegetables kept in the galley.

Rawbone had maintained an accurate fire, slow and deliber-ate. He had found the range and angle and managed to skip three balls into the schooner's starboard quarter at the water-line. Frost had been pacing the lee side of his quarterdeck, watching the dirty slate-gray waters as anxiously as had thou-sands of other ship's captains around the treacherous Sable Island, so named for the color of its sands, scoured from the shallow bottom of the Atlantic Ocean and heaped here by the confluence of currents and winds. The color and turbidity of the sullen waters, with so much roiled sediments in sus-pension, made it impossible to gauge the depth. A prudent mariner having business near Sable Island would have hove to long before and sent a boat ahead with a sounding lead on a short line, perhaps even a sweep, to find the depth. But the slow, steady cannon fire from the cat kept the Royal Navy schooner, which Frost had definitely identified as such an hour before when the schooner raised a red ensign, crowded ever nearer the shoaling waters without benefit of such critical information.

"Thoughtful of the schooner's commander to identify that shoal for us so handily," Frost said to Ming Tsun and the three ship's gentlemen who were gathered near him. He whipped his telescope to his eye quickly enough to see the sails shiver and flog with the sudden arrest of the schooner's forward speed. But the force of wind trapped in her sails heeled the schooner far over on her larboard side, tumbling her people all "agley," as Struan Ferguson would have said, had he been there to see the schooner's strike.

"Immediately shorten sail!" Frost called out to Acting Bosun Collingwood. "We don't wish to follow the schooner's example!" He watched through his glass as the schooner was swept over the shoal by the press of wind in her sails and righted herself in the slightly deeper water beyond. "I expect she's lost her rudder," he muttered to himself. The schooner moved another hundred yards, much slower now, before she grounded on another shoal. Frost consulted his watch. An hour earlier he had confirmed it against the Kendall chronometer and had been eminently satisfied that the watch had been off only five minutes from the time he had last confirmed it, before going ashore at Louisbourg. He judged the mean low tide was just now.

"How many of your cannons are ready to give fire, Mister Rawbone?" Frost shouted through his speaking trumpet. He did not expect Rawbone, with his impaired hearing, to hear him, but those standing near would.

A gunner nudged Rawbone and repeated the question into his ear, and Rawbone shouted back, "Three cannons, sir!"

"Fire as they bear at your order, Master Gunner!"

Rawbone waited until the cat slowed perceptibly, then the three cannons spat their balls in unison, all three balls striking the schooner, armed with four cannons a side as Frost had long deduced, most likely 4-pounders. The schooner was vastly outgunned by the cat, the disparity being far greater than the advantage of metal HM *Lark* had over the cat. Still, Frost knew those popguns could hurt him, if the schooner's commander so chose. "Employ the rest of your larboard battery, Master Gunner," Frost commanded. But then he saw the red ensign start down the ensign staff. "Belay firing! Reload and run out only, Mister Rawbone!"

Frost pondered whom he would send over to take the schooner's surrender. "Mister Dance, have you any objection to crossing to yonder vessel and accepting her commander's capitulation? I propose sending you and a sufficient force in the long boat."

"Capitulation, sir?"

"Surrender. Her commander I ken will be a very junior lieutenant, and he may be somewhat surly at the prospect of surrendering to a barefooted lad, not even a stripling. If he is a gentleman about his adversity, you may allow him to retain his sword. If not, keep it for your own future employment. Sway out whatever boat the schooner possesses, and direct her complement into it. Permit food and water only—no, you may allow hammocks and sailcloth for shelter, but no arms of any nature. Bid them ashore on the Isle of Sable. Scour the schooner of all charts, logs, code books, arms, and valuables that can be returned to our vessel in the long boat. Then burn the schooner."

Nathaniel did not blink. "Yes, sir. Ashore the crew, scour for items of value, then burn the schooner. I would like to have Mister Ming Tsun with me, sir, and Tilling Pickerel, Cato Calite, Cronin Abernathy . . ." Nathaniel continued to name the men he wanted.

Frost noted with satisfaction that Collingwood had already given the necessary orders to sway over the long boat. "I provide Ming Tsun only reluctantly, since I am so accustomed to having him near. Your choices for a boarding crew are excellent. Serve out muskets, pistols and cutlasses quickly. Mount a swivel gun in the bows of the long boat, and keep the match well lit. You shall need such show of force, since I misdoubt the crew of yonder schooner will face the thought of a maroon with equanimity and may show argument."

Nathaniel Dance grinned. "Once the schooner's crew be embarked, sir, I'll comfort them with the thought that the smoke from their burnin' vessel will shortly bring aid."

"Precisely so," Frost responded soberly. "And that is why we must be away ever as quickly as we can. I shall work our vessel as close to the schooner as prudent, but haste you away, Mister Dance, for the tide is on the turn. It would not do for yonder schooner to float free and fly from us."

Frost signed to Ming Tsun, and Ming Tsun acknowledged his understanding.

"Mister Collingwood, jib and stays'l only, and two men in the foremast chains with sounding lines. Though the tide is on the rise, we shall lay to at short anchor when we find two feet of water under our keel."

Herbert Collingwood glanced at the shoals to confirm his amazement at his captain's accurate assessment of the tidal state, then bustled forward to supervise the placement of two men with sounding leads, and to prepare for coming to short anchor. The long boat, completely filled with grim-faced, heavily armed men and a properly fierce-looking Ming Tsun armed with his fearsome halberd, was already pulling away.

Frost examined the schooner carefully through his tele-scope, focusing on the person he took to be her commander. For a moment he felt sorry for the officer. His undisciplined eagerness to go baying away after the cat had been his un-doing. The moment passed. The schooner's commander had only himself to blame for bringing about this pretty state of affairs.

"Three fathoms to bottom, three fathoms straight down to bottom," the leadsman in the larboard foremast chains chanted.

"This will do, Mister Collingwood," Frost snapped, "please see to the anchor detail." Faith, he had no way of knowing how rapidly the water was shoaling, and Frost was decidedly uncomfortable with the cat's keel so close to bottom on an uncharted shore, especially what could quickly become a lee shore. The wind was still directly out of the west, parallel to the lie of Sable Island, though it had abated somewhat; his only comfort was the knowledge that the tide was on the rise. The long boat had almost reached the schooner, and Frost watched the schooner's crew carefully through his telescope as the long boat drew alongside.

The diminutive Nathaniel Dance was first aboard, followed by Ming Tsun. A moment later there was some sort of scuffle on the schooner's deck—the distance was too great for Frost to observe the details. But he did see Ming Tsun's halberd descend, and the rest of the boarding party swarmed onto the schooner. A minute later a few of the cat's men clambered back into the long boat, then members of the schooner's crew were being unceremoniously ushered—tumbled was a better word—into the long boat.

"Mister Langdon! Mister Bowditch!" Frost called. The ship's gentlemen presented themselves before their captain. "Spy glasses and into the mainmast crosstrees with you, and a careful eye all around," he commanded. The lads took off at a run, pausing only long enough to collect telescopes.

The long boat was full of men and cast off from the schooner, rounding its stern and pulling for the Isle of Sable. Frost fretted. The schooner was obviously without its own boat, so Nathaniel Dance was sending the schooner's crew ashore in the cat's long boat. If Frost had led the boarding party and found the schooner without a means of landing the crew, he would have locked the crew below deck, cast the cannons overboard and hacked away the schooner's masts, leaving her derelict and unable to harm the cat or another vessel of the United Colonies for a long time. But Frost had nominated Nathaniel Dance to lead the boarding party, and Nathaniel was exercising the authority thus conferred well within the boundaries of his discretion.

Still, it was Frost's nature to fret, though he concealed his agitation by pacing his quarterdeck calmly, hands clasped contemplatively behind his back, judging the first low spit of sand connected to Sable Island to be at least half a mile beyond the schooner. Fifteen minutes to pull to the island and discharge the schooner's crew—by the Great Buddha, had Nathaniel been able to send away all the schooner's crew in the one boat, while still keeping sufficient guard to prevent the schooner's men from taking the long boat? Frost calculated the crew of an armed schooner bearing eight cannons in the service of the Royal Navy would be no more than forty men. If that were indeed her complement, the long boat would have to make two trips. So be it.

Frost turned to Helmsman Amiable Grossett, who now that the cat was riding to a very short anchor had no duties. Acting Bosun Collingwood was still forward with the anchor detail. He did not have to glance at his watch to know the time. "Amiable, I collect our men require their noon meal. Report to Cook Barnes and ask him to serve the men's rations at their stations. Cider and small beer only, and I would appreciate a cup of tea if Cook can oblige with hot water." Frost paused at the breast rail and regarded the cat's main deck. Though the crews were lounging beside their assigned cannons, Rawbone was making another of his ceaseless rounds of the iron beasts under his charge, checking breeching cordage, oaken trucks securely fitted to their axles, elevation quoins in place, all loading equipment easily to hand.

Amiable Grossett hastened to the quarterdeck with a mug of tea. Frost thanked the helmsman. "After you have eaten, please ask our master carpenter to join me here." Frost sipped the tea. No honey flavored it, and the tea had long been in the pot, but the liquid was hot and otherwise agreeable.

Dios! The long boat had touched at the schooner again and was already pulling away—with more of the schooner's crew, and what appeared to be several provision barrels—toward Sable Island. That had been a very lusty trip to and from the beach. Frost saw Ishmael Hymsinger standing diffidently in the break of the waist and beckoned him to the quarterdeck. The man was marked with extreme fatigue, but he drew himself up to his considerable height and waited Frost's pleasure.

"You have a report of our ship's casualties," Frost said. It was a demand, not a request.

"All still live, Captain Frost. The two men with amputations and two others of our wounded are feverish, but I believe it is the desire of the Almighty that all shall live. Surgeon Green is presently asleep on his operating table, so overcome by his labors is he. I looked in a moment upon Captain Whipple. He had earlier been awakened by the cannon fire, but now he sleeps."

"A venue you must pursue," Frost said.

Hymsinger smiled slightly. "Once Surgeon Green has awakened." He knew himself dismissed and stiffly walked down the companionway. Frost watched the man's tired progress back to the main hatch leading down to the lazarette.

A shout intruded upon Frost's thoughts: "Long boat's castin' off from the schooner!" He made a point of turning slowly and handed his cup to Amiable Grossett before taking up his telescope. The heavily loaded long boat was moving away from the schooner with oars flexing almost to the point of breaking. Behind the long boat a faint tendril of whitish smoke arose, then the tendril grew larger and turned brownish-black, and then brilliant orange flames spurted, angrily licking upward at the flogged sails.

"Mister Collingwood, snub to the anchor cable!" Frost shouted into his speaking trumpet. The hands sitting or squatting beside the capstan sprang to their feet and leaned onto the bars. The schooner was completely aflame now, sails already consumed and the two masts appearing to writhe in agony through the heat shimmer boiling up from her deck.

"Stand by the stay tackle," Herbert Collingwood bawled, anticipating the order that Frost was about to give. Frost nodded approvingly; Collingwood was proving himself to be an able bosun.

"Mister Collingwood, jib, stays'l and fore topgallant loosed as soon as the long boat is secured to the stay tackle. Bows around to lay us on a larboard tack. Win the anchor and raise only after the sails are a-draw. I would appreciate a lead overside to learn our depth."

"Three fathom and the half," the leadsman in the larboard foremast chains called fifteen seconds later.

"If your wound troubles so that you cannot wrestle the helm, Amiable Grossett, tell me now," Frost said.

"Don't trouble none a'tall, Capt'n," Amiable Grossett grunted.

The long boat was less than one hundred yards away, and Frost surveyed it quickly, though the boarding crew was too densely packed for him to determine what kind of stores Nathaniel Dance had borne away. Behind him Hannibal Bowditch coughed quietly. Frost turned.

"Begging your pardon proper, Capt'n, sir, but I thought better to tell you quiet like rather than shout it from the crosstrees. Darius—I mean Mister Langdon—and I descried a sail to the north, well hull down, but her course appears to be southerly—toward us."

"Quite right, Mister Bowditch. Please fetch a piece of bread and a wedge of cheese aloft for you and Mister Langdon to share. You shan't have to importune Cook Barnes; he shall have it ready for you."

The cat had pivoted on her anchor and the wind was coming over her larboard bow, so the long boat approached the starboard entry. The boat touched and the boarding party began debarking, Ming Tsun among the first. "I did as you asked," he signed. "The shoes are somewhat large for the present, though he shall grow into them. He has two pair."

"What trouble?" Frost signed.

Ming Tsun shrugged and signed in return. "The fool of a commander did not wish a lad to accept his surrender. He and another behaved badly. The threat of the halberd—actually, the flat of it—reminded them of their manners."

Frost glanced at Nathaniel Dance, just clambering onto the main deck, and awkwardly holding a sailcloth bag, containing his newly acquired shoes, and a regulation British sea-service cutlass. Nathaniel saluted his captain with a bob of his head and a knuckle to his forehead. "The lieutenant commanding the Royal Navy's armed schooner *Walrus*, of eight 4-pound cannons, threw his sword into the ocean rather than give it to me, sir, but I fetched along the best cutlass I could find, 'n' the schooner's log, what charts she had, though not much, a sextant, no code books, 'n' . . ." Nathaniel said with a plea in his voice, "I fetched along a prisoner from aboard the *Walrus*, man who had deserted from the British Navy 'n' been recaptured." Behind Nathaniel a wreck of a man, who was saved from total nakedness only by a wretched strip of rags, weakly pulled himself through the entry and onto the cat's gun deck. He threw himself supine at Frost's feet and stared up at Frost with anguished, pleading eyes.

Frost quickly took in the man's gaunt ribs, thin shanks, and the large "R" branded on the man's right cheek, only partially obscured by his rank, filthy beard. In his time at sea Frost had seen the "R" for "run" branded on the cheeks of several other men who had deserted the Royal Navy but who were living comfortably out of its reach in Macao or the Dutch Cape Colony. With that mark this man was gallows bait, or worse, destined for a flogging around the fleet upon capture. A hundred lashes administered by a bosun's mate from every warship in port as the punishment launch made its way around the anchorage would lay the run man's back open to his nipples, killing him hideously long before the circuit of all warships would be completed.

Frost quickly took in the suppurating wounds on wrists and ankles left by the manacles that Nathaniel Dance had somehow been able to chisel off. Unbidden in his mind's eye rose the specter of the black men who had been brought up from the slaver's hold, the dead and the not-yet-dead, their hands and feet manacled . . . their eyes holding the same dumb, anguished pleadings as this wretch. His gorge rose, and he cried out so that his voice could be heard by all on the gun deck. "Behold, yet another example of the brutalities exercised by the British government that now bestrides the globe like a colossus; a run man, liking not the tender mercies of the Royal Navy, now branded as a felon and waiting only delivery to a courts-martial that shall surely find him guilty of rebelling against his sovereign, and so his life be forfeit! Mark you this man well, as you have marked the prisoners we conveyed away from Louisbourg. If you believe you can accommodate yourself to the yoke and chains of ministerial tyranny, throw this man overside. If not, throw overside his pitiful garments!" Frost glanced at each and every crewman within his gaze, completely unaware that his face was aflame and his countenance most horrible: they all, to a man, shrank away and avoided his intense, burning eyes.

Then to Nathaniel Dance, "We haven't time to rig a hose, Mister Dance. Scrub the fellow down with buckets of water from overside, and the soap of lye we shipped to scour the galley pots and kettles. Cut away that beard and hair. Once you are satisfied he harbors no lice or other pestilential creatures, take him to Cook Barnes and give him nourishment. Send for Hymsinger. He is sadly experienced in looking after men so treated. And fling away those rags! I'll not have such rags on my ship one second more! I'm sure there are many among us who'll gladly share a shirt and breeches for one so unfortunate."

And the skin and bones that was the released prisoner under sentence of death threw itself at Geoffrey Frost; the wretched man sobbed as he fastened his gaunt arms around Frost's ankles with an awful grip. "Gawd love ye, soir—be naught but a poor fisherman, Cricket Dalrymple by name, but this day ye save my life, 'n' I will gift ye a secret make ye wealthy as a prince, I swear it."

## VI

"**W**E BELIEVE IT TO BE A MERCHANT VES-SEL, SIR,**" HANNIBAL BOWDITCH AND NATHANIEL DANCE SAID IN UNISON.

"I BELIEVE I CAN RELY UPON YOUR combined judgments, gentlemen," Frost said. "Have you formed any opinions as to why she charges toward us so boldly?"

"I believe she be drawn toward the smoke of the burnin' schooner, sir," Nathaniel ventured.

"Exactly so, Mister Dance. Yonder approaching vessel possibly has had some sort of fright and flees toward us for succor. Back to your stations in the mainmast crosstrees, and keep me informed of events as you deem proper." Frost turned to Herbert Collingwood. "Mister Collingwood, I am going below to refresh myself. Our course is as straight toward the approaching vessel as the cat can point into the wind. Please summon me for a wind shift, or if the approaching vessel alters her course."

Time later to think upon the approaching vessel. Duty had kept Frost on his quarterdeck until the armed schooner had been dealt with, but now, despite the fact that he was completely pumped, he had the luxury of a few moments not given over to caring for his ship; it was essential to check on his wounded, to learn if he would have yet another New Hampshire or Maine man's body to commit to his maker and the eternal sea. And to gauge afresh the tenor of his crew. He signaled Darius to accompany him.

Frost's first call was the lazarette, where he was met by a very tired yet triumphant Ezrah Green. "I give you joy, Captain Frost; the two amputees survived their terrible ordeals, and barring unforeseen complications I expect them to thrive." Frost nodded gravely. "Survived their terrible ordeals" was a phrase most apt for pain-crazed, writhing, screaming men who went under the surgeon's knives and saws. And yes, the phrase "to thrive" was also appropriate, for he had seen many seamen with various portions of their arms or legs amputated, grateful nevertheless to have escaped the lingering, torturous death by degrees of gangrene. Their amputations had irrevocably changed their lives, but they had lived, and they had adapted, as witnessed by Cook Barnes.

"I amputated the right leg just below the knee of Amos Sherman, and the right arm just above the elbow of Barnaby Lucent. Their fevers have subsided. The other wounds mostly involved splinters, though one man, William Felton, was heavily concussed by some sort of fearsome knock," Ezrah Green paused to blow his nose noisily on the blood-stained apron he still wore. He shook his head in wonderment. "The poor dear's right eye was dislodged and suspended on his cheek only by the great artery and nerve that nourish the eye. I prepared to excise the eye away and cauterize the socket, but the giant Indian," Ezrah Green nodded his head toward Ishmael Hymsinger, who slept, curled into a warmth-conserving knot, on the sole beside a hammock in which one of the amputees, Amos Sherman, lay, "he dissuaded me. He carefully cleaned the dislodged eye and gently manipulated and introduced the orb back into its intended orifice, lubricating the eye all the while with his own saliva! A short while ago, when I removed his bandages, Felton exulted that he could distinguish shapes and shadows! I have never seen the like!"

"Thank you, Doctor Green," Frost said gratefully, "thank you and Mister Hymsinger. Doubtlessly the amputees cannot now be moved from your lazarette, but our other wounded may enjoy the late afternoon sun and air on the quarterdeck, where they will be away from the bustle of the gun deck."

"That would be appreciated, Captain," Ezrah Green said.

Frost turned to Darius. "Please make it so, Mister Langdon. Calculate the number of hands you will need to shift the wounded Doctor Green appoints to the quarterdeck. Remain to ensure our men's comforts are attended, and until Doctor Green dismisses you." It would do the men with lesser wounds a world of good to leave the airless confines of the lazarette for the sunshine and air of his quarterdeck—and it would do his crew a world of good to see how their wounded mates were thriving. As soon as he possibly could, he would have the prisoners released from Louisbourg, and the amputees as well, brought on deck, and he would order the lazarette thoroughly scoured with lye and sulfur.

Ming Tsun had a basin of hot water waiting in Frost's cabin and was stropping the razor, but first Frost looked into his night cabin, where Marcus Whipple lay sleeping. He brushed his teeth with salt and soda, then seated himself wearily on the settee and gratefully gave himself over to Ming Tsun's ministrations and a refreshing shave, marveling at Ming Tsun's deftness in avoiding the bruised area of his left cheek. He pondered the nature of the approaching ship while Ming Tsun plied the razor. When Ming Tsun finished shaving Frost, he brushed and reclubbed Frost's hair. Frost signed, "Please lay out my blue tai-pan's coat."

Ming Tsun moved about the cabin quietly so as to make no noise that might awaken Marcus Whipple. "You have taken the measure of this approaching ship," he signed. It was not a question but a statement.

"I believe so," Frost signed in reply. "I believe it will prove to be a merchant vessel, independent of a convoy, that has been affrighted. If the vessel owes allegiance to the British Crown, and if our joss is right, we may add her to our prize list."

"You know how the Dyaks capture the monkey," Ming Tsun signed, somewhat abruptly and therefore crossly.

Frost nodded before he shrugged into the coat Ming Tsun held for him, then signed, "When the Dyaks wish to capture a monkey, they take a coconut shell and put a light line through the end of it. They scatter fruits the monkey likes in the front of the coconut shell, and then put several fruits in the coconut shell itself. The monkey will find and eat the fruit. Not being satisfied with the fruit scattered as bait, and too avaricious to leave well enough alone, the monkey will put his paw into the coconut shell and enclose the fruit with his hand. The monkey will keep his paw closed around the fruit and will not withdraw his paw from the coconut shell, which entraps his paw. The Dyaks come and kill the monkey."

"When all the monkey had to do was relinquish his grasp of the fruit, and upend the coconut shell to spill out the fruit," Ming Tsun signed with particular emphasis.

"I understand your concerns well, my dearest friend in life," Frost signed affectionately. "And if I am tempted to entrap my hand inside the coconut shell, I shall depend on you to chastise me properly—and force me to withdraw my paw from the coconut shell long before the hunter comes."

"You are always ever so froward," Ming Tsun signed, before he fell to an industrious sponging and straightening of Frost's sadly wrinkled blue tai-pan's coat.

"The sooner this war is accomplished, the sooner we can resume our rightful occupations as traders," Frost signed with finality. He consulted his watch. Half past five in the afternoon. The cat would close with the approaching ship just at dusk. He took off the tai-pan's coat and lay down on the settee, then signed, "I can manage an hour's sleep. Awaken me then with tea and a biscuit. Awaken me also if another sail is sighted."

Frost was marvelously refreshed when he, attired in his light blue tai-pan's coat, mounted to his quarterdeck an hour later. The day was far advanced, lacking slightly more than an hour to sundown, but the approaching vessel was well hull-up, identifiable as a three-masted square-rigged vessel of substantial size, larger by far than any of the snows or brigs in the Halifax-bound convoy. She was not as large as a typical East Indiaman, but she was larger than the dear old *Salmon* and obviously not a warship. Frost mentally computed the closure angles, distances and times, and calculated that the vessels would come within hailing distance just at dusk. He gratefully accepted a cup of pea soup brought by Ming Tsun and then drank a cup of tea sweetened with honey.

He brusquely ordered the wounded men on deck taken below, then ordered Rawbone to assemble his gun crews and feed them at their stations. Hannibal Bowditch scampered down the lee main shrouds as rapidly as ever he could to report to Frost.

"Nathaniel . . . beg pardon, sir, Mister Dance and I esteem her to be mayhap one hundred tunns more than the old *Salmon*. She be a merchantman right enough, and her armament be piddling. Men be standing to the small cannon, but they have the mark of men who don't know their careers."

It was an hour to dusk, but Frost ordered the stern lantern lighted. The cat shouldered through a heavy swell, and spray blown back by the building wind into which the cat was pointing high on a starboard tack rattled along the weather bulwark. Frost caught Hannibal Bowditch's eye. "Mister Bowditch, I would be obliged if you would raise the red ensign on the ensign jack, and please ask Mister Mansfield if he could spare a moment to confer with me." Frost studied the approaching vessel through his telescope. He regretted that he was not all that well acquainted with the West Indies trade and for a moment considered bringing Marcus Whipple to the quarterdeck for his advice, but he decided his brother-in-law was better left to the recuperative powers of sleep. On the basis of his limited experience in those waters, Frost judged the vessel to be a packet of the type that plied between the West Indies and England. She was definitely a merchant vessel, though far more seaworn than he would ever have permitted his *Salmon*, his dear, dear old *Salmon*, to become. Now that she was closer, the vessel, as nearly as Frost could compute, would shade the old *Salmon* by a good seventy tons. Easily consistent with the estimates of Nathaniel and Hannibal.

Simultaneous with Hannibal Bowditch's bending on and raising the ensign on its staff, Caleb Mansfield, gnawing on a beef bone, appeared in the twilight. "Ye be thinkin' of takin' that 'er ship, now ain't ye, Capt'n?" Caleb posed a question, not an accusation.

"She be far larger than the armed schooner driven ashore on the Isle of Sable and burned a bare six hours ago, Caleb," Frost said easily. "We shall hail each other in fifteen minutes time. I intend to go across and inspect her cargo. If she be British, and indeed I believe her to be a packet out of the West Indies, and well laden, we shall but pluck another whisker to mortify the British lion if we escort her home to Portsmouth."

Caleb finished gnawing on the beef bone and flung it into the sea, remembering in time to throw it to leeward, not weather. He rubbed his hands on his already greasy buckskin jerkin to clean them. "Might'n be bitin' off more of the plug 'n we kin chew," he said doubtfully.

The same sound advice had already been offered by Ming Tsun, but Frost had already weighed the risks and was determined to know the nature of the approaching ship and its cargo. "I know not the composition or mettle of the crew," he said, "that is why I must have a strong complement of your woods-cruizers to ensure we'll encounter no problems with her crew. The crossing will be brief but wet in this sea. Your woods-cruizers will want to protect the locks of their long rifles."

"Waal, my 'cruizers be fearsome enough to terrorize a British general most proper, so I reckon they can terrorize the crew of yonder barky. I'll git my 'cruizers ready, but yere right, it'll be sure some wet getting' over to that 'er barky in this kind of sea."

"You are learning how to gauge the temperament of the sea," Frost bantered. "Soon you will be ready to undertake a command of your own."

Caleb Mansfield shook his head scornfully. "Hardly likely, Capt'n, but me 'n' Gideon be with ye. I'll see to it." He brightened perceptibly: "Last time I wus in a church, the deacon, he preached a sermon 'bout if God thrust out His hand to grasp yorn don't just hold out yere finger in return. Give the hand a right proper shake. Come to think on it, that was the first time I wus ever in a church. Got nothing against the place, just the parson."

"Mister Collingwood," Frost commanded. "Please order two reefs in the forecourse, prepare to bring the fore tops'l aback, and ease the jibs. I believe yonder vessel wishes to speak us, and while we are preparing to lay-to, I would appreciate the long boat hoisted out on the starboard side. My intention is to go aboard her, and during my absence you shall be next senior to Mister Rawbone aboard our cat."

The vessel, oncoming on the cat's larboard side, was already doused topsails, and hands were on the yards fisting up the main and fore courses into loose hanks. The waves were cresting at four feet, and tendrils of sea fog were beginning to form to join with the overcast sky rapidly shading into darkness. "Mister Dance," Frost said to the youth just clambering down the lee shrouds from the mainmast crosstrees, now that the light was insufficient, "you had the joy earlier today of leading a boarding party. Mayhap my efforts will be as successful as yours. You and your fellow ship's gentlemen shall see to the muster of hands for the long boat. A swivel gun in the bows shall present a proper martial appearance as we cross over. Enumerate the people Caleb Mansfield shall embark, for we shall need a proper show of force to subdue yonder vessel, then add sufficient hands to ensure every oar is pulled. Mister Bowditch shall act as coxswain. Mister Langdon shall accompany me. You shall remain aboard to give every assistance Mister Collingwood shall require . . ."

Frost broke off as a voice hailed the cat: "Ahoy the British warship! You are a welcome sight indeed! We would be honored to have your captain join us for dinner!"

Frost's face, at first startled, almost disbelieving, broke into the caricature of a grin. "Why, gentlemen, we may dispense with that swivel in the bows of the long boat. Martial ardor is not called for. It seems that we have a dinner invitation to speed our way." He picked up his speaking trumpet and stepped to the larboard bulwark: "Delighted, sir!" he responded to the hail. "Permit me a few minutes to clear away a ship's boat."

The long boat was now heaving up and down alongside at the cat's starboard waist entry, and men were filing down into the long boat under Caleb Mansfield's wary eyes. Ming Tsun handed Frost his double-barreled Bass pistols. Frost thrust the pistols into the sash he wore around his waist and clambered down into the pitching long boat, exercising prudence and both hands. "Oars up, shove off," Frost commanded curtly as soon as he reached his station with Caleb Mansfield in the bows. He heard the short bark, and a moment later the mumbled curses, as the Newfoundland dog jumped into the long boat, his weight tumbling several men into the bilges. "Mister Bowditch, bring the latest crew member to join us under your control," Frost snapped.

The sea was becoming more agitated, and the long boat was heaving and pitching. What twilight there was would be gone by the time the long boat reached the packet. Frost was alone with his thoughts now. Was he doing the right thing? Was he gambling too recklessly with the lives of his men and the safety of his vessel by pursuing this fifth prize? Should he not be content with having taken four? Did he still have any prizes? Had the two brigs and two snows, victuallers taken from Louisbourg, themselves been retaken by the Royal Navy? Dios. He thought of Caleb's comment about meeting God's extended hand with one equally firm. Insh'allah. Frost was extending both hands fully in this venture.

"I shall go aboard first at the larboard waist entry, and you and your men immediately at my heels, Caleb," Frost, holding his tricorne tightly to keep it from being blown away, said just loudly enough to be heard. "Half ranging toward the bows, half toward the stern—as quickly as ever you can! We must cower the vessel's crew into submission by quickness and surprise."

The long boat crossed the bows of the cat and bore down on the packet, then crashed through a wave crest, the spray thoroughly wetting the crew. Caleb, his spirits vastly improved now that action was in the offing, passed Frost's order to his woods-cruisers. Each woods-cruiser clutched his long rifle, locks swathed in canvas or soft leather, all the more closely. Then the long boat was alongside the high, wet, slippery hull of the packet and Frost, timing his leap and grasp nicely, went up the entry steps and onto the main deck, lighted only fitfully by dim lanterns. He removed his tricorne in a sweeping bow to the two men standing near the mainmast. Behind him Caleb's woods-cruisers were swarming onto the packet's main deck from the cat's long boat.

"Why, sir!" the nearer man, dressed in an elegant frock coat that appeared peach-colored in the fitful lantern light, exclaimed, "you are strangely attired to be the captain of a British warship!"

"I regret I do not meet your expectations of a British naval officer, gentlemen, but I cannot. Rather, I am the captain of a private man-o-war duly chartered with privateer warrants and letters of marque by the American Continental Congress and the Legislature of New Hampshire."

"Now see here . . ." the man in the elegant frock coat began. He was something of a dandy, with satin breeches of a lighter peach color, a well-powdered and expensive wig, a frothy spray of lace at his throat, and a gold-headed walking cane that he was twirling in his hand.

Frost looked around in the fitful light of half a dozen lanterns at the startled seamen on the main deck, their disbelief written large on their faces as Caleb Mansfield's woods-cruisers pushed and jostled them into a knot that was rapidly becoming sullen. "I must ask that you order your crew to offer no resistance to my men. I'm sure we equally eschew the shedding of blood," Frost said evenly.

Just then the huge Newfoundland dog scrambled up onto the main deck and promptly bowled over two of the cat's boarding party. "Damn it, Hannibal," one of the men knocked down loudly grumbled—from his voice Frost identified the man as Tobin Tuttle, one of Caleb's woods-cruisers—"keep that beast off'n me!"

"Cannibal!" the man in the elegant frock coat virtually wailed, more than a trace of panic in his voice, dropping the walking cane and pulling a scented handkerchief from his coat pocket to mop his face, "Cannibal! Is that animal a cannibal?"

Frost immediately seized the advantage the dog had given him. "If we examine the word semantically, a 'cannibal' is one who eats the flesh of his own species. I misdoubt if this animal, weighing upwards of fifteen stone, has ever consumed one of his own kind, but I do assure you, sir, that this dog, as does a wolf, indeed relishes the tender parts of the human body."

The man in the elegant frock coat raised both hands in horror, dropping his handkerchief to join his walking cane on the deck, as the Newfoundland dog ambled toward him. No one of the sullen, bewildered crew of the packet stirred, nor did any of the boarders. "Easy, easy," Frost whispered. The great Newfoundland dog circled and sniffed both men, their fear evident in the dog's nostrils. Then the dog nonchalantly lifted a rear leg and urinated on the stockings of the man in the elegant frock coat.

"He has marked his property for future attendance," Frost said, giving his voice an ominous tone. "I am grateful no one of you has provoked him." He turned to Caleb Mansfield: "Search the berthing deck for weapons, anything that can be used as weapons, even billets of wood," he added, recalling his own recent experience in dealing with an incipient mutiny. "Then turn the crew below and confine them there. Quickly! Mister Bowditch, the pull will be hard in these seas, and I can spare you only a minimum crew, since I must keep most here as surety. But return to our cat and request Mister Collingwood to bring the cat around to hold station on this packet during the night. We can expect this fog to lay heavy until the morrow."

Frost bowed to the two men again and permitted himself his caricature of a smile at the incongruous knowledge that the mere presence of the giant but gentle Newfoundland dog had subjugated the crew of the packet far more effectively than his armed woods-cruisers. The late prison keeper Whip Loring had well understood how the physical size and appearance of the dog could intimidate. He would have to find a name for the dog. He had to think of a name for the cat. Later—no time now. "I fail in my manners, gentlemen. I am Geoffrey Frost, and the current unpleasantness with the British Crown has cast me in the unfamiliar rôle of a privateer. May I have the pleasure of knowing your names?"

"Perkins, George Perkins, master of the *Royal Retort*, packet out of Tortola for Bristol," the older of the two men said sourly, keeping his bulbous eyes fixed on the Newfoundland dog.

"And you, sir?" Frost inquired of the man in the elegant frock coat, when the man did not immediately speak. He chirruped just loudly enough for the men and the dog to hear him; the dog perked its ears.

"George Marlborough," the man said quickly enough. "Owner of the *Royal Retort* and its cargo."

"Gentlemen, as you are doubtlessly aware, the ancient law maritime provides for the apprehension by one belligerent of vessels and cargo belonging to another . . ."

"By God, sir!" the man in the elegant frock coat cried in stupefaction, "Your insouciance knows no bounds! This vessel and its cargo represent my entire fortune—my life's work—and I am exceeding loathe to surrender them as prize to any upstart, self-styled private man-o-war!"

"Life is oft-times unfair, and ultimately one dies," Frost said evenly. "You need not concern yourself with surrendering your vessel and cargo to me. I have already taken both. I pray, do not let this unexpected, and admittedly unpleasant, event rob your ability for pragmatic thought. Pray, escort me to your cabin, Mister Marlborough, and there produce your cargo manifests." Frost opened his coat to reveal the butts of the two Bass pistols in his sash, but he did not attempt to draw either. Instead, he chirruped to the Newfoundland dog. "I collect this animal requires a feeding evening as well as morning. Have either of you a preference for whom shall be devoured first?" On cue, the great black dog began salivating.

"Below then," the dandified George Marlborough said curtly. "On condition your horse of a dog remain on deck."

"I misdoubt you are in any wise to dictate terms," Frost said with some asperity. He had come aboard this packet prepared to feel sorry for the captain and crew who stood to lose everything through capture by a privateer except their personal possessions. But the supercilious prattle of the owner nettled him. "I had not intended to turn you out of your cabin, but failing your cooperation, you'll leave me no recourse but to confine you with your crew."

That prospect gave George Marlborough pause; he turned on his heel and began walking aft. Frost, accompanied by the Newfoundland dog, followed, though bidding Ming Tsun to precede Marlborough, for he knew well enough the arrangements of such a vessel, and the way to the owner's cabin was simple enough to twig.

The owner's cabin was altogether too elaborate for Frost's tastes. He found the heavy brocade drapes covering the stern lights and quarter badges, the satin-covered settees to starboard and larboard, and the heavy aroma of the cloying perfumes emanating from pomanders attached by ribbons to silver candelabrums to be gratingly effete. The heavy desk that served also as a dining table was covered with a silk tablecloth, and two places were set with exquisite bone china and delicate crystal all laid inside a brass fiddle to keep the dinnerware in place against the slow roll and pitch of the ship. A pasty-faced fellow with a heavily starched stock knotted around his neck above his mauve servant's coat placed a large silver tureen on a sideboard and shrank back in alarm as Ming Tsun threw open the cabin door.

"Here now, what is that rogue doing?" George Marlborough said, bustling across the sole of his cabin to grasp Ming Tsun's arm in a vain effort to restrain him from throwing open the drawers of the massive desk. Ming Tsun shrugged the man aside easily but with enough force to propel Marlborough several paces across the cabin to collapse on the starboard settee.

"He is searching for weapons," Frost said reasonably.

"He'll find none here," Marlborough said irritably.

For answer, Ming Tsun threw a dagger with a jeweled hilt onto the desk's top, where it rang musically against a plate.

"A letter opener," Marlborough sneered, "a bauble." He shrugged. "If you'll allow me . . ." Marlborough crossed to the desk and removed a large wooden casket with brass corners from a bottom drawer. He removed a leather portfolio from the casket and handed it to Frost. "These are the manifests of cargo freighted aboard *Royal Retort*. Now I ask that you be gone, sir!" He gestured toward the desk set for dinner. "I had expected to dine with an officer of the Royal Navy, but I find that I have been gulled bitterly by a colonial pirate."

Frost took the leather portfolio. "I am certain Captain Perkins will make an admirable dinner companion, Mister Marlborough. You are entitled to the quiet enjoyment of your quarters without hindrance from my men or me—so long as you offer no resistance." Frost crossed to the sideboard and sampled the soup in the tureen, making a wry face. He signaled the servant to place the tureen on the cabin sole, then chirruped to the great Newfoundland dog. The dog lapped the soup enthusiastically, and momentarily the soup was gone, with the dog pushing the tureen across the sole.

Frost sighed, "Alas, sirs, an infinitely small morsel, scarce able to take the slightest edge off the animal's prodigious hunger. We'll repair to the galley forward in expectation of locating more substantial sustenance, hopefully in the form of a half-barrel of pickled beef. I would ask that you remain in this cabin until summoned on the morrow. My woods-cruizers with their wondrously keen scalping knives and sharp-edged hatchets will be rigorously marshalling the vessel throughout the night."

Frost did indeed go forward to the galley in hopes of finding a kettle of boiling water and some tea, which after some length, Ming Tsun produced from the properly horrified and subdued cook. The Newfoundland dog made a proper meal on several pieces of cooked salt beef, then slaked his thirst at the scuttlebutt. Ming Tsun had found several oranges and lemons, and a slab of Portuguese bacalhau soaking in a tub of water, and while Frost pored over the cargo manifests spread before him on a hanging table, at length managed to produce an acceptable codfish stew, though a bit salty for Frost's taste, with the oranges as dessert. The great Newfoundland dog arranged himself at Frost's feet while Frost, whistling softly to himself, reflected on the wealth of the cargo freighted in the Tortola Packet. As always, when in the presence of great wealth, Geoffrey Frost was singularly unmoved.

Frost ate half the codfish stew and, taking a lantern and a blanket Ming Tsun draped around him as a cloak, went on deck. The sea and wind were calming, the reduced motion in the galley had told him that, but he was disturbed at the impenetrability of the damp and chilling fog in which the *Royal Retort* was swathed. Coming on deck up the main scuttle Frost could see neither helm nor bowsprit. He could just barely make out larboard and starboard bulwarks. Frost made two compete tours of the *Royal Retort*'s upper decks, noting as much as he could discern about her condition and equipments and approving the doubled watch standers of woodscruisers Caleb Mansfield had stationed in the bows and to both sides of the break at the waist. He stopped at the helm, where Caleb Mansfield was keeping the watch stander at the ship's wheel company near the blurred glow of the binnacle.

"Ain't seed a light from our cat since young Hannibal pulled away 'n the long boat," Caleb said softly. "Been listenin', listenin' hard." Caleb let the silence complete his sentence as he chewed on the coffee beans he used to keep fatigue at bay.

"'Tis a particularly dismal fog," Frost agreed, grateful for the blanket's warmth, though knowing that Caleb had been on deck all evening with only his buckskin tunic to shield against the chill damp, he quietly slipped the blanket around Caleb's shoulders. "We find ourselves at the point in the high Atlantic where the winds caressing the waters brought up on that great warm stream from the Caribbean clash with the frigid temps of this Current of Labrador to produce this all-encompassing vapor. Ming Tsun, Struan and I have encountered many types of fogs in our Oriental voyages, but until we were compelled by British perfidy to journey to these latitudes I have never experienced such opaque vapor. All of our complement, myself in particular, shall be glad once rid of it."

Frost fretted that he was not aboard the cat but put the matter out of mind. He had confidence in Herbert Collingwood's seamanship, though he would be glad enough to regain his own vessel on the morrow. "Grateful to your woodscruizers for standing such earnest watch, Caleb. There is food and small beer for them in the galley. I'll make certain the captain and owner are secure in their cabins and plotting no mischief, then relieve you to sup and find a place near the galley stove to sleep." Frost drew out Jonathan's watch and stepped to the binnacle light to note the time. Lacking fifteen minutes of midnight. He went below to conduct a thorough inspection of the Tortola Packet, starting with the owner's cabin, then to the berthing deck to ensure the vessel's people were accepting their unexpected rôles as captives.

Then he relieved Caleb Mansfield and sent him below. Frost was fatigued, the fatigue that lay so close to the bone that sleep, while longed for, was impossible to attain. So he paced many times that night around the main and quarterdeck of the Tortola Packet, listening often, straining to hear something, anything, in the engloomed dark to indicate the cat was near, but being rewarded only by the sounds of the muted workings of the packet's hull, masts and riggings. Several times when he paused overly long, Frost found himself close to slumber. But he fought off the drowsiness and resumed his pacing, through all the changes of the watch.

## ✿ VII ✿

✿✿✿✿ ROST KNEW THAT DAWN HAD ARRIVED
✿   F   ✿ ON THE TORTOLA PACKET'S DEW-HEAVY
✿     ✿ DECKS ONLY BY A FAINT — VERY FAINT —
✿✿✿✿ INCREASE IN VISIBILITY AND A SLIGHT
lessening in the oppressive darkness of the all-encompassing
fog. He could see the knighthead timbers from the waist but
not from the quarterdeck. Ming Tsun and Darius Langdon
joined him on the quarterdeck, Ming Tsun bringing a cup of
hot tea, the warmed-over remains of the codfish stew, and a
scowl, indicating his displeasure that Frost had not slept during the night. Frost smiled at them both. "Mister Langdon, I
would be obliged if you would roust out Mister Mansfield
wherever he be a-snoring and bid him bring up a few charges
from the magazine. We should assay a blank round or two to
alert our colleagues aboard the cat of our location, and to
ascertain theirs."

A grumpy Caleb Mansfield presented himself on the main
deck shortly, leather bucket with baize tubes of gunpowder in
one hand and his double rifle in the other. "All this wet has
me to thinkin' on how to make the firin' o' cannon go forward
when's needed," Caleb announced sourly. "Slow match ain't
got it by half. I'm thinkin' of nailin' a flintlock to the cannon
'n' lettin' her have a right good spark in the touchhole that'll
get her goin' fer sure!"

"See that you do so, Caleb," Frost said soberly. "Master
Gunner Rawbone will welcome your ideas doubtlessly, since I

constantly challenge him to new heights of accuracy and reliability. But for the nonce, I am interested only in creating sufficient sound to attract the attention of our mates aboard the cat that, perforce, must lie nearby."

"As ye like it," Caleb said, somewhat mollified. He felt among the cartridges in the leather bucket to find one to his satisfaction. "Any preference to yere cannon fer signalin'?" he demanded.

"As you see fit," Frost responded in kind, finishing the cup of tea. "For signaling one cannon is as like another. The decision lies with the cannon easiest to bring to signaling order."

"All's cannons I see be fit only as anchors fer moorin' a gig in calm water," Caleb grumbled, but nevertheless he gave his attention to a 4-pounder on the starboard side that seemed reasonably free of encumbrances such as drapes of hawsers and balks of timber that rightly should have been stowed elsewhere.

Caleb cleared away the wrack of spare cable draped over the 4-pounder and directed his woods-cruisers to tail onto the tackle and ease the cannon into position for loading. Caleb drew the tampion from the muzzle and thrust in the bag of powder. He whispered a few words to Darius, and Darius hurried away toward the main scuttle. By the time he returned from the galley with a slim wire poker heated red hot from the galley fire, Caleb had rammed the charge home and thrust in a pad of oakum as wadding. Three woods-cruisers tailed onto the lines and ran the cannon to its bowse. Caleb inspected the wire poker and confirmed that it was small enough to fit into the touchhole. He nodded, assigning Darius the pleasure of thrusting the slim wire down the touchhole into the cartridge, at the same time growling an admonition for Darius to stand clear of the recoiling carriage.

The small cannon barked a most satisfying blast of reverberating noise that Frost knew would carry far in the still, damp air. Caleb swabbed out the cannon barrel and thrust in another cartridge. Frost listened intently but heard no answering discharge. He nodded for Caleb to continue the reload.

The 4-pounder was run to its bowse, and Caleb inspected the wire critically to judge if it was still hot enough to ignite the powder. Deeming it so, he again signaled Darius the honor of firing the cannon, and just as Darius thrust the wire into the touchhole there was an answering blast that the 4-pounder's firing almost obscured.

Instantly Frost was at the breast rail, gripping it tightly. "Whence did the sound come?" he asked Ming Tsun. Ming Tsun gestured toward the starboard bow. Frost stepped to the helm and gauged the force on the rudder. The Tortola Packet was moving, imperceptibly, but moving as a piece of flotsam caught on the broad bosom of the Labrador Current in a leisurely flow toward the northeast. At least they were pointed toward the signal cannon heard off the starboard bow. Was it his imagination, or was there a gradual decrease in the opacity of the fog toward the east?

Yes! Frost could discern the knighthead timbers now from the quarterdeck, and even the bowsprit as far as the spritsail yard. What was more, the merest, most tentative touch of wind ghosted across the quarterdeck, causing a drapery of distracted fog to swirl momentarily. "Another signal whenever you are ready, Caleb," Frost said.

Another cannon's report from starboard ahead. "Commendable forethought on Collingwood's part," Frost said to himself. "He's cleared two cannons."

Caleb Mansfield touched off another cannon blast and was rewarded with an almost instantaneous reply that reverberated eerily in the fog. As with all sounds muffled and echoing in a fog, the direction of the signal cannon was difficult to fix, though Frost deduced Collingwood and the cat were somewhere in the arc from dead ahead to broad on the starboard bow, at a distance no greater than a sea mile. The set of the current was slowly but inexorably moving the Tortola Packet toward a heartily welcome reunion with his vessel.

Frost released his grip on the breast rail, surprised at the stiffness of his fingers from the tightness of the grip. "I believe we need no further signal, Caleb, the location of our cat is now established." He turned to Darius. "To the main crosstrees with you and your keen vision, Mister Langdon. Oft times a fog lays heaviest at deck level, and dissipates first at some height." A rope, invisible in the cloying fog, slapped against a sail. A window sash in stern lights squealed as someone raised it, then came the splash of a chamber pot's being emptied, all sounds unnaturally loud. A moment later Marlborough, the packet's owner, appeared on the main deck. Marlborough saw Frost on the quarterdeck and shot him a look of utmost disdain while making an elaborate, theatrical bow.

Toward the east the fog was perceptibly lighter, and Frost estimated visibility at a good one hundred yards. The fog was lifting, for he could see as high as the main course yard. He stretched luxuriously and began to pace the quarterdeck of the Tortola Packet. The packet heeled slightly as an unexpected rush of wind scurried up from the south and whisked aside a massive curtain of fog, rolling it northward.

"Deck there!" Darius Langdon cried from above. "Ship fine on the bows!"

But Frost had already seen it. Emerging from a fogbow directly to the east was a ship with a cat's cradle of rigging. The sail plan was exceedingly unorthodox, no foremast, the main and mizzen masts approximately the same height, a much patched driver, abbreviated main and mizzen courses, the main course even more so since its yard was scarcely the size of a forecourse — Frost guessed that it was the scavenged forecourse yard — and two large, much patched triangular sails rigged as staysails from the mainmast top to the bowsprit. Unconventional, and very likely unable to point very high into the wind. A bare two cables' length away, the slow current unerringly drifting the Tortola Packet directly toward her, lay HM *Lark*, all cannons on her larboard side run out, and slow match clearly smoldering.

Frost grudgingly admired the quickness with which *Lark*'s commander had repaired his vessel. Two days' time — less than two days, for HM *Lark* had covered some fifty leagues from the site of her engagement with the cat.

George Marlborough immediately rushed to the quarter-deck to stand triumphantly beside Frost. "A wrathful God and the Royal Navy conspire to exact punishment for your iniquitous, outrageous crimes, sir!" Marlborough gloated, his face suffused crimson and his eyes widely bulging.

"On the contrary, sir," Frost replied, "God has a neutral view of this chance encounter, and it is left to us to make of it what we will." Frost turned to Caleb. "Restrain Mister Marlborough, please, Caleb. See that he utters no sound."

Frost turned again. "Mister Marlborough, you would do well to heed the counsel of the ancient Luqmaan, to whom the Prophet devoted a chapter of the Muslem Sacred Book."

"What counsel could a Mussulman possibly give a Christian, sir?" Marlborough, not heeding Frost's earlier warning, sneered.

"Lower your voice," Frost snapped, "for the worst of sounds is the braying of an ass."

Caleb clapped onto Marlborough with a rough hand. Darius descended the mainmast starboard shrouds, and Frost signaled him to the quarterdeck. "Repair below and fetch the British colors, quickly now."

By the time Darius hurried up with the flag, the current had drifted the *Royal Retort* to within a cable's length of HM *Lark*, and by the time the flag was hanging limply from the ensign staff, the two vessels were within hailing distance. Frost wryly recalled his signed conversation with Ming Tsun about the Dyak method of hunting monkey as he picked up a speaking trumpet and stepped to the weather bulwark of the *Royal Retort*'s quarterdeck. "A right good morning we bid you, sir. You are just in time to join us for breakfast," he shouted across to the British warship. The fog to east and south was dissipating rapidly. Frost looked northward anxiously: there, a scant cable's length away, the fog was still banked densely. Were Collingwood and the cat concealed in that fog? Would the fog lift and reveal his vessel to the British warship? How close was the cat? Had the two signal cannons sounding so close together been fired from HM *Lark*, or one from *Lark* and one from the cat?

There was a quick conversation between two figures on *Lark*'s quarterdeck, and then one figure lifted a speaking trumpet: "What ship? Where bound?" came the abrupt, pre-emptory challenge.

"*Royal Retort*, packet from Tortola with general stores, bound for Bristol."

"Send over your captain with your ship's papers. I'll examine them while we pass news over my poor table."

"Accepted with pleasure," Frost shouted back. Then quickly to Ming Tsun: "Conceal my pistols in your tunic. Darius and Cato Calite, you shall row us across in this vessel's gig. Please see to its swaying out. Once aboard the British warship—her name be *Lark*, and she is commanded by a right mariner—you must speak no English, give no evidence that you speak or understand English. Yet you must keep every faculty alert for any intelligence that comes to ear." He looked directly at George Marlborough, "We have only a moment to gather your papers. They were returned to your keeping after I perused them."

"Now, me 'n' Gideon, we don't put no faith in the trustiness of any British," Caleb Mansfield said, draping an arm over Marlborough's shoulder. "Atter Mister Marlborough here gathers them papers fer ye, he 'n' me 'n' Gideon be takin' our ease outside the magazine atop a barrel o' powder with the head stove in. If there be treachery worked, Mister Marlborough 'n' I soon be arguin' afore Saint Peter the right of it." George Marlborough's face reflected his horror and consternation.

Frost followed George Marlborough closely down the companionway and into the owner's cabin. Marlborough took the wood casket with brass corners from his desk and removed the leather portfolio. "And, sir, what are the rewards of my acquiesce in your pernicious scheme, and God's truth, I am loathe exceedingly . . ."

"You are bargaining only for your own life and the lives of your crew, sir," Frost interrupted, in no mood to hear any more of George Marlborough's whining. "Your ship and cargo are irretrievably lost. You must appreciate that, having just released my brother-in-law and a few other pitiful survivors from a prison so horrific that no words exist to describe it, the fate of your vessel and all within her truly reposes in the hands of each man of your crew. I sincerely hope there will be no treachery worked on your part or any of your men, sir. You should communicate to your men the desperation of my fellows. They have sworn never to be taken by the British. This gentleman," Frost indicated Caleb, "and my servant," he indicated Ming Tsun with an incline of his head, "were prepared to destroy our vessel by applying fire to the magazine should we not have succeeded in taking the British sloop-o-war from which we hailed you yesterday."

Frost scanned the documents in the portfolio briefly. Seeing a small pouch in the wooden casket, Frost hoisted it experimentally and was rewarded with the musical clink of coins. He dropped the pouch into the portfolio. "As we remarked yesterday, sir, life is filled with ironies and inconsistencies, and in the end we die. I sincerely hope you have not resolved that life is so desolate of hope you wish to be shut of it today. But if that be your resolve, you shall be accommodated—depend upon it."

Frost gathered the portfolio to his bosom. "Caleb, it is a hard task I levy upon you. If we cannot intrigue the *Lark*'s commander, Ming Tsun and I shall engage the British as best we can. No doubt we shall be aided as best they can by Mister Langdon and Cato Calite, though we shall be only a forlorn hope. Your woods-cruizers, none of whom, I'm sad to relate, are right seamen, must take charge of this vessel and maneuver up to her, whereupon, hulls touching, you must kindle this vessel's magazine into explosion."

"Right enough," Caleb agreed. "That air British captain, he be well favored by nature, 'cause I had him fair in my sights two days past. Given the choice of dyin' as free men, and kickin' out our lives at the ends of British hemp, never fear, we'll take the British with us," Caleb grinned his wolfish grin, "'n' of course Mister Marlborough will be the first of many British subjects to ascend to heaven—or hell—today."

Frost made Marlborough a small bow. "Delighted you can entertain my prize crew so heartily." He gestured toward Caleb: "I believe he summons you toward the bowels of your ship and your gunpowder magazine. By my reckoning you have a minimum of ten tons of powder in your magazine. Sufficient to provide us with a wondrous pyrotechnic display! You will, I'm sure, wish a few words with your crew to place them on their best behavior."

"I'll pledge you my word that all aboard the *Royal Retort* will acquiesce in your demands," George Marlborough said weakly.

"Not to mention my woods-cruizers will be on deck, noses a-twitch fer the first sniff of treachery," Caleb growled.

As they came on deck Frost handed the portfolio to Ming Tsun and rubbed the stubble of his beard, wishing there was time for Ming Tsun to shave him. He clambered down into the gig and winked at Darius and Cato Calite, who had removed their shirts, stockings and shoes, the better to appear like ordinary seamen: "Your best speed across to yonder warship would be appreciated," he whispered, "we should not keep her captain waiting breakfast." He flipped his coat tails into his lap and settled in the stern sheets as Ming Tsun pushed off. The fifty yards to HM *Lark* were covered quickly, and just as quickly Frost climbed up the larboard waist entry.

Frost bowed to the stripling in a threadbare midshipman's uniform who waited at the entry: "George Marlborough, your servant, sir. I'd be obliged if you would let my gig's crew wait my return on your deck. The sea's chop is especially indelicate in a small boat."

The midshipman glanced knowledgeably overside. "Caribees, I've seen their like many times on the Jamaica station. They can come up all right. Caribees make excellent hands."

"Excellent hands, indeed," Frost said. "Extremely diligent." His heart sank. Was this midshipman obliquely threatening to press his men? He stepped aside to let Darius and Cato Calite on deck. "I am fortunate to have them as freemen employed in my service, even though they do not possess two words of English between them."

The midshipman muttered under his breath, though Frost heard him well enough, "A rope starter will teach them sufficient English in a week's time," then he swept his left arm toward the *Lark*'s quarterdeck: "This way, if you please. Captain Smith is already at breakfast."

Frost glanced northward before following the midshipman. The bank of fog was still stationary. The midshipman escorted Frost to the captain's cabin, nodded to the marine sentry on duty, said, "Good morning, McCoy," as if the sentry should be grateful the midshipman had recognized him, and rapped on the door panel.

"Yes?" came a voice from within.

"The captain of the *Royal Retort* awaits your pleasure, Captain Smith."

"Show him in, by all means, Mister Livingston," came the voice.

The midshipman opened the door and stood aside for Frost to enter, then attempted to bar Ming Tsun.

"I beg you, sir, he is my confidential servant and accompanies me everywhere I go." Ming Tsun effortlessly brushed past the midshipman. A spare, ginger-haired man with a deeply cleft chin, approximately thirty years of age, with one large gilt epaulette on the left shoulder of his uniform coat, rose stoop-shouldered from the table fitted between two cannons, long nines, Frost calculated, and extended his hand. He was heartily glad to have avoided the sting of those cannons during the cat's brief engagement with *Lark*. Although the *Lark* was a much larger vessel than *Jaguar*, the main cabin was surprisingly small for the vessel, hardly larger than the cat's main cabin, and far more spartan, with decidedly less headroom.

"Richard Smith, commanding His Majesty's frigate *Lark*. And you, sir?"

Frost took the extended hand and shook it warmly. "George Marlborough, at your service, sir. Of Bristol and the Macao, though I have seen Bristol only twice in the past twenty-odd years."

"Marlborough! A happy name, though yet a dark one also for me."

"How so, sir?" Frost asked solicitously. "Is it too forward of me to inquire into your reasons for saying thus?"

"A calamity, sir, of the first water." Smith waved Frost to the seat across the table from him. He cocked an eye at Ming Tsun when Ming Tsun pulled out the chair for Frost. "Your man may sit on the settee so he won't get a crank neck."

"The gentleman's gig was rowed across by two Caribees, sir," Midshipman Livingston said hopefully, "all the marks of prime hands, even if they do look like cannibals." Frost looked up sharply at the midshipman's use of the word "cannibals."

Smith laughed heartily. "We'll leave talk of pressing hands for later, Mister Livingston. Pray leave me and Captain Marlborough to our breakfast. I would rather a proper foremast and suitable spars, not to mention a suit of foresails, than a dozen prime hands however pressed." Smith signaled to the servant waiting at table, who obligingly uncovered the tureen on a sideboard. "Unfortunately, we've been so long at sea that a burgoo is all I can offer you, I'm afraid."

"Might I inquire the circumstances of the calamity, Captain Smith?" Frost inquired, anxious to steer the conversation well away from the impressing of hands from a merchant vessel, as well as the burgoo he loathed as virtually uneatable. Burgoo, that thick noxious gruel of oatmeal, crushed hardtack, molasses, and left-over scraps of pork or beef, all boiled together, had been a staple because it was cheap aboard the East Indiamen on which he had served his apprenticeship in the Orient trade. Frost calculated that Captain Richard Smith would have been hard pressed to serve something a bit more palatable were he entertaining an officer senior to him in the Royal Navy rather than a merchant factor. Smith did not appear to Frost to have sufficient personal funds to have laid in special provisions for a personal larder at the onset of his convoy duty, and he imagined Smith was sharing the same breakfast as his crew.

Smith dipped a spoon into the burgoo and chewed several moments before replying. "I was first lieutenant on the *Marl-*

*borough*, 74, but a guardship in Portsmouth, so infirm a vessel, and hard aground on a reef of her own beef bones! The scurvy master gunner thought to enrich himself to the tune of three barrels of powder pilfered from the magazine. There was an explosion to confound the scoundrel. The captain was ashore, a large number of my stout fellows were killed, and maimed in the horrific explosion. As senior aboard I was able to rally enough men to save the old *Marlborough*. Coincident with this grimace of fate, the captain of *Lark*, and well over half of his crew, came down with the ship-fever. My Lords at the Admiralty needed an escort captain to be sea-shepherd to a convoy of victuallers, but there were none to be had. So my Lords at the Admiralty fastened upon me."

Smith paused for a long sip of tea. "This ship, I tell you in all honesty, sir, was a right mess! Not the fault of her former captain, of course. The ship-fever struck suddenly. *Lark* himself was among the first to die, even before he could be invalided to hospital. I could not take such a plague ship into the dockyard until I had thoroughly ventilated and fumigated her, even to the remove of all the shingle ballast and replacing with new . . ." Smith glanced sharply at Frost. "Like you not the burgoo, sir? I apologize if it is not to your liking, otherwise you shall make your breakfast of tea. At least I can still command a pot of tea from the finest Chinese leaf."

"A burgoo sits not well on my stomach, I fear, Captain Smith, and you serve an excellent tea. However, it derives not from the fabled land of China, but the singular highlands of the subcontinent of India, from the Darjeeling region."

Smith harrumphed and cleared his throat. "I must trouble you for a look at your documents. The tea was not my purchase, but a small store gifted to me by my mother when she learned I had been promoted to this command. How come you, master of a packet outbound from Tortola, to be so expert on the subject of tea?"

Ming Tsun placed the portfolio in front of Frost. Frost untied the portfolio and pulled from it the sheaf of manifests. "I hope I have not misled you, sir. I am the vessel's owner, not her master. He has been confined to his cabin this week past with a dangerous fever and the flux that generally presages the pox, and the poor soul has been unable to stir except to take nourishment."

"Have you much pox in your vessel?" Smith asked anxiously.

Frost waved a hand dismissively, though grateful he had been afforded the opportunity to plant a seed of doubt in Captain Smith's mind about the potential health of Darius Langdon and Cato Calite. "Not any more pox than one generally associates with a voyage from the Antilles, and only a man or two down with the yellow jack. I attribute not my lack of appetite for your excellent burgoo to a touch of the pox, but then, I am well salted. My knowledge of the China and India trades has been gained as a factor there, mostly on the Macao. On my most recent voyage the ship of the Honorable John Company, on which I had taken passage, was blown far off course by a hurricane, and heavily damaged. Luckily we reached Tortola just as our pumps failed. In Tortola I learned of this war of rebellion against His Majesty's ministerial government, and I bought the *Retort* and her cargo on speculation."

Smith looked up from his perusal of the *Royal Retort*'s manifests and signaled his servant to pour more tea for Frost. "I'm quite sure your Caribees would fancy the rest of this burgoo. God's my life, but I'm tired of it myself. Would you bid your servant to light along the tureen and two bowls to your men?"

Frost hesitated for a moment; he knew Ming Tsun would not want to leave him alone in the cabin of the *Lark*'s commander—it could be a clever ploy to separate them, and there could be a dozen hands on the other side of the cabin's forward partition, waiting to spring upon him once he was alone. But it was exceedingly kind of Smith to make the offer. "Capital of you, sir, to offer up the remainder of your breakfast."

"My man will assist. That way he can bring your servant past the sentry." Smith spread the *Royal Retort*'s cargo manifests on his desk and began scrutinizing them. "A wealthy cargo you purchased, far from 'general stores' as you will admit now," Smith said, smiling knowingly, and then he changed the subject. "What do you know of this rebellion?"

Frost shrugged his shoulders. "I've been away from England for many years and have devoted my efforts toward the mercantile, not the political. I know aught of the rebellion's origins, though I've heard tell that taxes on tea had something to do with the choler of dissatisfaction."

"Sometimes there is little, if any, distinction between the interests of the mercantile and the political," Smith said in a guarded tone.

"I have not set foot in England for five years," Frost said truthfully enough. "I retain all my interests in the Orient, sir, but I thought this purchase of a cargo a prudential diversification, given the fact that war with the French and Dutch will make the voyage around the Cape extremely perilous."

"There you have it," Captain Richard Smith cried, slapping the table with the palm of his right hand. "The French are our native, our natural and rightful enemy, sir! Even now they—perfidious race—prepare for war and England's ruin! Assistance to our rebellious cousins be damned! Let the fractious colonies win but one significant battle and Louis the Sixteenth will throw himself bodily upon the Third George! And for what reason, sir, do we fight so among ourselves? The cost borne by the exchequer to outfit and deploy the fleet of victuallers under my escort vastly exceeds the paltry sums Government sought to extract from those proud people! The people of British ancestry in North America should be our allies, not our enemies!"

Frost studied Richard Smith cautiously. Was the man seeking to entrap him into saying something injudicious? "I am but a factor of cargoes, and little acquainted with the political, but it was not too long ago that the John Company was facing bankruptcy, if not complete ruin, and that led to the infamous scheme of tea importation into North America, and tax to which—at least, such is my understanding at the great remove of half a world away—the colonials took great exception." He ventured a bland aside: "Reports I heard in Tortola gave me to believe the colonials would have welcomed the taxes could they have been empowered to levy themselves."

"Precisely so, sir!" Captain Richard Smith brought his open hand down again hard on the sheaf of manifests. "No right-thinking person disagrees with the notion that those who benefited from the Crown's protection during the last war should assist in paying for those benefits. Our Parliament has but to name a fair contribution to the exchequer, and permit the colonials to raise it by taxing themselves! But Government has gone about it very heavy-handed. To gain a corn of pepper, Government is wagering an empire! No one is prescient enough to know whether the wager will pay out or no."

Smith signaled his servant, just returning with Ming Tsun, to pour more tea. Ming Tsun signed that the fog was still dense to the northward. Frost was grateful that the swift movement of hands would have meant nothing to Captain Richard Smith, even had he marked it. "I know a thing or two about these colonials, sir, though I have never yet set foot in North America—my naval service thus far has involved only the Mediterranean and the Baltic. My father served in the British Army in North America during the last war. He was attached to Braddock's ill-fated forces as an artillery officer—though the Dear knows there was little place for an artillery officer in that debacle. But for a colonel of colonial militia, name of Washington, who covered the retreat, none of Braddock's forces would have survived—my father included. Father always spoke well of the colonials, especially this George Washington. Father caressed him much. My father did not, however, ever talk about the horrors of that retreat."

Smith paused to drink off his cup of tea. "You have the advantage of me in knowing the origin of this tea, but it is a capital beverage, whether it comes from China or India." He turned over several of the manifest pages and pretended to examine them minutely.

"Capital indeed," Frost agreed, though he wished for some honey to stir into his cup of tea.

"And as I confirmed two days ago in a brief engagement

with a most saucy fellow, some among the colonials do possess skill in nautical matters. He saw me off good."

"Oh?" Frost said cautiously, hoping he was able to inject the proper note of incredulity into his voice: "You mean to tell me that an American warship had the temerity to attack such a vessel as this? Perhaps it was the same one that chaced my vessel just yesterday. The *Retort* is far more suitable quarry for the Americans than a Royal Navy frigate mounting thirty-two massive cannons. "

"I don't know how the rebels did it, but somehow they've got hold of Hugh Stuart's *Jaguar*. Never met the man, more's the pity, though he was reputed to be an able and honorable officer—had commissioned a sloop—no, his father had—eighteen cannons, a true beauty, and a most distinctive figure-head, unlike anything else in the Royal Navy, so I'm reliably informed. Gulled me proper, I'm ashamed to say. I challenged this strange vessel intruding into my convoy. He discomfited me by slinging casks with fuses a-smolder from his yards. To what degree was I hazarding my vessel and crew by closing with a terrier insolent enough to hoist infernal devices? Was the intention to destroy himself and my Lark contemporane-ously? Or was that cheeky fellow merely blowing smoke up my petticoats?" Smith drummed his fingers on the table to attract his servant's attention and pointed to the teacups.

"I shall have some more presently, sir," the servant mur-mured.

"Be sure to use the water from my still."

Sensing the moment to be opportune, Frost quietly slipped the cargo manifests off the breakfast table into the portfolio and handed the portfolio to Ming Tsun. "Was this *Jaguar* of which you speak a vessel with a most peculiar figurehead," Frost prompted innocently, "one in the shape of a crouching tiger?"

Richard Smith put down his cup. "What know you of a ves-sel with a leonine figurehead?" he asked suspiciously.

"Why, sir," Frost replied evenly, "I told you earlier, I would not be in these high latitudes had not a vessel with a catlike figurehead chaced me hither. My Tortola Packet was saved only by the intervention of an armed schooner that, providentially, appeared in the offing, causing this cat vessel to discontinue the chace. The last I saw of this vessel she was bearing away hard to the south, with the schooner in pursuit."

Smith nodded in satisfaction. "The *Walrus*, tender to this convoy. After my sharp engagement with the American chap I signaled *Walrus* to take up the chace. I would have liked to go in chace myself, though damage to my riggings and sails, my duties as sea shepherd, and the fact that my *Lark* is freighted with one hundred thousand pounds in specie as payroll for Lord Howe's troops unfortunately recalled me to my duty, counseling discretion rather than aggression."

"Utterly amazing!" Frost exclaimed, knowing that Ming Tsun, who had taken his seat on the settee behind him, had stiffened at the mention of the incredible treasure aboard the *Lark*. His mind raced, and for a moment avarice consumed him. How could he maneuver to capture this prize? He could throw over the table, draw the Bass pistols from beneath Ming Tsun's robe, hold Richard Smith captive, order the *Lark* sailed to Portsmouth . . . Or, once he had returned to the cat, he could go in search of *Lark* . . . Then reality intruded harshly, but properly. His primary mission, his only mission, was to get Ming Tsun, Darius, Cato Calite, and himself safely back to the Tortola Packet, and then the cat's crew, Marcus Whipple and the other rescued prisoners, and the prizes crewed by New Hampshire, Massachusetts and Maine men safely back to Portsmouth. There lay Frost's duty. He allowed himself a half-smile. The otherwise virtuous Richard Smith had neglected to mention that he could not have pursued the cat in any event due to the *Lark*'s virtual dismasting by the cat's two broadsides of shot, chain and langrage.

"Yes, foxed me proper, and threw me off my stroke," Smith continued. "Whoever gained Hugh Stuart's *Jaguar* replied to all my signals properly, save one. But so arrogant and cocksure of himself did the fellow appear, and knowing his father's close ties to the Crown, I deigned to force the matter of seniority and proper signals etiquette. Instead, I bore away to inspect the four victuallers that had miraculously reappeared in my convoy. Four victuallers had become separated from the convoy during a recent storm, and I had sent Mortimer in the *Scimitar* to look into Louisbourg to see if they had sought shelter there."

"You freight quite a treasure indeed, Captain Smith," Frost said. "I am not familiar with these waters, but I have heard of the *Tilbury*. Do you collect the vessel as well?" Frost wanted very much to question Smith further about Hugh Stuart, but he dared not.

Smith nodded soberly. "Aye, every Royal Navy officer of my age has heard of *Tilbury*. She was a fourth-rate, commanded by a chap named Barnaby. Driven ashore on the south coast of New Scotland in September of 1757 by a hurricane. Carrying the payroll for the entire British Army in North America she was. Barnaby and most of her crew perished. The specie has never been reclaimed by the Crown, though I daresay the locals thereabout have seen away the majority of it. Blackguards and villains all!"

"I admire your prudence," Frost said simply. He was inwardly fidgeting and was tempted to steal a glance at his watch. How long had he been aboard the *Lark*? Thirty minutes? It was evident Captain Richard Smith was satisfied with the *Royal Retort*'s documents, and Frost would very much have liked to be on his way. His restless eyes fixed on a book in the sparse collection of navigational almanacs held behind the brace of the single bookshelf in the cabin. "I see, sir, that you are a student of the Portuguese."

Smith followed Frost's gaze. "No, I'm afraid not. *Lark*'s former commander, Captain Crane, God rest his soul, had been first lieutenant on a frigate ordered to India. The frigate was forced to refit at the island of Moçambique. There Captain Crane learned the Portuguese." Smith stood up, keeping his shoulders well stooped due to the lower overhead, and fetched the leatherbound volume. He laid it on the table as the servant bustled in with a fresh pot of tea. "You know the title and author, Mister Marlborough? By all accounts Captain Crane enjoyed the book hugely."

Frost picked up the volume. "One cannot engage in the Orient trade without becoming acquainted with the *Luisiads* of Luis Camoëns, a contemporary of our peerless Shakespeare, sir. I must confess I have sought this noble tome for many years. It is the only literary work in the Portuguese language that requires an understanding of the verb conjugation 'pretérito mais-que perfeito do conjuntivo.'"

Smith nodded appreciatively as his servant, shoulders stooped also, poured from the fresh pot of tea. "My predecessor was a pious and honorable man, sir. He spent much time on the beach at half-pay while awaiting a ship. 'Tis said he could recite copiously from this tome. I dare say no one else in the Royal Navy has such facility in the tongue. It bodes ill for all to sell the effects of a dead man, but you are very welcome to the book, with the compliments of Captain Crane, God rest his soul. He would be pleased properly, depend upon it, to know the book lodges in the possession of one who cherishes it."

"Cherish it I most certainly shall, sir! But I cannot accept its bestowal without adequate recompense in return!" Frost reached back to retrieve the portfolio from Ming Tsun and removed the purse. He spilled the contents onto the table. "Am I to understand that the venerable Commission for Sick and Hurt Seamen still exists? I learned of it when I last was in Bristol, but does the Commission still conduct its charitable work for the seamen who have borne injury and disease in the vicissitudes of serving at sea?"

"Yes, the Commission founded so nobly almost eighty years ago by the Lords of the Admiralty still admirably serves to defray the pains and pangs of British seamen . . . and I must say with infinite sadness, it serves likewise to assuage pains similar suffered by American seamen confined in Mill and Forton prisons in England."

Frost carefully counted the coins in the purse into piles. Exactly fifty pounds in gold guineas. He pushed the coins across the table to Captain Richard Smith. "I have only fifty pounds cash money, but I wish to contribute this small sum to the Commission for Sick and Hurt Seamen in memory of Captain Crane, Royal Navy, in recompense for his gift of the *Luisiads*." Frost shrugged slightly. "I would like the memorial to be greater, but after five years' absence from Bristol I would not trust my bank to honor my draft."

Smith took the coins and formed them into one pile, then slipped them into the purse. He opened a drawer in the desk and drew out a receipt book. "Nobly spoken, sir! A munificent gift and handsome sum indeed for a book by some chap who's been dead, I wager, some two hundred and fifty years. I shall prepare you a receipt." He scribbled for a moment: "Tell me again, sir, whom shall I signify as the donor?"

"George Marlborough, sir, of Eighteen Apothecary Court, Bristol, and Nine Rua Vasco de Gama, the Macao. And since at these latitudes I shall have a following wind to Bristol, and hopefully shall encounter no more American private men-o-war, I believe I may be able to spare you a main course yard, should you think it useful." Frost had noted a main course yard on the gallows with a few other spars during his inventory of the *Royal Retort*.

Smith looked up, surprised. "Why, sir, that is generous of you indeed! I had been wracking my poor brain for some tactful way to implore you for any spars or timber you could spare. Generous to a fault, the hallmark of a true English gentleman!"

"Why, sir!" Frost exclaimed. "It is every Englishman's duty to assist the Royal Navy in its efforts to clear the seas of challenges to the ministerial powers. If an unused spar—hopefully I shall have no need of it in my crossing—can assist you in pursuing the rogue vessel with the catlike figurehead, then the spar is gladly given! I must give you warning, though, that the spar likely was cut in the Havana, and I cannot vouch for its temper."

Smith smiled ruefully: "A spar from the Havana cannot be any worse than the sticks the Admiralty has been getting from the Baltic. This war with our colonies has stopped our source for the best timber, damnation! Had I masts and spars of New England–grown trees, I do believe I could have prevailed against that cheeky rebel! And as for haring away in pursuit of him, I'll have to depend on Lieutenant Gurtman in the *Walrus* to surveil the rebel and discover his eventual hide. When *Walrus* smokes the rebel, Lieutenant Gurtman will convey that intelligence to HM *Diamond* and *Ambuscade*, similar to my *Lark*, of thirty-two cannons, escorting another convoy coming shortly behind. I regret to say, sir, that Britain can no longer fight her own wars, for that convoy brings mercenaries obtained from various of the Germanic princelings. Whether they arrive sufficient to assist my Lord Howe in this year's campaign is beyond the knowledge of a simple sailor. My duty as sea shepherd is to see the convoy of victuallers safely into Halifax Harbour, a task that will be difficult enough with this jackass rig I'm forced to spread. Without the ability to point more readily into the winds prevailing south of New Scotland, the dear *Lark* will have many a wearisome short tacks to keep her charges properly headed toward the fold."

Frost stood up, remembering in time to keep his head down. Yes, this frigate afforded its captain much less headroom than his cat. He knew that Lieutenant Gurtman would not be reporting the whereabouts of the cat to anyone anytime soon, but he was enormously grateful for—and dismayed by—all the intelligence he had gleaned from *Lark*'s affable commander. He realized, grudgingly, that he had come to like the bluff, open man. "To spare you the necessity of launching a boat, if you'll permit me to tow a messenger line behind my gig, I'll have the spar overside and tied off for you to retrieve. The quicker for you to regain your station."

"Capital idea!" Smith exclaimed. "Launching and recovering *Lark*'s own boat will consume time I can ill afford. I already have a plan for the spar's placement that I'll discuss with my carpenter directly." He signed his name to both receipts, stuffed one into the bag of coins and extended the other to Frost. "You understand the vicissitudes of the naval service may result in some months' delay before your gift can benefit the sick and hurt, but whenever it reaches the Commission, it shall be well applied."

"Of that I have no doubt," Frost said earnestly, handing the receipt to Ming Tsun for inclusion in the portfolio of the *Royal Retort*'s papers. The portfolio was large enough to accommodate the marvelous poetry of Luis Camoëns. Ming Tsun was as inscrutable and impassive as always, but Frost knew he was equally anxious to avoid the presence of British sailors, no matter how briefly, on the Tortola Packet.

"On deck, then," Smith said, draining his cup and pushing back his chair. "I'm grateful to apprehend the true source of the tea I've just enjoyed. There is little enough left in my captain's stores, though chests and chests of it reside in the convoy's holds for the sustenance of my Lord Howe's forces."

"While not directly necessary for sustenance of the body, tea does soothe and comfort to a remarkable degree," Frost said amiably, though anxious to be away and glad to follow Captain Richard Smith past the marine sentry, who came smartly to attention with an elaborate flourish. Once on the main deck, he sought first Darius and Cato Calite, grateful to see them seated inconspicuously against the larboard bulwark, and then the Tortola Packet, heaved to, and now some one hundred yards away from the *Lark*. Midshipman Livingston stood nearby and turned toward his captain.

Captain Richard Smith spoke first: "Mister Livingston, sixty fathoms length of light manila flaked down at the larboard entry, and paid out as Mister Marlborough's gig returns to his vessel. He is gifting us with a main course yard that we can put to excellent use."

Midshipman Livingston hesitated for a moment, Smith cocked an eyebrow at the delay. The midshipman saluted hurriedly and hastened off to do his captain's bidding. The *Lark* rolled slightly and its sails rattled as a light gust of wind passed through the rigging. "Aah! Some wind at last!" Smith said. He and Frost exchanged formal bows, and then Frost followed Ming Tsun into his gig. Darius and Cato Calite were already at their oars. A morose-looking Midshipman Livingston threw the end of a light line down to Frost; Frost smiled and raised his hand in mock salute: "A pleasant voyage to you, sir." The midshipman's dour expression did not change.

The gig fairly flew over the water as if propelled by six rowers and not two. "Capt'n Frost," Cato Calite whispered as soon as they were well away from the *Lark*, "that young officer wanted to press us bad."

Frost roused himself from his thoughts, reviewing the orders he would be giving as soon as he reached the Tortola Packet, as Darius looked at him, waiting permission to speak. "Yes, Mister Langdon?"

"I heard some of the crew talk of 'pressing us,' joking about what 'prime hands' Cato and I would make. Sir, what means this word 'pressing'?"

"'Tis but yet another particular name for a form of slavery, Mister Langdon, yet another barbarity the human animal has devised to deprive others of their natural worth and dignity," Frost said grimly.

"I got my freedom now, Captain Frost. I don't intend to be no slave, ever again."

"Then we ever shall have to be smarter, and exert ourselves more, than those who would enslave or press us, Mister Langdon."

"Aye, sir," Darius Langdon said, his voice raspy from the physical demands of pulling his oar. "I ain't going to forget that."

## ❦  V I I I  ❧

"✺✺✺✺✺ AITH, BUT IT IS A RICH HARVEST
✺  F  ✺ YOU HAVE WRESTED FROM KING
✺  ✺ GEORGE, AND BRING TRIUMPHANTLY
✺✺✺✺✺ TO US IN PORTSMOUTH THIS FIRST
week of this pleasant month of June!" John Langdon,
Geoffrey Frost's cousin and Continental Agent for New
Hampshire, effervesced vast enthusiasm and evident satisfaction as he clambered up the steps at the cat's starboard waist
entry and onto the cat's main deck. Arguably the most important man in New Hampshire, he spoke loudly to be heard
above the hubbub of noises made by men discharging cargo,
bringing aboard new stores, or effecting repairs. His barge
with its plum-colored canopy, rowed by Prosperous and
another Langdon household slave, bobbed up and down
beside the cat. Langdon's barge was grand indeed amidst the
gaggle of lighters and launches that had freighted in the master
mechanics and shipwrights levied from Langdon's dockyard.
Struan Ferguson had gone ahead to Portsmouth with Frost's
orders in the brig he had commanded, once Frost, aboard the
*Royal Retort*, had rendezvoused with the cat and then the
other four prize vessels.

Frost, harassed beyond all measure, was particularly irritated
at the number of Portsmouth dandies and their ladies brought
by carriages to Fort William and Mary, who were speculatively
regarding the cat through the surveillance of spyglasses. "You
should be a-ship on your own vessels in pursuit of your own

British prizes rather than envying my crew's good fortune," he said under his breath, anxious to be rid of the problems borne out to him from the land. Then he sighted Darius leaning over the cat's starboard bulwark, waving delightedly at his father. And as any father would in similar circumstances, Prosperous was gazing up anxiously at his son. Across the Piscataqua from the Pool where the cat lay to a single anchor, the raw, unpainted hull of Langdon's frigate *Raleigh*, launched a fortnight before, was moored alongside her fitting-out wharf at Rising Island. *Raleigh* was conspicuously lacking her masts, yards, or any of her designed complement of thirty-two cannons—a silent, smarting reproach to Frost for not returning from New Providence Island with the cannons captured from Fort Montagu by Commodore Esek Hopkins.

He scanned Portsmouth town, small in the distance, its church spires, and smoke from the breakfast fires, knowing the attractions and allurements the ports of Piscataqua had for his crew now that the cat's five prizes—exceedingly rich prizes, it was conceded by all—had safely berthed. At another time Frost would have enjoyed the raucous antics of the raft of herring gulls searching for tidbits of food from the pails of galley leavings Cook Barnes' mate had just emptied into the river. Or smiled at the naked tangle of young boys jostling and pushing each other into the bay's waters off the smoothed bark of the timbers and old masts shackled nearby to form the log boom protecting the harbor, perhaps even envying their rough game of "king of the log" and reflecting upon a childhood he never had. But not now. He was a-lather to quit the shore and seriously take up the rôle of a private man-o-war.

The heavy netting containing the last barrels of the five tons of powder Frost was unlading was being guided under the critical supervision of Struan Ferguson over the larboard bulwark into a lighter alongside. Simultaneously, a coop of indignantly squawking chickens and a wall-eyed nanny-goat with swollen udders were being pushed toward the manger through the press of workers by seamen under the direction of Daniel O'Buck. The launch bearing the litters on which lay Marcus

Whipple, feet laced into the incongruous baskets of split bamboo woven by Ming Tsun to immobilize the severed tendons while they healed, and the two amputees, Amos Sherman and Barnaby Lucent, was pulling strongly for the wharf at the north end of the Pool. William Felton, his eyesight improving daily, had petitioned Frost to remain with the cat's crew.

Joseph Frost, seated between the barrel-like Roderick Rawbone, tricorne planted squarely, as if measured with an artillery level, on his scarred head, and the lesser bulk of Slocum Plaisted, was following in Frost's gig. Rawbone and Plaisted were under strict orders to deliver Joseph directly to Marlborough Frost, with subsequent orders to see Joseph properly off to Saugus, where he was to concern himself with the manufacture of cannon balls, and not with further escapades of a warlike nature. Joseph grinned hugely and waved his hat at his brother. Frost, engaged in the formalities of welcoming John Langdon aboard the cat, was unable to return the wave.

"The richest harvest I wrested from King George is Marcus and our fellow New England men," Frost said tightly, nodding toward the launch bearing his brother-in-law to Portsmouth. "You cannot fathom my distress when I relate that far less than one half of the prisoners lodged in the vilest of gaols by the British have lived through their mistreatment—nay, torture, by the vilest of gaolers—and are miraculously alive to describe their horrific captivity."

"Your sister is beside herself with joy complete, as well Charity should be," John Langdon said with a self-important smile, as if he were somehow responsible for the happiness of Marcus Whipple's wife. "But why lie you here at anchor in the Pool? Why not come forward to moor before your own warehouse? Or at my dockyard, where the refit you demand can be done properly, rather than having your fellow Ferguson descend on my master mechanics and shipwrights like the wrath of God and spirit them out with all the well-seasoned timbers I had at hand to meet you off the Isles of Shoals?"

Frost saw the wherry bearing Ming Tsun gliding in behind Langdon's barge, a sea chest perched on the thwart in front of

Ming Tsun, and judged that the note taken ashore by the first snow to dock at his wharf had been delivered to Juby, and Juby had collected some clothes for him. Frost was powerfully short of decent clothing since he had given all except the clothes in which he stood to be parceled out among the former prisoners rescued from Louisbourg, so they could go ashore for their homecoming in some semblance of dignity. "Why, Cousin," Frost said mockingly, escorting John Langdon down the ladder to his cabin where were laid out the vessel manifests collated by Ming Tsun. "Recall you not that my cruize was to intercept a handsomely laden ship belonging to the Honorable John Company? This foray was but a diversion."

"Well, I dare say your designs are abundantly known to the British," Langdon snapped as he seated himself in front of Frost's desk in the day cabin, the warm June sunshine flooding in through the stern windows. "All too well known, as I must in honesty advise you."

Frost merely raised an eyebrow.

"Lieutenant St. John Lithgow, basely disregarding his given parole and irrevocably besmirching any honor he may have possessed, is run, along with that foul fellow Reedy Stalker. You know the chap, pretended to be a Piscataqua pilot, while all he did, we now realize, was gather intelligence on our Piscataqua shipbuilding programs to pass to the British. King George himself now knows that you are at sea in a sturdy sloop-o-war captured from his own Royal Navy." The Continental Agent waved an aristocratic arm in frustration. "Have you no Madeira, no port wine, man, to offer your poor afflicted cousin? I have newspapers, scarce a week old, and fresher intelligence as trade goods."

On cue, Ming Tsun knocked and then stepped into the cabin, preceded by the diminutive Nathaniel Dance, looking wretchedly uncomfortable, since his feet, even encased in two pairs of stockings, were nowhere near to fitting into the shoes borne away as a personal prize from the armed schooner *Walrus*. Regardless of his personal discomfort, Dance gravely set the tray containing the crystal decanter and elegant goblet he was bearing onto the desk and ever so carefully poured tawny port wine into the goblet. Ming Tsun placed tea in a delicate cup in front of Frost.

"I take it from your dour mood that the British officer who held his honor and parole so lightly, and the Piscataqua pilot whose services were mediocre at best, and who, having declared his true colors, will not be missed, are not the only people who've run, Cousin?" Frost sipped his tea appreciatively. Indeed, he well knew the identities of the others besides St. John Lithgow, Lieutenant, Royal Navy, and Stalker, who had decamped from Portsmouth. He had spoken with two cod-fishing boats as his small flotilla lay to off the Isles of Shoals while he switched the men he did not want with him on the rest of the cruise into the brigs and snows. The loquacious fishermen, their tongues made even more pliant and voluble by the two bottles of rum Frost had ordered passed down to them, had been only too anxious to convey all the gossips and scandals of the quality's doings in Portsmouth.

"Woodbury's gone off also," Langdon said quickly, the pain thick in his voice: he could not bring himself to say the hated word "run" with all its dreadful connotations. "His wife with him. A British merchant vessel under a flag of truce—how arranged I know not, and I am the Continental Agent for New Hampshire—called for them in this very harbor. So great was the turmoil of their leaving that it was only the day later that the decamping of that base fellow Lithgow and the knave Stalker was discovered." John Langdon wiped his florid face with a large kerchief and downed the goblet of port wine in a single long swallow. Nathaniel Dance obligingly refilled the goblet.

"Such a scandal reflects most adversely upon me, Geoffrey, as you can well imagine. My brother's sympathies are discovered to lie with the British, and thus my own are suspect, very suspect."

"Don't allow these events to agitate you, John," Frost said quickly. "After events in Louisbourg I shall forever be loath to believe the word of any British officer. The only British officer

I might have trusted unfortunately was killed in the desperate taking of this vessel and now rests many fathoms deep in the Gulf of Maine." Frost paused, suddenly thinking of Captain Richard Smith of the *Lark*. "There is probably another who would honor his word, but I evidence no surprise that this Lithgow fellow has run, and the Piscataqua is well shut of Stalker. But as for Woodbury, things surely must not be what they seem on first examination. I cannot believe Woodbury has declared himself for King and Crown. He has substantial investments and interests in London. You know that as well as I.

"My father's bank has substantial funds on deposit in England. Mayhap those funds may escheat to the Crown if this accursed war persists. So be it. But Woodbury—he is a dilettante, John, neither of us can deny that, but I cannot in my true heart believe he shall ever dishonor the proud name he bears."

Langdon laid his hand on Frost's arm impulsively. "Then you are the only man in Portsmouth who thinks thus, Geoffrey," he said gratefully.

Frost finished his cup of tea and stood, gathering up the cargo manifests of the prize vessels and extending them to Langdon. "John, the two snows are less than three years built, the same for one of the brigs, the other hath not been at sea much past five years. The Tortola Packet, I confess, is a different matter. *Royal Retort* served the British in the French War. I've no idea of her age, but she has seen long and hard usage. I think it would be a great service for the court of admiralty to knock her down to her true owner for a few pounds and permit Mister George Marlborough to resume his voyage to England in ballast and hope. I would not take her the short distance to Falmouth on the fairest wind possible, so punky are her timbers.

"The victuallers freight cordage, sailcloth, flour, onions, preserved beef, salt, sugar, cobblers' wares, clothing, needles, thread, wine, vinegar, oyl pressed from the Spanish olive, a dozen score stand of muskets—the tallies are here."

John Langdon separated the manifest of the Tortola Packet

from the others. "*Royal Retort* has a handsome cargo indeed! One thousand hogsheads of sugar, fifteen bales of cotton, and one hundred hogsheads of rum. She mounted six cannons when you took her as prize, though she has ten iron cannons of unverified condition as additional ballast."

Frost shrugged: "Perhaps those cannons will make partial amends for the cannons I shipped at New Providence for your *Raleigh* but was unable to deliver."

"Equal to, and more, Geoffrey!" Langdon exclaimed. "Faith, such rich cargoes have never been landed in Portsmouth during my life." John Langdon paused: "But the marvel greater than the four prizes fetched from Louisbourg, and the rich prize of the Tortola Packet, is your total destruction of a British sloop-o-war of twenty cannons, an armed schooner mounting eight cannons, and the severe mauling administered to a light frigate of thirty-two cannons."

"The Tortola Packet also bore as cargo two of the large sea turtles from the Caribbean," Frost continued. "Seeing that these turtles were intended for the sustenance of our enemies, I thought it best to bring them before the Continental Agent for appropriate disposition. Perhaps you will accept one for your table and gift the second to His Excellency General Washington." Frost paused. "When we were hove-to last eve off the Isles, I drew some stores for this vessel's use, as witness the minute in Ming Tsun's bold hand at the bottom of the last manifest." Frost handed Langdon two more documents. "If it had been prudent to shift the powder I freighted and Marcus and Joseph and the other New England men into the prizes, off the Isles, not to mention your master mechanics and dock workers levied upon by Struan Ferguson, I would not have brought this vessel to Portsmouth. I would now be five hundred sea miles closer to British shipping."

"Elegant of you in the extreme, this gift of succulent sea turtle, my dear Cousin! I'm certain His Excellency will find his turtle very acceptable."

Frost sighed and handed John Langdon more parcels. "These be the log and signals code book of His Britannic

Majesty's sloop-o-war *Scimitar*, now stoppering with another vessel, a schooner whose name I neglected to ascertain, the channel leading into Louisbourg Harbor." Frost looked pointedly at Langdon. "You need not enumerate that vessel with HM *Scimitar*, or the schooner *Walrus*. And as far as the confrontation with HM *Lark*, John, I admit it was a near thing. Let not her innocuous name mislead you. More like a bird of prey she be than a bird of song. She is commanded by an able officer who would prefer fighting Frenchmen to Americans, though his preferences will not blind him to his duty."

Frost shrugged again. "Perhaps you may wish to dispatch these documents to His Excellency with the turtle, or this Marine Committee, or is it called now the Naval Committee —you are always talking, Cousin, about some commission or committee that may glean intelligence from these pages." Frost had read *Scimitar*'s log: it told of nothing but the dreariness of convoy duty, shepherding reluctant and poorly crewed transport vessels en route to Halifax in the late spring storms of the high Atlantic.

"And this," Frost said reluctantly, adding a large folded letter to the stack of documents, "is the list of dead in my service, and those wounded badly enough to be put ashore. There are amounts entered against each name to be paid directly to kin from my accounts with Marlborough's bank. The unwounded men I have put ashore with the snows, fifteen or so, are people not fitted for life aboard a private man-o-war. Their promised wages advanced against that wretched abomination of prize money, so akin to the wages of piracy as virtually indistinguishable, to be paid immediately, and prize monies to be shared out once the cargoes and vessels are condemned and auctioned, are likewise indicated by their names. I depart as this tide turns."

"But Geoffrey," Langdon said with some exasperation, even bewilderment, in his tone, "presently I respond to instructions issuing from the Marine Committee of the Continental Congress. But surely you must rest ashore, this talk of rushing immediately to sea is madness! Your vessel has need of refit, replenishment, rest for your crew—there is much happening in Philadelphia. Our Continental Congress is meeting. We are resolved to stand up a nation of our own. Within the month, my colleagues advise me, Congress will declare our unilateral defiance of the British Crown—we are declaring our independence from British rule!"

"There is amazement in how long a truth is known, though studiously ignored, before it is finally acted upon," Frost said tersely. "When you dispatch the *Scimitar*'s log and code book to your Marine Committee, John, kindly advise the Committee that German mercenaries are at this very moment on the Atlantic en route to Howe in Halifax. As for me, the business of a private man-o-war is business, though perhaps not in the form normally associated with trade," Frost snapped. "We ruin the British trade as a spur to their increase, and the British warships we draw off or destroy are those less to pursue us. The cat at sea, the British in a panic, wondering where this cat might next strike, might next appear—the cost of cargo insurance ever rising on the Exchange, more British men-o-war told off for convoy duty—the cat at sea is worth far more than all the silly posturings of this so-called 'Congress' of yours in Philadelphia."

"I cannot say nay to you, Geoffrey, but you must take due cares. There is no useful intelligence that the Ministerial Government—no, damnit, no more of this silly pretending that George Three is the innocent pawn of corrupt ministers! It is the British Government that the King heads—to perdition with him! And his Royal Navy declines to recognize the validity of a privateer's warrant or letter-of-marque issued by a colony—now a state—in rebellion."

"On that score my men and I must take our chances." Frost chose his next words carefully: "I have never foreseen any situation where I would surrender any ship I command." His voice conveyed his determination, and he thought of his instructions to Caleb Mansfield just before he and Ming Tsun had crossed over to HM *Lark*.

"Still, you have to exercise great caution, Geoffrey. There

are several New England captains, at least three have been named to me, who have deigned to apply to state legislature of united government for privateer warrants. They fall upon any vessel of any flag as their rightful prey. They also care not a whit that you have privateer's warrants granted by the New Hampshire legislature and the Continental Congress."

"Then they be pirates operating without what little benefit the laws of Admiralty provide, and pirates, of any description, should keep their distance from me." Yes, Frost had endured far more than what he considered his rightful share of pirates, of various nations or tribes, along the trade routes from Macao to London, Saint Helena, Recife, Angra, Saint Eustus, and Portsmouth.

"There is more, Geoffrey," John Langdon said ominously. "The British Crown is set upon extirpating this rebellion as quick as rot can be cored from an apple. The purchase of German mercenaries by George Three in the same wise planters in Jamaica purchase Guineamen, as you have reported, shows but one aspect of British intent."

"Thank you, Cousin," Frost said formally, but with a hint of humor in his voice. "As our mutual friend, Benjamin Franklin, has observed in his excellent almanack, 'to be forewarned is to be forearmed.'"

John Langdon could not help noticing that Nathaniel Dance had quietly and efficiently refilled his goblet with the port wine while he had been conversing with Frost. He drank, sipping this time, with relish. "A most excellent port wine, Geoffrey," he said, then returned to the subject of pirates. "For the life of me, I cannot see why people like Morgan and Tackett don't take out the necessary warrants from New Hampshire, Massachusetts, Connecticut, or the Congress. It is little enough we ask in the way of a warrant, and the bonds certainly are minimal."

Frost smiled mischievously, feeling the muscles stretch in his cheek and shoulder without undue discomfort. "It is not the initial expense that deters them, most like, John, but the prospect of having to share their gains with an agent of prizes."

Langdon ignored the jibe but harrumphed several times as if clearing his throat. Finally, he said, "Geoffrey, I trust you do not mind—your being at sea for a cruize of unknown duration, I could scarce consult you—but I shared the draughts of your vessel with an especial friend of mine, John Roche; you may know of him, a prominent captain engaged in the West Indies trade. Currently he is an officer of the Continental Navy serving aboard one of His Excellency's schooners, *Lynch* by name."

Frost cocked an eyebrow. "I have never met your Captain Roche, though I am acquainted with his reputation. Being a reputation only, and knowing not the man, I possess no judgment of his person or character. But to what purpose have you shared out the draughts of this vessel, which I collect are derivative of the genius of a French naval architect, as elaborated upon by a Scottish dockyard?"

Langdon did not look directly at Frost. "Cousin"—the use of the term of relationship instead of his Christian name, which he knew to be calculated, did not escape Frost—"you well know how comely this vessel is, and the enthusiastic reports I heard immediately when Ferguson brought in the first prize brig and levied upon my master mechanics praised most extravagantly her sailing and fighting qualities."

Frost smiled thinly. "For that you can thank the quality of men like Struan Ferguson, and New Hampshire men by the names of Chasse, Collingwood, Lacey, Nason, O'Buck, and Plaisted, to name but a few. But the attributes you describe are certainly possessed in full measure by this cat, and a crew of determined, resourceful men embarked upon a staunch vessel indeed forge a formidable weapon."

"Your name is noticeably absent from the list just enumerated, Geoffrey," Langdon said. Frost did not reply but led John Langdon, who had to finish his port wine hastily, back to the cat's main deck.

"Mister Langdon," Frost commanded Darius when he and his cousin emerged on deck, "please summon the Continental Agent's barge."

John Langdon looked up sharply: "You have given Darius my surname."

Frost nodded. "That is how the young gentleman is entered in the muster books of this vessel. I surmise Captain Roche and you aspire to construct a vessel similar to this cat, and surely in your yard, now that *Raleigh* is launched and the building way is vacant. If that be the case, you cannot have chosen a vessel more worthy of emulation. This cat is a wondrously fast and robust ship that cyphers my intent before I know it myself. You and the Continental Navy and your Marine Committee are ungrudgingly welcome to her draughts with all my heart."

Langdon gripped Frost's hand firmly. " 'Thank you, Cousin! So worthy a sentiment was what I indeed expected of you." Then, gesturing toward Darius, "I would rather you had given him your own surname, Geoffrey, though mind, I fully comprehend the honor." He nodded toward one of the prize brigs at anchor nearby. "Is that the one three years off the stocks? I think I might purchase one, perhaps more, of your prize vessels and go privateering myself. What think you of this notion, Cousin?"

"As your fancy is suited, so be it, though I misdoubt, John, that so high a personage as yourself wishes to risque his person on a private man-o-war." Frost stood aside as four burly crewmen hustled up with the two sea turtles, each strapped to two heavy lathes, stretcherlike, upside down on their carapaces, mouths wired closed, their expressions lugubrious, as if already divining the fate awaiting them. "I trust you do not mind freighting these turtles in your barge, John. I have no further communication with the land once I send your dock workers ashore and must ask your indulgence in their appointed delivery."

"There are many competent mariners, Cousin," Langdon said waspishly, ignoring the sea turtles for the moment. "Marcus Whipple is a name that springs readily to mind. Once his wounds mend he would make a capital privateer's master."

"Let Marcus be," Frost said harshly, staring his cousin

unflinchingly in the eye. "He will never walk again as God created him. He'll walk, aye, Ezrah Green, Ming Tsun, and the giant Indian all assure me of that, but with caution and a limping stride. It would take many a day for him to learn again the trick of a steep quarterdeck in a stiff breeze. Let him be."

John Langdon shrugged but said nothing. Frost gravely saw the two mournful looking sea turtles lowered overside, and then his cousin into his barge. Langdon, carefully avoiding the turtles, ordered Prosperous to move the animals strapped to their lathes as far forward in the barge as possible. He peered up earnestly at Frost, picked up the parcel of cord-wrapped newspapers lying on the plump cushion of the middle thwart and threw the newspapers up to him. "My fresh intelligence I've already delivered; these be the newspapers promised." Langdon peered up earnestly at Frost. "Surely one night as our guest, Geoffrey? Elizabeth misses you sorely."

"The business of a private man-o-war is business," Frost repeated. And with a glance toward the westward sky, "I suggest getting the barrels of powder just landed for His Excellency into warehouse as quickly as possible, Cousin, for sure a blow is coming on. All of your mechanics and shipwrights are to follow you." He lifted his hand in farewell. Langdon shrugged, flipped his coat tails into his lap and took his seat.

The barge stroked way, and Frost turned to face Ming Tsun, Struan Ferguson, Ishmael Hymsinger, Hannibal Bowditch, and Nathaniel Dance. Darius Langdon waved a hurried farewell to his father and joined the group. "Mister Ferguson, order all dock workers off our ship and into their boats. Quickly, else they sail with us! Prepare to weigh anchor. We have one hour before the outflooding tide, and we must be away. Our people in the launch are now returning." Frost did not wish his crew to dwell upon the fact that he was holding them to their articles for a six months cruise rather than paying off with the five prizes in harbor.

There was a great confusion on the main deck of the cat as the mechanics and shipwrights ceased their work and hurried for their barges alongside. Frost concealed his pleasure at seeing Langdon's dock workers cease their tasks and flee so quickly, though Daniel O'Buck thoroughly searched each dock worker personally before permitting him into a barge.

"Beg pardon, Captain," Struan Ferguson said diffidently, "but the lads have a proposal for ye."

"A proposal for me?" Frost stared at each of them in turn, then Ishmael Hymsinger. "Mister Hymsinger, I confess I thought you had gone ashore with Captain Whipple. His need for nursing remains great, and I have not given you permission to join this crew."

"Beg pardon for not petitioning sooner, Captain Frost, but while Captain Whipple's need for skilled ministration of physic remains great, he has a loving, devoted wife, and others far better equipped and skilled than I to return him to health."

"I know not how you would be employed in my crew, sir. I already have a surgeon, and a minister of the gospel . . ."

"Mayhap Surgeon Green could again employ me as his mate, as was done off the Isle of Sable. I have some training as a carpenter, also, Captain, a worker of wood as was our Lord and Savior Jesus Christ afore he got the call."

"We'll discuss this later, Mister Hymsinger, and before we do, kindly trim your beard—a proper shave would be better— if you have any hope of joining this vessel." Frost, frowning, turned to Darius, Hannibal and Nathaniel: "Now, what is this proposal of yours?"

All three lads pointed to Hymsinger and chorused, more or less in unison, "It be Ishmael's proposal, Captain, sir."

"Yes, Hymsinger?"

"A smelling-out, sir."

"A what?" Frost demanded, his frown deepening. "With anchor almost a-trip this be not the time to have sport with me, Ishmael Hymsinger."

Hymsinger raised both hands beseechingly. "Sir, there is yet one among this crew who sought to take your life at Louisbourg—and nearly succeeded. He bears you desperate malice enough to attempt again, surely with more cunning."

"You cannot know that," Frost snapped. Insh'allah, Deo

Gratis: he had been far too busy during the voyage from Louisbourg, the altogether too close brushes with the Royal Navy, and the capture of the Tortola Packet, to give the second sniper who had attempted to take his life any thought at all. "Campbell died for his crime, that's lesson hard enough for any man. And I have set fifteen men ashore this day as unwilling to pull their weight. That potential assassin is likely among those slackers."

"That is not the sentiment of the crew, sir. They wish to be shed of one who bides his time to strike again when your leadership will be needed most."

"Then let the crew name this assassin."

"The crew cannot, but yonder dog can," Ishmael Hymsinger said, pointing to the Newfoundland dog stretched out luxuriously full length on the main deck, his massive head resting contentedly against the truck of a 6-pounder.

"How so?" Frost demanded.

"Some lore I possess from the Mi'kmaq, and other of the northern tribes among whom my father and I lived as missionaries. It be not witchcraft, though some, upon seeing it, might think it so."

"I have a tide to catch, Hymsinger . . ."

"This smelling-out shall delay you less than ten of those precious minutes, and upon its completion the men shall work all the more willingly, knowing that the danger posed by a disaffected one in their midst is grubbed out, branch and root."

Frost looked at Struan Ferguson, who nodded acquiescence. "The men have developed a remarkable affinity for Hymsinger, Captain. He has won them over, much as our good Ming Tsun has." The three youngsters bobbed their heads in vigorous assent.

"Very well, gentlemen, I ken plainly that you have discussed this among yourselves betimes. You have ten minutes—no more—and those ten minutes begin now." Frost displayed Jonathan's watch and marked the time.

The launch thumped softly against the cat's hull and Roderick Rawbone's huge bulk filled the starboard waist entry.

Slocum Plaisted, carrying a large wicker basket, heaved up behind him. Two men stood ready to pass sling tackle down to hook onto the launch.

"Belay that!" Struan Ferguson shouted. "All hands muster on the main deck. Form ranks by your watches and divisions. Lively now!" The crew of the launch swarmed aboard the cat; the topmen who had gone aloft in preparation to cast off gussets at the call slid down from the yards; and men, including old Cook Barnes, came pushing and jostling each other from below decks, wonderment on every man's face. In half a minute the entire crew of the cat, one hundred and eighty-two men as Frost reckoned, less the woods-cruisers, was marshaled in four more or less straight lines, though vastly cramped together, on the cat's main deck.

"Open ranks!" Struan shouted. "Front rank, two steps forward; second rank, one step forward; third rank, stand as ye are. Fourth rank, one step backward." The men, unaccustomed to hearing, much less complying with, such martial commands as indeed Struan Ferguson was in giving them, jostled further for uneasy position somewhat akin to the lines of formation Struan had ordered. Then each man froze in place as an apparition, leather phylacteries bound to forehead and arms, shoulders draped in a soft, tanned deerskin cloak on which strange ciphers and symbols were painted in bright hues of red, black, indigo, yellow and green, clutching a forked deer antler, bounded up from the main hatchway and onto the main deck.

The apparition paused for a moment, drawing itself to its considerable full height, then brandished aloft the branched antler and gave voice to a long shriek which ululated like nothing Frost had ever heard before, causing the hair on the nape of Frost's neck to prickle, and a shiver to course down his spine.

The apparition began a strange shuffling dance, all the while continuing its high-pitched ululations. Frost saw the great Newfoundland dog lift himself in one fluid motion from his position of ease and trot over to fall in step with the apparition.

Frost sensed a presence at his elbow and knew without turning that Caleb Mansfield had joined him. "What do you make of this, Caleb?" Frost whispered, unwilling, or unable, to take his eyes from the apparition that was cavorting and bounding about the deck in front of the lines of men, who were all distinctly uneasy.

"Kint rightly say, Capt'n. I wus in a Iroquois village once, tryin' to trade furs, only they'd been promised to the Frenchies, and I got nothin' for my troubles. I saw somethin' akin to this, to divine which man had lain unbidden with a maiden."

"And was justice served, Caleb?"

"I wouldn't know about thet, Capt'n, but one man wus pointed out, then clubbed to death. Thinkin' on it, the maiden wus clubbed to death betimes."

The apparition shot out both arms dramatically toward Frost, and Frost realized with a start that he was comprehending the story the apparition was telling in pantomime. Against his will Frost saw again the gray stone walls of the houses inside the quay at Louisbourg, the desperate fighting, the deadly, hateful thud of bodies against bodies; felt again the stone chips spat up by the bullets' impact biting into neck and face, so convincingly that he raised his right hand to touch the bruises and cuts on his face, only partially healed. Every man in the crowded ranks was likewise absorbed into the story being played out without words.

Frost realized the apparition was Ishmael Hymsinger as Hymsinger drew out Ming Tsun, and Ming Tsun went through the pantomime of swinging his halberd; and gazing down from his quarterdeck at the crew in their rough lines on the main deck, Frost saw the absolute, abject fear in each man's face—fear that nearly matched his own during the savage fighting with the British soldiers and Whip Loring and the almost successful attempt on his life.

Hymsinger paused dramatically and gestured toward the Newfoundland dog. He touched an antler's tine to the dog's nose, and brandished the antler triumphantly aloft. Hymsinger leaped high, releasing yet an even higher-pitched ululating shriek, then began pacing menacingly along the front rank of men. The Newfoundland dog followed closely at Hymsinger's heels, neck hair bristling, a growl forming low in the dog's throat.

A man started to step backward, paused with foot lifted, then thought better of it as both Hymsinger and the dog glared fiercely at him. He stood quivering as the Newfoundland dog sniffed him carefully, then Hymsinger and the dog passed down the rank. Hymsinger paced the deck in front of the first rank twice, then abruptly turned and moved along the men in the second rank.

A man in the second rank was seized by a fit of coughing, but Hymsinger glared at him, and the man's coughing immediately stopped. Hymsinger held the forked antler in both hands now, much like a witching rod for the divining of water, and like a witching rod the forked antler jerked and oscillated in Hymsinger's hands. Hymsinger and the dog, the dog licking chops heavy with saliva, turned the second rank and, carefully sniffing at every man, began walking down the line of men in the third rank.

Suddenly, a man near the end of the third rank broke away from his mates and raced across the deck to hurl himself despairingly over the starboard bulwark before anyone could stir to stop him. Frost rushed to the quarterdeck starboard railing and watched as a head emerged from the froth of water and began flailing away with a lusty overhand stroke. Well, at least David Sweeney was a passable swimmer. Beside him Caleb was raising Gideon to his shoulder. Frost stopped him. "We are best shed of him, Caleb. I reckon he won't be much welcomed in Portsmouth."

Frost drew Jonathan's Bréquet from his waistcoat pocket and clicked open the cover. "Mister Ferguson!" he shouted, "We have the tide in exactly three minutes. Anchor weighed if you please. I suggest tops'ls, driver and sprits'l to work the vessel into the channel. Do not worry, we shan't be a-frolic on the Piscataqua as we were on our initial cruize." Frost grinned at Struan, whom he knew was aghast at the thought that Frost would attempt the madcap running of the Piscataqua as he had little less than a month previous, setting out on the cruise to Louisbourg. Frost had defied the odds then to show the cat's clean heels to the gentlefolk of Portsmouth, and, it could not be denied, to show off to John Ayres of His Excellency's schooner *Lynch*. Frost was deeply grateful that his impetuosity had not brought harm to his crew or vessel. But he had learned . . .

"'Tis coming on a blow, Mister Ferguson, and I wish to be well off soundings when the weather arrives. Once we are a league offshore, please have the storm sails broken out and made ready." Frost glanced around the main deck so suddenly abuzz and saw the three ship's gentlemen petting the Newfoundland dog profusely.

"Masters Bowditch, Dance, and Langdon, a word with you, if I may." The youngsters dutifully made their way to the quarterdeck, followed by the dog, who sniffed hungrily at Nathaniel's pocket. "Please detail for me your rôles in this charlatan's display," Frost demanded sternly, knowing intuitively that the three youths had plotted the smelling-out with Hymsinger.

Hannibal knew the meaning of the word, though the other two lads did not. "Oh no, sir," Hannibal said, speaking for the three, "it was naught the charlatan nor a monkeyshine, sir. George was all primed to smell out this Sweeney chap good and proper."

"George? Who is this George?" Frost broke in quickly.

"Why, the dog, sir. We've named him George, for the British King," all three ship's gentlemen said, speaking as one. "Sometimes we call him Three, for George Three," Nathaniel said. "He answers to both. All the men know his name."

Frost nodded as if the naming of the dog was something he had known but had momentarily forgotten. He likely had heard some of the crew call the dog by name, though in truth, he had been too engrossed in other cares about his crew and vessel to remark it. So be it. The problem of naming the dog had resolved itself. He said, "David Sweeney broke and ran, attesting to his guilt, which on the thinking of it, especially his being a running mate of Campbell's, who had lost his head at Louisbourg to Ming Tsun's halberd, was only too obvious. I'll warrant he rightly feared being smelled out, for fear has its own foul odor. But inform me, please, gentlemen, why you and Mister Hymsinger were so certain this 'George,' as you have named him, a right name I might add, would smell out this Sweeney above all the rest that you would resort to this trickery?"

"Why, sir," Nathaniel Dance spoke for the three, "Ishmael believes his antler can divine corruption 'n' treachery, but we . . ." Nathaniel paused conspiratorially to include Hannibal and Darius, "had smoked Sweeney long betimes as the one who attempted yere life." The diminutive youth paused to draw an onion from his pocket and held it out to George Three, who nipped it softly from the boy's hand and chewed it with relish. "We ware precautionary enough to slip an onion into Sweeney's shirt. George rightly dotes on onions, he does."

HE STORM CAUGHT UP WITH THE CAT BEFORE SUNDOWN, AFTER THE COAST HAD DROPPED FROM SIGHT, THOUGH NOT WITH ALL THE DISTANCE RUN that Frost wished. It was not a proper nor'wester, though any vessel less well found than the cat would have been excused for thinking it so. The winds and seas coming from the northwest continued to build for two days, intensified on the morning of the third, and diminished below forty knots and heavy, tumultuous, uneasy seas just before darkness of the third day. There were two more days of what Struan Ferguson called *dreich* summer weather before the storm really subsided, and Frost was almost ready to order down the heavy storm sails and return to regular canvas.

Frost was awakened from his first four hours of uninterrupted sleep in as many days by mumbled curses and drunken shouts. The noise arose from the crew's berthing deck forward, but there was, after all, very little that happened on a ship one hundred and twenty-five feet in length overall, into which two hundred and four men were packed cheek to jowl, that did not make its way aft. Frost stuffed his feet into his shoes, grabbed his brass-backed cutlass, and, taking the one Bass pistol fortuitously loaded, was up the companionway, on his quarterdeck, and standing by a shocked Jack Lacey, the helmsman, thirty seconds after he had been awakened.

In the dim half-light of a mist-shrouded morning just before dawn Frost saw two men joined in a tight embrace of head-locks and clumsily propelling themselves up the main access hatchway. A knot of men, following up the hatchway, stopped immediately when they saw Frost. The two men joined to-gether continued their writhing on the main deck. Struan Fer-guson charged onto the main deck clutching his backsword and an Andrew Strachan all-metal pistol. Except for the weapons and the shoes on his feet, the cat's officer immediately subor-dinate to Geoffrey Frost was stark naked.

"Mister Ferguson! Give each of those men a knock on the head or a prod in the guts if you please!" Frost shouted. Struan happily obliged with a kick to the stomach of the man who had rolled atop the other and then with an equally swift kick to the man underneath, with the happy effect of separat-ing the clumsy ball into two puking, convulsing individuals. Frost walked slowly down the starboard companionway to the cat's main deck. "Thank you, Mister Ferguson. You may repair below to dress yourself more fittingly."

Struan Ferguson glanced down, his face dissolving into hor-ror as he turned on heel and flew toward the nearest compan-ionway. Frost paced over to the nearer man, lying face down, and turned the man over with the toe of his shoe. "Bruce Bel-mont," he muttered to himself, "farmer from Exeter." He turned the second man likewise. "Owen Pushaw, cider maker from Kittery." He could smell the liquor surrounding both men like the rank fog of a polecat's essence. It was plain enough that somehow Belmont and Pushaw had gotten access to the spirits room.

Frost's eyes fell upon the frightened, wide-eyed face of young Nathaniel Dance peering through the legs of the press of men who had flowed up from the berthing deck. Nathaniel would know. "Mister Dance!"

"Sir!" Nathaniel Dance cried, struggling to his feet and slip-ping through the press of men to stand before his captain.

"Does this cat possess a kitten?"

"Beg pardon, sir?"

"A flogger, a scourge, a cat with at least nine tails. Something, anything, to whip a disobedient, insolent, besotted sailor."

"Yes sir, this cat has such a . . . kitten."

"Please fetch it, Mister Dance," Frost said coldly. "You!" he continued, indicating with his cutlass a loose group of four men standing slightly apart from the rest of the crew, formed now in a rough half-circle on the main deck, "Drape these squalid excuses for private men-o-war over those two cannons."

Nathaniel Dance returned quickly with a bag cut from coarse red baize. Frost took the bag from Nathaniel Dance, untied the strings at the bag's neck and drew out a regulation Royal Navy cat-o-nine-tails. The crew, to a man, was watching him fixedly to see what Frost would mete out as punishment for drunkenness.

Frost handed his cutlass and pistol to Nathaniel Dance and palmed the deadly flogging tool. The muscles along his spine tingled as the knotted thongs slipped through his fingers. Frost took a step forward and lashed the mainmast with the cat-o-nine-tails, making a sound that fell like multiple pistols shots in the absolute silence. He lashed the mainmast again.

"How does the Royal Navy maintain discipline in its service, Mister Dance?" Frost demanded.

"With the lash, then rum, then sodomy, sir." Nathaniel Dance replied meekly.

"Then not on this ship, Mister Dance. No floggings on my ship . . . but no drunkards either!" Frost stepped to the leeward bulwark and threw the murderous whip into the sea. He tossed the red baize bag to Nathaniel Dance. "Keep this to carry all your gold coins, Mister Dance."

Frost stood over the two men draped over the cannons. He lifted Owen Pushaw's head by the man's hair, peered into the man's blankly staring face, mouth rimmed with vomit and nose a-bubble with snot.

"All of you!" Frost shouted, staring round at his crew. "The Dear knows I've shipped no angels, but men who break into the ship's stores of spirits, stealing from their shipmates and debauching themselves, will not long be members of this vessel's complement!" Frost glared, seeking Slocum Plaisted and finding him: "Mister Plaisted! Prepare to sway out and stream the gig astern. First chain each of these men to thwarts. Two days shall they have to contemplate the demons of rum without food or water, before we shall deign to determine if they be fit to rejoin our company."

Frost glared around at his crew, who shrank back from his fierce countenance. "Who are Pushaw's mess mates? Who are Belmont's mess mates? Come! Identify yourselves!"

Here and there among the gathered crew, hands were raised reluctantly. "Your rum rations are stopped for one week. As for Pushaw and Belmont, their rum rations are stopped for the rest of this cruize. If ever again you allow your mess mates to make such infernal asses of themselves, all of you shall join them for two days in tow behind this vessel."

Frost turned on his heel, began walking toward his quarter-deck, then turned to Slocum Plaisted, who in Struan Ferguson's absence to dress himself was the next ranking deck officer. "Mister Plaisted, as soon as the gig is streamed, all plain sail, starboard tack, course to be made good will be southeast by south."

Two days following the incident with the two intoxicated hands, Frost was braced on his quarterdeck, taking his noon sight, calling off the numbers to Hannibal Bowditch, who noted them on a chalkboard. He was pleased that his deduced reckoning of the cat's drift during the storm had been off less than half a league. This business of finding longitude with an accurate clock was infinitely easier than the laborious lunar sights. Still, it would not do to place all trust in the delicate Kendall chronometer, which so far had been meticulous in its recording of time, though of course the winding of it was punctual and scrupulously logged. Frost's ingrained caution, and fifteen going on sixteen years at sea, had long ago taught him the value of using all navigational resources to hand. He was still taking lunar sights as often as the weather permitted—and he had detected another round dozen of errors in Moore's calculations. He frowned as he thought of the recently confirmed mathematical errors, added to those he had discovered in the last two years; he simply had to find the time to transcribe those errors and advise Moore's publisher.

The storm had borne the cat a good five hundred sea miles southeast of Boston, and the ship was on a strong reach to fetch the westernmost islands of the Açores in less than a week. Frost lowered his sextant into the case that Hannibal Bowditch now held for him, and his eyes fell on Ishmael Hymsinger, who was doing his best to saw a board under the disproving eye of the elderly carpenter, John Brandon.

"I understand, Mister Bowditch, that our inestimable friend, George Three, has found most amenable berthing accommodations with Mister Dance, Mister Langdon and yourself, than elsewhere in this vessel."

"Oh, sir," the youth piped, "we chose not George as a berth mate, he chose us, though as you can't but notice, he has become a great favorite of the entire crew, so gentle he is, and all. Many a man of our boarding party aboard the Tortola Packet laughs to think how George cowered that entire crew."

Indeed, Frost had noticed. Half an hour previously, he had seen Roland Pickering, the sailor who had tried to drown the Newfoundland dog in Louisbourg Harbor, give the big dog a piece of biscuit spread with butter. Evidently all the crew was kindly disposed toward the dog, for he went about the ship as he pleased, and any mess he created was instantly cleared away by the nearest hand. "I am glad he has chosen you, Mister Langdon and Mister Dance," Frost said. "He is a credit to this ship and portends good fortune for all our company, but have a care to his diet; I collect the weight he carries at this moment is optimum for him."

Hannibal Bowditch momentarily turned sternward; his eyes widened as he exclaimed: "Sir! Sir! A shark is following the gig!"

Frost followed Hannibal Bowditch's gaze and saw the dorsal fin of a huge sea animal paralleling and keeping station two fathoms to the leeward of the gig. He noted with amusement that both Pushaw and Belmont were sitting rigidly on their thwarts, unmoving, hands tightly grasping the gig's gunwales, too frightened to cry out. Frost recognized the animal immediately. "That be a northern bottlenose whale, Mister Bowditch," he said quietly. "Quite common in these climes, though belike our brave lads, so recently having forsaken plow and axe, know it not for its true self. Despite its size and appearance, it is no more offensive than George. Mark you the distinction between the shark on the one hand, which is a fish, Mister Bowditch, and a whale, though a small one such as this, which is a mammal. You shall doubtless see your fill of both animals before you return to Salem."

Frost allowed himself the luxury of a chuckle. "Our lads have had sufficient time, sun and rain, to gain their sobriety. Their second day astream ends this eve. Still, it would do no harm to hand them in now, and make that my generosity was more to spare the 'shark' a bellyache than succor them. Ask Mister Plaisted to give you sufficient hands to draw the gig once sails have been backed and we're briefly hove-to."

"I twig your drift, sir, but your sextant below first." Hannibal Bowditch scuttled for the companionway to Frost's cabin.

"Mister Ferguson!" Frost shouted, his voice easily carrying, even without a speaking trumpet, to Struan standing amidships. "Turn into the wind and sails aback while we recover our errant lubbers. Mister Bowditch reports a thumping great shark is intent on ingesting them for dinner, and I believe we should spare the poor animal surfeit of indigestion." The cat's parrels squealed and protested as Struan Ferguson bawled directions for hands to their proper lines and hauls. The helm put the cat smartly into the wind; sails flogged and snapped, and way came off her abruptly.

Hannibal Bowditch raced aft with two sailors, one of whom brandished a long boat hook. One sailor braced the other as he leaned far out over the stern and hooked the bight run through the massive iron ring stapled to the sternpost, hauled the line over the stern bulwark, untied the double bowline, and with the line free raced to the larboard, the lee, waist entry, where a knot of men waited to tail onto the line.

Frost was pleased to see that the men waiting at the entry were mostly Pushaw's and Belmont's mess mates. Efficient husbandry, nay, the absolute safety of a ship at sea depended upon the crew's loyalty to the ship and each man's loyalty to his mates. He judged the loss of rum rations for yet another five days would have a salutary effect upon the manner in which their mess mates looked upon Pushaw and Belmont.

The line was handed so quickly by more than a dozen men that the gig fairly boiled over the sea's surface, and in less than a minute the gig bumped against the cat's filling strake and two hands jumped down to attach lifting tackle. Immediately the gig rose from the water to the screech of blocks, and once it was high enough to clear the bulwark, willing hands seized the gig and brought it inboard.

Frost saw Ezrah Green at the edge of the press. "Doctor Green, please examine these men, perhaps some grease for their parched skins. They have avoided giving offense to the belly of Leviathan, so they should willingly join their mates in the proper husbandry of this vessel." Frost turned sternward to hide his smile from the crew and saw the bottlenose whale stroking leisurely away to the north.

"Mister Ferguson, brace round the yards, if you please, we have dallied far too long. And see if the fore course won't draw a bit easier if we ease the starboard leech." Frost turned to the helmsman. "Make the course as before. Southeast by south."

"Southeast by south it is, sir," the helmsman replied.

Frost stepped to the breast rail and gazed down at the wizened carpenter who, scowling, was running a knowledgeable thumb down the edge of a board that Ishmael Hymsinger had just sawn. "Mister Brandon," Frost said in a conversational tone, "if you can spare your carpenter's mate, I would like a word with him."

"He lacks much being a mate of mine," Brandon said with resignation, then addressed Hymsinger. "The captain wants to gam with you; report to him like a proper seaman."

Hymsinger ascended to the quarterdeck, his feet, clad in worn, shabby Indian moccasins, making no sound, and stood respectfully in front of Frost. "Please promenade with me, Ishmael Hymsinger," Frost said, clasping his hands behind his back and stepping to the weather rail, then pacing from stern bulwark to breast rail several times, Hymsinger pacing silently beside him, before saying: "I do believe carpentry is not your calling."

Hymsinger dropped his shoulders slightly. "Work with wood I have done with axe and drawknife, but I confess to having seen no adze, saw or auger until the English invaded the poor village on the island of Abegweit where I lodged with my Mi'kmaq brothers and conveyed me in captivity first to Quebec, thence to Louisbourg. Though I do love the Jewish carpenter mightily."

Frost stopped at the breast rail and scanned the horizon for some moments before resuming his pacing. "Grateful I am that an exceedingly benevolent Providence placed you in Louisbourg to aid my brother-in-law, Marcus, for without your ministrations he would doubtlessly have perished long since." Frost glanced sideways and arched an eyebrow. "I am always reluctant to question a man too closely about his origins, Ishmael Hymsinger, but a carpenter's mate you'll never be, so now that you are shipped, I must find useful employment for you aboard this vessel. Forgive me if it is unseemly that I satisfy my curiosity as to how you came to live among the aboriginal inhabitants of New France."

"My father, Eziechel, was the instrument the Divine One chose to bring me to the 'Indians,' as you English are prone to call them. Late in the last century, so I was reliably informed, a minister returned from the New World to the humble village in Cornwall where my ancestors long betimes had dwelt. This worthy person had been associated with that most gentle clergyman, the Reverend John Eliot of the Massachusetts Bay Colony. This minister, whose name I'm informed was Cutts, Trembling Cutts, to be precise, told of the great work Reverend Eliot had done in setting the feet of the Algonquins on the path to Christianity."

Frost paused, musing against the breast rail, and took in all that was happening on the crowded main deck, noting with satisfaction that everyone had a task and was diligently prosecuting it. "I am familiar with the name, a distinguished one in the Massachusetts Colony. Yet the Reverend Eliot was unable to keep the Massachusetts men from falling upon the Algonquin and Abanaqui tribes during Philip's War—and butchering them."

"Yes, the story be horrific, though by my reckoning a century has passed. A number of young men from my village, inspired to make amends for the Massachusetts men's blood thirst, took ship to the New World to be missionaries to the Indians. A generation later more young men followed, and it was in '46 that my father, a lad of thirteen at the time, heard his call and made his difficult way to Massachusetts."

As the cat's stern lifted to a gentle swell from the southwest, Frost thought he saw a sail flash momentarily on the far northern horizon. He glanced quickly aloft; the lookout in the main topmast crosstrees was peering due eastward. Frost called out, summoning Nathaniel Dance, who was helping Will Sawtelle, the sailmaker, lay out a studding sail for mending. "Mister Dance, add another pair of eyes aloft. Remind the lookout in the mainmast crosstrees not to concentrate so fixedly in one direction that he fails to direct his gaze elsewhere.

"And once landed in the New World, your father took up a very cold trail of those few Indians who had survived the savagery of the Puritans, God's own anointed fanatics," Frost breathed harshly, turning to examine Hymsinger even more closely.

"Oh yes, sir, but my father found them, the remnants of some Christian Wampanoag from Chelmsford, their descendants actually, who had trekked far into New France, all the way to the southern shores of the great Fleuve de Saint Laurent."

Frost was listening keenly but his eyes were following Nathaniel Dance's rapid progress up the main shrouds, the youth's easy, fluid transfer to the main futtock shrouds, going outside the main top, of course, rather than through the lubber's hole, and up the main topmast shrouds to the ratlines that culminated just below the main topmast crosstrees. "Youth is truly wasted on the young," he said pensively to himself.

From the corner of his left eye Frost saw the Newfoundland dog jump daintily to the larboard bulwark just aft of the waist entry, gain his balance against the ship's slow roll until the mainmast inclined slightly to starboard, then heave himself into the ratlines.

Ishmael Hymsinger gasped: "Le chein est extra!"

Frost answered, "Oui, mais incapable d'être á la hune."

The dog, fairly caught in the ratlines, first whined, then barked. Eighty feet above the deck Nathaniel Dance heard the bark; in a twinkling he was sliding down the larboard mainmast backstay at an astonishing rate of descent. Nathaniel hit the larboard bulwark with a heavy thump that surely must have knocked all breath from him, but with only a slight pause he threw himself into the ratlines beside the great Newfoundland dog.

"George! George! What hey! Don't struggle so!"

The dog was very frightened now, struggling to move his legs, hurting from the pressure of the lines in which he was becoming even more hopelessly enmeshed, flopping and heaving as frantically as a fish gill-caught in a net. He snapped at Nathaniel, fierce teeth barely missing the surprised boy's face.

"George!" Frost shouted. "Halt!"

Ishmael Hymsinger was beside the giant Newfoundland dog now, talking to him in a low, soothing voice in a language Frost had never heard before. Almost immediately the dog quieted. Hymsinger stroked the dog's flank, and the dog's body sagged in the shrouds.

There was no lack of hands to help untangle the dog, for George Three was certainly much loved by the crew. Hannibal Bowditch was there, as was Daniel O'Buck, and of course Roland Pickering. George remained quiet until he had been freed and lowered to the deck. Once on the deck he barked frantically and raced around in a circle, bounding upon the men within reach in a frenzy of excitement, then happening upon Nathaniel Dance and Roland Pickering, bowling both of them to the deck, where he stood over them, licking their faces, then chancing upon Nathaniel's chaffed and rope-burned hands and switching his full attention to the bloody furrows in the boy's palms. The men were laughing at the dog's antics.

Frost had not moved from his place on the quarterdeck but glanced aloft at the lookout, still waiting for the lookout's report. The lookout's attention was focused on the deck. Frost shook his head in irritation and shouted in the loudest voice he possessed. "Masthead there! The time for lollygagging is long past!" The men gathered around the dog were startled; they ceased their simple play and eyed their captain nervously.

The lookout heard Frost easily. "Masthead aye!"

"How many sail do you see?" Frost roared.

There was a slight pause while the lookout glanced anxiously about him, then: "On deck! Three sail, on the larboard beam!"

Frost's eyes sought out Hannibal Bowditch. "Mister Bowditch, take a glass and lay aloft. When you believe you know the sail plans of the ships to our north, report to me."

Seizing a telescope from its beckets on the binnacle and thrusting it through his belt, Hannibal sped aloft with all the agility that youth, enthusiasm, and a liking for one's task lend to hands and legs. George the Newfoundland dog rose to his feet, looked up at Hannibal's rapidly diminishing figure, shook his head in a mighty sneeze, then strolled over to the shade of a cannon, where he settled down contentedly.

"All of you men!" Frost bellowed, "Watch that George has indeed learned he is not suited for the foretop! Mister Dance, off to the surgeon to have your hands dressed." Frost nodded to Ishmael Hymsinger, indicating that he was to rejoin Frost in pacing.

"Oô avez-vous appris le français?"

"Avec l'abbé Le Loutre, qui m'achehé comme esclave aux Mi'kmaq. L'abbé m'a enseigné le français, le meilleur moyen de me convertir á sa religion."

Frost resumed his pacing and reverted to English. Hymsinger instinctively kept a respectful half-pace behind him. "So, you were with the Mi'kmaq when the Abbé found you, though your father had originally fallen in with some Christian Wampanoag."

"Yes, Captain, because the Mi'kmaq did battle with the Wampanoag, whom the Mi'kmaq accused of invading the Mi'kmaq ancestral lands. All had been well between the two tribes until there came a time of famine. Being a man of God, my father could not lift an offensive hand. We were taken prisoners, along with half a dozen other men and a score of women. My mother, a Wampanoag, of gentle and kindly disposition and blessed spirit, was unable to keep the march and was murdered by our captors before my horrified eyes."

"Your father?" Frost asked, though he had already guessed the answer.

"Not he, nor any of the other men, survived the gantlet. I alone—I know not how." Impulsively, Hymsinger turned aside half a pace and lifted the bottom of the plain homespun woolen shirt Roderick Rawbone, the only man near his size among the cat's company, had given him to wear, to bare half his back and his midriff.

At Louisbourg when Hymsinger had been tending the men released from Whip Loring's gaol, Frost had seen the intricate, glazed tracery of deep welts laced all around Hymsinger's torso, so Frost said nothing. Frost had seen the results of severe floggings of run men from various navies in a dozen ports. The marvel was that Hymsinger had survived the Mi'kmaq gantlet!

"And you were then a slave to the Mi'kmaq?" Frost said matter-of-factly.

"Until the Abbé purchased me."

"And then?"

"And then the Abbé died as is all our due, and ascended into Heaven, being preceded of course by my blessed mother and blessed father—but I had his books and all his teachings. So I remained with the Mi'kmaq on Abegweit, and made my captors my pupils. Until two summers ago, when the English, who had conquered from the French, and settled the south part of Abegweit, discovered me with the Mi'kmaq, seized me, and sent me first to Quebec, and then to Louisbourg."

"Etres-vous bon en calcul? Addition, soustraction, division, multiplication?"

"Oui."

"Tenez-vous bien la plume?"

"Oui."

"Pensez-vous que vous puissiez tenir un livre de comtes?"

"Oui. Je ne l'ai jamais fait mais je crois que j'en suis capable."

"Good," Frost said. He had scanned the mast top every time he made a turn as he paced his quarterdeck and had seen Hannibal Bowditch descending from the main crosstrees. "You can instruct others as well?"

"My father taught me when we were among the Wampanoag. Then among the Mi'kmaq I taught their children stories of the Christian God in addition to the stories the Abbé and other Catholic missionaries had taught," Hymsinger said simply. "When they were killed by the English because they were nominal allies of the French, they died as Christians."

Frost faced the man directly. "You are to take up your duties aboard this vessel thusly: you are to work as a purser. What you have yet to know Mister Ferguson, Ming Tsun or I shall show you. You are to continue in your understudy of Surgeon Green, to assist him and yet learn all you can of his form of the healing arts. You are seconded as schoolmaster to the ship's gentlemen on those occasions when I cannot serve. You shall shift your berth into the gun room to be nearer your pupils, Mister Hymsinger—after you are properly shaved. It is my intention to maintain you incredibly busy, Mister Hymsinger —after you are properly shaved. You may retain your braids, they are much like a double queue and club, but shave you surely must."

## ꬉ X ꬷ

❖❖❖❖❖ ANNIBAL BOWDITCH JUMPED FROM
❖ **H** ❖ THE STARBOARD MAINMAST SHROUDS
❖ ❖ ONTO THE MAIN DECK AND RAN UP
❖❖❖❖❖ THE COMPANIONWAY TO THE QUAR-
terdeck; all out of breath, he saluted Frost with a knuckle to his
forehead. "Captain, I have spied out four sail, and they be
three-masted, square-rigged, of great burthen, though they
appear overly slow. I have never seen the like."

Frost smiled: "Belike you have not seen all that many great
ships in your young life, and this be only your second cruize,
Mister Bowditch. Could you spy a hull?"

"Not truly, Captain, but I stared at the four sail long enough
through the glass to affirm they be slow sailors indeed."

"And their courses are set toward the west, Mister Bowditch?"

"As you say it, sir. All four pointed high to the north,
northwest on a larboard tack."

Frost nodded in satisfaction. "Mister Ferguson! Helm hard
up if you please, prepare to come about on the larboard tack."

Frost thanked Hannibal Bowditch, then dismissed him and
waited for Struan Ferguson to join him on the quarterdeck.
"Unless I am sadly mistaken, Struan," he said with relish, but
softly so the helmsman would not hear, "the Great Buddha has
brought us a convoy of merchantmen, I believe the smaller
East Indiamen chartered off the trade by the Crown as trans-
ports for soldiers and supplies to our coasts. Bear away to the

northwest, for I believe the recent storm which caused us so much discomfort has separated the merchantmen from their sea shepherds."

The merchantmen were over the horizon an hour before nightfall. Frost altered course to the north-northeast and reduced his vessel's speed slightly by taking in fore and mizzen topgallants, and one reef in the main course. He left Struan Ferguson on deck and went below for the dinner of sauerkraut, bread, cheese, onions (he thought amusedly of George Three and the "smelling-out"), olives and tea Ming Tsun had waiting for him.

After dinner, Frost returned to his quarterdeck and ordered the log cast. Satisfied with the cat's speed of seven knots, he ordered a slight course alteration two points to starboard and returned to his cabin, where he confronted the delightful choices of studying his chessboard or delving into the volume of the *Lusiads* he had purchased aboard HM *Lark* with a gift of fifty pounds to the venerable Commission for Sick and Hurt Seamen. He chose the *Lusiads* and browsed entranced for an hour among Camoëns' verses. Frost was particularly smitten with a simple elégia, "O poeta Simónides, falando,"

> And if our fate be cruel,
> We must endure
> With spirit brave and ever present cheerfulness.
> What serves it to remember
> What is past,
> Since all passes soon or late,
> And to brood bring but great heartache
> In its train?"

He then performed his evening ablutions and instructed Ming Tsun to awaken him two hours before dawn.

When Frost emerged from his cabin the half moon was well down, but Venus was a brilliant yellowish-white diamond low over his shoulder in the west. He ordered Slocum Plaisted, who had the watch on deck, to extinguish the stern lantern, and he walked the larboard side of the main deck all the way to the knightheads in the forepeak. Frost returned to his quarter-deck by the starboard side, paying close attention to and taking keen delight in the workings of his ship, the hiss of water parted by the cat's bows, the faint phosphorescence of the wake, the sighing rustle of taut sailcloth, the slap of rope, the creak of a yard and its parrels. Absorbed in watching his old and familiar friends among the constellations, he almost bumped into a hand moving to adjust the tension of a lee halyard.

"Ye son of a fornicatin' whore, watch . . ." the man began, as he reached to pluck a belaying pin from its rack.

Frost spoke quickly. "Pleasant evening, Robbins, though I expect the breeze to freshen before morning. Think you we may have rain before noon?"

Robbins instantly recognized Frost's voice and was quick-witted enough to understand that his captain was overlooking his transgression and was not going to upbraid him. "Touch of dampness in the air, right enough, sir. More we'll know at sunrise. When I leave the barn after milkin' I can alus tell by lookin' at the sunrise what kind of day it'll be. Rightly steadies a body, it does, knowin' what kind of day it'll be."

Frost nodded sagely, though he knew Robbins could not see the movement. "It pleases me to have a man like you in this crew, Robbins. You have made a wondrously quick transformation from a farmer to a sailor." He gripped the halyard. "Let me hold the tension while you belay."

"Pays better to be a sailor with ye, betimes," Robbins answered gruffly, "specially yere advancin' wages against prize money so my family don't go without while I'm privateerin'. But I look toward the day I can return to my cows 'n' plough, that I do."

The pull and tuck was quickly done, and Frost walked back to his quarterdeck, climbing the eight steps of the centerline companionway ladder and moving to the weather side of the quarterdeck, where Ming Tsun waited with a mug of hot tea swaddled in a napkin. Frost sipped the tea appreciatively, for it was just as he liked his first tea of the day, fragrant, scalding hot, and heavily sweetened with honey.

Frost paced the windward side of his quarterdeck, enjoying the darkness and the tea hot in his throat and belly, savoring the freshening breeze foretelling the morning and coming steadily from the south-southwest, as the breeze always did this time of the early day in these latitudes. For the past half-dozen hours he had been thinking like the captain of an East Indiaman, a task with which he had more than casual acquaintance. The ships were out there to the northeast, that he knew. Unlike the leisurely routes to and from Canton when the ships of the John Company would lie to at night, the need to hurry to the rebellion in the colonies, and the exorbitant charter fees paid by the Crown, would have demanded that the vessels spied the day before carry sail through the night, though, he was certain, with greatly reduced canvas.

On the high Atlantic passage the ships would be beating constantly against the prevailing winds, and with the typical foul weather of these parts, most likely the fleet of which the four vessels discovered yesterday were a part had been at sea for two months or more. Frost handed the empty mug to Ming Tsun, hearing as he did so the faint tread of someone ascending the center companionway. He turned, knowing that it would be Struan Ferguson, having already made his rounds of the cat a good half hour before he was due to relieve Slocum Plaisted.

"A very pleasant good morning to you, Struan," Frost said briskly, before Struan Ferguson reached the quarterdeck. "Please rouse the watches below and send all hands to breakfast. Ming Tsun has already alerted Cook Barnes to prepare the meal. In thirty minutes all cannons to be ready for running out. Caleb and his woods-cruizers are to stand by in the waist."

Struan murmured, "Aye, sir," and turned down the companionway toward the main access hatchway. Frost cast back over the spherical geometry problem he had been mulling since he ordered the course change to the northwest the evening before. He reviewed his calculations one more time and factored in an extra knot of current setting from the southward, for the cat was afloat on the bosom of that great river in the Atlantic that welled up from the Gulf of Mexico and the Caribbean. He instructed the helmsman to fall off the wind a point. Several hands were heading forward to the seats of ease in the roundhouses. He could smell the great rashers of bacon beginning to fry, and the aroma of coffee, as well as newly made bread, floating aft from the galley. Bless Barnes! A good cook aboard any vessel was a treasure, but doubly so for a private man-o-war with its greatly augmented crew. The cat's crew was eating better than they would have ashore, and Cook Barnes tended to their feeding with just one hand and one cook's mate.

Fresh bread! Frost was confident that the men of his crew would meet the new day with full stomachs and cheerful dispositions. The new day would also reveal whether his geometrical solution would be accurate or not.

Exactly thirty minutes later, as recorded by Jonathan's Bréquet, the main deck reverberated with the ominous rumblings of eighteen 6-pounder cannons being run out, the truckle of the two 9-pounders on the quarterdeck quite lost in the hubbub of the main deck, which ceased as suddenly as it began when each cannon was bowsed into position.

In the dim, fantastic rumor of dawn, Ming Tsun came up the main access hatch and glided across the main deck, the knots of men obligingly opening for his passage, then closing behind him. Ming Tsun bore a small, cloth-covered tray, and when he stood by Frost on the quarterdeck he whisked away the cloth to reveal a magnificent half-loaf of crusty bread well slathered with melted butter and another mug of thick, dark, well-honey-sweetened tea. Frost signed his deep thanks, bit into the bread and chewed it slowly, with relish, as he gazed aloft to the partially reefed fore topgallant, watching with the gratitude and awe he never failed to experience as the high wind-formed canvas was the first to pick up and reflect the beauty of the dawn's magical colors.

Frost washed down the crusty buttered bread with the honey-flavored tea and watched the morning expand around his ship, absorbing himself in the subtle play of soft lights sparkling at the foaming crests of the now visible waves, contrasting with the dark gray bosom of the morning sea. The twang of rigging, the creak of blocks, the delightful roll and graceful lift of the cat as she surged through a larger than normal wave all told him that the vessel he commanded was not an inanimate block of wood but a vibrant, living thing possessed of its own noble soul. He was so completely lost in his thoughts that the call from the masthead took him completely unawares, and he almost choked on a mouthful of tea.

"Deck there!"

Frost nodded at Struan Ferguson, who was watching him closely, signaling that Struan was to respond. "Deck aye!"

"Three sail! Broad on the starboard bow! No! There be four!"

"Main and foremast topgallants, Mister Ferguson, mizzen topgallant as well. All plain sail. Starboard tack, if you please."

"Aye, sir. Topmen aloft! Look lively, all of ye!"

Frost took a ship's telescope from its beckets by the Judas binnacle and swung himself into the starboard mizzen shrouds: he gained fifteen feet above the deck before snicking open the tube. Through the oscillating ellipse of magnification Frost could see the lead ship in the flotilla, well hull up, beating to the northwest on a larboard tack.

Yes! It was an East Indiaman! And not one of the great eight hundred tonners built to get around the new British tonnage laws, which assessed taxes and port fees on the basis of a ship's beam and consequently prompted the John Company to build its newest ships narrow, deep and long. Instead, like all the John Company's ships with which Frost had any acquaintance, the one caught in his glass was crank, wallowing with that lurching roll that made even experienced topmen seasick. He moved the glass onto the other three vessels, searching for a warship escort. He breathed a sigh of relief; all East Indiamen, and sailing as close to the wind as East Indiamen could.

Above him the mizzen topgallant sail was unloosed by its topmen, then immediately sheeted home by the eager hands tending lines on the main deck. Fifteen seconds later the main topgallant shook out, snapped and filled with momentarily trapped air, adding its thrust to the sails already drawing fully. Frost studied the four ships approaching the cat at an oblique angle for another five minutes, formulating his plan of engagement before descending to the quarterdeck and assembling his officers.

"They are the John Company's vessels," Frost said tersely. "I could discern no escorts, though there could well be frigates playing the shepherd's role just over the horizon. We shall be among them in thirty minutes!" He glanced around the half-circle of his officers: Struan Ferguson, Roderick Rawbone, Slocum Plaisted, Daniel O'Buck, and Caleb Mansfield, with the three ship's gentlemen gathered respectfully at one side to await Frost's orders. He took the chalkboard from a binnacle. "We have the weather gage. I mean to cross the lead vessel, immediately tack, and come down her starboard side."

Frost sketched the maneuver in a few sparse strokes of chalk on the slate, indicating the positions of the four British ships, the relative wind, and the course he intended the cat to take. "Mister Rawbone, you shall direct the fire of all main deck starboard cannons. Your object will be to sweep the lead vessel's gun deck. These Indiamen are a good eight feet taller off the water than our cat, so aim directly at the bulwarks and the cannons themselves."

Frost turned to Caleb: "All your woods-cruizers in the main and fore tops; concentrate your fire, as you have always, on the quarterdeck. Dan O'Buck, your station will be the two 9-pounders on this quarterdeck, both of which I desire to have shifted to fire over our stern. As we draw away from the lead vessel you are to fire directly into her rudder at the waterline. As we are passing astern, the helmsman will luff to bring our stern around momentarily. You must time your shots for that luff. We shall run down to the next vessel and treat her accordingly with our larboard cannons. Caleb, I trust your woods-cruizers will have had time to reload, as well as you, Mister O'Buck, for you must get two cannon balls into the rudder of the second vessel as well."

"And then, Captain Frost," Rawbone said hesitantly.

"And then, Mister Rawbone, we immediately wear ship and, coming from astern, bring your starboard guns into play against the larboard side of the second vessel. Then we run up to the first vessel and you throw our larboard broadside into her. Mister O'Buck, I must ask you to reload the long nines as such cannons have never been reloaded before, for as we pass the second vessel's bows I shall expect you to rake her decks with both of the cannons you command."

Daniel O'Buck visibly paled as Frost said this. "You will luff again, Captain?"

"Expecting that your long nines will be ready, the helm will luff."

"And the same raking maneuver upon reaching the first vessel, Captain?"

"Right you are, Mister O'Buck!" Frost smiled at the small knot of his officers. "You are doubtlessly wondering what we shall do with the other two vessels. We shall leave them to their own contretemps. I'm a trader, gentlemen; I'm gifted with no special insight into the conduct of naval battles, nor am I—thank God—a farmer. However, I have heard it said by sage farmers that when the fox has gained entrance to the hen house, those chickens not immediately favored with the fox's attention will be seeking to escape, not coming to the aid of their companions in the fox's clutch."

Caleb Mansfield showed his gapped teeth in what passed, for Caleb, as a grin. "Ain't no farmer meself, Capt'n, never hope to be one, but the same be true fer wolves in a moose yard. I ain't rightly ever bethought meself as a wolf, but . . ."

"Deck there!" A lookout screamed.

"Deck aye!" Struan Ferguson immediately replied.

"Deck! The foremost vessel be breaking out French colors!"

Frost raised his telescope and focused, catching the run of the golden lilies of France on their white background up the jackstaff at the stern of the vessel in the van. "Mister Ferguson! Please hoist our rattlesnake flag."

Frost turned to Rawbone, who was all agape. "To your station, Mister Rawbone! Less than five hundred yards divide our vessels! Caleb!" But Caleb Mansfield was already scurrying toward the main top, moving remarkably swiftly for a landsman who devoted one hand for his beloved rifle and the other for his ship.

"Captain Frost . . ." Rawbone began hesitantly, "the French . . ."

"The French are neutrals, you were going to say, Mister Rawbone," Frost said sharply. "But when do Frenchmen come to command the John Company's vessels? Yonder vessels be no more French than I be the Emperor of China! I expect your cannons to demonstrate their worth before the quarter hour is out."

Still, Frost held his telescope on the fleur-de-lys of France, wondering in his heart of hearts if this display was a clever ruse of the British captain to throw him off his stroke momentarily, or if the vessels really were sailing under the French flag. Another distraction: he realized that none of the vessels had convoy numbers painted on their hulls. "Well, I am fair committed," he told himself fiercely, "for I know these fellows surely to be British built. They have been taken up on charter so quickly time lacked to paint the numbers." Insh'allah. The Great One would have to sort out the guilty and the innocent. Frost knew of no other reason for this group of vessels to be sailing in company in these latitudes but as part of a greater convoy. Frost glanced sternward, where the rattlesnake flag crackled proudly in the breeze, not trailing astern, the entire ensign standing out boldly for the oncoming vessel to see, and clearly.

Frost beckoned Nathaniel Dance to his side and curtly ordered him below to secure the chronometer in a mattress and then report to the lazarette to assist Doctor Green and Ishmael Hymsinger. Then the vessels were two hundred yards apart, and equally curtly Frost ordered the helmsman to bring the wheel hard up to larboard, hold the helm there for the count on thirty seconds, then ease the cat's helm and let her fall off . . .

"Deck there! Capt'n Frost!"

"Aye, Caleb!" Frost easily recognized the woods-cruiser's high-pitched twang.

"Ther' be a passel o' men lowerin' a'hind the side o' the ship! I make out redcoats and green 'uns ain't nev'r seed!"

"One point to larboard," Frost ordered crisply. The bows of the two ships were one hundred yards apart now, but the last order to the helmsman caused the distance between the vessels to open slightly. Frost wanted one hundred and fifty yards distance as the cat passed the first British vessel—yes, it was truly a British vessel! The East Indiaman had yet to open its gun ports. The East Indiaman's captain was certainly peeling his onions fine, but he had soldiers, sharpshooters probably, hidden, though poorly, below his starboard bulwarks. Insh'allah. There was no reason to change his orders, only to reinforce them.

"Caleb!" Frost shouted aloft through his speaking trumpet. "Recall to concentrate your fire against the officers on the quarterdeck! Spare nothing for the men beneath the bulwarks! If they have muskets they can do naught but annoy us at this distance!"

The vessels were close enough now that through his glass Frost could distinguish the captain standing on the other ship's quarterdeck, regarding the oncoming cat through his own telescope, so close that Frost recognized the distinctive cut of the East India Company's cloth. He had once worn it himself. And the insight burst upon him that the vessel before him was ill prepared to exchange broadsides with any vessel, much less a vessel like the cat mounting twenty cannons.

Frost glanced at Rawbone, who was moving, self-assured now that he was going into action, hunched over down the line of starboard cannons, exhorting each gun captain and crew, looking up repeatedly over the cat's starboard bulwark, like a preening turkey in a pen, to gauge the position of the East Indiaman. Behind Frost, Daniel O'Buck had placed a tub of slow match between the two 9-pounders now squatting in the embrasures opened in the stern counter on either side of the ensign standard. Frost refocused his telescope, ranged the length of the main deck of the East Indiaman, looking for the telltale wisp of smoke rising from slow match. No smoke. And the gun ports were still closed . . .

That last observation was lost in the assault of horrific sound from nine 6-pounder cannons belching flame, smoke and ball that hammered at Frost with a physical blow, deafening him though he managed to keep his telescope focused on the other vessel's main deck. He noted with satisfaction the great chunks of wood chewed out of the East Indiaman's starboard bulwark by the cat's broadside. Here and there along the rail tops he saw men rise to shoulder muskets quickly, saw the small, angry blossoms of musket smoke dissipate in the brisk wind as quickly almost as they formed and, having fired wildly, the men wielding those muskets rapidly cowered out of sight below the Indiaman's bulwark.

Frost's hearing had partially returned, enough for him to hear the angry spat of rifle fire—the sharp crack of a long rifle, so different and so easily discernible from the flat bellow of a musket. He swept his telescope along the Indiaman's quarterdeck and saw with relief how effectively Caleb's woods-cruisers had swept that deck with their own rifle fire. Only three men were standing; all the others had been scythed down.

Then the cat's stern was passing the East Indiaman's stern, and the quickest glance at Daniel O'Buck showed him crouched, oblivious to all else but the 9-pounders that were the center of his universe. "Luff your helm!" Frost shouted to the helmsman, a command that the man, expecting it, executed with alacrity. The cat's stern pivoted immediately to starboard with sufficient thrust that Frost was instinctively forced to shift his footing to maintain balance as the cat's bows arched toward the wind.

Immediately the two stern chasers fired as one, the concussive wave of sound causing Frost to close his eyes but open them in time to see both balls so well centered on the East Indiaman's rudder that the back piece from the rudder chain's ringbolt to the first brace was battered into splinters. The East

Indiaman had not fired a single cannon shot, though a glance along the cat's starboard gun deck showed one man slumped alongside his cannon. Frost stared at the man anxiously, but the man roused, fighting off his mates' attempts to aid him, whipping a kerchief around his upper left arm, knotting it into a crude bandage with the aid of his teeth, seizing a cannon ball from the rack beside him, waiting while the cannon's tube was sponged out and the bag of powder thrust home, then rolling in the ball while another member of the gun crew rammed the charge home.

Thankful that the man had sustained only a superficial wound, Frost turned his attention to the second East India-man coming up on the cat's larboard side as the helmsman brought the cat back before the wind. The second vessel, like the first, had no gun ports open, no cannons run out, but was desperately attempting to alter course to the north—no! The captain of the second Indiaman was attempting to wear ship, to get the wind behind him, and in so doing he was going to present his unprotected stern to the cat!

"Yonder master is placing his vessel in great hazard," Struan Ferguson said in wonderment.

Frost did not reply but attentively gauged the wind and the draw of the cat's sails. Aloft, Caleb and his woods-cruisers had reloaded their fearsome long rifles. Below Frost on the main deck Rawbone was repeating his macabre dance of checking each larboard cannon's aim in turn. All right, now to deal with this second vessel . . . "A dozen spokes to larboard, helms-man!" he commanded. "Caleb! Are there soldiers hidden below her bulwarks?" Then, not waiting for that answer, for the second vessel's frantic maneuver made the position of any sharpshooters on her main deck irrelevant: "Mister Rawbone! We shall have her stern-on in a minute! She cannot wear com-pletely before we are upon her! Pound her stern, Mister Raw-bone, work on her rudder—disable her!"

Frost kept his telescope trained on the East Indiaman, for it was most definitely an East Indiaman, one he recognized, for he had spoken this particular vessel two years previously, off

Saint Helena. He searched his memory for her name: "Princess, Princess something," he muttered to himself: "*Princess of Tuscany* . . . no! *Tuscany Countess*!" A John tea-wagon right enough!

The cat, running with the wind behind her at a good eight knots, was crossing the East Indiaman's vulnerable stern at a distance of one hundred yards, steady on with no roll or sway, as boldly as the right angle stroke of a pen casually scratched on parchment to form a "T." Rawbone judged the moment of firing with exactitude; having raced to the larboard bow, Rawbone paced down the line of cannons, ordering each gun captain to fire as that cannon came perpendicular to the East Indiaman's stern.

One by one the 6-pounder balls, whose velocity of twelve hundred feet per second over the one hundred yards separating the two vessels made the strike of ball almost instantaneous with the roar of cannons and the raucous, high-pitched squeal of trucks, pummeled the East Indiaman's stern. Rawbone had directed the cannons' fire against the waterline; the rudder was gnawed away, and the East Indiaman shuddered under the impact of nine cannon balls striking in a compact area, right on the waterline, little more than the breadth of a hogshead!

A glance sternward confirmed that Daniel O'Buck had the two 9-pounders reloaded and run out. "Hands to the braces!" Frost shouted, then repeated the order through his speaking trumpet. "Mainsail haul alee! Down helm!" The cat, groaning and protesting, pivoted away from the wind to southward. "Add your weight of iron to the work so nobly wrought by Master Gunner Rawbone, Mister O'Buck!"

Daniel O'Buck had reacted instantly to the maneuver and was peering intently over the barrel of the cannon to starboard, then his linstock slashed downward, the linstock of the other 9-pounder following O'Buck's lead instantaneously so both cannons roared as one. Both balls threw great gouts of wood from the East Indiaman's stern just at the waterline.

"About ship!" Frost shouted through his speaking trumpet. "Braces 'round!" The cat came round to starboard and hesitated as her sails spilled their wind, yards swung round to lay her on a short starboard tack. Frost smiled at the way in which Rawbone was berating the starboard gun crews, striding along the main deck, shouting orders that were incomprehensible to Frost due to the distance and the constant chirping in his ears. "More of the same, Mister Rawbone!" Frost shouted; then to the helmsman: "As fine into the wind as ever she will point."

A quick survey of the second vessel showed that she was drifting before the wind, her vulnerable, oh so vulnerable stern still at a right angle to the cat's course. There was never a better time to try for a dismasting: "Mister Rawbone, if you please! Try your next three balls into her masts—they will be a-line—I'll bring the cat as close as she will bear!"

Frost saw a few soldiers aiming muskets over the East Indiaman's stern rail, heard the flat, whiplike cracks of the long rifles, and saw the soldiers—disappear. The cat was crossing the Indiaman's stern at less than fifty yards distance. Then the first three starboard cannons fired in a sequence so close they sounded as one, and the mizzenmast a dozen feet above the stern lamp quivered and shuddered, then began to topple.

"Stout work, Mister Rawbone! Twenty Spanish dollars for each gun crew to be shared out! Her waterline now, if you please!"

From somewhere on the stern works of the East Indiaman a musket banged, and Frost's tricorne was tugged smartly from his head. He turned instinctively to grab it and saw Nathaniel Dance chasing the hat across the quarterdeck. "Belay that, Mister Dance!" he shouted. "Get yourself back to Surgeon Green's and Hymsinger's aid . . ." The rest of his sentence was lost in the roaring of the next six starboard cannons, firing sequentially.

"Ease off two points to larboard!" Frost commanded. The helm went over promptly, and the cat began to tack briskly toward the first Indiaman. Rawbone was running back and forth behind the larboard cannons, cajoling and threatening by turns, but the cannons were already reloaded and run out, the gun crews standing eagerly, yet relaxed, beside their great iron beasts.

Frost drew out Jonathan's watch: "I make it ten seconds less than two minutes, Mister Rawbone!" he shouted with an enthusiasm he hardly knew he possessed.

Rawbone mopped his forehead with a powder-begrimed kerchief: "Aye, sir! Near as good as Royal Navy-men with a year's hard gunnery drill a'hind 'em!"

"No, Mister Rawbone!" Frost roared into his speaking trumpet and stepped to the breast rail so all the men on the main deck could hear him: "As good as any Royal Navy-men with a year's hard gunnery drill behind them! But we must shave another twenty seconds off the reload if we are to be better than the Royal Navy-men!" He noted with immense satisfaction that the crews tailing onto the starboard cannons had not paused in their work but were preparing to tail on and run out their cannons.

"Starboard cannons reloaded in one minute forty-five seconds!" Frost exulted. Actually, the starboard cannons lagged the larboard cannons by a second or so, but the two sides would be competing briskly against each other now, and the competition would be good for everyone, but most of all for the ship. There were a lot of efficiencies to be gained, a lot of wasted motions to be refined; Frost fully expected to have his gun crews reloading their cannons in one minute thirty seconds before he ended the cruise and paid off in Portsmouth.

Frost glanced back toward the second East Indiaman. That vessel was down perceptibly by the stern, but the crippled mizzenmast had already been cut away. He imagined the Indiaman's stern post and lower counter planking had taken a right pummeling in areas where it would be difficult for carpenters to reach quickly. Most likely the bread room had already flooded . . . a launch appeared from behind the East Indiaman's starboard quarter. Her captain was putting a crew to work from the outside to plug holes before the stern was too far down to reach the holes without putting a man in the water. No! The launch was crowded with men! Could it be that the crew was abandoning ship?

The cat was rapidly leaving the second East Indiaman astern, and that vessel posed no problem for the moment. Frost turned toward the first Indiaman, which was half a mile ahead and had not made appreciable headway since taking the cat's first broadside. A quick glance through his telescope confirmed that the two 9-pounders so admirably served by Dan O'Buck and his gun crews had largely reduced the Indiaman's rudder to kindling.

Frost lifted his speaking trumpet upward: "Caleb! Advise me when you can see musketeers on her main deck!" His voice was creaking from strain and the foul-smelling powder smoke; beside him Ming Tsun offered a cup of honey-sweetened tea. Giving over his speaking trumpet and telescope briefly to Struan Ferguson, Frost signed his thanks and while sipping his tea surveyed the set of the cat's sails, the speed with which his vessel cut through the water on her larboard tack, and the tenor of his crew. He was satisfied with all he saw, and his men were of a certainty solidly with him. Frost gave the empty cup to Ming Tsun and reclaimed his telescope and speaking trumpet. The cat was within easy cannon shot of the East Indiaman, but his questing glass revealed still not a single gun run out.

"Mister Rawbone!" Frost's throat was much refreshed by the tea. "We shall continue to work on her gun deck, though if your first three gun crews are of a mind to topple a mast, as did their mates on the starboard cannons so handily, they may try!"

Then, reminded by the nagging of guilt that he had enjoyed a cup of tea while his men went without, Frost addressed Struan: "Mister Ferguson, please pass the word to Cook Barnes that if he has some quantity of cold coffee, I would take it kindly if he would serve it out in buckets with pannikins—and a pint of rum added for flavor—to each gun crew."

"I know for a certainty that Cook Barnes has been keeping a barrel of coffee handy for your call—bread and cheese also," Struan said enthusiastically, "and though it be as cold as a witch's tit, a pint of Jamaica per gun crew would make the coffee palatable, most palatable indeed."

"Having not your experience in those matters, I shall perforce take your word for the degree to which the coffee has cooled, Mister Ferguson," Frost bantered with his second in command. Yes, he would not trade this day on the quarterdeck of his ship, among the crew serving him so willingly, for anything, not in this life.

Frost turned to his stern gunner: "Mister O'Buck, on this tack you'll have no rudder as a target, but after we have given this fellow a broadside, I shall round into the wind quick, and you can bring down such masts, yards, sails and cordage as you are inclined." Gracias a Dios, but this cat was such a marvelous sailor that Frost would even consider such a maneuver! And the cat, he knew, would unhesitatingly undertake it.

"Deck there! Capt'n Frost! She's haulin' down them lilies!" Caleb Mansfield bellowed from the main top.

Frost swung around: the distance to the East Indiaman, which for all practical purposes was dead in the water, had narrowed to five hundred yards and was closing rapidly. The French colors were being pulled down the stern jackstaff with all speed. There was a pause as the flag collapsed on the quarterdeck, and then a white flag, actually a bed sheet, as Frost's telescope confirmed, was hastily bent on and pulled up the jackstaff. "Yes," Frost reflected, "East Indiamen do have proper beds from which a sheet can be robbed."

"Mister Ferguson, I intend to come alongside the John Company ship and confirm that she has, in fact, yielded to us. You shall go aboard and bring her under your command. Take twenty seamen and six of Caleb's most ferocious woodscruizers as your prize crew. Sequester all small arms on the quarterdeck and confine all her people below after searching them properly. Determine her inventory—Helmsman! Ease the helm a point to windward. Come up on her from larboard."

The helmsman put the wheel over, broadening the tack to run behind the East Indiaman and come up on her undamaged larboard side. "Mister Rawbone! Keep your linstocks smoldering properly! At the first sign of treachery . . ."

"Capt'n Frost!" Caleb's now familiar hoarse bellow: "Them redcoats be throwin' chests into the sea!"

"Discourage them, Caleb!"

The words were hardly uttered before at least three long rifles cracked, then another. Through his glass Frost saw two large wooden chests slide overboard from the larboard waist entry. A redcoated body followed.

The cat's bow was nearly even with the East Indiaman's stern: "Mister Ferguson! Prepare to back sails, if you please."

Struan Ferguson gave the preparatory order; hands leaped to the braces, and a moment later Frost ordered, "Back sails, Mister Ferguson." The cat immediately lost headway and eased to a halt forty yards from the Indiaman. Frost lifted his speaking trumpet: he had already identified the vessel's captain, standing with his right arm in a bloody, makeshift sling, supported by a sailor on either side.

"Sir!" Frost shouted through his speaking trumpet, "May I assume you have yielded?"

"Damme, sir, ye may so assume," the East Indiaman's captain shouted, audible clearly without resort to a trumpet, "and damme, sir, I must protest that ye fired into me after I had struck, killing men of my complement."

"Throwing cargo overboard once a vessel has struck is four-square contrary to the ordinary usage of the sea, sir," Frost shouted back. He had absolutely no idea if that was the case or not, but he was not going to let the East Indiaman's captain paint him in the wrong. "I am sending my second officer to take command in your stead, sir. May I have the honor of knowing your name?"

"Cowmeadow," the East Indiaman's captain shouted back irritably. "John Cowmeadow, captain in the service of the British East India Company, commanding the Company's ship *Sagittarius.*"

"Once third officer on the *Lord Cardiff*?" Frost shouted across the forty yards separating the cat and the Indiaman.

"Ye have the advantage of me, sir," Cowmeadow shot back, "and whom might ye be?"

"Proper introductions in due course, Captain Cowmeadow. In the meantime have I your parole you'll not interfere with the prize crew I'm sending aboard?"

"And have I yere word, sir, that from henceforth ye'll respect the common and ordinary usage of the sea?" Cowmeadow shouted across sarcastically.

"My word on it, Captain Cowmeadow, so long as your complement does not engage in unfreighting cargoes rightly claimed prize."

"Struan," Frost said quietly, noting with satisfaction that Struan Ferguson already had the long boat rigged to the main hatch tackle, "trust not this fellow with such an incongruous name for one who follows the sea. I recall his reputation in the Macao and Canton; an altogether unsavory one. He appears much wounded, but I wager it is not more than a splinter in his shoulder. I would not be averse to his close confinement, for it may be some time before I am able to return."

"Return, sir!" Struan Ferguson said, unable to keep the tone of surprise from his voice.

"Why yes, Struan, there are two sail to leeward which we have yet to engage. Send the long boat back quickly, make repairs to the rudder of *Sagittarius* and all else you deem necessary, then make your way to the second Indiaman, who seems, for all the world, to be sending off her people as if she feared sinking. Keep station here against my return, maintaining this exact latitude and longitude. Under no circumstances attempt to take aboard any embarked already in yonder vessel's boats, nor let them board you. It seems that these ships of the John Company have been dispatched *en flute*, with cannons struck below to make more deck room for troops."

Frost watched the coffee laced with rum, and bread and cheese, being served to the men of the gun crews at their stations, and waited impatiently, though hoping he avoided all outward manifestations of impatience, for the long boat to be rowed back, hooked on, and swayed in.

⚙⚙⚙⚙⚙ VEN THOUGH THE TWO BRITISH VES-
⚙    E    ⚙ SELS WERE HULL DOWN AND BROAD
⚙         ⚙ BEFORE THE WIND WHEN THE CAT
⚙⚙⚙⚙⚙ TOOK UP THE CHASE, FROST RAN THE
third East Indiaman to ground well before sundown. Frost
came in quickly on the chase's larboard side, closing to a bare
one hundred yards and preparing to discharge his starboard
cannons in quick sequence, when the British colors the ship
had been displaying were hauled down abruptly without cere-
mony, and the chase smartly backed sails without a shot having
been fired. Rawbone and the starboard gunners were vastly
disappointed. Frost was vastly relieved.

After determining that the captain of the East Indiaman
*Triton* had indeed yielded, obtaining the captain's parole,
sending over Slocum Plaisted as prize master and thirty men
as prize crew with orders to join Struan Ferguson, and recovering the long boat, Frost went haring away to the southeast with all plain sail set in pursuit of the remaining British
vessel.

This vessel's captain was more resourceful, or more desperate, for her wake was marked with the jetsam of bales, bags
and barrels heaved overside. An hour before dusk, when the
cat was but a mile behind, the Indiaman began swaying up the
horses, cavalry mounts and draft animals for pulling cannons
that were part of her cargo. Through his telescope Frost saw
the animals pushed from the starboard waist entry and sent

sprawling into the sea, neighing and thrashing the water in helpless, hopeless terror.

The cat was in among the first of the horses a few minutes later, the farmers in Frost's crew shouting in protest at the wanton waste of good horseflesh—many a farmer temporarily turned privateer's man saw in the frantic, wall-eyed, doomed animals beasts eminently suited for pulling a plough or wagon. "Silence!" Frost roared. "Caleb—the woods-cruizers you have—do what you can!" The long rifles began to crack, and here and there among the closest, a horse ceased its agonized struggles. Five minutes later Frost saw the first fin cutting through the water—then another, and another.

"Mister Rawbone!" Frost shouted loud enough for his voice, without benefit of the speaking trumpet's amplification, to carry all the way to his master gunner standing in the fore-peak. Frost was angry at the needless deaths of the horses but understood the desperation of the chase's captain all the same, grimly recalling how it was that the "horse latitudes" to the southward of their present position came to bear that name. He was glad dusk was approaching and the carnage of the sharks among the horses was falling behind. "I'm going to fall off to larboard as soon as you have the forward cannon on the starboard side run out. I'd like to skip a ball into the vict-ualer's hull." What Frost would not give for a proper bow chaser! He would think on that problem.

The cat veered and the starboard forward cannon boomed, but in the gathering darkness Frost did not see the fall of the shot. The shot spurred the Indiaman to start her water, though, which jetted from her hoses in steady streams until the sun was below the horizon. The moon would rise late this night.

But while there was no moon as yet, there were no clouds either; the chase's sails were colored steely gray in the bright starlight. The cat gained steadily until she was three hundred yards astern the chase. Frost summoned Rawbone to his quarterdeck. "Mister Rawbone, the master of yonder vessel should be well satisfied that he has assayed all in his power to avoid his vessel's capture and salve his honor. But for every hour we sail down wind, three will be necessary to beat back to our friends. Elevate the two forward cannons starboard to fire high into the chace's riggings. Signal when you are ready to fire, and we shall luff the helm. Should the whistle of shot through her riggings not cause her master to forego this chace, I'll lay you along the Indiaman's starboard side in thirty minutes, and your matrosses may resume their excellent work." Yes, Frost would have to solve the problem of proper bow chasers once back at his cousin John Langdon's shipyard. Luffing to bring a cannon to bear was too costly in lost time and headway.

Fortunately, the two cannon balls into the chase's lower riggings convinced the captain of the East Indiaman that further flight was futile. The chase backed mainsails and turned to larboard into the wind, waiting listlessly for the cat to draw alongside.

"Mister O'Buck," Frost said, his voice so hoarse now that he could scarcely be heard by the helmsman and keenly aware that he had been on his quarterdeck for the better part of twenty hours, "would you do me the honor of crossing to yonder vessel and taking possession of her in the name of the New Hampshire Legislature? Select twenty men and the rest of Caleb's woods-cruizers. You have already heard my admonitions on securing enemy vessels to Mister Ferguson and Mister Plaisted, so I need not repeat them again. Follow in my lee while I sail back to our rendezvous . . ."

"Oh, Captain Frost, Captain Frost, may Nathaniel and Darius and George and I go over, too?"

Annoyed at being interrupted, Frost turned sharply, seeing in the dim starlight Hannibal Bowditch, hopping from one foot to the other in a frenzy of excitement, and the great dog George Three, sitting, body quivering, next to the helmsman. Nathaniel Dance and Darius hovered just at the edge of vision, and Frost felt rather than saw the boys' intensity.

"Why yes, Mister Bowditch. A capital idea! It strikes me that an animal as fierce appearing as our George will do wonders in keeping the crew of yonder prize, surly at their rude treatment, fixated on their captivity. Why, recall the wonders he worked on the crew of the Tortola Packet." Frost strode to the breast rail and shouted: "Roland Pickering!"

"Sir!" a startled voice answered from somewhere in the waist.

"If you please, Roland Pickering."

A breathless Roland Pickering, face much begrimed with powder, clambered up the centerline companionway. Frost drew Pickering and O'Buck aside, out of the boys' hearing. "The lads have asked to go along as prize crew. I wish them yet such little childhood as can be snatched from this mad world we inhabit, yet they seek to be valued for their own worth. I charge you with their special care, Roland Pickering."

Pickering grinned, teeth protruding from the stubble of his beard. "I twig your drift, Captain Frost. I be their angel, sure. No, George and I both be their angels, and they'll never be the knowin' of it."

"Dan O'Buck," Frost said, looking intently at the man, "during this cruize have you formed opinions of the worth of certain of the men in this ship's company?"

"Aye, that I have, sir, and I would be pleased if you was to name Roland Pickering as second to me on this prize."

"Done!" Frost said. "Mister Bowditch, Mister Dance, Mister Langdon! All have a care that George looks the part of a most fearsome partisan for American liberty . . ."

"I have his collar with the spikes, right enough, sir!" Darius said gleefully. "We un's have taught George how to growl proper!"

"Good!" Frost exclaimed, though he thought that Whip Loring had probably goaded the dog's education in growling. "Then your mates, George, and you will be the equal of Caleb's woods-cruizers. Away with you in the long boat! Mister O'Buck, it won't be necessary to accept the master's sword should he want to give it to you. And commanders of East Indiamen rarely possess swords, in any event. Just disarm and lock all of yonder vessel's people below—you may find singular accommodations for her officers in the mangers that have recently been so violently vacated—and follow me closely. We are a long ways from Portsmouth."

Once Frost was certain that O'Buck was having no trouble with the captain and crew of the fourth prize—the longboat returning brought her name, *Generous Friend*—he ordered the guns secured and two watches off duty to sleep. The duty watch he set to trimming sails and yards as the cat wore 'round. Frost ordered Jack Lacey to the helm, leaving him with orders to steer northwest by west and to call him at any change of wind or apparent deviation by the prize following. Then he descended to his cabin and gratefully sat down to the dinner of fish stew, bread and onions, washed down with a pot of hot tea, that Ming Tsun had laid on his desk table.

Immediately after supping, the lure of his cot was overpowering, but he resisted long enough to pull the cat's log onto his desk, open it, and begin, "Aboard the . . ." Frost stroked his stubbled chin with the quill's feather tip: surely there had to be a better name than *the cat* for the vessel that was serving him, New Hampshire, and the United Colonies of North America so well. Yes, there had to be—but he was at a loss as to what that name should be. Frost shrugged. Joss. A name would suggest itself in due course. He dipped the quill in the ink well, and just as he put quill to paper he was struck by the thought that, being in rebellion against their colonial master, the colonies of North America were actually no longer colonies of England. Frost cast about for a proper noun, shrugged off the brain-numbing weariness, and without further thought on the matter elected henceforth to use the word "state" wherever he had formerly used the word "colony." He continued,

Ex-HM *Jaguar*, now private man-o-war, State of New Hampshire charterd: 37 degrees 45 minutes N, 54 degrees 20 minutes W: 5:30 AM sightd four Sail SSE. Gave chace. Moderate wind NNW. Engagd East Indiaman *Sagittarius* 10 AM. Ditto *Tuscany Countess* 11 AM. *Tuscany Countess* taking water. Not responding to helm. *Tuscany Countess* musterd her people into boats. *Sagittarius* struck 12 AM. First Officer S. Ferguson into *Sagittarius* as P. Master. Chaced East Indiaman *Triton*. Struck

4 PM. Boatswain S. Plaisted into *Triton* as P. Master. Chaced *Generous Friend*. Fired two cannons 9 PM. Struck. 37 degrees 33 minutes N, 53 degrees W. D. O'Buck, coxswain, D. Langdon, H. Bowditch, N. Dance and G. Three as P. Crew.

Frost consulted Jonathan's watch against the Kendall chronometer. Five minutes shy of midnight. He confirmed the date, then added the day of the week and the date at the beginning of the log entry: Thursday, 4 July 1776.

The date pleased him. "Four prizes on the fourth day of the month," he said, half-aloud. For half a second Frost was tempted to write "four on the fourth" at the bottom of the log entry but dismissed the thought. Most likely when the cat beat back to the area where Struan Ferguson was holding *Sagittarius*, the *Tuscany Countess* would have sunk. Besides, it would be just so much vainglorious boasting.

Frost sanded the ink, closed the log, brushed his teeth with soda sprinkled with a drop of sea water, then sprawled face down on his bunk, falling instantly asleep as his body contacted the oakum-filled mattress. He slept so soundly he never knew that Ming Tsun entered his night cabin, quietly removed his shoes, and covered him with a blanket.

Up before dawn on Friday, the morning of 5 July, bleary eyed and yawning but walking among his crew as they performed the morning ritual of running out the cannons, for Frost knew not what dangers the morning would reveal. He sat on a cannon, gratefully accepted the pannikin of hot coffee John Mugglesworth, the gun captain, timorously offered him, and listened to the voices of his crew and the workings of his ship. His ship. Then he remembered the man who had been wounded at this very cannon: "There was a man wounded from out your crew, his left arm, I collect."

"Why, yes, Captain," Mugglesworth said, apparently surprised that Frost remembered such a mundane incident. "Loader name o' Robert Knapp. Spent musket ball, did no more'n break the skin. But Doc Green, he came by in the night, seems like he wus lookin' for wounded. Mighty glad he wus to find Knapp. Hauled 'im below, Knapp bellowing all the whilst about how he didn't want to lose his arm, but Doc Green was shoutin' that since no wounded had been sent below, he wus bound and determined to find some body to tend."

Frost sipped the atrocious coffee; the fact that it was hot was its only saving grace. He looked for a way to pour the pannikin overside unobtrusively. "I judge our Mister Knapp still has his arm."

"That be true indeed, Capt'n, sir, we have that word from the Indian Hymsinger. Knapp has been cryin' out to rejoin his gun crew, that he has, but Doc Green, he's bound 'n' determined to keep Knapp in his hammock. Sez he won't let Knapp out of his hammock 'til he's seen the laudable pus."

"Indeed," Frost said noncommittally, catching Ming Tsun's eye and handing him the pannikin of coffee. "I fear that with our complement so greatly reduced with the capture of three prizes, I shall have to ask our good surgeon to restore Knapp to his mates, laudable pus or no."

"Why, thankee, Capt'n Frost, Knapp wants to be back with his mates, that's asure," Mugglesworth said, vastly relieved that his captain saw matters as he did. "Three prizes we have, aye, Capt'n Frost? Think ye one be sunk?" Mugglesworth did not wait for Frost's reply. "We be a long way from Portsmouth."

Frost clapped the gun captain on the shoulder, glad that Mugglesworth had not seen the transfer of the pannikin of coffee to Ming Tsun or Ming Tsun's surreptitious pouring of the vile liquid down the pissdale. "The voyage is not over, John Mugglesworth," Frost answered, smiling confidently as he continued on the circuit of his vessel. "We are a long way from Portsmouth, sure, and on such a long voyage to the ports of Piscataqua we can hope other prizes will cross our bows ere we sight the Isles of Shoals again."

The winds tended light and capricious, and it was Sunday afternoon, 7 July, before the cat and the *Generous Friend* raised the *Triton* and *Sagittarius*. Just at sunrise that morning the masthead lookout had reported two sail well to the north, though they had dropped below the horizon in less than fifteen minutes. As Frost had surmised, the *Tuscany Countess* was nowhere to be seen, though there was a cluster of ship's boats and crude rafts gathered in a loose huddle a mile or so southeast of the *Sagittarius* and *Triton*, both keeping station under jibs and half-furled fore topgallants.

Frost focused his telescope on the knot of boats and rafts, quickly estimating the number of men in them. Perhaps one hundred and ten, one hundred and twenty. If the *Tuscany Countess* had been a troop ship and not a victualer, the boats she carried would not have been sufficient to take off a quarter of the men aboard her. Frost was mystified by the sight of several strange uniforms he did not recognize, and he ordered the helmsman to make for the boats, though deeming it prudent to order the cannons run out and slow match lighted.

The cat was soon at the edge of the knot of boats and rafts, and Frost ordered sails a-back; main course snapping occasionally in the light air, the cat fell off until she was barely maintaining steerageway. Frost studied the men crowded tightly in the closest ship's boat intently. They were a surly looking lot, with only a handful of men he took for British sailors among them. The majority of the men were shirtless, shoulders and torsos burned brilliant flamingo crimson by the pitiless sun, the bodies of men from cold climates unused to regular exposures to the sun. Theirs was the cloying stench of long unwashed bodies, and Frost realized he was looking at a contingent of Great Britain's German auxiliaries. He suddenly recalled Captain Richard Smith's and his cousin John Langdon's words about the British Crown's purchasing mercenaries from German princelings, and Geoffrey Frost knew anger as he had rarely known it before.

Frost directed his speaking trumpet toward the closest boat and shouted, "Who is your officer?" He received no reply, only expressions of absolute hatred from the faces turned upward toward him. Frost switched to Dutch: "Wie is Uw officier?"

Frost knew no German, but he had certainly traded enough with the Dutch in their East Indies and their Cape Colony at the southernmost tip of the African continent. In trade one can buy in any language, but a trader can sell only in the language of the prospective buyer.

No one in the boats stirred.

"Caleb!" Frost shouted. "I require the services of your friend, Gideon."

In a moment Caleb Mansfield was beside Frost on the quarterdeck, long rifle in hand, hesitantly proffering it to Frost. Frost checked the priming of the uppermost barrel, then threw the rifle to his shoulder, eased back the cock until the sear caught, sighted briefly down the rifle's barrel, aiming at the tiller on which a soldier's arm rested negligently. He judged the distance to be fifty yards, waited for the cat's slight roll to steady out, and caressed the trigger. The crack of the shot was almost masked by the anguished yelp of the soldier whose arm had been resting on the tiller. The soldier jumped to his feet, cursing and rubbing his elbow, causing the boat to wallow at a frightening rate. His mates quickly pulled him down.

"Wie is Uw officier?" Frost repeated.

The men in the boat stirred apprehensively, then one man, wearing an extremely dirty, sweat-soaked linen shirt that still had a trace of lace at the throat, rose to his feet and said hoarsely but defiantly: "Ik ben Heros von Fendig, majoor, onder het gezag van majoor-generaal Baron von Riedesel, die in dienst staat van Prins Ferdinand van Brunswick." The German major's Dutch was good, better than Frost's command of the language. Frost noted the heavy stubble of beard that did not quite conceal a handsome dueling scar on the man's right jaw, the heavy rime of gum caused by being long without water gathered thickly at the corners of the man's mouth, the thickened tongue. Geoffrey Frost was well acquainted with the physical effects of prolonged thirst.

Caleb Mansfield, who possessed a smattering of Dutch from his unsuccessful wooing of a stout burgher's daughter in the upper New York grants, translated for the benefit of his woods-cruisers. "Says he's a Brunswicker major name o' Fendig, servin' under a general name o' Riedesel."

"U hebt geld van George de derde geaccepteerd om zijn plannen in Noord Ameerika uit te voeren."

"Capt'n says the Brunswickers have taken King George's silver to do the King's biddin' in North America," Caleb translated.

"Wij gehoorzamen de bevelen van onze Prins."

"The Brunswicker allows as how his men obey their Prince," Caleb said.

"Die jullie aan de Engelse koning verkoch heeft."

"Capt'n says the Brunswickers be sold to the British crown by their Prince," Caleb continued quietly.

"Wij zijn beroepssoldaten, een eervol beroep . . ."

"The Brunswicker says his troops just follow soldierin'," Caleb translated freely.

"Jullie zullen een graf in Amerika vinden," Frost snapped.

"To a grave in America, Capt'n just said. That's tellin' 'im, Capt'n!"

Frost glared at Caleb, but Caleb merely grinned.

The German officer shrugged. "Als onze Prins ons naar een Amerikaans graf stuurt, zullen we met plezier gaan."

"The Brunswicker says if their Prince sends 'em to a grave, they'll go happy." Caleb did lower his voice.

"In dat geval is een graf in the Noord Atlantische oceaan net zo goed."

"Capt'n just said that a grave in the North Atlantic be just as good."

Frost had watched Caleb often enough rotate the rifle so that the second barrel came under the cock. He depressed the spring-loaded button that held the barrels locked in alignment, rotated the barrels one hundred and eighty degrees around the rifle's spindle until the button snapped into its corresponding slot on the second barrel and locked the second barrel, rigidly in place. Frost took satisfaction that no one, not even among his own crew, knew this was the first time he had essayed this maneuver.

"Ye be needin' primin'," Caleb said tersely, partially divining Frost's intention but not daring to look at him. "Bottom pan ain't got primin'."

"Priming powder, please, Caleb."

Caleb flipped back the frizzen with his callused thumb and held his small priming horn over the pan, tapping the neck of the horn to shake just the right amount of fine-grained priming powder into the pan, all the while avoiding Frost's gaze. Caleb closed the frizzen.

Frost cocked the flintlock very deliberately and raised the rifle to his shoulder. The brass patch box was cool against his left cheek. The fine brass front sight blade settled into the notch of the rear sight; Frost squared off the top of the blade so that it was even in height with the top of the rear sight, forming an "E" laid on its side, then concentrated on the front sight so that the blade was in sharp focus while his intended target, the Brunswicker's throat, was slightly blurred. There was no sound aboard the cat except for the brisk snap of a rope against a sail. The cat rose on a swell, and the boat with Major Heros von Fendig answered the surge a moment later. The front sight blade of Caleb Mansfield's long rifle was still firmly on the point of the Brunswicker's chin.

Frost was almost overwhelmed by the swift, insane, giddy rush of power that came from knowing that he held the German mercenary's life absolutely captive on the meaty pad of his left forefinger. Slowly the front sight lost its focus and Frost found himself staring sharply at the German's throat. Even at the distance of fifty yards Frost could see that the man was perspiring copiously, though he did not flinch and continued to face Frost resolutely.

"He has no choice," Frost told himself, "save to throw himself into the mass of partially naked, partially clad men huddled so fearfully in that boat, trying to hide from this bullet, and ever afterward mourn his diminishment in the eyes of his men, and his own." Frost shifted the front sight, seeking another target. There were a few things worse than death, he knew, such as living with dishonor. The front sight blade had aligned with the head of the rudder where the tiller had been inserted until his first shot had so weakened the tiller shaft that it had broken under the weight of the man's arm.

Frost expelled half his held breath and, once the front sight steadied, took up the final slack on the trigger while concentrating his aim fiercely on the head of the rudder. Caleb's rifle bucked against his shoulder, though Frost did not hear the shot as he watched the rudder twist sharply and break away from its top pintle. Frost handed the long rifle to Caleb. "My thanks to Gideon, who most surely was never meant to do murder."

Then he shouted to the German officer: "Majoor von Fendig, U heeft Uw leven en het leven van al Uw Brunswickers, aan mij verbeurd tenzij U Uw erewoord geeft om de wapeus tegen the Verenigde Stateen neer te leggen gedurende dit jaar, zeventien hondred zes en zeventig."

"Capt'n just told the Brunswicker his men must swear a parole not to take up arms against us United States fer the rest o' this year," Caleb translated loosely, as he methodically applied himself to the task of reloading Gideon.

"Ik . . . Ik kan geen enkel goevernement mign erewoord geven."

"Brunswicker's sayin' he can't give no parole to no government . . ."

"Nee, maar tegenover mijn geschut heeft U Uw erewoord aan mij gegeven. Het is nu een persoonlijke erezaak tussen U en mij."

"Capt'n says that by standin' up like a man when he thought the Capt'n wus gonna shoot him, the Brunswicker done give parole as a matter of honor between the two o' 'em." Caleb centered a lead ball on its patch of thin deerskin on the muzzle of a barrel and thrust the patched ball down the barrel with one smooth stroke of his ramrod.

"Dat geef ik toe," the German officer said thickly.

"The Brunswicker says he understands," Caleb translated, withdrawing the ramrod.

"Goedendag," Frost said, turning to the helmsman and

preparing to give the order to fall off to larboard so the sails could fill on a larboard tack.

"Wacht!" the German officer shouted.

Frost turned back to the starboard bulwark.

"Ons gevoel van eer is bevredigd, maar we hebben nog steeds honger en dorst. We zijn zonder water of eten van het zinkende schip ontsnapt. Mijn manschappen hebben al vier dagen niet meer gegeten of gedronken."

"Somethin' about honor bein' satisfied, well and good, but the Brunswickers ain't had nothin' to drink no' eat fer four days."

"Kom langszij," Frost shouted back. "We zullen jullie twee tonnen water geven. Met eten zul later vandaag moeten wachten."

"Capt'n's goin' to give 'em two puncheons of water now, and some vittles later in the day."

"Dank U," the German officer said simply.

Frost ordered two puncheons of water brought up and rolled to the starboard waist entry. He felt no need to explain to his crew that the pitiful one hundred and twenty or so men fearsomely overcrowded in the boats and makeshift rafts were all that remained of the ship's complement and half a regiment of German mercenaries embarked aboard the *Tuscany Countess*. "Jack Lacey, sway over my gig and load the puncheons into it," Frost commanded his acting bosun. Then, looking along the cat's main deck and seeing the gun captain: "Mister Mugglesworth, do you think you can find a bucket of Cook Barnes' excellent coffee?"

"Immediately, Capt'n!" Mugglesworth scurried away, and returned quickly enough with a bucket of coffee. The boatload of Brunswickers was in the cat's lee now, and Frost whispered a word of warning to Rawbone, anxious lest the Brunswickers were of the desperate mind to attempt to board the cat.

"Pannikins there!" Frost said. "What you can spare, into the gig with the water!" The work was quickly done, and men in the waist let out line so that the slight wind took the gig fifty yards down to the German soldiers. Then, momentarily foregoing Dutch: "Major von Fendig, do not let your men drink too quickly, and avoid destroying the puncheon, just start the bung . . ."

"Zoals U zegt," the German officer said, stepping up onto the stern sheets to make room for the first puncheon to be rolled into his launch. "We bedanken U voor dit kostelijke geschenk." Heros von Fendig stared across the fifty yards of water at Geoffrey Frost. "We ontmoeten elkaar wel weer, Amerikaanse kapitein."

"The Brunswicker thanks us fer the gift o' water," Caleb translated, " 'n' he's told the Capt'n they'll meet again."

"Ik hoop oprecht dat we dat dan in vredestijd doen," Frost said.

"Capt'n hopes the meetin' be in peacetime," Caleb said to his woods-cruisers, then finished reloading and thrust the ram-rod down into its thimbles.

"Dat hoop ik ook," the German officer said. He raised his right arm in salute.

Caleb Mansfield sidled up to Frost and spoke softly: "Ye shine the Brunswicker can keep his part of the bargain, Capt'n?"

"I devoutly hope these Germans keep their paroles, Caleb. It goes hard against the grain for these stiff-necked Brunswickers, but the major's loyalty to his men overcomes his loyalty to his general and his prince in this case." Frost paused: "I cannot abide seeing men die of thirst, Caleb. Though whether these Brunswickers may wish they had found their graves in this North Atlantic on which we tarry rather than the soil of our nascent American states is impossible to know."

Thirty minutes on a larboard tack brought the cat to the *Sagittarius* and *Triton*, and scanning the *Sagittarius* through his glass as the vessels closed, Frost was startled by evidence of a fire in her forepeak. He scanned the quarterdeck anxiously for Struan Ferguson and saw him finally, tightly holding onto the great stern lantern. Struan managed a feeble wave with one hand, though he did not loosen his grip on the lamp stanchion. Struan had evidently encountered some difficulties.

"Mister Lacey, place us fifty yards from Mister Ferguson's

vessel and keep station on her, if you please." Frost was glad he had not ordered his gig recovered but towed astern. He ran through his officers still aboard; Rawbone was now the next most senior.

"Mister Rawbone!" Frost shouted, "You command in my absence. Mister Mugglesworth, four men from your gun crew to row my gig, if you please, and I'll thank you to be my coxswain."

"Yere leave, Capt'n," Caleb Mansfield interposed, "but ye'll likely be needin' me 'n' Gideon."

"Into the gig then . . ." Frost dropped into the bow of his gig an instant after Mugglesworth and his four men had tumbled in and run out the oars. He was followed quickly by Caleb Mansfield and Ming Tsun, who had armed himself with his fearsome halberd. Behind them, unheeded, Roderick Rawbone stared about himself in consternation as the realization that Frost had once again left him in command of the cat struck home.

The fifty yards between the two vessels was covered in less than two dozen strokes of frantically pulled oars. Even before the gig was properly alongside the Indiaman, Frost leaped for the entry ladder steps and pulled himself up into the starboard waist entry before anyone from the *Sagittarius* had thrown a line to the men in the gig. As he pulled himself onto the main deck, Frost looked up into the dear, anxious, wane, gaunt face of Struan Ferguson. "I ha'e failed ye miserably . . ." Struan began, whispering hoarsely.

Frost cut him off brusquely: "Are you all right, man!" He stared at the stiff, blood-soaked bandage wrapped around Struan's throat. "What of our men who boarded with you?"

"Three dead, six wounded . . ."

Joseph, Mary and Jesus! Frost turned to lean over the Indiaman's bulwark: "Mugglesworth! Immediately back to the cat, return even more quickly with Surgeon Green and Ishmael Hymsinger." Ming Tsun was already standing behind Struan, gently probing and kneading Struan's collarbone and shoulders with his strong, blunt fingers.

"The bullet went through the fleshy part of my neck," Struan whispered. "I've bled out . . ."

"You can recite all at your convenience," Frost snapped. "Let's get you below out of this sun, which does naught for your composure." His eye fell on Cox Pridham, one of Caleb's woods-cruisers, standing nearby. "Pridham! Clap onto Mister Ferguson. Let him fall at your peril." But Ming Tsun had already gathered Struan into his arms, forcing Pridham aside.

"Companionway thar, Capt'n," Pridham pointed. Frost led the way to the Indiaman's great cabin, staring soberly, but only for a moment, at the splintered bullet hole in the door, the shattered panes of glass in the stern windows, and the great splotch of dried blood on the cabin sole. Ming Tsun laid Struan on a settee beneath the starboard quarter gallery in the spacious quarters and unwrapped the bloody bandage from around Struan's neck. Ming Tsun sniffed at the blood and pus caked on the rag, scowled, and then moved swiftly around the cabin, unerringly locating the captain's private spirits locker.

Ming Tsun signed for Frost to support Struan's head with a pillow, then liberally doused brandy on the gaping wounds. He signed again.

"Fire," Frost ordered. "Pridham, bring us fire. No! Coals would be more helpful. Coals from the stove in the fo'c's'le. Go, man!" Then to Struan: "You have not been good to yourself, Struan."

Struan grimaced at the brandy's sting. "Lucky we were to have Slocum at hand, Geoffrey. After securing his own unruly crowd of British sailors below decks, he sailed his prize down on us, his fightin' tops fair bristlin' with every man who could aim a long rifle or a musket, firin' into the crowd we were bare holdin' off. His assistance was most timely, otherwise the highlanders would have retaken this vessel."

"Highlanders?" Frost said incredulously.

"Aye, Geoffrey, highlanders," Struan Ferguson said bitterly. "My own countrymen fightin' for the British, though as ye collect there was Royal Highlanders in Boston when Marcus was taken prisoner. God rot the lot who took the shilling after the Culloden amnesties. Loyal, fawnin' subjects now they be of the British Crown. That not be the worst my countryman ha'e done." Struan coughed great wracking spasms, gritting his teeth as Ming Tsun kneaded the brandy through the inflamed channel of his wound.

"'Vast talking, Struan. Sufficient time for telling all later."

Pridham burst into the room, a small iron frying pan containing white-hot coals hastily dipped out of the galley stove nestled in a towel held out gingerly in his hands. "On the desk," Frost commanded brusquely, "don't let the brazier overtip."

Ming Tsun seized a writing quill from the ink pot on the desk, took up the pen knife laying nearby, stripped off the barbs with his teeth, and neatly sliced the shaft into a three inch length. He thrust one end of the quill's shaft into the wound at the front of Struan's neck, then selected a coal from the frying pan, breathing on his fingers to form the moisture so necessary to the task. Caleb held Struan firmly while Ming Tsun touched the coal to the wound, sealing the quill into the wound. Struan fainted. Ming Tsun then seared the wound at the back of Struan's neck, the cabin filling with the cloying reek of scorched flesh. Ming Tsun threw the coal through the broken stern windows.

"The same with that brazier, Pridham, if you please, before we fire the ship," Frost said tersely. Pridham, who had been standing with mouth agape, collected his wits and stepped to the wide gash in the stern windows, ready to hurl the coals into the sea. Ming Tsun signed quickly, and Frost countermanded his order: "'Vast, Pridham. We shall need the coals to brew tea for Mister Ferguson. Caleb, off with you to intercept our surgeon and his mate. Doubtless there are wounded among our men or the British prisoners who require their ministrations far more than our Struan, now that Ming Tsun has seared him. Send someone with a kettle of fresh water— not the muddy scrapings of some barrel long in transit."

Caleb hurried away and Frost turned to Pridham. "How did this happen?" Frost demanded.

Cox Pridham swallowed nervously several times. "Capt'n, that Britisher, you know, the fella in charge of this 'ere overgrown wooden bucket, he had a pistol hidden in that bandage of his'n, and once you were hull and gone, he shot Mister Ferguson."

Frost glanced at the bullet-splintered door. "Obviously, Mister Ferguson was sore wounded."

"He killed the Britisher, Mister Ferguson did. I didn't see none of it since I wus fightin' for my life on the back deck. But my mate, Wright Blount, was 'ere, 'n' he seed it all, and Wright Blount be most reliable, so I got the full twig off him."

"Threw the ship's captain through the stern lights, I take it," Frost said.

"Yes sir," Pridham said, greatly surprised. "How'd you twig that, sir?"

Frost did not bother to explain the clues: bloodstains on the glass shards still held in the panes, threads of blue cloth also snared here and there in the shards. "Continue, please, Pridham."

"Wal, sir," Pridham began reluctantly, then with greater enthusiasm as he warmed to his story, "that shot war the signal for a bunch of redcoats, women we thought they wus at first, sir, God's my witness, sir, 'cause they wus wearin' skirts and all. It wus only a'ter they wus comin' at us that Mister Ferguson said they warn't skirts, but the way the Scotlanders dress. Can't see it nohow, sir, that men would wear skirts, and that be God's truth! But anyway, we held the back deck, the place wher the steerin' be done 'n' you be shoutin' orders, sir—pardon me, sir, but fortune-like they warn't able to come at us a'many at a time. Otherwise, they war cut us up, liver 'n' lights, right proper, a'fore Mister Slocum came ballin' up with all his men hangin' from them masts and cut down a power of them men in skirts, that he did! It war right tuck 'n' nip war we to see Portsmouth agin, sir, but Mister Ferguson kept cuttin' down anyone who got up on the back deck, that big sword of his'n, until, what with Mister Slocum's men and the ruckus we put up, the fight just went outa 'em."

"And we have three men dead out of our vessel, and seven wounded, including Mister Ferguson, is that your tally, Cox Pridham?"

"That be a true tally, Capt'n, far as I kin judge."

Frost sighed. "Name them—wait! Ming Tsun must find paper to transcribe. Continue, the names of the dead first, and their homes if you know them, then the men wounded . . ."

So there it was again, three men who had walked through the wall between life and death for Geoffrey Frost. But these men should not have died. Frost thought of Captain Cowmeadow and felt a great rush of anger. He had known the man for a cheat and a scoundrel from a chance encounter in Macao, all but ostracized by the other Europeans in that strange, wondrously barbaric city, a fantastical blend of Portugal and China; he should have been forewarned. Frost kept his thoughts to himself as Ming Tsun wrote down the names and home places of the dead, and then the wounded.

"We'ze had to bury our men in the water, Capt'n," Pridham said reluctantly after he had told the list of dead and wounded. "Mister Ferguson waited for twa' days, a-hoping yere return, knowin' you'd want to say the words o'er 'em right, but then we'ze buried 'em all proper, sewed inta sail cloth, and Mister Ferguson sayin' the words o'er 'em 'n' all."

"Quite properly done," Frost said bleakly. No, he had never wanted to "say the words" over any dead, though it would have been his duty. "Our wounded must be removed to the cat. Pridham, please find Surgeon Green and advise him to make our men ready to go across."

Behind him Struan Ferguson coughed and repeated the words he had uttered before fainting. "That not be the worst my countryman ha'e done."

Frost was struck by the use of the singular noun. "Why do you say 'countryman,' Struan? Have you someone particular to name?"

Struan Ferguson struggled to rise: "Aye, Geoffrey, and particularly gallin' it be, for Patrick Ferguson is my cousin from Aberdeenshire."

Ming Tsun signed that the wound was well sealed, and none of the great blood vessels or tendons in the neck touched, though he indicated that the ball had missed the great blood vessels by less than half the thickness of a feather's quill. Struan Ferguson had been incredibly lucky, or Cowmeadow had been an exceedingly bad marksman, which equated to luck. Frost nodded with satisfaction as Caleb Mansfield bustled into the cabin with a kettle, steam rising above it, and set it quickly upon the coals in the iron frying pan. Ming Tsun and Caleb Mansfield assisted Struan to sit upright on the horsehair-padded settee.

"Caleb," Struan said in a barely audible whisper, "ye, more than any man I ken, are well acquainted with firearms. Fetch the rifle from the cot in the sleepin' cabin."

Caleb returned, holding out a firearm that to Frost seemed to be a musket with a shortened fore stock.

"I'll wager ye can fathom her secrets, Caleb," Struan said tersely. Ming Tsun held a cup of tea, liberally laced with Captain Cowmeadow's brandy, all steaming, to Struan's lips; he drank the cup in two swallows, and Ming Tsun replenished the cup with tea and brandy.

"Waal, this shines! A right marvel it be!" Caleb exclaimed. "No looby conjur'd this!"

"No looby indeed," Struan said in the weakest of voices, "my cousin, Patrick, whom last I knew was fightin' Caribs in the West Indies. Geoffrey, see if ye ken the trick of it."

Frost took the firearm from Caleb, noting the long metal rod beneath the barrel, thinking it first a ramrod, then divining that the rod was spear-pointed and slid forward—a bayonet! "Most unusual design for a bayonet," Frost murmured to hide his confusion. He thought himself tolerably well acquainted with firearms. Now how could this musket be loaded without a ramrod? No, a glance at the muzzle revealed the presence of shallow rifling. This firearm was a rifle, not a smoothbore musket. "I collect the bayonet must somehow also serve as a ramrod . . ."

"No, Geoffrey," Struan said, "but from his exclamation Caleb has smoked the trick of it, I warrant."

Caleb Mansfield nodded soberly and took the firearm from Frost. Caleb grasped the projection at the end of the trigger guard—Frost had thought it no more than a stop to keep the shooter's hand from slipping too far rearward—between thumb and forefinger and startled Frost by rotating the trigger guard one full rotation anti-clockwise. Caleb pointed to the deep chamber that had opened in the thick metal of the breech immediately to the left of the cock.

"I warr'nt the ball be placed here, the barrel bein' held down'rd, then powder pour'd in a-hind, 'n' . . ." Caleb rotated the trigger guard clockwise, and Frost saw the ten-pointed breech plug revolve quickly and smoothly into position, sealing the chamber. Caleb opened the frizzen, simulated the addition of priming powder to the pan, snapped the frizzen closed, and shouldered the rifle.

"It is the invention of the devil!" Frost exclaimed, seeing immediately all the weapon's horrific implications.

Struan sank back wearily on additional cushions that Ming Tsun had fetched and plumped up for him on the settee. "Nae, Geoffrey, 'tis but an evolution in the armorer's craft, though truly a most cunningly diabolic one. I suspect my cousin believes otherwise, that it be a superior weapon to chace his King's wayward American brethren back to the shelter of the British Crown."

"So rifles such as these were in the chests going overside as we closed with this wretched *Sagittarius*," Frost guessed.

"Aye, ninety rifles all told overside, though the one chest of ten arms already at the waist was prudently spared when Caleb's men got the range. This rifle, and another like it, was in the baggage of a Highlander lieutenant charged with their safe delivery to General Howe."

"And he revealed the secrets of this arm?" Frost asked.

"Most assuredly. After we had forced the British back below decks followin' their captain's treachery, I dinna mind tellin' ye, Geoffrey, that we disposed of the British dead by throwing them overside. There followed a glorious conglomeration of sharks. I report happily that Captain Cowmeadow's body had not sunk, and his was the first torn asunder by the brutes. That sight was a wondrous laxative of the tongue; we had but to dangle the lieutenant over the lee bulwark and the maelstrom below, and he quickly related all he knew of the workin's of my cousin's infernal invention."

"What be the quickness of its fire?" Caleb asked, twisting the trigger guard first one way, then another, marveling at how smoothly the breech plug rose up and down on its interrupted threads.

"The lieutenant of Highlanders—as perfidious as . . . as Judas," Struan fairly spat the hated words, "said a skilled soldier can load and fire at least six aimed shots in the minute, though seven aimed shots was common enough."

"Belike," Caleb said with a sharp intake of breath. "I can feed both o' Gideon's barrels inside the minute, if'n I hold th' balls in my mouth and not be consarned with th' 'xact measurin' o' powder."

"I have timed your woods-cruizers, Caleb, during their musketry drills," Frost said, taking the rifle from Caleb's hands to hold in his own, admiring the rifle's deadly beauty, noting how it differed so efficiently and singularly from the smoothbore muskets borne away from Louisbourg with which his crew, save Caleb's woods-cruisers, were armed. "From the discharge of the ball already in the arm until the next aimed round is generally on the minute."

"Aye," Struan said, gratefully swallowing his third cup of tea and smiling wanly to signal his gratitude to Ming Tsun, "and muskets can be fired within the minute—if ye have powder and patience enough to train the man, though the undersized ball rattlin' down that piece of gas pipe is apt as not to miss its mark at fifty paces."

"It be harder 'n' harder to keep a hot fire," Caleb interjected, pointing a dirty forefinger at the top of the breech plug, "'cause the brimstone in th' powder fouls th' bore somethin' awful. Got to keep the foulin' soft, with spit o' whatever's handy, or yore ramrod's like to break. But this," he tapped his forefinger on the breech plug to emphasize his point, "be a right marvel. See, Capt'n, th' slots 'round this plug—they help grind th' foulin' from the earlier shot, then th' foulin' drops out the bottom when th' plug opens agin."

"The lieutenant pointed out with grand pride," Struan said gloomily, "what immediately becomes obvious upon the thought. My cousin's rifle can be loaded as handily when the soldier is lyin' on his belly as when he's standin'."

"And did your lieutenant count the number of these rifles being conveyed to the British Army in North America?" Frost asked.

"Aye, there were three hundred divided among this small flotilla, chartered to make all possible speed to land the arms and men at Halifax. The one hundred stand on the *Tuscany Countess* won't do General Howe any good. Meanwhile, Patrick is in London drivin' Durs Egg and Billy Hunt to make as many of 'em as they can, as fast as they can. He'll be in the next flotilla to be formed, armed additionally with a letter directly from George Three to General Howe sayin'—all this according to the Highlander lieutenant—Patrick's to form a Rifle Corps, and carte blanche in the bargain."

If Frost were a betting man he would have bet, perversely, that the other one hundred Ferguson rifles would, more likely than not, have been shipped not aboard the *Triton*, now under Slocum Plaisted's care as prize master, but aboard the *Generous Friend*, and beyond all recovery, having been jettisoned during the lengthy chase of that vessel.

"I shall have my brother, Joseph, find a smith who can duplicate this arm," Frost said quickly. "Joseph is an ironmonger, not an arms smith, but surely there are among us smiths with the cunning to fashion a rifle such as this."

Caleb Mansfield scooped up the penknife and a quill from the desk and whittled a pick tooth. "Ain't sayin' we got ner'n, but this be close work, 'n' th' like never bin don' in our part o' the woods afore . . ."

With a sinking heart Frost realized no gunsmith practicing the craft in North America had the abilities or the tools to copy the Ferguson rifle. He thought of his pair of Bass turn-off fire double-barreled pistols—more than once he had sought American gunsmiths who could duplicate the work. The answers had always been regretful shakes of the head. A few, a very few, long rifles were made completely by American gunsmiths, but the vast majority of long rifles were assembled, not made. Oh, the gunsmiths in the colonies were generally excellent, able to do skilled broaching and rifling operations, even deep-hole drilling, of imported welded barrel blanks. A few gunsmiths had even mastered the art of welding twists of iron and steel around a mandrel to form barrels on the Damascus principle—the barrels of Caleb's Gideon had been so wrought by a Pennsylvania smith.

But the great majority of gunlocks to make American long rifles were imported from Britain, less frequently from France or Belgium. It was easier, and far cheaper, thus than to fabricate the frizzens, cocks, springs, and sears, the small parts, on a forge in Exeter or Rumford. The workmanship of wedding barrel and lock to native maple was exquisite—and deadly— in proper hands, but to expect that an American gunsmith using any metal smelted in America could fabricate a copy of the Ferguson rifle—no.

But by the Great Buddha, there must be an effort! Frost thrust out the Ferguson flintlock rifle to Ming Tsun and signed: "Find the size of its ball and make up cartridges, though I imagine somewhere on this vessel there should be a chest of cartridges. I shall dispatch one to Joseph, with instructions to attempt its duplication with every diligence he can command." Then to Caleb: "Doubtless you would be loath to lay Gideon aside, but if your fellow woods-cruizers . . ."

"Naw, Capt'n, none o' mine will want the changin' o' the familiar. But I've had my eye on a couple of likely lads who could, pardon my sayin' it, make ye a right smart crack o' marines."

"Make it so," Frost said. "Pridham, I trust that in the three, almost four, days of leisure you've enjoyed while your mates were chacing other prizes to enrich you, someone has come up with the bills of lading of this vessel's cargo."

"Wal, Capt'n, with this bucket's people still locked below, 'n' . . ."

"I hae a fair copy of the *Sagittarius* manifests there," Struan Ferguson whispered hoarsely and pointed toward the captain's desk. "Artillery and their trains, powder 'n' musket balls by the cask, flints, uniforms, salt pork, flour, tallow . . . all the provisions for an army of invasion and occupation . . . no rum or hard spirits, though, those are to come from the West Indies."

"The same as the other victualers," Frost interrupted. "Enough from you for the nonce. You are in my gig when next it crosses to the cat. I have this plan . . ."

✹✹✹✹ FTER THE ENTIRE CREW OF THE *SAGIT-*
✹ A ✹ *TARIUS* AND THE REMNANTS OF THE RE-
✹ ✹ INFORCED COMPANY OF HIGHLANDER
✹✹✹✹ GRENADIERS EMBARKED ABOARD HAD
been transferred to *Generous Friend* to get them out of the
way and keep Captain Barnstead MacMillan and his people
company in the close and odoriferous stables so recently
vacated by their chevaline charges, and by working through a
night illuminated by every lantern possessed by the cat and
the three East Indiamen prizes, at dawn the next morning all
the cargo from *Sagittarius,* including the forty absolutely
priceless 12-pounder artillery tubes and their trains, had been
shifted into *Triton.* Frost had given Ming Tsun and Ishmael
Hymsinger specific instructions of what to look for as the casks
of provisions were swayed up from the holds of *Sagittarius.*

The barrels of spoiled provisions were easily detected, either
by the swollen, leaking and discolored staves dribbling their
fetid soups onto the deck or their distinctive cadaverine aroma
of salted meat that had quite gone off. On an even dozen
barrels Frost was amused to see the large letter "C" for
"condemned" burned deeply into the barrel staves with a red
hot musket ramrod. Very possibly those particular barrels had
made a dozen trips across the Atlantic and had been put up
a dozen or so years ago during the French and Indian Wars.
These barrels of spoiled provisions were set aside on the cable
tier, as well as an even four dozen hogsheads of rancid water.

At sunrise, with all cargo transferred, Frost ordered Caleb and his woods-cruisers to cut down Sagittarius' main and mizzen masts, an order the woods-cruisers obeyed with enthusiasm, not stopping until both masts, though not their yards, had been reduced to lengths that required only slight additional splitting to be ready for the cook's stoves aboard the cat, *Triton*, and *Generous Friend*. The sails were unbent, folded, and distributed equally between *Triton* and *Generous Friend* for later delivery to Portsmouth.

Even before the main and quarterdeck of *Sagittarius* had been cleared of the masts and yards, Frost ordered Slocum Plaisted to bring over the slovenly rabble of British seamen from *Triton* and *Generous Friend* and the Brunswick mercenaries in the boats and rafts off the *Tuscany Countess*. Frost passed orders to Major von Fendig through Caleb Mansfield. He did not give this task to Struan Ferguson, due as much to the infirmities of his wound as to the rancor of his abandonment on the beach at Batavia by the cheeseheads—he resolutely refused to acknowledge he had ever spoken the language. Von Fendig, in the role of senior military commander, was to deal with the provisions and water as he deemed fit.

Then Frost set the boats, rowed by British sailors but carefully superintended by Caleb Mansfield's woods-cruisers, to ferrying back the people taken off *Sagittarius*, though diverting the cutter conveying Captain Barnstead MacMillan to pause momentarily at the cat, where a scowling and deeply unhappy Captain MacMillan met Frost on his own quarterdeck.

"You behold your next command, sir," Frost said without preamble, gesturing abruptly toward *Sagittarius*. "Her former commanding officer paid with the coin of his life for his treachery. If there is some dispute whether you or your compatriot out of *Triton* are more senior and therefore rightfully command," Frost shrugged to indicate any quarrel over whom the proper master for *Sagittarius* might be was of absolutely no concern to him. "The Brunswickers, with Major von Fendig as the senior military officer embarked, have already gone aboard, and I hope have not made too free with the provisions apportioned for the benefit of your combined crews." Frost signed to Ming Tsun, who copied a series of figures from the chalkboard by the cat's binnacle and handed the scrap of paper to Frost. Frost extended the paper to MacMillan, who did not extend a hand to take it.

Frost shrugged and wadded the paper. "This, sir, is your exact position. As you see, your next command possesses only a foremast, which is ample to see you back to England with the following wind I've never known to fail in these climes. You may, of course, continue on to North America, though the provisions provided by the generosity of the British Admiralty may not admit of that voyage's length. I do remark that you have enshipped in your next command more than seven hundred souls, and given that you are essentially in ballast, I would keep as many below as ever I could. I would also keep a weather eye on your rudder, sir. It was bunged a few days ago, and without attention paid to it, you will find it somewhat tender."

Frost made as if to throw the wadded paper overboard, but stopped: "Major von Fendig has pledged his word that his troops will not take up arms against Americans through the remainder of this year. I do not know if that promise will assist you in calculating a landfall."

Shooting Frost a glance of utmost distaste, Captain Mac-Millan snatched the wadded paper from Frost's hand and glanced suspiciously at the latitude and longitude written there. "Is there a sextant or quadrant left aboard my next command, sir, or has that, like all else, been plundered as booty by you rebels?"

"Your own sextant has already been delivered aboard *Sagittarius*, sir," Frost said, half turning away to signal that he was through talking with MacMillan. "Good day to you, sir, and I wish you a quick and kindly voyage to wherever you believe destiny should lead."

"Beg pardon, sohr, it's bin ages 'n' all, but do I ken ye to be Geoffrey Frost, out of the old *Bride of Derry*?" A man pulling stroke oar called up from the heavily laden cutter paused at the lee waist entry for MacMillan to return aboard. Frost turned, scowling, and paced to the lee rail, for the *Bride of Derry* was a name he had not heard for many years, a name that was anathema to him.

"And who, sir, may you be?" Frost scowled down into the cutter, scanning every face.

"Lamb Wilkes, sohr, from Truro, down on the Cape of Cod. Course, ye woldna ken me from the old *Bride*, ye being but a nipper at the time, 'n' all, but ye was pointed out to me years back, after ye got yer growth, when ye vittled at Saint Helen's, and I was a hand what rowed out a turn of water barrels from the town."

Frost glared at the seaman; somewhere in the vicinity of fifty years, he judged, bald, pudgy belly, most assuredly a hernia, moderate to severe, less than five teeth in his head, rheumy eyes faded from decades of squinting against sunlight at sea. A man long acquainted with defeat and despair. He was typical of several thousand hands Frost had known in his lifetime at sea. Frost had no particular remembrance of this seaman.

"Who was the master of this *Bride of Derry*, Mister Wilkes," Frost demanded, "at the time you knew of me?"

The man paused: "I darn't mention the name, sohr, lest ye give me leave."

"My leave you have," Frost said curtly.

"Wick Nichols, sohr," Lamb Wilkes said quietly, though Frost heard the name well enough.

"And what lesson did Captain Nichols teach, Lamb Wilkes?"

"That the master of the vessel was to be obeyed at all times, and in all things, sohr." Again the voice was low, but Frost heard every word.

"How do you come to be here, Lamb Wilkes, and from which company come you?"

"I be out of *Triton*, sohr, taken two years ago out of a fever ship in Freddie Po. Proper salted gint the fever I be."

"Do you wish to join my people, Lamb Wilkes?"

"Aye, sohr, seein' who ye be, and I know a power of hands who'd like to join like'ise."

"If you can vouch for a man duly breeched in one of the

North American states now in rebellion against the magisterial government of George Three, then he is as welcome as you, Lamb Wilkes. But no man not known personally to and vouchsafed by you shall be permitted to join my people, do you ken?"

"I kin bring yer barky this cutter right full of *Triton* hands, all fair breeched in North American colonies."

Frost turned to Nathaniel Dance: "My compliments to Doctor Green. I wish him to attend this man to the *Sagittarius*, and if he can indeed fill the cutter with men born within or without the former colonies, well and good, though I shall ship only men without hernias, the pox, or other maladies. Men who shall be scoured in water and vinegar to cleanse them of lice and other small creatures of inconvenience before joining us." Frost saw his remark about hernias caused Lamb Wilkes to wince. "Not to worry, Lamb Wilkes, I don't believe your hernia is so particular grave as to prevent you from being rated quartermaster."

As Nathaniel Dance scurried away to carry his message to Ezrah Green, Frost's eyes fell on Hannibal Bowditch: "Mister Bowditch, lay below to my cabin. You'll find there a sextant in its case, a gift to you from the late Captain Cowmeadow of the *Sagittarius*, and my *Moore's*. You are to go aboard *Triton* as navigator to Mister Plaisted, her prize master. Take our present position from Ming Tsun. While we shall convoy together, the vagaries of the sea are such we may become separated. If so, it shall be your task to navigate *Triton* and *Generous Friend*, who shall keep particularly close company with you, to Portsmouth."

Frost granted himself the briefest of smiles as Hannibal Bowditch skipped away as nimbly as a fawn, wholeheartedly delighted at being entrusted with such an important task as navigator of a prize. Frost watched Captain MacMillan climb down into the cutter, stiffly and hesitantly; Frost had noted—but not remarked—on the hand drawn into a claw by arthritis, and suspected the Britisher's knees were equally affected. By all rights MacMillan should be sitting by the fire in his parlor in some town like Deal or Bath, bouncing grandchildren on his knee, telling them stories about weathering heavy gales off the Cape of Storms, belike. But here he was pressed into his King's service, as effectively as Major von Fendig's Brunswickers.

Frost shook his head; with the ministerial government of George Three willing to commit military forces of such magnitude to the campaign in North America, the British strategy was clear: overwhelm the rebellious colonies quickly through sheer force of numbers. It was going to be either a very short war, or a very long war. "Mister O'Buck," he said, and Daniel O'Buck stepped to his side. "I hope to see thirty men in yonder cutter when she pulls back. If we be so gifted, you will take the charge of them as they touch here, sending equal numbers into your *Generous Friend*, *Triton*, and this vessel. The cutter falls as your due. You are to keep company as close to *Triton* as you possibly can, both of you proceeding to Portsmouth with all dispatch." Frost smiled thinly: "I may be elsewhere engaged betimes."

Frost dismissed O'Buck with a nod and began pacing his quarterdeck, glancing with a sense of wonder that he successfully concealed from anyone watching him at *Generous Friend* and *Triton* hobbyhorsing on the moderate mid-Atlantic swells, keeping steerageway under twice-reefed main topsails—his legitimate prizes! Too bad there was not a deck gun between them.

And one hundred yards away rode *Sagittarius*, a woeful sight, to be sure, the scorched bulwarks, the pitiful foremast standing alone—and close to seven hundred souls crowded aboard her. Rancid rations for half that number for one month, no more. If MacMillan could eke three knots an hour downwind from that rig, he would be most fortunate indeed. MacMillan would sail northeast, back toward England, of that Frost had no doubt. MacMillan had been long enough at sea to know that he could not beat against the trade winds with his greatly abbreviated sail plan, and by heading to the northeast he might at least encounter some of the other vessels in this massive convoy.

Who was the commodore of this particular invasion fleet? Struan had told him: Hotham. Yes, that was the name, William Hotham. Frost supposed this Commodore Hotham had some sort of title granted by the British King as well, but by the Golden Buddha, he had sworn never to apply a patent or title of nobility to anyone. A dignified "sir," or "mister," or reference to an earned rank: that was the cast of democracy.

Frost saw the cutter shear away from *Sagittarius* and come strong for the cat, rising heavily on a swell, then dipping almost out of sight. The cutter was crowded with men. Frost doubted if another could have been forced in with a shoehorn, men who had had quite enough of the Honorable John Company and were joining him, sight unseen. And just who was this Lamb Wilkes? Frost had no recollection of the man, and why had Joseph, Mary and Jesus chosen this moment to throw Lamb Wilkes across his bow? He could not name a single man among the crew of the *Bride of Derry*, her officers, yes, but crew, no. Yet he had sensed the crew had all been with him during that terrible ordeal that had near cost him his life, now sixteen—seventeen—years in the past. Frost shut his mind resolutely against the memory. Joss. Insh'allah. The Prophet.

"Mister Lacey," he said in a conversational tone, turning now toward his acting bosun, "as soon as we have taken a third of that cutter's complement into our vessel, courses and main jib until *Triton* and *Generous Friend* catch up to us. Our initial heading shall be west by north, one-half west." Frost watched his vessel take life through the bawled commands of his acting bosun, nodded in satisfaction as the cat's head swung round sharply, and did not spare a glance at the hulk of *Sagittarius* that the cat was rapidly leaving in its wake.

## ❦ XIII ❧

"▓▓▓▓ T IS MY WISH TO AVOID PREJUDICE ▓ I ▓ TO YOUR RECOVERY, STRUAN, AND ▓ ▓ THE WIDOW CROCKETT WOULD SUM- ▓▓▓▓ MARILY DISPOSSESS WITHOUT QUALM any boarder from that fine corner room on the second deck of her tavern you so particularly favor." Frost spoke earnestly to his first officer as he focused his glass on the snow, a tremendous grand union flag, the same as was first flown by His Excellency, General Washington, upon taking command of the Continental Army at Cambridge, streaming from her jack staff, reaching broad from the mouth of the Piscataqua.

With her present course and speed, Geoffrey Frost reckoned the snow would reach the holding ground off Smuttynose Isle in thirty minutes. The cat lay at short anchor, with launches, barges and cutters plying industriously around and among *Triton*, *Generous Friend*, and his most recent prize, a brig-rigged dispatch vessel taken three days before. *Neptune*, under the command of a Lieutenant Stanley, en route from Halifax to the Virginia Capes—with dispatches—and freighting the incredible sum of twenty thousand pounds in specie! Not to mention the dozens hogsheads of rum sent to relieve the tribulations and tediums of Lord Dunmore and his floating town in the Chesapeake. Fair consolation for the vast, untouchable treasure that had been in Captain Smith's possession aboard HM *Lark*. The boats were consolidating the ship's company and various provisions Frost would be freighting for his next cruise against the British.

"Thankee, Geoffrey, I'll nae deny that the attractions of the vastly estimable Widow Crockett are quite beyond measure, and that corner room has a thumpin' great bed with thick goosedown quilts into which one man, nae, an entire fleet can sink without leaving so much as a spar to mark its disappearance. Not to mention the widow sets the best table in Portsmouth. I recall with especial fondness the lobster bisque Mrs. Crockett prepared the night before we sailed to Louisbourg. Could George Three but taste that bisque, he would empty the Germanic principalities of mercenaries and contract with the Spanish and Portuguese as allies—all the sooner to subdue us and gain the secret of the widow's recipe."

"Far better, then, t'would seem, Struan, to ship Mrs. Crockett off to London to prepare vittles for George Three," Frost said in jest, cutting off his first mate. The grievous wound to Struan Ferguson's neck had changed Struan's voice, permanently, to a low husky baritone that, fortunately, could still reach from main deck to masthead.

"I would nae rest easy ashore, Geoffrey, knowin' that Patrick and a power of those infernal rifles of his may appear with the next convoy out of the British Isles. My duty be plain; betimes, Ming Tsun has physicked me twice now with his needles, and swallowin' brings very little pain, to the everlastin' dismay of our dear surgeon, who believes this business of twistin' needles as balm and salve to pain be codswallop. Methinks Ezrah be jealous that my wounds turned not gangrenous." Struan self-consciously fingered the heavily starched stock that encircled his throat.

"A most interesting amputation may have ensued," Frost said dryly. "The type which the medical gents term a success, though the patient expires."

"Was never worried about this wound, Geoffrey. In truth, I know that, havin' survived the battle in which ye took this cat, I know that I be destined to die ashore, peaceably, at a ripe age, most like in a deep feather bed such as the one in the Widow Crockett's corner room . . ."

"Or run through the gizzard at age seventy by a jealous husband," Frost bantered. "By the Golden Buddha, that is Tommy Thompson on the quarterdeck of the snow! I'm glad of it; had Cousin John come out to greet us, I fear the gam would be long and tiresome. Tommy is a right sailor, all a-fret, I'm sure, to get away to sea in his *Raleigh* once she has sufficient cannons. I can pass my letters and the captured dispatches to Tommy, and he can shepherd these three prizes to join the Tortola Packet and Louisbourg vessels to be condemned under the Admiralty Court's hammer. Look! There is Jack Lacey in the waist! Bless him! He made capital time to shore with the *Neptune*'s gold and silver. So all her specie should be shut safe in Marlborough's bank. I just hope he was able to lay by a store of young corn, though regrettably the season is not achieved for potatoes, pears and apples."

"Mister Bowditch!" Frost shouted through his speaking trumpet, glimpsing Hannibal's diminutive figure perched atop a tidy pyramid of beef barrels coming over in a long boat from *Triton*, the case containing his sextant and Frost's *Moore's* held tightly in both hands. "I trust you recorded your noon sights every day. Please bring them to me at your leisure for comparison against mine." The sheep and geese, the residue of *Triton*'s manger sharing the launch with Hannibal Bowditch, were unanimously vociferous in protesting their unceremonious transfer.

Hannibal heard and waved excitedly like the youth he was, quite forgetting that upon his young shoulders had rested the awesome responsibility of navigating *Triton* and *Generous Friend* to the rendezvous in the Isles of Shoals. Young Bowditch had done an admirable job, as Frost had known he would.

"Give you joy, Geoffrey Frost, estimable privateer!" Tommy Thompson boomed in his gravelly voice as the snow came within fifty yards and rounded into the wind to lose way, the maneuver startling into flight a gaggle of double-crested cormorants that had been solemnly nodding up and down like black-habited nuns genuflecting at vespers, drying their wings on the rocks of Smuttynose. "Never before has such been seen in the Ports of Piscataqua! First the Halifax Packet with her wondrous sterling, and now the wonder of seeing first hand these two great East Indiamen. Are you not surfeited with prizes enough to berth at your own wharf rather than lie off these Isles and send them in?"

"Come aboard and I'll tell you more, Captain Thompson, but you must be quick, before I've shifted my men out of the prizes, leaving just enough to work them up the Piscataqua. This vessel's company is on the wing for the mid-Atlantic while this wind holds fair." As Frost stepped away from the cat's weather rail, closely followed by Ming Tsun with his portable secretary, his eye fell on Lamb Wilkes, who was seated on a cannon industriously darning a stocking.

"Mister Ferguson," Frost said to his first mate, "please inquire of Lamb Wilkes if he can spare a moment from his needlework to gam with me."

An apprehensive Lamb Wilkes knuckled his forehead, British seaman fashion, nervously as he reported to Frost's quarterdeck.

"Lamb Wilkes, your rupture is a grave affair indeed," Frost began without preamble. "I've observed the pain it causes you, and I fear you are no longer suited for the rigors of further service at sea."

Lamb Wilkes stood speechless, his jowls working as he tried unsuccessfully to form words, his forehead sheened with sudden perspiration.

Frost motioned the man to approach closer. "Your days at sea are past, Lamb," he said kindly, in a voice low enough that only Wilkes could hear. "You should have gone ashore before you were taken out of the fever ship. The wonder is you've lasted so long."

"I . . . I've got no trade but the sea, sohr," Lamb Wilkes said, finding his voice. "It don't hurt 'tall when I bind this stocking stuffed with a bit of sand close agin the bulge, atter I done poked the sausage back in my belly—I kin still reef, hand

and steer with the best o' hands, sohr! Ye must credit me with a right job of handlin' the helm of this barky."

Frost held up his hand, signed for Ming Tsun to bring the portable secretary, opened the ink pot to wet the nib of a herring gull's quill, and wrote steadily for the time it took Tommy Thompson's gig, rowed by John Langdon's slave, Prosperous, to cross from his snow to the cat. Frost shook and blew upon the paper to dry the ink. "This is a letter to Mister Silas Rutherford, the superintendent of my warehouse. He is directed to employ you as a watchman at a salary of fifteen New Hampshire dollars per month. As watchman you shall be entitled to your own accommodations in my warehouse, as well as provisions, same as aboard a vessel of the Frost Trading Company. You were a crewman of this vessel when she took the Halifax Packet. The prize court will take some weeks to libel all the prizes this cruize has fetched us. So this," Frost affixed his signature precisely to a second letter, "is a draft on my father's bank for two hundred New Hampshire dollars to be paid immediately to you as advance against your share of the Halifax Packet."

Frost looked sternly at the seaman, who hesitantly took the two pieces of paper and held them at arm's length as if they were contagious as the pox. "Anyone who was before the mast on the *Bride of Derry* deserves a turn ashore, Lamb Wilkes, particularly a hand who's spent thirty and more years at sea, betimes." Frost smiled at the man. "I know you have no kit to delay you, so you're up to Portsmouth with Captain Thompson on yonder snow. He'll ensure you are taken to my warehouse as soon as his snow gains her berth. Good fortune to you, Lamb Wilkes."

Frost clapped a hand on Lamb Wilkes' shoulder, then turned away and hurried down the central companionway to the larboard waist entry, into which Tommy Thompson was just now thrusting his imposing bulk.

"Geoff!" Thompson shouted, his florid face a rich port-wine red from the exertion of heaving himself aboard the cat: "Joy, oh joy, to you! Is it true that you have duck and cordage?

I understand you have taken cannons? If so, I may yet get my *Raleigh* to sea." He and Frost bowed formally to each other, then Thompson had Frost in a great bear squeeze, fairly lifting him from the deck. "Great news! I have newspapers, and this, which John Langdon wanted most particularly for me to show you. He entrusted it to me to give you as he rode away to Providence to seek cannons for my poor *Raleigh*."

"What of the cannons I brought from Louisbourg, Tommy?" Frost interrupted. "Surely those cannons went directly aboard your commission? I have taken cannons, but they are 12-pounders with trains for artillery, and it seems sure they are bespoke for our army."

Thompson scowled. "So you would think, but that rascally bookseller with pretensions to being an artilleryman, Knox, claimed some for His Excellency's forces now in New York, and some others were sent to the Lake, where a nutmegger name of Arnold, a New Yorker named Schuyler, and a certain Horatio Gates, all styling themselves generals, are a-building a great fleet to keep the British from seizing the Lake and doing our cause great harm. Can you imagine it, Geoff, generals with impertinence enough and independence enough to contemplate naval affairs? Who would give it credence?" Thompson snapped his fingers, and Prosperous, who had followed him closely aboard the cat holding a leather portfolio, dutifully handed Thompson a rolled broadside of foolscap that Thompson held up with a flourish.

"Speaking of independence, Geoff, this is the Unanimous Declaration of Independence of the Thirteen United States of America, declared on the fourth of July, so your cousin John tells me, in Philadelphia, by all the nabobs of our Continental Congress. This broadside was printed by one Dunlap, styling himself official printer to the Congress. John declares it was first read on the sixth or the eighth—damme, actual date fair escapes me—by a chap named Mifflin—damme if I know who he be—in the square before the State House to the people assembled. Grand, grand words, these, Geoff!"

Thompson was startled at the sight of Struan Ferguson,

standing at a discreet distance by the mainmast. "Why, Ferguson, the wags had it that you were at death's door, fairly perched on the stoop, though deigning all the while to accept the invitation to enter the Devil's Parlor! Heartily glad am I that those rumors be given the lie!" Thompson threw the broadside to Prosperous, who replaced it in the portfolio, and crossed to the mainmast in two strides, thumping Struan mightily on his shoulder. Struan almost buckled from the onslaught but grinned gamely.

Frost moved between the two men quickly. "Tommy, would you be so kind as to release Prosperous to seek his son," and, without waiting for a reply, he spoke directly to John Langdon's slave: "Prosperous, Ming Tsun will assist in locating your beloved son. Thence I suggest you make your way to the galley, where I have no doubt Cook Barnes will have coffee and toasted biscuit for you. I'll delay Captain Thompson no more than ten minutes." Frost stepped closer to the black man and said in a low voice: "Darius' share of monies for prizes taken thus far in this cruize stands near five hundred pounds, and he intends to purchase your freedom; go to your son now." Then, more loudly: "Once you've found Darius, ask that he charge one of his associates to bring coffee and biscuit to my cabin for Captain Thompson, and tea for me." Frost took the leather portfolio from Prosperous, whose radiant smile bespoke his happiness.

"Coffee!" Tommy Thompson exclaimed, aghast. "Have you naught to offer an old comrade than the bilges of coffee grounds strained through a cast-off stocking? And tea—spare me if you will the boiled leaves of that noxious weed that you quaff, and lie like a Philistine that you find such vile brew a tonic. It's honest rum from Jamaica or Trinidad or Saint Martin's Islands that I thirst for."

"I opened one hogshead of rum out of the Tortola Packet taken earlier to share out among my company, and I'm reliably informed it is of tolerable quality, with the lot likely to knock down to advantage," Frost said. "I doubt, though, if that rum is more than two months from the cane press. However, there were several bottles in a basket bearing the seal of the Tory Goodrich, owner of the Halifax Packet, of a more settled age, all destined for Dunmore. Since it was intended for the sustenance of our enemies, I had no option but to sequester it. Perhaps, Tommy, you'll be good enough to give me your frank opinion of the quality." Frost signed to Ming Tsun and led the way to his cabin.

Thompson whistled softly when he saw the simple but elegant appointments of Frost's cabin. "You've done yourself up proud as a lord, me bucko! God's truth, nine-tenths of the captains on the List of the Continental Navy—wherein I stand sixth in order of rank," Thompson said unabashedly, "would gladly submit to eunuch-hood to live in such luxury." Thompson's color rose perceptibly as he realized what he had said. "Geoff, I didn't mean . . ."

"Ah, here's Ming Tsun with one of those rare bottles of rum I mentioned on deck, Tommy," Frost said, unperturbed and studiously ignoring Thompson's awkward turn of phrase. Hannibal Bowditch timorously peeked around the door and handed Ming Tsun the borrowed copy of *Moore's* and a slate covered with calculations. Ming Tsun passed the bottle to Thompson, who drew the cork with a dexterity that spoke of long practice. Ming Tsun placed a silver tray conveying two delicate crystal goblets on Frost's desk. Frost took the bottle from Thompson and poured one goblet over half full; into the other he tipped only a splash.

Frost handed the first goblet to Thompson and saluted the man with the second. Thompson drank down half the glass in one toss, smacked his lips appreciatively, and drained the rest. "By God, Geoff, this is capital stuff indeed. I truly fear it is too good to be let out to the Continental Army and must be reserved solely for the Continental Navy."

"Very well, the residue of this lot of bottled rum that was distilled by Callwood escheats to you as the senior officer of the Continental Navy in Portsmouth." Frost set down his goblet without tasting the rum. "Returning to your exposition of the situation on the Lake, Tommy. Is this Arnold the chap who ascended the Kennebec, then traversed the heights o' land and the Dead River to assault Quebec?"

"The same," Thompson acknowledged.

"It was a noble effort, Tommy. I know naught of the tactics involved, though the physical labors confound the imagination. I believe this Arnold could have brought it off had he embarked in the much lighter, more manageable Indian canoes, rather than heavy bateaux of green, uncured wood. If a man of his temperament guards the Lake, I think the British will find they have a catamount on their hands."

"The same Arnold," Thompson said, almost contemptuously. "Permit me to say, Geoffrey, that the true mind behind that campaign was a chap named Montgomery, who would have carried the fortress had he not the unique—perhaps not so unique—misfortune of being killed before it. More's the pity."

Frost shook his head. "Pray, where is this wondrous document over which you are all a-hob?"

Thompson pawed among the papers in the portfolio that Frost had placed on his settee and held up the broadside, which he unrolled with another flourish. "Ah, Geoff, how is this for high style?" Thompson placed the document on Frost's desk, weighing down the sides with ink well and books. "Who is this chap Moore?" Thompson asked, briefly holding up the well-thumbed book Ming Tsun had placed on Frost's desk. "It seems you have done a power of scribing 'n' it."

Frost collected that Tommy Thompson had primarily been a coastal mariner as a ship's master, though Thompson had made numerous voyages to the Caribbean as a mate. The coastwise trade needed little in the way of open-water navigation; the ability to read currents and clouds, the local knowledge of rocks, reefs and shoals, knowing when to stand in toward land before a storm struck—these were the traits much more highly valued in the coastwise trade than the ability to fix longitude through lunar triangulation. But now John Harrison had proved the longitude through the precise capture of time, and nearby in its sturdy walnut case on a cushion of velvet was that marvelous chronometer so painstakingly and lovingly crafted by Larcum Kendell.

"It's a book for the aid of navigation, though with a lot of inaccuracies. Given its authorship and its wide distribution in the warships of George Three, may it equally confound the perfidious British."

Frost sat down at his desk and scanned the Declaration with interest. Nathaniel Dance, carrying a plate of toasted biscuit, entered the cabin after knocking and receiving Frost's permission. Frost continued scanning the document for some moments while Thompson helped himself liberally to the biscuit—and the rum. "We hold these truths to be self-evident, that all men are created equal, that they are endowed by their Creator with certain unalienable Rights . . ." Frost laid the document aside. "Strong words, these, Tommy. Aye, treacherous words, certainly hanging words once George Three catches wind of them. But what of my young colleague, Darius Langdon? Is this document of which you are so proud writ broadly enough to include him, and his father?"

Tommy Thompson had been devoting himself to the toasted biscuit. "What's this you say, Geoff? Darius, Prosperous created equal? No, of course not—there are classes of men, and then there are classes of those who are other than men, though to all outward aspects they appear to be men—but they ain't men like you and I, people like John and Sam Adams, who had quite a say in the draughting of this Declaration, they feel the same way about women and children, madmen, criminals and debtors. Not our equals at all. Do you twig my drift?"

"I'm afraid I do not, Tommy," Frost answered somewhat testily. "Of the three men of Struan's prize crew who suffered death on my behalf in beating back the desperate attempt to retake the *Sagittarius*, one was Bloodsworth's Tiberius, enrolled in my crew as Tiberius Bloodsworth, freedman from Newburyport. I grieve his death as keenly as the deaths of his white colleagues, Nicholas Auger and Robert Kelly. And unless we acknowledge the equality granted to all peoples under

God's Great Heaven, this document conveys no more independence or freedom than that of a hog set a-skate on an iced-over pond." Frost did not attempt to conceal his irritation. "And we shan't have longer to entertain ourselves with such discussions, since, unless I'm mistook, my company is even now preparing to raise the anchor of this New Hampshire warranted private man-o-war . . ."

"By God, you've got to hear of the great victory in the Carolinas," Thompson said explosively, sweeping up most of the toasted biscuit from the tray and popping the pieces hurriedly into his mouth. "It was capitally done . . ."

"Only as we stroll along to the main deck, Tommy. Here," Frost extended a neat pouch sewn from old sail cloth, daubed over with pitch, bound with ribbon and certified with Frost's signet chop on a wafer of red wax, which contained letters to his father, his mother, his brother Joseph, his sister and brother-in-law, and his cousin John Langdon. "There is also a large parcel wrapped in duck that is destined for my brother. And not to forget, this separate packet contains the dispatches found aboard the Halifax Packet so fortuitously laden with gold specie. Perhaps these dispatches can be mined for more worth than the payroll the Halifax Packet carried. John will know what to do with it. Finally, an old shipmate happened to cross my bows, and he, as well as these letters and parcel, I'll trouble you to deliver to Silas Rutherford. Silas will conjure my desires."

"I'm afraid your parcel won't reach Joseph anytime soon, Geoff. He is away to the Lake. The artillery master of the Continental Army summoned your brother to reverse himself and convey cannons to Ticondyroga. He and Knox fetched the cannons that caused General Howe grief enough to quit Boston. Now your brother has adapted to the muleteer's and ox driver's trades, freighting cannons that rightly should be sitting on elm gun carriages on the decks of my *Raleigh* to this Arnold fella on the Lake for the benefit of his flotilla."

The news was a physical blow to Frost. He had no idea— no, that was not correct. There had been premonitions, vague ones, that he had disregarded. Where had been all his fey instincts?

"Delivery will be made within the hour of my old barky's laying alongside the Frost Trading Company's wharf at Christian Shore, but have you read more of this wondrous Declaration?"

"Yes," Frost answered truthfully. Years of trading in half a hundred ports had taught him how to scan a document quickly for its worth. "That section about George Three's transporting large Armies of foreign mercenaries to our shores is true enough. I plucked these Indiamen from a convoy freighting a legion of George's Hanoverian colleagues."

"You may clap hold of that copy of the Declaration," Tommy Thompson said magnanimously. "You must read it to your crew 'stead of church the Sunday coming, and of course the newspapers." Frost led Thompson out of his cabin and had a course laid to get Thompson up the companionway, to the waist, and into his gig inside of two minutes, at which time Frost expected the cat would be snug against the anchor rode, ready to trip the anchor free. Great Buddha, whatever had possessed Joseph to go away to the Lake when his mother depended completely upon him and there was the technique of casting cannon balls at Saugus to perfect?

Thompson paused and looked around at the men hurrying to ready the cat for departure. "Bye the bye, Geoff, these men work willingly enough, but it strikes me they would fain reach into Portsmouth on the next tide."

Frost ignored the comment. "I could not help but note that the broadside you've so kindly tendered to me bears no signatures, Tommy. No signatures, but obviously writ with much recourse to Descartes and Spinoza." Aye, without doubt the majority of his crew had already thought out how they would spend their prize money, that staggering sum of prize money that was to be theirs—whatever portions they might retain after the usury of easy credit and the lure of the ale house. However, while sullen to the extreme that Frost was not concluding the cruise and putting into Portsmouth, they were not mutinous and were going about their duties efficiently enough, though grudgingly.

"No signatures, eh? No, course not. The nabobs of Congress, Adams, our own Billy Whipple, Marcus' brother, John Hancock, that whole lot, had to get the thing declared and promulgated before actually affixing their signatures to it. Treacherous, aye, you said so earlier. Mayhap some may be overcome by second thoughts when the time comes to put goose quill to parchment—but the thing's done, Geoff! After spurning George Three so spitefully, we new Americans have no choice but to strike the British wherever British are to be found, or be laid by the heels. And who be these chaps De-cart and Spin-osa you've just mentioned?"

"I don't recollect the dates René Descartes lived among us, but Benedict Spinoza was a Dutch Jew who lived one hundred years ago." Frost saw Prosperous standing at the leeward waist entry and signed for Ming Tsun to give Prosperous the hamper he had carried up from the cabin. "There are a dozen bottles of that excellent Callwood rum you've just enjoyed, Tommy. Be so kind as to share them with my cousin, John Langdon."

"Capital, oh, capital, Geoff! Share with your cousin John? Well, I don't know, no, I'll bribe him with half the rum, not an outright gift you understand, he'll have to bestir himself more on my *Raleigh*'s account. Billy Hackett done a prodigious right job of designing my *Raleigh*. Can you imagine it, thirty-two gun frigates a-building in these now United States? Another of Billy's designs—I think it's going to be named after John Hancock—is a-building in Greenleaf's Newburyport yard."

"I'm sure John is bestirring himself mightily on your *Raleigh*'s account, if he is in Providence attempting to pry cannons from the Rhode Islanders. I sorrow that you could not retain the cannons brought with the Louisbourg prizes. And that the forty artillery pieces brought in *Triton* cannot be adapted for naval uses. Without cannons your *Raleigh* is just seven hundred tons of mute wood."

"Aye," Thompson said gloomily, "as useless to the Continental Navy without cannons as tits on a boar hog." Struck by a new thought, Thompson asked, "And why do you mark a Dutch Jew who's been dead a hundred years?"

"Spinoza helped lay the foundations of constitutional democracy, Tommy, along with Descartes, John Locke, and a host of others who infected our strict Puritan forebears with the yeast of rebellion against tyrants."

Darius and Prosperous embraced quickly, and Prosperous went over the side into Thompson's gig. Prosperous apparently bethought himself of something he had forgotten to pass along to Frost, found a large basket under a thwart, and held it up to Darius. Darius took it and peeled back a corner of the napkin covering the basket's contents, exposing the contents briefly to Frost. "Strawberries!" Frost exclaimed to himself. "Why, of course, it's summer right enough, and time for wild strawberries!" In fact, he recollected, the first name applied to Portsmouth had been Strawbery Banke, because of the wild strawberries found there in such profusion.

Prosperous mouthed the words "Miss Charity," though Frost already gleaned who likely had sent the strawberries.

Thompson rounded once more on Frost, desperate to utter a few last words he considered of importance and eloquence: "The British fleet sent to invade South Carolina was itself totally defeated. I know not how many British warships—the accounts are in the papers I've left for you—commenced an attack on a fortified island in Charles Town Harbor, an island, mind you, mounting only thirty cannons, only half of which could be worked at any time, since the garrison was only two hundred stout fellows under the command of a Colonel Moultrie.

"The British General Clinton, attempting to take the fort from the rear, had landed not less than a thousand and a half troops to do so. But, bless him, our General Charles Lee, who came over to us from the British, recognizing and cherishing this cause of liberty, interposed himself and drove the invaders back to their boats."

Thompson chuckled and broke his narrative to listen to the merry clink of the bottles of rum as the hamper was stowed by Prosperous. "Every vessel the British placed in action was sorely wounded; one frigate was burnt, the rest sailed away very tatterdemalion-fashion . . ." Thompson gave a great guffaw: "But the British Admiral, Peter Parker, lost his pecker, or nearly so, being shot in the buttocks and reportedly near death—sounds quaint, don't it, Geoff—Peter Parker lost his pecker? So by the Great and Eternal and the Just and Merciful God, may all the enemies of America perish."

Thompson paused at the entry: "And where are you off to in such an all-fired hurry, Geoff? Wherever it is, please be good enough to fetch back some proper naval cannons to go with the field pieces and sailcloth you've brung in. Neither His Excellency Washington nor your brother will be able to winkle any cannons you fetch back for commissioning my *Raleigh*."

"Why, wherever good prizes are to be had, and cannons for sure, but misdoubt it not, Tommy," Frost said, heartily shaking hands with Thompson before Thompson gingerly lowered himself into his gig. "The British intend to overwhelm us with vast forces. This is not a game of chess to George Three or his ministers, though he has all of his capital pieces still on the board, and all his pawns. We in rebellion are hard pressed to muster a few pawns, and at most one knight, one bishop, and perhaps a castle, though the latter is slow, oh so slow, to get into proper employment. You will have your bait of fighting, Tommy—and then some."

Thompson moved to the stern sheets of his gig, causing it to rock alarmingly. "I'll have dozens and dozens of prime young men flocking to enlist into my *Raleigh* once your prize flotilla comes to berth in Portsmouth," he shouted at the top of his voice, sweeping off his tricorne and waving it lustily.

"Have them read *Thucydides*," Frost muttered under his breath, acutely conscious of how gallant and glorious war must appear to those who had not seen it, though he smiled and waved once. Then he turned to give the order to win the anchor home: "Shake out jibs and tops'ls, course to be east by south, one-half east." He was fair salivating for a taste of the first strawberries of summer that his sister had sent him. Frost turned and came face to face with a fairly apprehensive Surgeon Ezrah Green, who was clutching two books. Behind Ezrah Green two hands stood by the surgeon's sea chest.

"Geoffrey . . . Captain Frost, I must beg leave to depart your ship," Ezrah Green said.

Frost was quite taken aback by this unforeseen event. "Doctor Green," he began lamely, "I had no idea you were dissatisfied with service aboard this vessel."

"I confess no dissatisfaction," Ezrah Green said, "indeed, service aboard this private man-o-war has been eminently satisfying. But Geoffrey . . . Captain Frost . . . given the healers you have enshipped already, I fear I am redundant and fain would go where my surgeon's skills are more needed."

"Doctor Green, I must tell you in honesty that a full explanation is required before I can allow you to quit this cruize," Frost said in exasperation. "And even then it mayn't do."

"Believe me, Geoffrey," Ezrah Green said, drawing close enough to Frost that no one could overhear them, "it is not professional jealousy, and yet it is. When we were off the Isle of Sable I had a very bad moment during the final surgical amputation. I know not what maneuvers you were forced to execute, but I was thrown violently to the deck of the lazarette, and in some manner struck my right arm, rendering it most numb indeed, totally without feeling. I had just detached some poor wretch's limb . . . I can remember neither the wretch nor the limb taken off, I was so numbed—and fatigued, I confess that also. Without so much as a 'by your leave,' your giant Indian made the necessary ligatures and led the ligatures outside the stump, flemishing the flap of skin I had left attached, with sutures as neat as any surgeon at Harvard's College. I have previously described to you how Ishmael Hymsinger saved the sight of a man whose eye was detached violently from its socket."

Ezrah Green shrugged. "Geoffrey, the fact simple and plain is that with your fine man, Ming Tsun, and Ishmael Hymsinger, you have no need of me. Hymsinger is an apt student and bids fair to be a prodigious surgeon's mate. It would be fruitless and foolish for us to argue otherwise."

"I began this cruize with a surgeon, and I am reluctant in the extreme, particularly on the account of the crew, to continue without the services of a person skilled in the surgical and medical arts," Frost said. "Though I cannot bring myself to hold you aboard against your will."

Ezrah Green smiled. "You've no idea how scant our knowledge is of humanity's sores and sicknesses, Geoffrey, however much we physicians may pretend otherwise. Ming Tsun's knowledge of the efficacious herbs, not to mention the benefits of the low diet you adhere to so assiduously, and Hymsinger's abilities to look at the mind, will serve you and your vessel better than I. I have not given up the sea, but I heard Captain Thompson talking about Joseph's going in some glorious enterprise on Champlain, and I've a mind to join your brother on the Lake." Ezrah Green thrust out the two books he was holding. "I shall leave for your surgeon's mate Jones' book *Plain, Concise, Practical Remarks on the Treatment of Wounds and Fractures*, published within the year in New York, showing that our North American born and trained physicians need stand in the shadow of no one. And here is a book describing the diagnosis and treatment regime of the Dutch physician Boerhaave. All of my pharmaceuticals and implements are left aboard for the use of your surgeon's mate. I can re-equipment myself easily enough at Mister Greenleaf's Apothecary in Boston."

Frost nodded in defeat and acquiescence. He took his speaking trumpet and turned to hail Tommy Thompson, who was bustling about preparing his snow for departure, requesting the favor of his gig for an unexpected passenger. He saw Doctor Ezrah Green and his sea chest into the gig and bade him farewell with a heavy heart.

## ❧ XIV ❦

**T**HERE WERE NO SOUNDS ABOARD THE CAT SAVE THE OCCASIONAL SIBILANT SLAP OF ROPE OR SAIL AS THE SHIP ROLLED SLIGHTLY, OR THE FAINTEST, random chuckle of water against the starboard hull as the vessel surged in a long, slow, uneven swell. The cat was wrapped in fog so thick that Frost could not see the foremast from his quarterdeck, as the ship ghosted along at a bare half-knot, and that as a push from a swell that had its origins somewhere deep in the Caribbean. Fore topgallant, a closely clewed up main topsail and fore staysail, were rigged, though quite invisible from the quarterdeck, but had not captured a cup of wind since midnight. Since he had happened upon HM *Lark* in the thick fog south of Nova Scotia, Geoffrey Frost had developed a marked distaste for fog, a distaste he knew had no basis in rational thought.

Frost was pacing the starboard side of his quarterdeck, confident that the wind, when it came, would come from the southwest. His cloak, tightly drawn around him, was heavy with dew, as was everything on the cat's decks. The sound of cannon fire, faint and muffled by the fog, came again; not the regular, monotonous firing of powder only to give notice of a ship's lying becalmed in fog, but four reports, and then a fifth —a ragged, sullen demi-broadside. Frost had been hearing it, irregularly, for the past two hours.

"Mister Ferguson," Frost said quietly, "please relieve the

man in the foretop and the two men in the bows. Please have the hammocks sent up and stowed in their nettings, but quietly, oh so quietly, and ask our good master gunner to exercise equal quietude in making ready our cannons." As he always did when lying-to in fog, Frost had a hand stationed in the foretop, for frequently the fog would lay heavy against the sea's bosom for only fifty feet or so, with the topmasts in clear air. Two men minimum were always kept in the bows, as well as other stations about the vessel, to watch for the loom of a ship, any shape or shadow in the engloomed fog.

It had taken some doing, getting his crew to roll their hammocks and pass them up for stowing in the nettings along larboard and starboard bulwarks forward of the quarterdeck, British man-o-war fashion, but Frost had succeeded. However, the majority of the hammocks had yet to pass through the iron hoop designed to gauge their diameters for proper stowage. The maneuver created infinitely more space on the berth deck, and Frost was keenly aware of the benefits of closely laid hammock canvas as barriers against musket shot, and some passable protection against splinters. Frost was not in the least averse to borrowing sound tactics or techniques from wherever he could, even the British Navy, which was, he readily acknowledged, a crack outfit greatly to be feared.

Frost pulled Jonathan's watch from his waistcoat pocket and consulted it. Ten o'clock, and the fog showed no signs of dissipating, though he knew that when the fog began to disperse from the sun's heat, the lifting would begin gradually, then increase rapidly. "Mister Ferguson, I do not expect this fog to lift much before noon, though there is a possibility that we may have some intelligence from the tops before then. Please send the hands to dinner by divisions. I collect Cook Barnes intends to serve sauerkraut this noon."

Struan Ferguson was close enough for Frost to catch his first officer's grimace. "Yes, sir, it has been twenty days since we departed the Isles of Shoals, and proper time to begin servin' out the scorbutic, though no hand really relishes it."

"I'm not the least interested in whether the hands relish

sauerkraut or not, Mister Ferguson," Frost said, a bit sharper than necessary. He was uneasy about the intermittent firing, wondering whether he should close or lie away. He was instantly sorry for the sharpness of his tone and lowered his voice. "Sauerkraut is to be served ahead of other rations of meat, bread, and cheese, before they be drawn. No rum for the noon meal, mind, though small beer and cider, as much as the men wish. Take the name of any man who refuses his cabbage; he'll have no more rum this cruize."

"Well, though they relish it not, one thing Doctor Green, before leaving us, convinced all who passed through his dispensary was that sauerkraut, at least the kind prepared by the dear ladies from Exeter, will preserve against cannon balls an' bein' took prisoner."

"Then increase the sauerkraut ration by half," Frost said, trying not to smile. "I've not seen it, having never any occasion to venture that far to the north, but as a student Ming Tsun traveled to a country above China where dwell a race called Ko-reans who subsist primarily on cabbages mixed with hot peppers and spices and fermented in large pots buried in the earth. I shall ask for a recipe, so the first opportunity comes to hand we may ask the good ladies of Exeter to make their sauerkraut more palatable."

Frost turned away, so that Struan Ferguson would not see the worry that flitted across his face. He might well be moving slowly into an engagement with another vessel, and he was without the services of a surgeon. Did Ishmael Hymsinger possess a passably adequate knowledge of surgical intervention after the briefest of apprenticeships under Doctor Ezrah Green to serve his fellows as a surgeon's mate? Frost could rightly have insisted that Ezrah Green finish out the cruise as agreed. Should he have? Frost trusted well enough Hymsinger's gifts as a natural healer, but did he possess the skills to arrest hemorrhage? Guard against gangrene? Treat the ship-fever? Insh'allah. Joss. The Prophet. The future would bring the answer.

"I believe I am acquainted with the dish," Struan said, "for

I traded once into a Ko-rean port. The cheeseheads had failed in their attempt to call at the forbidden ports of Ja-pan, and we repaired to Ko-rea for victuals. Locally the cabbage is called 'keem-chee,' and all sense of taste deserted me for near two weeks after havin' swallowed but one mouthful."

"You are walking proof, then, Struan, that fermented cabbage keeps men's teeth firmly in their heads, for your teeth are the envy of all who stand in the radiance of your smile. I shall be holding school for the ship's gentlemen in the gun room the next hour, but I am to be called immediately this fog begins to lift. I wish to hear no noises while I hold school."

Struan touched his forehead and replied in all seriousness, "The hands know not what is out there in the fog, sir. We can trust to their quietude."

When Frost entered the gun room, lighted by two lanterns with well-polished glass, bending almost double to duck beneath the massive beam running the length of the room, Hannibal Bowditch, Nathaniel Dance, Darius Langdon and Ishmael Hymsinger rose to their feet respectfully, as did George Three, who uttered one small, gruff, joyous bark of greeting. Darius was the only one of the three youths who had to hunch his shoulders to keep from striking his head against the gun room overhead; the other two, being younger and shorter, could stand upright without fear.

Based upon their conduct before Louisbourg and subsequently, Frost had rated the three youths "ship's gentlemen," that is, quarterdeck material. Hannibal Bowditch was already a keen scholar, quite remarkable with ciphers and celestial observations. Nathaniel and Darius were completely unlettered, save for the few school sessions Frost had been able thus far to eke out of the hectic pace of husbanding a private man-o-war. Though Nathaniel was possessed of keen powers of observation far beyond his age, gained during the years he had already been at sea. And Darius was possessed of an inordinate desire to please and a quick, inquiring intellect of which the youth was unaware but which Frost trusted would mature quickly. Frost knew that Hannibal was sharing his formal education with the other two lads, while Nathaniel was sharing his knowledge of the sea.

And the contributions of Darius? Frost trusted that some of the young black man's graceful manners and deportment would take root in the two younger ship's gentlemen. All in all, the various intelligences of the three youngsters complemented and enhanced each other. And all three lads were constantly consulting Ishmael Hymsinger.

"Gentlemen, all of you, George included," Frost acknowledged them, "pray take your seats. Mister Hymsinger will shortly be expanding his already daunting duties as our surgeon's mate to encompass the duties of ship's pedagogist. I am quite certain you gentlemen shall heed him as you have heeded me." Frost seated himself at the tiny trestle table that had been unlatched from the bulkhead and let down to form a desk for him. "Mister Bowditch, I'm sure you have got the answer to the question I put to you last about measuring the tonnage of a vessel, given the vessel's length on the keel, range of the lower deck, beam, and depth of hold."

"Oh, yes, sir!" Hannibal cried, his face even more aflame with pimples than Frost had ever beheld him as he bobbed to his feet and thrust out his slate for all to admire his small, precise hand: "One hundred and ten feet, seven and one-quarter inches on the keel. One hundred and thirty-one feet and five inches on the range of the lower deck; thirty-four feet and five inches on the beam; and eleven feet exactly for depth of hold. Her burthen works up to six hundred and ninety-seven ton." Hannibal darted a small, triumphant glance at the other two students, who, having never experienced formal education until brought into Frost's lycée, were just beginning their foray into the unknown terrors of penmanship, grammar, and basic addition and subtraction.

"Very good," Frost mused, studying the meticulous calculations on Hannibal Bowditch's slate. He laid the slate aside and turned to Darius: "Mister Langdon . . . have you any thoughts on the exactitude of such a measurement?"

"Yes, sir," Darius said, "well, it seems like, when Hannibal . . ." Darius remembered in time the formalities of the classroom, "I mean Mister Bowditch, was doing all his cyphering, admirable it all be, I warrant, but all wood don't weigh the same. Pine be heavier than oak . . ." Darius gulped, "I mean, oak be heavier than pine, and if you got oak and pine and other woods . . ."

"Like elm, there's loads of elm on a ship knocked together in a British dockyard . . ." Nathaniel Dance interrupted excitedly, stopping just as quickly when Frost raised an eyebrow. "Beg pardon, Mister Langdon, for interruptin'. Ye was doin' capital."

"You are absolutely certain that you have deduced the correct answer when the cyphers are properly done, Mister Bowditch?" Frost's tone was slightly accusatory.

Hannibal hesitated: "I was most attentive to my cyphers, sir."

"And so you were, though your fractions could bear more scrutiny." Frost rubbed a fragment of chalk to a point and placed a minute tic by a calculation on Hannibal's slate. "You omitted the fraction for the last proportionate inch in the range of the lower deck when you applied the formula calculation, which, had you not done so, would have given you the tonnage of six hundred and ninety-six and eighty ninety-fourth's."

"But what does the fraction signify, sir?" Hannibal queried stubbornly.

"It signifies much, or it signifies little," Frost said. "On the one hand you have a proven formula, a precise calculation that if applied scrupulously in all its parts, omitting nothing, assuming nothing, gives you a result of absolute exactness. On the other hand, there are certain variables that may be incapable of exactitude—the varying densities of woods, as Mister Langdon, reinforced by Mister Dance, noted aptly, may alter the actual, if not the theoretical, computable results." Frost broke off as Ming Tsun entered the gun room, bearing a tray that he placed on the trestle. Ming Tsun flicked back the napkin covering the tray, then poured Frost a cup of tea.

Frost made due note that the eyes of all three youngsters grew wide at the sight of the plates standing revealed on the tray. "Gentlemen, I assure you that Cook Barnes has saved back ample portions of this excellent sauerkraut for the three of you." Frost lifted the plate laden with sauerkraut and sniffed its pungency appreciatively. "But why, pray, should we cherish preciseness while admitting of variables—belay that question, Mister Langdon—other than by the use of rote formula, how is it possible to calculate the tonnage of a vessel?"

Darius shook his head. "Master John, he had a scale and yard for weighing stuffs like hogsheads of flour, puncheons of rum, and once I went with him to Mister Revere's down in Boston when Master John was having coin melted for his table silver. Mister Revere had a small cross that measured to a hair."

"A balance it may be called," Frost said. "I believe you are entitled to refer to my cousin as 'Mister Langdon' rather than 'Master John.'" Frost paused briefly to let his remark sink home. "Think you there exists a balance large enough to weigh this cat of ours?"

Darius scratched his scalp and glanced sideways, moving only his eyes, covertly seeking assistance from Nathaniel or Hannibal. "Maybe somewhere in the world where you and Mister Ferguson and Mister Ming Tsun have been, there might be such a one, but I know of naught anywhere near to Portsmouth."

"So until we can construct such a balance, we must content ourselves with mathematical formulae, is that your deduction?" Frost had eaten half of the excellent Exeter sauerkraut and turned his attention to the second plate, a fine ripe tomata plucked carefully from a vine growing in the narrow trays of loam fertilized by manure from the chickens, sheep and geese in the manger and tended conscientiously by Ming Tsun. It had been thinly sliced, appealingly arranged on the plate, and then lightly sprinkled with sea salt and vinegar.

Frost had not directed his question to any particular youngster, and they all spoke simultaneously: "Yes, sir."

"Recognizing that there may be variables incapable of quantification that may result in some final inaccuracy?" Frost forked half a slice of tomata into his mouth, savoring the firm, fresh taste on his palate, the fruit and the seasoning.

The three youngsters nodded in harmony, unable to speak, their eyes wide in horror.

"But riddle me this, Mister Bowditch: it is a night without any moon due to sullen cloud, and a heavy sea is running from two points abaft the beam; the wind is from the east-southeast. The last cast of the log gave us seven knots, four fathom. Our last observation at noon the day before gave us twenty leagues due east of the Isles of Shoals, as we hope to fetch the approaches to the ports of Piscataqua. As we calculate the distance run since our last observation, should we be meticulous to the fraction, or may we, in all good conscience, parse and scrimp?"

The door to the gun room opened, and Jack Lacey ducked under the transverse beam and bobbed upright: "Mister Ferguson's compliments, Capt'n Frost, sir, and he believes the fog be liftin' . . ." Lacey's eyes accommodated to the lantern light, and he saw Frost in the process of lifting a slice of tomata to his mouth. "Nooooeee!" Lacey shouted, thrusting the youngsters aside and knocking them from their chairs as he threw himself across the gun room to strike the fork violently from Frost's hand. He swept the plate of tomata off the trestle.

"Saved ye, sir, I did! Know ye not them love h'apples be poison, absolute poison they be! I've seen men bloat up all black and hard green like, deader than Adam's off ox, atter one bite of a love h'apple. Gawd, sir, who among the crew convinced ye to eat this pi'son dish? Identify him, Capt'n, and we'll have him overboard in a flash!"

Frost retrieved his napkin from the deck and patted his lips slowly, a ploy to gain time to compose himself, for the fear stamped bold on poor Lacey's earnest face could be allayed not by anger, or worse, laughter and ridicule, but by reason. "I greatly appreciate your kind concern, Mister Lacey; it does you much credit. But surely the fact that Ming Tsun has been tending four trays of tomatas, parsley, cucumbers, turnips, potatoes, carrots, and squash did not escape your notice? Belike, you have tailed onto a tray once or twice this cruize to rise it from hold to quarterdeck. Be that not true?"

"Waal, yes, sir, but I thought the love h'apple be an ornament of yore mother's affection, not something a Christian would eat, sir."

"Indeed, Mister Lacey, leaving aside for the moment the consideration of whether I am or am not a Christian, though I thank you very kindly for generously considering me so," Frost passed a hand before his face to conceal the smile that had begun to swell at the corners of his mouth, for George Three had pounced upon the spilled plate and was greedily lapping up the tomata slices and vinegar, "the bloodthirsty Cortez found the 'tomata' had been cultivated for centuries by the peoples of the Andes. The native peoples called it 'tomatl' and the fruit is most highly regarded by the Spaniards and Italians to this day, I do assure you. The tomata's unfortunate connection with some poisonous nature is the herbalist's mistaken association of the plant with belladonna and nightshade. I have indulged myself with the fruit of the tomata by the dozen on voyages to China, Mister Lacey, and you may judge for yourself whether or not the effect upon my health has been deleterious—better yet, watch carefully over George Three the next several days, for he has eaten the tomatas I coveted. If he falls not down dead by tomorrow forenoon, perhaps you may be persuaded to try a slice."

"Never in life, sir!" Lacey exclaimed, aghast.

Frost shrugged. "Would you please name me the times and places when you have seen men 'bloat up black and hard green like' from consuming the love h'apple, Mister Lacey?"

Jack Lacey stood with mouth agape, then slowly lifted a tar-stained hand to scratch his cheek thoughtfully: "Well, sir, I . . ."

"You don't rightly recollect, Mister Lacey?" Frost got to his feet, remembering just in time the low overhead in the gun room, quite different from the luxurious headroom he enjoyed in his cabin. "Mister Langdon, Mister Dance, I shall have to comment upon your cyphers at a later time." In fact, he had already cast his eye over their slates. Both youngsters' chalk scratches could hardly pass for letters or numerals, but they exhibited aptitude and perseverance—and the marks of heroic struggle. Startling progress had been made over the two months their formal studies had been encompassed by these two lads; a former slave for whom education of any sort had been forbidden and a powder monkey whose formal education had been deemed sufficient when he learned to mark an "X" against what he was told was his name in a pay ledger. Frost took that as proof that Hannibal was tutoring both Darius and Nathaniel. He would have to rely now on Hymsinger's taking up their general education, while he would continue with mathematics.

"Mister Bowditch, when next we convene school you shall present a list of all the different woods incorporated into this vessel. Mister Langdon, you are charged with keeping an especial eye on George Three. If he succumbs to the poisons of the love h'apple within twenty-four hours—the time I fancy any poison should work its mischief—then he shall be buried in a hammock-shroud. If not," Frost glanced significantly at Jack Lacey, "Mister Lacey shall eat an entire tomata while standing on the windlass . . ." Frost rather enjoyed the expression of horror stamped on Lacey's face, "or else he shall continue to encourage all hands by his example in devouring the excellent sauerkraut prepared by the ladies of Exeter."

"Sauerkraut!" Jack Lacey fairly shouted, "Yes, sir, capital in every respect! Most exceptional dish if I may say so, sir. Prodigious, prodigious, toppin' in fact, sir! Can't get enough of it, sir, wish we had tubs more! Why, with sauerkraut and a ration of salt cod issued to all hands, we can sail this barky to the British Islands handsomely, that we can, and spit in the eye of King George himself, right enough, sir!" Lacey peered anxiously at Frost: "I'm sure our dear George will survive right enough, no harm in 'em love h'apples, now ye've explained the gist of it, but all the same, beggin' yere pardon, sir, love h'apples ain't something I'd particularly like to mouth, catchin' my meanin' as I'm sure ye do, sir . . ."

"By all means," Frost said briskly, ducking under the transverse beam, "I'm not one to deny any man the consolation of a double ration of sauerkraut. Now, if you gentlemen will excuse me—oh, Mister Langdon, please be so kind as to inquire of Mister Rawbone the number of charges he has prepared. I should like to know that figure within the next five minutes." Frost stretched out his arm to scratch George's head vigorously; the dog, sitting on his haunches, massive tail thumping against the deck, gave a mighty yawn and panted appreciatively.

"I hope you enjoyed that tomata, George, because there are no more than two left in Ming Tsun's horticulture."

Frost went through the gun room door that Jack Lacey held open for him and walked swiftly along the passage and up the scuttle onto the main deck, noting that the fog had thinned just enough to permit him to see stem and stern of the cat but naught else. Frost went up the center companionway to his quarterdeck. Struan Ferguson smiled his usual warm greeting.

"Not much increase in visibility here on deck, Captain Frost, but Shuntcock here," Struan nodded in the direction of a hand standing nearby at loose attention, "came down from the foretop two minutes ago with word that visibility aloft is much improved over what we can discern here."

Frost looked sharply at the man, who was actually a youth still in his teens. In the two and a half months since he first enlisted them into his complement, Frost had learned every one of his one hundred and seventy-six remaining crewmen—augmented by the volunteers solicited by Lamb Wilkes—by name, and connected their faces to the names entered in the cat's muster book. He had marked Shuntcock before as an excellent topman. "Abraham Shuntcock, it is, from Salisbury. Your father is a caulker in Billy Hackett's yard. I've no need to question your eyes. Tell me what you ken from the mast head."

Shuntcock was rated able seaman, though he had been employed only in the coastal trade until shipping with the cat.

He had behaved well enough before Louisbourg. Frost recalled that the man's mess mates called him "Short Dick," but the man bore the nickname goodnaturedly.

Shuntcock nodded quickly: "Me dad be the best culker Mister Hackett ever had, sir. And hard work it be. But concerns them sail: best I could see, sir, two sail, close together, two points off the starboard bow, I make the distance not far off a league. I could make out only the topgallants up'ard. One sail larger than the other, and 'less I'm mistook, the smaller be firin' more into the larger, rather than arsey-versa, sir."

"Thank you for coming down quietly with your report, Abraham Shuntcock. I'm glad to have a man of your vision aboard this vessel. Return to the mast head and keep me apprised of both ships' positions." Frost glanced around his quarterdeck and spied Darius and Nathaniel, in animated, but low, conversation, leaning against the larboard bulwark. "Take Mister Dance with you. Send him down periodically with intelligence of the two ships."

The sullen, ragged broadside came again, five cannons, almost thirty seconds between each blast. Frost was distinctly uneasy, but he was resolved to take the cat closer. "Mister Ferguson, I think we may spread the jibs'l to assist the fore stays'l, and I'd be obliged if we could stretch the main topgallant stays'l. I've no doubt but we'll see a bit of wind toward noon, but do all quietly, quietly. I like not this uneven cannonade. Something sits not right, and I intend to approach closer as soon as wind permits."

Darius appeared crestfallen that Nathaniel had been chosen to ascend to the masthead rather than he. Frost thought for a moment. He had decided to send Nathaniel because of Nathaniel's far greater experience at heights, but Darius was progressing quite well in that regard. Frost walked over to the larboard bulwark. "Mister Langdon, I would take it kindly if you would fetch my best and next best glass from my cabin and join your colleague and Abraham Shuntcock at the masthead. You should retain the best glass for yourself, while Mister Dance and Abraham Shuntcock exchange the second glass between them, all the while quietly describing to you what they discern and what importance should be attached to the objects captured in your glass."

"Aye, sir," Darius whispered happily and was gone, reappearing almost instantly, so it seemed, with two telescopes in their leather cases, carrying straps crossed over his shoulder, springing casually into the ratlines and climbing quickly out of sight into the ceiling of fog.

Frost stood for a moment, glancing upward into the fog and listening, but he heard no sound. He shook his head briefly. "Yes, youth is truly wasted on the young," he thought to himself again. Then Ming Tsun was at his elbow, an exquisite porcelain cup decorated with fanciful dragons held out in both hands. Frost took the cup and gratefully inhaled the fragrance of tea and honey.

"There will be no further tomata," Ming Tsun signed crossly. Frost held a mouthful of the delicious tea for a moment in his mouth before swallowing it, then cocked an inquiring eyebrow. "The vile dog sought them out in their tray in the passageway outside your cabin and ate them both."

"If we have dried and preserved seeds, then we may sow again," Frost signed philosophically, handing his cup to the quartermaster at the wheel momentarily to free both hands for signing. "Though I confess the tomatas in this harvest were particularly succulent. I also regret most heartily the fact that we have eaten all the strawberries." Frost shrugged and caught Ming Tsun's sign of "joss" before retrieving his cup and beginning to pace the starboard side of his quarterdeck, marveling at the chill in these latitudes.

What had Struan said about the harsh winter in Scotland? Weather all cockamamie—Frost checked himself: when had the weather not been cockamamie? Still, there had been no hint of a hurricane thus far, and the season for hurricanes was well advanced. Frost drank down the rest of his honey-flavored tea. Joss. What would be, would be. His seaman's instincts told him the wind would arrive from the starboard quarter, not much at first and then strengthening before noon, though likely the fog would not dissipate completely for several hours. Enough time for the cat to shorten considerably the distance to the vessels two points off the starboard bow. If the two vessels were engaged in a sea battle—and how could it not be a sea battle?—chances were that their crews would be too busy to note the cat's presence in the fog-shrouded middle distance.

A cat's paw of wind ruffled the hair above Frost's right ear; he glanced upward, hoping to see the main topgallant staysail, but the ceiling of fog was impenetrable thirty feet above the deck. Somewhere in the fog above, a sail flogged momentarily. "Five minutes," he told himself. "Five minutes and the wind will steady."

Frost paced his quarterdeck, right hand in his waistcoat pocket, elbows tucked loosely into his ribs, left hand holding the cup of finest Chinese porcelain and turning it reflectively. "Mister Plaisted," Frost said quietly; without turning his head, he knew that his bosun was close enough to hear him.

"Captain?"

"Please be good enough to rig the log for a cast. Mister Bowditch will assist you."

"Aye, sir," Plaisted said, equally quietly, knowing as well as Frost how far sound could carry in a fog.

Ming Tsun appeared in the companionway: "I have loaded your pistols," he signed, then took the cup. Beyond Ming Tsun, at the head of the center companionway, Frost saw Ishmael Hymsinger.

"The day has begun inauspiciously, Mister Hymsinger," Frost said, "at least as far as the weather is concerned. However, I believe the forenoon will present a more pleasant prospect."

"That sound of cannons is very wearying, Captain Frost," Ishmael Hymsinger said. "I can't but imagine such sound portends evil."

"Sure, the cannons we hear are not in the nature of a friendly signal, Mister Hymsinger," Frost said. "Would you join me for a turn? Even if the wind springs briskly this minute, it shall be, at best, an hour until we are close enough to identify what those vessels be."

"I assumed there would be two such," Ishmael Hymsinger said wearily. "I could fathom no one vessel firing such blasts repetitively and repetitively."

"Right you are, Surgeon's Mate," Frost said, taking Ishmael Hymsinger by the arm and walking the man to the starboard side of his quarterdeck, into the teeth of the wind that suddenly sprang upon them, slowly rolling the cat to larboard before permitting the vessel to return to an upright keel.

"But surely, should something not have occurred from the profusion of such reports? By my reckoning those cannons have been hammering for the better part of the morning—surely something should have occurred . . ."

"It most likely has," Frost assured Hymsinger, "though what it likely is remains hid from view in the fog." Frost tugged Jonathan's Bréquet from his pocket and noted the time. Another loom of wind came over the starboard quarter. "I must ask that you make ready your lazarette." Frost snapped the watchcase closed. "In one hour's time we shall be close enough to the origin of such horrific sounds as to gauge their true intent."

Both Frost and Hymsinger turned simultaneously, having heard the splash astern. They both paced quickly the length of the quarterdeck to the taff rail near the stern lantern, where Slocum Plaisted was quickly bringing the log line hand over hand, keeping the wooden chip just barely ahead of the jaws of George Three, who was swimming behind the log at a furious rate, eager to seize it.

"It just be George, Captain," Hannibal Bowditch said quickly, thrusting himself in front of Frost, "he thinks we throw the log as a toy for him to fetch."

"Third time in a week fool dog's done it, Captain," Slocum Plaisted said, though not crossly, for he loved the big Newfoundland as well as any of the crew. "Caught the first one right proper and bent it with his jaws. Lucky, Chips has plenty made."

Frost looked away from the crestfallen Hannibal Bowditch, who was apparently expecting a tongue-lashing. Frost stifled a grin: "Mister Bowditch, I charge you strictly—and any man who may conveniently be at hand—to keep George below decks when the log is to be cast. We must have a true measure of our speed, difficult to assess, don't you think, when George is trying to snap up the log?"

"Just so, Captain," Hannibal Bowditch said, greatly relieved. "Below decks for George Three whenever we cast the log, sir."

"Below decks before we cast the log, Mister Bowditch," Frost emphasized the "before." "Hoist in the fellow however you do it, and soundlessly, mind. Something is awind."

"IT DOES SEEM REMARKABLY LIKE A SNAKE, SIR, A SEGMENTED SNAKE EVEN," NATHANIEL DANCE SAID EARNESTLY, "THOUGH IT IS NOT AT ALL like the snake we hoist." Nathaniel Dance cocked his head toward the flag with the coiled rattlesnake on its yellow field that fluttered lazily over the stern. The cat was making, at best, two knots in a fitful wind that had shouldered aside some of the fog, leaving great gaps here and there but still masking the hulls of the two ships that were less than half a mile away.

Frost lowered his telescope from his careful study of the masts standing up from the tendrils of fog. One vessel, the smaller, had lost its mizzen and most of its main mast above the main top but had succeeded in overtaking and coming alongside the larger. "There is not much wind where they lie, but it strikes me the banner on the second vessel has some sort of center device."

"A center device of certainty, sir," Nathaniel Dance said, "though I know not the meaning of it."

"It is a house flag, Mister Dance, a house flag of a Portugee trading house. The Portuguese are allies of the British crown, though as yet I believe they are regarded as neutral in our pitch-to with George Three and his ministerial government," Frost said. He did not add that he had more than once used a Portuguese house flag as a flag of convenience in the long voyages from Macao, itself a strategic outpost of the Portuguese empire.

"Yes, sir," Nathaniel Dance said, somewhat lamely, for he could provide no explanation for the strange sight of a small vessel of perhaps two hundred tons flying a snake flag and hammering away at a much larger vessel that trailed the flag of a neutral nation over her sternwork.

"I believe we have smoked a renegade, Mister Dance," Frost said grimly. "John Langdon advised me when we stood off Portsmouth following our return from Louisbourg that there are some seamen among us who could not, nay, would not lay out the thousand pound or so for the indemnity and bond in case of counter-libel. They bear no letter of marque from any colony—I must become accustomed to naming the so-called former colonies as states, as I previously vowed—but hope to profit, nevertheless, from this joint madness and snap up prizes, whether under the flag of our British enemy or a neutral such as yonder Portugee nau." Frost raised his telescope again, finding it difficult to believe that the cat had approached so closely, less than half a mile now, without anyone aboard either vessel having smoked the cat.

Well, he had the weather gage, what little the fitful wind would permit. Frost surveyed his ship, crews at all cannons, slow match smoldering, Caleb's woods-cruisers already in the fighting tops. Frost did not relish the thought of fighting Americans, either Tories or renegades, but that was the reality; the men attacking the Portuguese nau had placed themselves outside the norms of law. "A nicety, though it was a difference with more than a distinction," Frost thought to himself. "As far as George Three and his ministers are concerned, all inhabitants of our continent who have not openly professed their loyalties to king and crown are rebels against lawful British order. Were I his prisoner he would cheerfully, with his own hands, place a noose around my neck."

But the cutthroats aboard the vessel flying the snake flag of North American revolution were willfully violating the ancient law maritime, "and," Frost reminded himself, "if what we are striving to attain through this rebellion I did not wish is legitimacy, then accountability must be paid for violating such laws as nature ordains." And pirates these renegade Americans were, as surely as were the Malays who ran aboard shipping in the Straits of Malacca under cover of darkness, slaughtering all aboard with a fine disregard for any country's flag, British, French, Dutch, Spanish, or Portuguese. Or, for that matter, that infamous chap Blackbeard. And what would a person be called who had profited so handsomely from some of Blackbeard's ill-acquired treasures? Particularly the silver so coveted by the Chinese? Frost shook off those thoughts and studied the two ships again, though he had already puzzled through exactly how he would come at the renegade American vessel. He paced over to the group of men anxiously clustered near the cat's helm.

"Mister Rawbone," Frost said abruptly, without preamble, as was his wont, "you ken how the renegade is locked starboard side to the nau's larboard. I discern she has just begun to send men into the nau. My intentions are to come up astern the renegade, and you are to discharge our starboard cannons as they bear to rake her main deck. Guns discharged are to be reloaded with langrage." Frost's eyes drilled into Rawbone's; the matross lowered his gaze, unable to hold it steady.

"I shall scandalize the tops'ls to reduce way—Mister Ferguson shall take care of that order—cannons reloaded are to await my command to fire. I wish one broadside of langrage fired on her deck, then we must board in the smoke." Frost had not taken his eyes from Rawbone. "It may hap that the renegade's larboard cannons are discharged, but I cannot count that true. You recall, I misdoubt not, Mister Rawbone, that your fastest time to date in readying a side of cannons for concentrated fire has been a few seconds less two minutes. That will prove a very long near two minutes if those larboard cannons aboard the renegade indeed be shotted, with our vessels not fifty yards apart."

Frost turned next to Caleb: "I must ask for your woodscruizers' hottest fire to be directed toward any renegade who ventures near a larboard cannon. It would be best for all if no larboard cannon fires toward us from such a distance." Then to Struan: "Mister Ferguson, I must ask you to remain on the renegade and deal with her people. Mister Plaisted, you shall come with me aboard the Portugee and chace down those who have got aboard her to stop their harm."

Frost stripped off his coat and handed it to Hannibal Bowditch. Despite the overcast day's chill he was perspiring heavily and was glad to be rid of the coat. "The places for the ship's gentlemen," he said sternly, "are aboard this vessel to assist first Mister Rawbone, who shall be senior in my absence, as he directs, and to administer for Surgeon's Mate Hymsinger should we have casualties."

"I have no doubt my starboard cannons will shave the recharge handily, Captain," Rawbone said stoutly.

"Some o' my people cotton tew 'em Ferguson rifles," Caleb said slyly, "half 'n' half they be, 'n' ye've put up a cask of best Jamaica tew the half that maintains fire the best."

"Happily shall a puncheon of best Jamaica be served out—once ashore in dear Portsmouth," Frost winked at Caleb. "Your stations, gentlemen."

The cat bore down on the two vessels locked side by side, with hulls hidden again in the fog, maddeningly slow, and how could the approach of the cat have remained undetected? Two hundred yards bearing directly toward the stern of the renegade—yes, through his telescope Frost saw that someone aboard the renegade had spied them at last. "Mister Ferguson, we shall bring her up hard on a larboard tack, if you please," Frost said calmly, and in the same breath to the helmsman, "helm hard up."

The maneuver was executed as efficiently as Frost had expected, though there was an inevitable delay in bringing the bows around since the wind was so slight. But now the cat's bows were rounding up handsomely, and Rawbone was watching Frost expectantly. "As you deem proper, Mister Rawbone!" Frost shouted; no need for a telescope now, he could see the gaggle of incredulous men on the renegade's quarterdeck watching his vessel's tack. Then the forwardmost starboard cannon of the cat belched its 6-pound ball, and then its mate, and so on down the starboard cannons.

"Steer fine!" Frost ordered the helmsmen, hearing at the same time Struan's orders to the topmen to haul up the lower forward tacks of the topsails and scandalize them, slowing the cat instantly as the fitful wind spilled from her sails. Then the pressure of wind against her top hamper began pushing the cat down onto the renegade. Frost saw men running toward the renegade's larboard cannons, then saw them sag and fall as the rifles of Caleb's woods-cruisers began exacting their deadly tolls.

Frost tried not to appear anxious as he scanned the renegade's line of starboard cannons, Jonathan's watch held tightly in his right hand. Had he cut the timing too fine by half? He thought fleetingly of his lecture to Hannibal Bowditch and the other ship's gentlemen not three hours earlier about paying due attention to all factors in the equation.

He had sufficient downwind experience to have judged the drift to the foot, but the wooden bulwarks of the renegade were looming up now no more than thirty yards away, and men were clustered around a cannon sharp up against the break of the waist. There was a momentary lull in the firing from the tops as the woods-cruisers paused to reload, then one quick, angry crack, that of a woods-cruiser's rifle, and a man running from the starboard side with a length of slow match was arrested in mid-stride by the bullet's strike and tumbled like a rabbit, gut-shot, the slow match falling from his hands but caught up by another, who bore it triumphantly, desperately, to the cannon. Frost stared resolutely at the cannon's mouth, scarce twenty yards away, willing it not to fire. A renegade who had reached a swivel gun on the quarterdeck died with an arrow launched from Ming Tsun's bow protruding from his chest before he could slew the swivel around.

"All cannons reloaded, sir!" Rawbone shouted, waving his grubby tricorne to make certain he had secured Frost's attention.

"Fire!" Frost shouted, vastly relieved, pocketing his watch, noting with satisfaction that the time had been one minute, fifty-two seconds. By the Great Buddha, Rawbone would have the crews down to one minute thirty before too much longer —but that thought was borne away in the vast concussion of sound that whipped along the cat's main deck as nine cannons fired in unison.

"Grapples!" Frost shouted, his order repeated from the starboard bow by Struan Ferguson, and a dozen iron grapnels snaked across the ten yards now separating the two vessels. Two grapnels hit amid rigging and pulled out when strain came on their lines, but the other ten caught on bulwarks and held, and the gap separating the vessels slowly closed as human muscle pulled three hundred and fifty and nineteen ninety-fourths' tons Thames measurement, not including weight of cannons, ballast, stores or crew, sideways toward the renegade.

From the corner of his right eye, Frost caught the flash of an arrow and followed its brief flight to bury itself in the belly of a man on the renegade's quarterdeck who had aimed a musket in Frost's general direction. The distance between the vessels was five yards, now four. Frost leaped to the starboard fife rail, briefly tottered there to catch his balance, then threw himself at the renegade's larboard mizzen shrouds, smashing into the ratlines to arrest his fall, grasping the sternmost shroud with his right hand.

Frost rolled to his right out of the ratlines as soon as he was over the quarterdeck, releasing his grip to fall the five feet to the deck and coming down into the gore of what fifteen seconds before had been a living man, now decapitated and eviscerated by the horrific broadside of langrage into something only barely resembling a human. Frost slipped in the gore and crashed heavily to the deck but quickly got to his feet, tugging one pistol from his belt, his cutlass firmly in his left hand and the lust for battle shrilling like a blacksmith's bellows in his ears.

A body landed beside him; Frost threw up his blade in an instinctive parry, but saw that it was Slocum Plaisted. Other men from his crew were jumping down onto the renegade's main deck now that the vessels had touched. Daniel O'Buck was already fighting three renegades who were survivors of the crew serving the cannon in the waist. Frost coolly shot one renegade in the chest, then fired the second barrel into the back of a renegade who was straddled on the quarterdeck atop Darius, choking the youth with a belaying pin. Darius! Frost kicked the body off Darius and pulled him roughly to his feet, shouting as he did so, "Insolent pup! I should have let him finish the job! You deliberately disobeyed my order!" He flung the youth aside: "Slocum! Get him back aboard the cat!"

Frost threw himself fiercely against a renegade armed with a dirk and beat him to the deck with two quick blows of his cutlass, slashing the man's throat with a third thrust and looking for a way to board the nau; a shouted warning of danger behind! Frost spun around to parry a pike and saw beyond the renegade wielding it two additional pikemen thrusting their way toward Slocum Plaisted.

Slocum thrust Darius behind him, shielding the youth with his own body, and hacked at the head of one pike with his cutlass. Frost had to deal with his most immediate danger first: he feinted beneath his opponent's pike, letting the wooden shaft slide harmlessly over his shoulder while he struck his man in the belly, then smashed the pike upward. Frost turned to see Slocum Plaisted retreating slowly and grimly along the main deck cluttered with bodies, living and dead, using only one arm to wield his cutlass, the other keeping Darius firmly behind him. A third pirate, bloody cutlass in hand, rushed toward Slocum Plaisted and Darius Langdon from behind. "Slocum! Behind you!" Frost roared, amplifying his voice by power of will sufficient to be heard above the tumult of battle.

Frost started toward Slocum Plaisted as quickly as ever he could, but two pirates with cutlasses blocked his way. Slocum Plaisted whirled to counter the new threat, momentarily uncovering Darius as he dispatched the pirate with the cutlass with one shrewd blow, then turned, batted aside one pike aimed to skewer Darius—but leaving himself open and defenseless against the second pike. "No! No!" Frost roared, willing his savage voice to distract the second pikeman but enveloped now in a vast dread of despair, knowing he would never reach Slocum Plaisted in time. Frost clubbed and cut down the pirates in his path, momentarily losing sight of Slocum and Darius. And then, powerless to do aught but watch in helpless rage, Geoffrey Frost saw his bosun, one of his three truest friends, skewered on the pike. The pike head protruded some foot or so from his back, but Slocum clawed his way with bloody hands down the shaft to the renegade, who watched Plaisted's relentless approach with panicked eyes.

Slocum thrust his cutlass into the throat of the pikeman, who held to his pike with fear-numbed hands. Slowly, both bodies toppled to the deck atop a terrified and speechless Darius Langdon.

Frost killed the last pikeman with a savage chop to the side of the man's head. He saw a length of rope laying free on the quarterdeck, scooped it up, and fashioned a quick bowline that he threw over Darius' shoulders as he pulled him from beneath the bodies. Frost snugged the rope under Darius' arms and threw the bitter end to Roderick Rawbone, who was anxiously leaning over the cat's waist, flanked on either side by Caleb's woods-cruisers, three of whom were wielding Ferguson rifles to great effect. "Pull him aboard!" Frost roared. "Keep him with the surgeon's mate!"

Ming Tsun and his fearsome halberd, and another man whom it took Frost a second to recognize, were beside him, fighting off half a dozen renegades as Frost stood defenseless, guiding Darius while Rawbone pulled away with great industry. A quick sideward glance at the man: a British seaman named Urquhart, at least he had marked his "X" beside that name, out of ex-*Jaguar*, with abnormally long arms and a rolling gait that gave him the appearance of a spider, hence the nickname by which all knew him. Because of his long arms, he was one of the best topmen now in the cat, perhaps even the best. Frost recalled Nathaniel Dance telling him the man had been pressed out of an East Indiaman within sight of

Plymouth after a two-year voyage to China. Spider Urquhart caught Frost's eye and winked.

"Strange thing it be, Capt'n, us rebels fightin' other rebels . . ." Urquhart applied himself industriously to hacking down a renegade who had ventured too near his cutlass. Then Frost saw Struan Ferguson charging from the renegade's bows, a score of men at his heels, the ululating cry of the Scottish battle song shrieking in the air above the curses of the men who were dying or would soon be dead, the basket-hilted backsword already bloodied to its hilt and renegades falling back into Daniel O'Buck and half a dozen men from the cat who had joined him.

Ming Tsun's halberd flicked, and a renegade with upraised cutlass who was screaming toward Frost sprawled in the scuppers, a look of terror, astonishment and release stamped upon his face. Frost broke the pike with a blow from his cutlass, twisted the haft from Plaisted's body and glanced wildly around for something to staunch the flow of his bosun's blood. His own rattlesnake flag had been clipped from the cat's ensign staff by a bullet and hung near at hand over the cat's starboard quarter badge. Frost grasped the flag in both hands and tore off a long strip of cloth that he wrapped hurriedly around the awful wound in Plaisted's belly. He cradled his bosun in his arms, desperately willing Plaisted's heart to continue beating. He felt no answering beat of heart against his breast, and he gently lowered his bosun's body to the deck.

"Slocum has walked through the wall," Ming Tsun signed quickly, but Frost, suffused with a rage he had rarely known, was already rising and turning away, seeing the grapnel lines that led from the renegade's starboard side upward to the Portuguese nau. "No quarter," he shouted behind him, "no quarter save to those who beg!"

Afterwards, Frost could not recall how he had gotten onto the main deck of the nau, some ten feet above the main deck of the renegade, but he was standing there, flanked by Ming Tsun and Jack Lacey, facing a dispirited band of renegades. Frost shot one renegade brandishing a pike, who was standing over a Portuguese knocked to the deck. "Throw down your arms!" Frost shouted. "I've taken your vessel!" Five or six men hastily obeyed; a seventh did not, and Ming Tsun sent an arrow into the man's ribs for his insolence. Frost glanced at the fallen Portuguese, noted that he was better dressed than a common seaman—an officer—and stepped over to bring the man to his feet.

"Onde está o capitão?" he demanded, when his attention was immediately diverted by the loud, agonized scream of a woman in extreme terror, a scream that broke off suddenly.

"As mulheres estão na sala de repouse," the Portuguese officer gasped. Frost had no idea where the sala de repouse was located, though he knew it likely would not be too far from the captain's cabin. He ran for the passageway in the loom of the quarterdeck, thrust open the door and instantly spied a dark human shape kneeling in front of a closed door several yards down the passageway. The human shape just as quickly glimpsed Frost, scrambled to its feet, and hastily scurried in the opposite direction. Frost's gorge rose as the vague human shape reminded him of Whip Loring, the hunchback gaoler of Louisbourg. The scream came again, seemingly near, though without direction. Frost, closely followed by Ming Tsun and Jack Lacey, raced along the passageway, lighted only by a small skylight. Thankfully the passageway offered at least six feet of headroom, and they did not have to run all hunched over.

Just in time to avoid stumbling over it, Frost saw a form huddled in front of the door where the human shape had been kneeling—no, two forms, two men, slender, middle-aged, wigs knocked askew, their throats slit as they had defended themselves or begged for their lives with sobs and supplicant hands. The human shape had been rifling the dead men's pockets. A scream—the same one?—came from behind the door in front of which the two dead men lay.

Frost cautiously pushed open the door into sudden silence. Another small skylight provided some illumination, and he paused involuntarily for several seconds to permit his eyes to accommodate the gloom. A shapeless bundle of cloth that was probably a woman lay sprawled just inside the door; another bundle of cloth, again a woman, was thrown askew over a table in the center of the salon. A hand emerging from this bundle of cloth ineffectually brandished a fiddle in small, erratic circles, attempting to strike a man who was rutting atop her, trying to force his way deeper into the mass of petticoats.

Frost stepped the two paces to the table, placed the barrels of the Bass pistol behind the man's ear, and cocked the hammer. The sound was ominously loud in the small salon. "The position is ludicrous, and the pleasure exceedingly transitory," Frost said quietly. The man jerked upright and ceased pawing the petticoats. He turned slowly, showing to Frost the snarling, incredulous, hate-filled face of Reedy Stalker.

"Secure the fiddle, Mister Lacey. Ming Tsun, search this man for weapons, then bind his hands." Frost thrust the Bass pistol into his belt, self-consciously reached out to smooth down the petticoats from which one delicate stocking-clad ankle protruded, immediately thought better of the idea, and knowing nothing else to do cleared his throat rather more noisily than was necessary.

Since he was aboard a Portuguese vessel and had not ascertained the woman's nationality, Frost spoke in Portuguese. "Bom dia, Senhora . . ."

The heap of clothing convulsed and rearranged itself into a quite presentable, pastel-colored violet and gold silk morning gown, culminating in a cream-colored Spanish shawl with gold-threaded morning glories twisted around the bosom and shoulders of a woman with extraordinarily honey-golden hair and eyes the color of amethysts. Down to the style in which her hair was worn, its color and the color of her eyes, this woman was the exact image of the small, exquisite portrait Frost had found among Hugh Stuart's possessions. And Geoffrey Frost knew that never in his time would he behold again so lovely or so tempestuous a woman. She said, "Puio semplicione al tuo fessacchiotto de mettere il violino nella valigetta che si trova su quella credenza. A quanto pare si tratta di uno Stradivari e al Signor Baretta piace davvero molto."

Frost curtly ordered Jack Lacey to place the fiddle in its case on the sideboard, though he did not bother to tell Lacey the woman had referred to him, in Italian, as a simpleton. He contented himself with thinking it passing strange that the woman, who moments ago had sought to beat off her assailant with it, to the instrument's destruction, was now so concerned for the fiddle's safety.

A small, delicate, and perfectly proportioned hand, with long, tapering fingers, twitched the Spanish shawl into place around the woman's bodice. It fell into place amazingly well. The woman shook herself with a flourish, not at all unlike a dog emerging from water, and slipped from the table to stand upright in the salon. A tiny pistol that she whipped from a handbag beneath her shawl was suddenly aimed at Frost's forehead.

Frost bowed, and as he did so, easily swept the pistol from the woman's grasp—as easily as Reedy Stalker would have done. "Your pardon, Madame," Frost said in English, having decided on the basis of her resemblance to the portrait first sighted in Hugh Stuart's night cuddy that the woman was English. He examined the pistol briefly, then tossed it to Ming Tsun. "I am glad to note that your pistol is loaded, for mine is not . . ."

"Ye miserable son o' a whore!" Reedy Stalker shouted. "Ye tricked me, ye tricked me! By god-dam . . . but all Portsmouth knows the high 'n' mighty Capt'n Frost don't have the spade to cultivate this little posset-garden."

"I prolonged your life only for a few minutes, Stalker," Frost snapped. "It seems the lady was quite capable of protecting her honor, once she learned the trick of cocking the hammer, and but for my intervention you now would be dead."

"Slut, foul slut . . ." Reedy Stalker's mouth was fairly foaming.

Frost whirled to face him and said quietly, "Mister Stalker, you have well less than thirty minutes left to you in this life. If you own a god you would do well to seek some semblance of reconciliation . . ."

Frost was interrupted by a shriek and yes, a rush of wind, as the woman threw herself beside the pile of clothes on the salon sole, somehow found an arm, and used it to draw out a human form, which the woman began slapping sharply on her face. "Amber! You shameless sack of bones! Disgraceful, disrespectful hussy—you! How dare you have let this unspeakable knave attempt to violate me so!"

Frost seized the woman's wrist and drew her roughly to her feet. "Madame! It is most impolite and unkind to strike a person I perceive to be your servant . . ."

"The wretch is not my 'servant', sir, but my slave, and I must protest in the strongest terms your impertinence!"

Frost pushed the woman into Ming Tsun's arms; Ming Tsun grasped her gently but firmly. Frost knelt down, gathered the woman on the salon sole, whom he saw for the first time was a light, brown-skinned woman with high, aristocratic cheekbones, into his arms, looked around, located a settee against a bulkhead, and gently lowered the woman onto the settee.

"Mister Lacey, I shall thank you to conduct Reedy Stalker to the main deck. I judge from the comparative calm that Mister Ferguson has convinced the renegades to lay down their arms. Deliver Stalker to Mister Ferguson, then search this vessel for any other renegades. There is at least one other lurking about . . ."

"Gaunt Hutson," Stalker spat, "captain of the barky *Zeus' Chariot*, and he not be lurkin'."

"I suggest you search the magazine as soon as you've delivered Stalker to Struan, Mister Lacey. Gaunt Hutson may have designs of fashioning some infernal device." Frost was all too well aware of the lengths to which a desperate captain would go. "Once you find this Gaunt Hutson, deliver him likewise to Mister Ferguson. Also beg of him an inventory of my casualties. I would then be pleased to make the acquaintance of whoever commands this vessel. Ming Tsun, please find some water, that we may revive this poor lady. If I mistake not, the captain's cabin lies through yonder door, and there should be a vessel of water located somewhere in the cabin."

The golden-haired woman stamped her foot in anger and interposed herself between Frost and the settee. "You are a blackguard of the deepest shade, sir, to interfere between a lady and her slave . . ."

Frost faced her down, seeming to grow and tower above the woman, marveling as he did so at the spaciousness of these Portuguese naus. He had last been aboard one two years past in the harbor at Mombasa, on the abbreviated trip to bring away a cargo of spices, teas and silks arranged especially for him by a factor on the Island of Moçambique. Their head-room was truly remarkable. "Madame, this woman is no longer your slave. You have two choices; either she belongs to me by the ancient rights of succor from peril, in which case my intention is to set her free immediately, or I shall purchase her from you, then set her at liberty. I truly recommend the latter course, since you will profit from it the more . . ."

The woman screamed and clutched both hands to her bosom: "What of signori Baretta and Garibaldi! They were without this chamber a few moments ago, before this, this vile . . ."

"Madame," Frost said evenly, seeing Ming Tsun emerge from the captain's cabin with a ewer of water and a large sponge, "two men lie without in the passageway, though I am very sorry to say they are both dead." Frost spilled water from the ewer onto the sponge and tenderly bathed the face of the woman called Amber.

"Ming Tsun," Frost said.

"No!" Ming Tsun signed quickly, instantly guessing Frost's intent. "It would not do for me to be the first she sees upon awakening."

"As you say," Frost agreed. "Here," he said, reaching out to grasp the golden-haired woman's wrist and pulling her down roughly to kneel on the salon sole. Frost thrust the wet sponge into the woman's hands. "Tend this lady, and tend her well. I charge you, Madame, to remember that she is no longer any-one's slave!" Frost rushed for the door of the salon; he had much to do. Every seaman's instinct and his fey intuition had suddenly told him that a hurricane of great magnitude was inexorably closing on the three fragile chips of wood afloat on the bosom of this deceptively calm ocean. There was very, very little time in which to prepare for all the tumult and violence that the hurricane would bring.

## ◆ XVI ◆

◉◉◉◉◉ N QUICK ORDER AFTER RETURNING
◉　I　◉ TO THE MAIN DECK, FROST LEARNED
◉　　◉ THAT THE CAPTAIN OF THE NAU HAD
◉◉◉◉◉ BEEN KILLED, THE FIRST OFFICER
severely wounded, and the second officer, Manuel Magalhães,
who was from a distinguished seafaring family, and whom
Frost had rescued minutes before from the mercies of the
renegades, was effectively the senior officer of the nau. He also
learned from Struan Ferguson that the casualties from the cat's
complement were two killed, fourteen wounded. Ishmael
Hymsinger had already sent word that nine were simple cases
of gunshots, shrapnel and splinter, but five were serious, and
Hymsinger was laboring feverishly in his lazarette to stop their
hemorrhaging. He would send word via Nathaniel Dance as to
the men's conditions as the day progressed.

"Struan, what is the condition of this nau and the renegade
vessel called *Zeus' Chariot*?" Frost demanded of his first mate,
as he bleakly surveyed the ruined top hamper of the Portuguese nau and the even more ruined top hamper of the
renegade.

"She swims, they both swim, masts and yards sorely
wounded—they had time enough to pound each other remarkably—but I've nae time yet to survey hulls." Struan
paused to look around the main deck. "This renegade *Chariot*
has rather puny cannons, and it appears her intention was
to fire away at the nau's riggin' rather than directin' her fire

against the hull. A sinkin' vessel does not permit the orderly removal of cargo."

"We are square in the hurricane season for these climes, and there is a hurricane making, Struan, I can smell it so surely I need not consult the mercury," Frost said with finality. "Still . . ." Frost had spied Hannibal Bowditch flitting about the deck of the renegade. "Mister Bowditch!" Frost commanded, using his cupped hands as a makeshift speaking trumpet: "Please consult the barometer in my cabin and bring me the reading directly."

"I make our position far closer to the continent than I do New England . . .," Struan began.

"In latitude thirty-two and longitude thirty-eight, my last good observation, putting us southwest of the Açores," Frost said quickly. "It is my intention to declare *Zeus' Chariot* a prize of this nau—you would oblige me extremely, Struan, if you could name me this vessel."

"*A Nossa Senhora de Graciosa*, as the second officer, Magalhães, who speaks very creditable English, informed me," Struan said, "bound from Rio de Janeiro to Lisbon with a cargo of hides, several hundred tons of sugar, possibly several small bags of raw emeralds—Senhor Magalhães does not know for sure, the bags were given over to the captain for his safekeeping—most handsome of Senhor Magalhães to have informed me, a complete stranger of this fact—some gold for the Portuguese mint—I've no idea how much—and fifty or so passengers. Some sort of operatic troupe and orchestra, according to Senhor Magalhães."

"Unless I am completely off the mark, Struan, the dead and wounded of this nau leave barely fifty effectives," Frost said. "Little enough to work a ship this size under average conditions, and certainly not in the blow I foresee . . ." Frost broke off when he saw Hannibal Bowditch dart across the renegade's deck.

"Captain Frost, Captain Frost, sir!" Hannibal cried, "The mercury stands at twenty-eight and one-half inches and rapidly trending down!"

"Thank you, Mister Bowditch. Please pass the word for my carpenter." Then to Struan Ferguson: "Struan, ask Jack Lacey to see to the transfer of all the renegades back to their vessel. I wish the count and condition of her crew directly."

Struan hurried away to do Frost's bidding. There was no need to send for Carpenter John Brandon, for he crabbed up from the forward hold of *Zeus' Chariot*, his clothes wet and sopping from the waist downward. The carpenter caught Frost's eyes and shook his head dourly, approaching the starboard waist to stare up at his captain.

"I don't know what yard turned out this miserable barky, sir, or what ill treatment she's received, for if ever she was fair, she was knocked together with green wood, and she belike a horse been ridden hard and put away wet many times. Her carlin's and knees midship both sides are punky. Decks beneath forward two larboard cannons are buckled, so punky those carlin's, spirkettin' and footwallin' be, and there be over three feet, near four feet, of water in her hold."

"Thank you for your accurate report, Mister Brandon," Frost said, running his eyes down the renegade's armament. Four 4-pounders a side, and half a dozen swivel guns. "You may have ten minutes to survey this nau." He stepped toward the Portuguese second officer, now acting captain. He noted that Magalhães had his right arm suspended in a sling. "Senhor Magalhães, I would take it as a great kindness if you would assist my carpenter in surveying your vessel's hull."

"Sir!" The voice jerked Frost around as the golden-haired woman with amethyst-colored eyes appeared from the companionway beneath the nau's quarterdeck. "I must have a word with you this instant!" The woman's maid hurried after her, attempting, vainly, to drape the Spanish shawl over the woman's shoulders.

Frost turned away irritably. "Madame, I regret extremely that I am presently not at liberty to do aught but see to the conditions of these two badly damaged vessels."

"But Signori Garibaldi and Baretta, they remain unburied,

and the customs of their religion demand that they be buried prior to sundown."

Frost's eyes narrowed as he faced the woman directly: "Madame, I do assure you they shall be buried well afore sundown, and in plenteous good company."

"But where, sir? There is no land nearby . . ." The woman stamped her foot: "You must put ashore immediately!"

"Madame!" Frost shouted in exasperation. "The nearest dry land—excepting that in some flower pots aboard my vessel—be almost three hundred leagues away, and the last thing you could wish is to go ashore in the blow we are about to receive. Your friends shall be properly consigned to their maker's mercies, and you will be doing them a far greater power of good, if you retire now to your cabin and pray for them . . ."

"But, sir, there is certainly no rabbi aboard, certainly no parson or priest . . ."

"Madame!" This time Frost, patience exhausted, did shout, much more volubly than any crewman who had been with him during this privateering cruise had ever heard him shout. "I can send you a well-read parson apprentice or an Indian mystic—No! In your present state the one would not do! You shall have both!" Frost scanned the nau's deck, settling on Daniel O'Buck. "Mister O'Buck! Light along to the cat. My wishes are for Nason and Hymsinger—if he can spare five minutes from his gruesome duties—to assuage this lady's griefs. They are to bring sufficient duck cloth to sew shrouds. Have them attend this lady and her company directly."

Frost slid down a grapple's rope onto the deck of *Zeus' Chariot*, grateful to be shut of the woman but cursing himself for a fool. He could ill afford to take two men away from their duties, particularly Surgeon's Mate Hymsinger. He strode over to Jack Lacey, who was holding three men under unwavering guard of pistols borrowed from Struan Ferguson. Frost glared at Reedy Stalker and the man he presumed to be Gaunt Hutson, and then his heart sank into his shoes; the third man with his hands tied behind his back was Benjamin Farnsworth, young Benny Farnsworth, who had shipped with him as a cabin boy on the old *Salmon*. When had that been? Two voyages ago? A bright, likeable lad; never an ill word in twenty thousand miles of hard sailing. A lad whom Frost had recommended without reservation to Tilling Pickering in Salem as a bosun's mate.

But this Benny Farnsworth was a vastly different Benny Farnsworth, face all bloodied and an open wound across his forehead swelling his right eye shut, copious blood stains, not his own, on his shirt, and unable to meet Frost's fierce, determined but disbelieving glare.

Gaunt Hutson walked forward two paces and bowed awkwardly, as well as he could with his arms bound behind him. "Captain Frost, I am your prisoner, and of course give you my word as a gentleman that I'll cooperate with whatever your endeavor may be regarding these vessels . . ."

"You are not a gentleman," Frost retorted, "though I'll be obliged if you'll name those you term your officers." Then to Jack Lacey: "Mister Lacey, please bring forward any crew of this barky able to stand or crawl."

Gaunt Hutson was taken aback, but he recovered quickly. "Well, I be captain, of course, and Peleg Scott be second to me, though he was killed by a splinter thrown up by a gun from the Portugee, and there is Mister Farnsworth here, acting as my bosun, and Mister Stalker, whom I believe you know, as my mate—I believe you are acquainted with both Mister Farnsworth and Mister Stalker."

Frost took a turn on the main deck of *Zeus' Chariot* to calm himself, then another, and yet another, giving Jack Lacey time to gather the renegade's crew on the main deck. Frost sized them up quickly. Forty-five men and boys able to walk; a silent, sullen, dispirited, but hostile group. Hutson had been desperate indeed, his punky vessel sinking beneath him, to attempt such a long chase far off the North American coast: a fine prize, this Portuguese nau. Frost had no illusions about the fates of all souls aboard the nau if Hutson had taken the vessel. A few hands might have been spared to help work the ship, but everyone, even that shrew—well, another two minutes and Reedy Stalker would have poxed her, though she would never have lived long enough to require the standard venereal treatments.

"Mister Lacey, three lines if you please, sixty feet minimum, a noose at the end of each," Frost commanded harshly. From the corner of his right eye, Frost saw Benny Farnsworth go pale.

"Gaunt Hutson, Benjamin Farnsworth, Reedy Stalker," Frost said bleakly, "you are heartless blackguards and pirates, and piracy is 'hostis humani generis.' You hold no letter of marque from any colony—state—in rebellion against the ministerial government of Great Britain. You have no right to fly a flag with the rattlesnake device. You have attacked and brought exceedingly close to ruin a neutral vessel engaged in peaceable commerce. You have violated the Ancient Law Maritime and offended the Law of Nations. As pirates you are the common scourges and enemies of all mankind, and for that you must be hanged."

Frost heard the collective intake of breath from the assembled renegade crew. "The penalty for piracy, enforced in all the civilized seas, is death, and that sentence extends to each and every one of this vessel's crew as well." Frost paused, knowing it was for effect, and hating himself for it, but he needed—he could not afford to hang the entire crew, much as he might wish. He spoke slowly but loudly so that the pirate's crew could hear him.

"But there is a blow coming, in the form of a hurricane, and live hands will profit me more than dead crew. I propose to put aboard the Portugee nau any hand from *Zeus' Chariot* who wishes to ship. If the nau survives the coming hurricane, which is problematic, then any hand still alive shall be landed on a neutral shore with ten English pounds in his pocket to make his way wherever he will. That only if he works the nau as if it were his own, for indeed the life of yonder vessel shall depend upon it."

"Frost, you are a cove, the weather is too chill to support a hurricane . . ." Gaunt Hutson began.

"These waters are too chill to breed a hurricane, aye, but the hurricane that will shortly ensnare us was born hundreds of leagues southeast of here in much warmer waters, with a sirocco from the deserts of Africa acting as midwife. Once fair underway, the chill of local waters matters naught." Frost watched impassively as Jack Lacey came up with coils of rope over his shoulder.

"Sixty feet they be, sir," Lacey said, ashen-faced, "three lengths, though the line not be the best hemp—but I'll need a moment to fashion nooses."

"There isn't sufficient time," Frost said, consulting his watch. "A bowline run back through itself will suffice for a noose. The forecourse yard appears staunch enough. Mister Lacey, shoot the three lines over the yard smartly, if you please." Frost glared at the assembled renegades. Forty-five men, which divided evenly into threes. "Fifteen of you tail onto each line, and when I give the order you'll walk away smartly. If any man-jack among you can't stomach the tasks, then I'll add a fourth, and a fifth, and a sixth line—whatever it takes to hang you all—you hear me?" He was answered only with blank, shocked stares.

"Now, Captain Frost . . ." Hutson began, in a voice that conveyed his incredulity.

"A stopper for this mouth, Mister Lacey," Frost said grimly.

"Sir . . ." Benny Farnsworth began lamely.

"A stopper here also," Frost said. He faced Farnsworth squarely and mentally recited verse nine from chapter seventeen of Jeremiah: "The heart is deceitful above all things, and desperately wicked: who can know it?" Slocum Plaisted had been especially fond of Farnsworth and had seen great promise in the lad.

"Capt'n Frost," Reedy Stalker fairly shrieked, "I've got information to trade for me life, information 'bout the high 'n' mighty Mister Langdon . . ."

"A third stopper for that man also, Mister Lacey," Frost said.

Reedy Stalker screamed insanely, struggling in his bonds,

almost breaking away from the two cat's seamen who had stepped forward to hold him: "I've information 'bout the mighty Mister Langdon's brother, that Woodbury, be yore kin also . . ." Stalker's voice was choked off as Jack Lacey roughly thrust a rag into Stalker's ruin of a mouth. Stalker somehow spat out the rag: "Woodbury be a spyin' for the British . . ."

Jack Lacey shoved the rag back into Stalker's mouth; Stalker's face turned livid from the blockage of air. A line snaking over the forecourse yard was brought up short, its end with a hastily tied bowline oscillated two feet behind Reedy Stalker's head.

"Affix the rope 'round the condemned man's neck, Mister Lacey," Frost said quietly. "Do the same for the other two condemned." He surveyed the forty-five men, divided into thirds, now ranged down the main deck in loose files, making no effort to conceal his contempt. "Goddamn them all to hell!" This time Frost made no apology for the curse he uttered under his breath. He should dump the lot overboard; clubbing the pirates behind the ears beforehand would be an unearned mercy.

"Done, sir," Jack Lacey said tersely.

Frost looked at Stalker, trying to keep the revulsion out of his face and voice. "You ran with my cousin and the British lieutenant," he said softly, so only Stalker would hear, "for they had need of you then, to arrange a British merchantman under a flag of truce for Portsmouth. And once they had no further need of you they cast you off." Frost was sure to a mortal certainty that Stalker had been a source of information to British sympathizers about the cruise of the *Salmon* to New Providence. Still, that knowledge made it no easier for him to do what he knew he must. Frost squared his shoulders. "Get on with it," he told himself.

"All! Step away handsomely!" Frost commanded, running his eyes quickly over the files of men, searching for anyone who was shirking his duty. When the files had walked some four paces Frost shouted: "Belay and tie off! Mister Lacey, set these miserable wretches to clearing these decks of their dead, then break these pop guns off their carriages and sway them over to our cat. Stow them below on the ballast. Nothing but the tubes, mind . . ." These 4-pounders were the same armament he had for *Salmon*. Pop guns, yes, but others could use them.

"Sir, sir!" It was Nathaniel Dance calling. "Here is a man sorely wounded, his guts laid on the deck, though still he breathes . . ."

Frost motioned toward two of the nearest renegades. "Mister Dance, I'll thank you to survey the holds; if there is aught you deem worth saving, please order it transferred to our vessel, so long as the task consumes no more than fifteen minutes. As soon as the cannons are aboard the cat this punky vessel shall be cast loose." The 4-pounders off *Zeus' Chariot* would be poor substitutes for the cannons from New Providence Frost had jettisoned from *Salmon*, but cannons, any cannons, were dear, and gunpowder was the life blood of revolution.

The two renegade sailors had divined Frost's intentions, but they hesitated. "Overside with your mate," Frost ordered harshly. He turned, much against his will, to glance toward the bows of *Zeus' Chariot*, willing himself to watch with dispassionate gaze the grotesque convulsions of the three men slowly kicking and strangling to their deaths.

Clutching a bloody rag, Hannibal Bowditch appeared at the cat's starboard forward quarter fife rail, to take a breath of air, most likely. Where was Hymsinger? Then Frost remembered that John Nason and Ishmael Hymsinger had gone over to the *Graciosa*, and Hannibal had volunteered to finish dressing wounds. Hannibal Bowditch glanced toward *Zeus' Chariot*, his eyes catching sight of the hanging men. He stared at them, mouth agape.

"Mister Bowditch!" Frost shouted to distract the boy from the awful sight, then walked toward him, "Are all our wounded as comfortable as we can make them?"

"Yes, sir," Hannibal answered tremulously, "all except a man named Cutts. He died just afore Ishmael Hymsinger was summoned for prayer services. A musket ball was lodged near his heart, Ishmael said, and Mister Cutts died from loss of blood, so Ishmael said. We had given him an infusion of the opium tincture to ease his pain."

"Pious Cutts," Frost mused, loud enough for Hannibal to hear him, "a likeable chap, from Barnstable, rated him able seaman because he had worked the banks as a cod fisher . . ."

"Here is Ishmael!" Hannibal said with relief, as Hymsinger came down the side of the nau.

Hymsinger turned his gaunt face toward Frost: "Many souls have gone to their gods this day, Captain Frost, and I fear we have many shrouds to sew. Thank you for the loan of young Hannibal; he had to endure horrid sights and sounds I fain he would have been spared. Just as I wish he could have been spared the sight of that massive tree branch's contaminated fruit." Hymsinger's eyes traveled to the now limp forms suspended by their necks from ropes over the forecourse yard.

Frost stepped close to Hymsinger: "Ishmael, you have two hours, no more, before we shall be in the midst of a vastly agitated sea. By nightfall we shall have a full gale, and before midnight I fear we shall be in the edges of a hurricane swelling up from the Caribbean. You must utilize that time to compose our wounded for their trials by the shock and pitch of a great tempest."

"Aye," Ishmael Hymsinger said sorrowfully, "two hours will be sufficient for seeing all my work done, Captain. I must return to the sorrowing lady aboard the Portuguese for a moment. I wanted first to check on the condition of our wounded." He plodded toward the hatchway that led to his lazarette. Frost glimpsed Darius standing stiffly in front of the cat's fore jeer bitts, facing sternward.

"Mister Langdon!" Frost roared, "Why in the name of all that's holy stand you lollygagging while your mates are splitting their guts to ready our departure—to me, sir, at once!"

Darius hesitantly drew himself along the cat's fife rail to the starboard waist planksheer, where he stood gazing, terror-stricken, at Frost. "Please, sir," Darius began, his voice breaking, "I was but reporting to the bowsprit . . ."

"By the Great Golden Buddha, Darius . . ."

"I disobeyed you, sir," Darius said, lips quivering and eyes tearing, "and you punish disregard of your orders at the bowsprit . . ."

Frost was aware that every hand from the cat within hearing had ceased his task of breaking the renegade's cannons from their carriages and transferring the cannons to the cat and was eyeing him covertly. He gritted his teeth: "Aye, Darius, surely you disobeyed my order and a goodly man, true friend to me for uncounted years died for it, and you shall be punished. But I have learned much since that unhappy day I bowsprited my own brother. I'll tell you your punishment later—it shan't be the bowsprit, never worry. Report now to Mister Grimes, the sailmaker. Your immediate task shall be to lay out on the larboard waist the two men of our complement who have walked through the wall between life and death for us and must be buried in cold water rather than warm earth.

"You are to assist Mister Grimes in sewing sea-shrouds for our dead, with a fine stitch, mind, and two 6-pounder shot at each man's feet. You are to begin with Slocum Plaisted, and as you encoffin him in our vessel's best linen duck, look upon his face lovingly, for due to him you live." Frost dismissed the shaken youth with a curt nod and turned to see who stood beside him.

"Sir, nothing in the holds of this barky but some barrels holding pressed oyl of the olive, and bales of cloth in the middle hold." It was Nathaniel Dance.

"Olive oyl, you say?" Frost demanded. "How many barrels? What size?"

"I . . . I did not count exact, sir," Nathaniel said, "tierces in size, above two dozen . . ."

"Very well," Frost snapped, "advise Mister O'Buck to shift the oyl into our forward and middle holds, the most going into the middle hold—all that can be stowed within the next ten minutes. If the ten minutes allow, shift the bales of cloth also."

Frost turned toward the Portuguese nau, momentarily

wondering from what vessel the olive oil and cloth had been looted by Gaunt Hutson, noting with distaste that all three of the hanged men had fouled themselves exceedingly as their bowels had relaxed at death. Some flies that had emerged from the *Chariot*'s empty manger to feast on the carnage of battle had already settled in a bustling mask on Reedy Stalker's hideously contorted and blackened face.

"Shall they be cut down, sir?" Nathaniel asked anxiously.

"No!" Frost pulled himself aboard the *Graciosa* with a grapnel rope and shouted for Struan, who came running up from the nau's main hold.

"She wasn't pierced in the hull, Captain," Struan said without preamble, "but she's an old vessel, bottom all wormy, launched in the Tagus before I was born, accordin' to Magalhães. She's been pumping all the way from the January River, but the pumps are all ahoo, chains thinned by rust and leathers sadly shrunk. And with the fightin' an all, she ain't been pumped the better part of the day."

"How much water in the well?"

"We ain't measurin' from the well, but from the hold, Captain, where there is three and a half feet, and makin' all too fast."

"Jesus, Joseph and Mary," Frost said, forgetting himself in the mild oath. Struan Ferguson was taken quite aback, for coming from his captain this was near blasphemy. "That be a great weight of water for this vessel! Tell off as many renegades as you need for the pumps. If there is a cook aboard, get something hot served up for all hands, renegades also. But no rum, beer if it can be had. Wine, this be a Portuguese vessel, so she shall carry wine. By the saints! Every hand on both our vessels shall need all his strength near midnight." Frost briefly turned over in his mind the idea of transferring the *Graciosa*'s people into the cat but dismissed it immediately. The *Graciosa* shipped some one hundred passengers of various stations, mostly the opera company, cast and servants, and fifty-some-odd members of her crew had survived the nau's mauling by *Zeus' Chariot*. And there were the forty-five men of the *Char-*

*iot*'s crew transferring into the *Graciosa*. The cat could not accommodate a fifth that number. The *Graciosa* would have to endure the unendurable, or whatever lay just below the southern horizon.

"I trust that Senhor Magalhães will be able to assist in the passing of orders to his crew, and you may have thirty men from the cat as soon as the renegade is cut away. I intend to place aboard this nau all of the renegade's crew. I believe they will assist you willingly, at least through the approaching storm."

Struan nodded; he had already accepted the fact that Frost would give the nau's care to him. "It is very likely the storm will separate us," Struan said simply.

"Very like," Frost agreed. "Your primary task shall be to remain afloat. I shall keep station on you. Should we be separated, Angra Town on the island of Terceira shall be our rendezvous. Make for Angra Town directly. I shall send over Hannibal to assist you with the navigation." Frost glanced over the nau's stern. The fog had mostly cleared, though the day was still heavily overcast; a mean swell had begun to build, and the horizon to the south was colored with a surly greenish-yellow tint. Frost felt the merest hint of wind on his right cheek, and then, unexpectedly, a light drizzle began. He thought about his promise to land the pirate crew on a neutral shore. With Angra in the Açores the intended destination of the nau, the Portuguese authorities might have ideas of their own about the fate of the pirates who had attacked a vessel under the protection of the Portuguese flag. Joss. The nau's crew had to keep her afloat long enough to reach the Açores.

"Next to last barrel of the pressed olive going over," Nathaniel Dance shouted up from the main deck of *Zeus' Chariot*, "Captain Frost, if you please."

"Leave the last barrel on the *Chariot*'s deck, Mister Dance. Give way on those grapple ropes holding the *Chariot* to this Portugee," Frost shouted back. "Slacken our grapples two fathom, and stand by to boom off. Send over the gig with Mister Bowditch and his navigation instruments, and to take me off." Then to Struan: "I believe it is possible to get this vessel's jibsail and fore staysail sheeted home to draw her bows to starboard." Frost saw John Nason and Ishmael Hymsinger emerge from the passage at the break of the quarterdeck. Both men looked properly funereal and somber as John Nason reported to Frost.

"The lady insists we bury her slain friends accordin' to the Jewish rites, which we would be at pains to oblige if we but knew . . ."

"I am familiar with the Jewish burial rites, but the ritual is the same for all who sleep in the abysmal depths where no sounding line can ever touch, John," Frost said. "If you have sewn their shrouds then, Ishmael, please tarry aboard the nau long enough to perform whatever rites you deem appropriate, remembering that whatever deity the dead acknowledged will be propitiated only by their life's works, not the words or forms designed only to comfort those of us who remain this side of the wall. John, you shall return with me to perform the same sad duty aboard our vessel . . ." Frost broke off as an ashen-faced Davis Cummings, one of Caleb Mansfield's woods-cruisers, fairly flew through the break passage and scuttled for the leeward bulwark. He was followed a moment later by the servant Frost had heard called Amber. She paused for a moment at the head of the passageway, saw Frost and the men around him, hesitated, then gathered herself and walked toward them.

"My mistress, the Lady Cygnet, commands me to ask if she may have two bottles of best distilled spirits."

"It is always a chagrin to disappoint a lady," Frost said, "but a search for distilled spirits must wait until this nau has been prepared—as much as she can—for the storm that shall strike us, without fail, in the late afternoon."

The woman named Amber sighed: "That is what I told mistress, but she commands me anyway, for she be afeared the hearts of Signori Baretta 'n' Garibaldi will dry out if not soon placed in proper spirits."

And Frost knew why the hardened woods-cruiser, who had

doubtlessly beheld untold horrid carnage during his life, had come running up from the salon where he had been assisting in the stitching of shrouds. "Your mistress may lay the hearts by, with assurances this vessel shall be searched for such spirits once the sea burials have taken place and Captain Ferguson can spare a pair of hands."

An impassive Ming Tsun was beside him now. Frost noted the fresh blood under his life's best friend's fingernails and cocked an eyebrow at Ming Tsun. Ming Tsun shrugged, then signed: "I did as the woman asked. My halberd was a crude instrument for such work; thus, I asked the man yonder . . ." Ming Tsun gestured toward Davis Cummings, "who was nearby, and I did but borrow his knife." Frost nodded bleakly; he had done the same for Jonathan at St. Helena, burying his brother's body in the English garrison's small cemetery but bearing Jonathan's heart back for interment in the Frost family's own burying ground. He heard the bump of gig against the nau's side, and in a moment an excited Hannibal Bowditch had run up on deck, sextant case and a roll of maps tightly clapped under his left arm while he saluted his captain with his right hand.

"I copied our position from your chart, Captain: thirty-two degrees, twenty minutes north; thirty-eight degrees, forty minutes west." Hannibal's enthusiasm was painful to watch.

"Exactly so, Mister Bowditch. Sail directly west on this parallel and you shall fetch the Bermudas, but I suggest a course somewhat northeast. The Açores are spread over a great span of ocean. Something like thirty-eight north and twenty-eight west will put you in the midst of the islands. There is an island in the archipelago named Graciosa, fortuitously the name of this Portugee nau. So it is foreordained that she shall reach harbor safely at Angra Town, though the voyage may prove somewhat circuitous, given her rig and the heavy storm approaching."

"Aye, sir!" Hannibal said, his pimply face all smiles. "I'll stow my charts directly and do as Mister Ferguson, that is, Captain Ferguson, orders."

"Yes, Mister Bowditch," Struan said gravely, "please stow yere charts in the great cabin aft which ye shall share with me, and then I would appreciate yere rummaging the ship for distilled spirits."

"Distilled spirits, sir?" Hannibal said, uncertainty in his voice.

"Yes, lad, distilled spirits, once you've stowed yere sextant and charts."

Frost could wait no longer; he sensed the nearness of the storm. He clasped Struan firmly by the hand. "In Angra Town we meet." Then he was overside and into his gig, taking the tiller, followed by Ming Tsun and John Nason. The four men at the oars began pulling away for the cat.

"You, sir! I have not done with you!" Frost, startled, looked up sharply at the woman with amethyst-colored eyes striking off sparks of purple at the nau's bulwark. The woman wrung her hands helplessly and stared down at Frost strangely: "My manners have been exceedingly wretched—I hope you credit I have been much distraught—and you bear a marked resemblance to someone—a relative, cherished when I was a child . . ."

Frost thought that the lady Cygnet was still very much a child, a very spoiled child. "Remember our bargain for the servant who is no longer your slave. We can settle the price of manumission later, in Angra Town," Frost said, with a confidence he did not entirely feel. Yet he knew that he wanted, very much wanted, to see this haughty woman again. Then he dismissed everything from his mind save preparing his ship and crew for the storm.

"Bring me alongside the renegade," Frost ordered curtly to the four oarsmen. If they were surprised by the order, they successfully concealed it and pivoted their oars. In five strokes or less the gig was alongside *Zeus' Chariot*, and Frost leaped upward onto the entry steps, slippery in the drizzle, so much so that he almost lost his footing, but then he gained the deck. "Ming Tsun, your halberd," he shouted tersely, knowing that Ming Tsun would not merely throw up his huge axe but would instead bring it. Frost indicated the barrel of oil of the pressed olive standing by itself on the main deck.

"Smash me that barrel," Frost ordered and looked around for a tub of slow match. No tub of slow match was to be seen, but he did spy a small section of slow match laying next to a large pool of blood now much diluted from the drizzle. Frost snatched it up, drew the match through his fingers to squeeze out excess water, reached a Bass pistol from his belt, placed one end of the slow match in the priming pan of the pistol, and cocked and snapped the pistol several times, blowing on the end of the wet slow match until it caught fire. Still blowing on the slow match to keep it alight, Frost snatched up a fragment of light duck, providentially dry, held the match to it until the cloth was properly aflame, then carefully dropped the burning cloth at the edge of the pool of olive oil spreading from the remnants of the barrel that Ming Tsun had sundered with three or four powerful blows of his halberd. The olive oil began to burn with a clear flame, and the fire raced to the broken barrel staves and began licking at the oil-impregnated wood.

Frost dropped into his gig, waited until Ming Tsun was aboard, then stood on the stern sheets for a moment, looking up at *Zeus' Chariot*. "Her flag, Capt'n, want I to haul it dow'?" One of the oarsmen volunteered. It was the British seaman nicknamed Spider, off ex-*Jaguar*. Frost allowed himself a brief, bleak smile: so the man's loyalties had transferred to the cat.

"No," Frost said after a moment, "Gaunt Hutson and his crew have dishonored it extremely. Far better that it be cleansed in the fire." And he ordered the oarsmen to get him to the cat as fast as ever they could.

**D**ESPITE THE DESPERATE NEED FOR HASTE, HASTE TO ADD ADDITIONAL PUDDING TO THE YARDS, HASTE TO REINFORCE THE STAYS, HASTE TO double breech the cannons, haste to reeve lifelines, and haste for the innumerable other items, some small, others large, that were absolutely necessary to prepare the cat for the onset of a hurricane of unpredictable fury, Frost paused all hands while John Nason spoke the burial service over Slocum Plaisted and Pious Cutts, the two men now bonded to each other in death. One of the old *Salmon* hands, Shank O'Riley, two voyages to Macao, face a tanned mass of wrinkles scrunched up so tight from crying that his eyes were hardly visible, appeared beside Frost with a book.

"Please, sir," Shank O'Riley said in a voice hoarse from crying, a voice so hoarse and low that Frost could scarcely make out what the man was saying, "the crew of the old *Salmon* alus 'joiced to have the bosun read to us. Ain't there be something in this book the bosun would like to hear 'side the Christian words?" O'Riley poked the book into Frost's hands.

Frost looked around for the other reason why he had to strain to understand what O'Riley was saying. Yes, the wind was rising, had begun to rise halfway through the brief service, and as John Nason was finishing his prayers he had fairly shouted to be heard. There was precious little time to prepare the cat and the Portuguese nau for the storm about to be unleashed on them. A curt "the Christian words are sufficient enough for the bosun" was on Frost's lips, but another look at the weeping O'Riley and he could not utter it.

"Anything in particular you or your mates would have me read?" Frost asked. He calculated there were no more than fifteen men left aboard the cat who had shipped with Slocum Plaisted to China. If he cared a whit about the lives of those fifteen men, Frost would now be exhorting them to labor to prepare their ship—Frost gently took the book from O'Riley's hands.

"We alus liked the gist of the tale about the boy 'n' girl what families didn't cotton much to each other . . ." O'Riley looked bewildered, "the bosun, he read it to us any power of times, but I can't . . ." O'Riley blinked away a fresh onslaught of tears, "I can't rightly 'call what it be named."

"I believe I know it," Frost said, leafing through the worn and smudged collection of Shakespeare's plays and sonnets until he found the *Tragedy of Romeo and Juliet*. Now where exactly was that quote by Juliet that he and Plaisted had once discussed during a week when the *Salmon* had been becalmed in the South Atlantic midway between Ascension and Saint Helena? Act two? No, it had to be act three. Frost found the passage, glanced around at the silent throng of sailors gathered at the starboard waist entry, cleared his throat, and began to read in a voice louder than the rising wind, a voice that could be heard clearly by everyone on deck.

"Come gentle Night, come loving black-brow'd Night, Give me my Romeo. And when I shall die take him and cut him out in little stars, and he will make the face of heav'n so fine that all the world will be in love with Night, and pay no worship to the garish sun."

O'Riley involuntarily clasped his hands in delight: "The very passage for the bosun, Capt'n Frost, sir. It'll tickle his fancy as much as the parson's Christian words."

Frost nodded slightly at Darius and Caleb Mansfield standing by the gratings, the signal to move the bodies forward to the entry, and he stood with head bowed until the grating bearing Pious Cutts' remains sewn into his eternal clothing was tipped to plunge the body overside on its way to the abysmal deep. Darius was weeping bitterly, though his tears were washed away by the blowing drizzle as quickly as they welled in his eyes, as he and Caleb Mansfield tipped the grating on which Slocum Plaisted's body lay. Frost recalled another line from Shakespeare, and he whispered it: "Be just and fear not; let all the ends thou aimest at, be thy country's, thy God's and truth's." And then the ancient Jewish greeting and farewell: "Shalom alei-chem." The Americans had a country now—if they could win and keep Slocum Plaisted's purchase.

Fifteen seconds after the souls of the dead men had been commended to their Maker and their bodies committed to the abysmal deep, Frost issued the first of a stream of orders that would prepare his vessel—as best he could—for the ordeal that was rapidly approaching.

"Mister O'Buck, strike topgallant masts to the deck immediately. Clew the main tops'l to its first reef. It will be exceedingly dangerous to do so, as you well know, but we must do everything in our power to remain with the Portugee. Once the storm is upon us fair, Captain Ferguson will doubtlessly have what canvas he may be able to spread on his abbreviated spars double reefed."

Frost turned to Jack Lacey: "Mister Lacey, triple lash our boats . . ." Darius had avoided Frost's gaze during the brief service and had assiduously remained out of Frost's way, but Frost looked around the deck, saw the youth, and summoned him curtly.

"Darius, you are turned before the masts and attached to Mister Lacey's watch. You shall take orders from him. First report to Cook Barnes and remind him to douse fires but that he is serve out all soup he has warming to the hands reporting by divisions as they can be spared by their watch officers."

Frost turned abruptly from Darius and resumed speaking to Jack Lacey: "Pass the word for the carpenter to meet me in the forepeak. I shall inspect the vessel. Mister O'Buck, get the deck watch into tarpaulin jackets and station two men at the helm."

In the fifteen minutes it took Frost and Brandon, the carpenter, to inspect the cat from stempost to sternpost, stopping in Frost's cabin only long enough for him to throw on the tarpaulin jacket and storm cap Ming Tsun had ready, the wind had grown to the force of a gale, and walls of angry green water were pouring over the cat's waist, wind and press of water heeling the cat sharply to starboard. To starboard: with any luck, the cat and *A Nossa Senhora de Graciosa* would stay in the western fringes of the hurricane as it revolved around its eye. The eastern winds were always more fierce, though the opposite held true in the typhoons of the southern oceans. Joss. Frost glanced about his ship, acutely aware of just how fragile and insignificant the cat and her people were in the immensity of the ocean and the forces warring for dominion over her. The westerly side of the hurricane could claim his vessel as easily as the easterly.

Men were still struggling to double the life lines on the main deck, one short lad being swept completely off his feet by a torrent of water; he was plucked out of the maelstrom by his mates and promptly ordered below by Daniel O'Buck.

Frost searched for the Portuguese nau, finding her pitching violently two cables' length off the cat's starboard stern quarter, though difficult to see through the driving rain that had succeeded the drizzle. Half a dozen men were bent precariously over the nau's fore yard, attempting to gather in and re-reef the fore course, whose head bolt rope and larboard robband gaskets, as nearly as Frost could judge, had blown out. "She is an old ship, sails, ropes, reef-points, rigging, everything about her rotten or frayed," Frost thought as he anxiously watched the men seeking to collapse and lash to its yard the fore course, which snapped and flailed with a life of its own.

Then the starboard robband gaskets blew out, and the flogging sail threatened to dislodge the men still attempting to master it.

"Order it cut loose, Struan!" Frost willed his friend and first officer, now entrusted with the fate of the nau. The cat descended into the bottom of a deep trough of water and Frost lost sight of the nau, though when the cat rose on the crest some thirty seconds later and Frost glimpsed the nau once again through the wall of rain, he breathed a sigh of relief, for the sail had vanished from the yard, whether cut away or snatched away by the wind it did not matter. But he counted one less man clinging to the fore course yard, and the sigh choked in his throat.

Frost kept station to windward of the Portuguese nau, though only with the greatest difficulty, until the onset of night. It took three men to kindle a light in the cat's starboard stern lantern, but it was an hour past nightfall before the most feeble of lights glimmered from the nau's stern, and then only fitfully, through the vagaries of wind, rain and the tumultuous seas.

Frost hooked his lifeline through an ear ring gammoned to the mizzen mast and stood with fingers hooked around the quarterdeck breast rail through uncounted reliefs of the helmsmen struggling to maintain steerage-way, straining his eyes for the faintest sliver of light that meant the Portuguese nau, Struan Ferguson, and all aboard her still swam. He slowly became aware that Ming Tsun stood on one side of him and Daniel O'Buck on the other. Frost unhooked his fingers from the breast rail, mildly curious that there was no feeling in them, and staggered back to check the binnacles. In the feeble, shrouded lamplight, the incessant drum and splash of rain against O'Buck's tarpaulin cape enlarged the man to twice his size, making it seem that O'Buck was clad in a suit of iron armor.

"May I relieve you, Captain?" Daniel O'Buck shouted, his mouth less than a foot from Frost's ear.

Frost sighed wearily but found the strength to shout back, "The wind and seas are setting us northeast by north, and I've lost count of the times we've almost been pooped. I charge you strictly to remain to windward of Captain Ferguson . . ." He stopped, then hesitantly clapped a hand on O'Buck's shoulder. "You know that right enough, Daniel. You have the deck, though you are to call me if men must be sent aloft. I would appreciate your sending a hand to sound the well with a report every fifteen minutes."

Frost allowed Ming Tsun to lead him below to his cabin, poorly lighted by the single candle in a battle lantern, and stood dumbly, clutching a handhold in the overhead to counterbalance the violent roll and pitch of the ship, while Ming Tsun stripped off his sopping clothes and rubbed him briskly with a coarse towel. Frost pulled a nightshirt over his body and was asleep even as he fell forward to meet his cot.

Soon enough he was awake and searching awkwardly for his clothes in the cold, clammy darkness that he knew presaged the dawn by no more than an hour. His eyes burned as if filled with sawdust as Frost felt his way out of his sleeping cabin, standing upright for only a second before being thrown to the black-and-white-chequered, canvas-covered sole as the cat's stern suddenly rose and fell off to starboard in a vicious corkscrewing motion.

Ming Tsun, who had been tightly wedged in the settee beneath the starboard quarter badge light, writing in his journal by the frail light of the battle lantern hanging from its gimbals above the desk, quickly stowed his journal and crossed the cabin to guide the sleep-beguiled Frost into dry clothing. A moment later he thrust into Frost's hands a mug of exceedingly cold tea, a crust of bread with an onion and a piece of cheese, and a yam as cold and as sweet as the tea.

Frost ate quickly, his senses awakening sluggishly at first, then more quickly as he listened to the shrieking, mournful keen of tortured wind that surrounded the cat. He felt the stomach-churning dip and roll, roll and dip of the cat's riding down the crest of one huge wave, being shaken nilly-willy by the random cross-currents lurking a-swirl in the trough, then rolling even more as the cat was borne up the crest where the winds and rains lay a-wait. Frost ate the yam, skin and all, acknowledging and giving in to his hunger and feeling the strength revive throughout his fatigued body. Frost drank off the cold, sweet tea, pulled on his sea boots, and got to his feet, eyes well accustomed by now to the dearth of light, wondering anew how Ming Tsun could see to write in such light or even hold a pen in the pitch and swerve of the ship. The line from Horace came unbidden: *Nulla dies sine linea.* Never a day without a line. Frost marked the compass over his desk, which was now indicating a course slightly south of east.

"Thank you, my friend, for the tea and the yam, they have restored me remarkably," Frost said to Ming Tsun, for it was still too dark for signs to be read easily and acknowledged. He let Ming Tsun help him into the dank, salt-encrusted tarpaulin cloak and tied the ribbons of the tarpaulin cap beneath his chin, casting one last, despairing glance at the barometer.

The quarterdeck was a cold, dark and dangerous place, though relatively dry compared to the main deck, which was swept from larboard by wind-pushed rain heavily flecked with spume every minute or so with monotonous regularity. The shrieking cacophony of wind almost drowned out his words as Daniel O'Buck tersely reported the events of his watch: number seven cannon had become unbowsed and had taken fifteen men to re-lash; a shift in the wind or, more likely, Frost thought, the cat was following a rough triangle inside the wind inside the hurricane and had reached the apex, where the wind angle changed from roughly north, northeast to northeast by east. Daniel O'Buck reported only intermittent use of the pumps—the cat was a remarkably dry vessel! He finished his report with the answer to Frost's unspoken question. "Not a glim of the Portugee, Captain, I'm sorry to say."

Frost nodded, instantly realizing the movement of his head could not be seen. "Bestir Cook Barnes and his mate, have bread, cheese, onions, small beer—absolutely no hard spirits—served out at first light. If Cook Barnes has swayed a barrel of cider out of the hold, there's no harm in serving that, one cup to a man, no more."

"Aye, Captain," O'Buck said with all the tiredness that standing a four-hour watch in the midst of a hurricane would invariably bring, and he shuffled off the treacherous quarterdeck toward the waist companionway, carefully clipping and moving his lifeline with each new reach.

The helm continued to be relieved every fifteen minutes by two fresh quartermasters, and twice Frost took a turn, mostly to keep himself warm with the silent, muscle-shrieking effort and strain of maneuvering the cat's rudder exactly so to keep the cat stern-to to the mountainous waves rushing up from behind, even though the brunt of the wind's force was almost directly opposite the direction of the waves. Any of the waves would have pooped the cat and shouldered her off to larboard or starboard at the wave's whim, rolling her under in less time than it would take to shout a warning. "A helmsman's task in the violence of a storm," Frost reflected, "is an unenviable one, but 'tis the most important task on the ship."

And then the dark began to lighten, almost imperceptibly, and Frost realized he could see as far as the breast rail, then the mainmast, and then the bowsprit. He stepped to the helm again, eager to pit his strength against the sea, though cautious that the sea not think him too eager or too brash, or disrespectful. He knew well the sea and feared it and loved it all at the same time. But even as he feared it, as he did now—the fear palpable and strong enough to taste—Geoffrey Frost still loved the sea more than anything else in life. And if there was any exhilaration in meeting the best the sea could offer with his own counter-maneuver, Frost kept that to himself.

When he staggered away from the helm following his third trick, Frost found that Jack Lacey had gained the quarterdeck, waiting patiently by the breast rail, wind whipping spray and foam around him, to be noticed. The cat was rolling and twisting but well under control. Visibility from the quarterdeck had improved only marginally. "Mister Lacey, get two men aloft, the one to help the other, as far as the mainmast cap, if possible. They are to spot for the Portugee under Captain Ferguson's command."

"Aye, sir, two men aloft, to the cap if possible, to spot for Captain Ferguson, immediately, sir." And Jack Lacey was gone, so quickly that Frost had to call after him: "Mister Lacey!"

"Sir?" Jack Lacey acknowledged, turning from the companionway to the waist.

"Have a care, Mister Lacey," Frost said testily, "and clap on with your lifeline. I can ill afford to lose a man, a single man, do you ken?"

"Aye, sir!" Jack Lacey shouted.

"Repeat my words to the men you send aloft, if you please, and see that they are well clothed against the wet and chill." Frost took a position by the lee rail, knowing in his heart of hearts that the Portuguese nau was still to the south of him, that there was no way the vessel could have somehow gotten upwind of him. And there was at least an even chance the nau was somewhere near. Though could she be seen in this weather and sea state? Frost heard two men but kept sweeping the shortened horizon to the south of the cat.

"Sail-ho, deck there, sail-ho, broad off the starboard bow!"

Frost heard the hail and his heart sank. The tremulous tenor voice carrying so faintly to the quarterdeck was that of Darius. "Dios, what have I done?" Frost thought frantically. "I should have ordered Lacey that under no circumstances was Darius to go aloft—no, it is right, Darius would wish to be aloft . . ."

"Helmsman!" Frost shouted. "Ease off a point! Mister Lacey!"

"Sir!" Jack Lacey called from the waist, his voice coming from a long, long way off.

"Mister Lacey! See if she will bear a closely tucked fore stays'l of our stoutest storm canvas."

"Deck there!" Again the tremulous voice of Darius Langdon, which cut to the pit of Frost's soul: "It be the Portugee, and she be dragging her foremast!"

Frost set his teeth. Nothing he could say or do would alter what was to be. He could order the staysail bent on with all speed, that was right enough, but first he had to see how much strain the staysail could take, and whether it would give him enough control over the cat to straighten her drift and work her slowly to the south. One peremptory order obeyed too slowly, and the cat would pitch-pole.

"Aloft there!" Frost caught up his megaphone and shouted through it: "How far away do you make the Portugee?"

The reply from the main top was blown away. "Aloft there! Send down a man to report!"

A moment later a body was sliding down the lee main top-mast backstay, landing with a harsh thud at the main backstay stool, then up the waist companionway to shout triumphantly at Frost: it was Darius! "Less than one sea mile, Captain, though she be rolling most fearful."

"Thank you, Mister Langdon," Frost said formally. "Please organize the heaving up of barrels of the pressed oyl of the olive from the hold, and their collection at the starboard entry. You may commandeer as many men as needs be in my name."

Frost watched fearfully as Darius hurled cheerfully from one shroud, one brace, to the next, though not recklessly, keeping one eye cocked to weather to gauge the arrival of the next greenish-white mountain of water poised to pour itself upon the cat. Frost cautiously let himself out to the extent of his life-line until he could encircle the weather mizzen topmast back-stay with his hand, a-tingle with its vibration and hum, com-muning with his ship through the tension and tautness alive in the tarred cordage gripped in the partial circle of his palm and thumb. He stood thus for several minutes while topmen made their ways warily forward to bend on the fore staysail.

"Down helm!" Frost ordered, as the fore staysail broke out to the tug of the hauls, bolt ropes immediately protesting their strain so loudly that Frost could hear the strumming of the stressed tackle all the way to his quarterdeck. "Hold her cross-to as much as she can bear." He drew himself by his life-line to his station by the quartermasters, who stood strained and grim-faced, muscles tightly bunched in the corners of their jaws as they fought to counterbalance the almost overwhelm-ing forces of wind and sea with the cat's rudder. Frost glanced anxiously at the taut, angry billow of the staysail, let out to less than a third of its full spread, willing the stout canvas to contain that portion of wind necessary to maintain a perilous track made good, yet spill enough wind to avoid overstraining seams, grommets and bolt ropes. If even one seam started the entire staysail would be blown to rags within seconds. And with it the delicate balance of the cat's bows, almost perpendicular to the fierce, relentless wind, at cross purposes with the tumultuous set of the waves to slow her drift and keep the vessel slipping sideways as much as possible.

It was a hard way to treat a ship, an easy way to strain her, open her seams, overburden her, broach her, roll her under; but Frost had to balance the cat across the wind rather than use the rudder to take a straight sternward drift toward Struan Ferguson and the Portuguese nau. The delicate balancing had to be done if the sea-quieting slick he hoped to create with the olive oil were to spread as quickly and as widely between the two vessels as ever it could—well, the staysail was holding, so Frost could think on other things.

A hatch was uncovered, a block with chine hooks dropped down, and a moment later, as half a dozen hands tailed on, a barrel of olive oil shot upward from the hold and flailed perilously above the main deck before being tackled by four men and wrestled to the deck. "Lash it alongside the number six cannon!" Frost roared futilely into the wind, unable to make himself heard further than the mizzenmast. But Daniel O'Buck and Darius were there, calmly directing the lashing of the first barrel, casting off the chine hooks, slacking the blocks sufficiently to hand the scissors into the hold.

"She comes!" someone shouted, and two men threw the cover over the hatch, then fell onto the cover, scarcely sealing off the hatch before a frigid spume-laden roller of green sea water rushed over the larboard bulwarks, clawing at the men on the main deck, heeling the cat sharply, threatening to lay her on her starboard beam. Then the heavy wave was across her; the cat rode the wave until it crested, and through sheets of rain and spume sweeping almost horizontally across the vastly agitated sea Frost glimpsed the nau, little more than half a mile directly to the southward. The nau was completely dismasted.

The two men on the hatch cover wrestled it off: Frost recognized John Nason and Caleb Mansfield. A second barrel of olive oil rose from the hold, thumped across the deck, and was quickly captured and snugged up; the chine hooks swayed down into the hold and grappled out a third barrel before the shout—"she comes!"—warned of another broaching wave. Caleb Mansfield's grip on the hatch cover was broken by the next one hundred and fifty ton anvil of sea water flushing over the cat's main deck, but John Nason somehow managed to seize Caleb by the nape of his sodden buckskin shirt. He held on to the woods-cruiser until the cat shrugged off its burden of seawater and rolled back to what would have to pass, in such a storm, for an even keel. Darius and Daniel O'Buck were hastily lashing the third barrel of olive oil against the starboard bulwark.

Frost dared a look toward the Portuguese nau: closer now. Insh'allah! How the wind was driving the cat southward at madcap speed! He glanced momentarily at the spars lashed in their gallows over the boats nested on the foredeck. Three spares, two sufficiently long for fore yards, one almost as long for the seldom used crossjack yard. Frost pondered whether he should offer up the cat's mizzen topmast, main topgallant mast, and fore topgallant mast, which had been struck down on deck and were lashed on the gallows as well. No. The cat would have need of those critical masts and their related spares whenever this storm abated. Struan would have to fashion some rig capable of bearing sail from those three puny lengths of New Hampshire pine that Frost could ill enough afford to spare.

"Mister Lacey!" Frost belatedly remembered his speaking trumpet: "Mister Lacey!" The shrill wind hurled his words back at him. A tug at his right elbow, and Frost looked down into the serenely solemn face of Nathaniel Dance. "I be yere runner, sir," Nathaniel shouted in his thin voice, holding up his lifeline to indicate he was ready to go wherever his captain sent him.

"With me then, Nathaniel. Follow me to the waist and you can return to the quartermasters with all speed the storm permits to deliver my orders. But first, nip below and ask Ming Tsun to fetch along his hatchet."

Nathaniel nodded once, gravely, then was gone. Frost clapped onto the earring line running from his quarterdeck to near the waist break and launched himself into the shriek of wind. It took Frost the better part of a minute in a crabbed, shuffling stumble on the pitching, twisting deck, left shoulder thrust into the moaning wind, to cross the distance he would normally cover in eight or less long paces. Frost kept a wary eye roving to windward for the next killer wave and straight ahead for the loom of barrels rising from the hold.

The men tailing onto the block and lifting gear hoisted the fourth barrel just enough to clear the hold coaming before the deck gang tackled it, uncoupling and flinging away the chine hooks and rolling the barrel the short distance to the starboard bulwark.

"She comes!" several men shouted in unison. Caleb Mansfield and John Nason clapped on the hatch cover and sprawled atop it. Frost sized up the looming wave and without hesitating grasped the lee main shroud batten with both hands. The wave swept him off his feet, upending Frost and almost taking his body over the bulwark. Frost set his teeth against the cold that swiftly clawed its way into his sopping clothing. Por Dios! The men on the main deck had already been inundated a dozen times at least by the cold water roiled up from the depths of the ocean by the hurricane, but no one was shirking his duty.

"Mister Ming Tsun and I are here, Captain!" Nathaniel Dance, a-tiptoe, shouted into Frost's ear. Frost anxiously searched out the nau. The wind had brought the cat within three cable lengths of the nau. Frost gestured at the barrels of olive oil and spoke to Ming Tsun rather than release the one hand with which he continued to grip the shroud batten to sign to him. "Hack them apart as fast as ever you can!" he shouted. "The staves overboard."

Ming Tsun wielded his halberd against these olive oil barrels as deftly and efficiently as he had battered the oil barrel left aboard *Zeus' Chariot*. The light oil, the color of chartreuse, spurted from the shattered staves, momentarily spreading over the deck, only to be washed overboard immediately when the next tremendous wave flooded over the waist.

"All the pressed oyl!" Frost shouted against the keen wind as soon as the cloak of water had cascaded over the starboard bulwark. "Every barrel brought up and cast upon the sea!"

Ming Tsun was a demon plying his halberd, three or four blows from which stove in the headings and reduced half the staves to splinters. The olive oil flowed through the starboard scuppers in steady torrents, instantly washed away and immediately dispersed by the goading spur and whip of wind and wave, though coalescent again into a thin sheen that spread perceptibly over the tumult, not calming it completely but slowing it, weighing it down. The remnants of a cask soared over the bulwark, enthusiastically propelled initially by the combined muscles of Daniel O'Buck and Ming Tsun and then taken further, much further, by the wind. A placid pool of oil spread and widened, laving outward in ever increasing concentric half-circles. The unbroken spread of the oil, a thin, all encompassing film perhaps a hair's depth, no more, weighed down the crests of the waves, reducing them to sullen peaks too heavy to dissolve into spume.

"More oyl!" Frost called, rolling one barrel, Caleb's assistance mightily welcomed, toward the bow so as to give more tangent to the oil's spread; Ming Tsun sundered the barrel in four strokes, and they heaved the barrel, spilling its liquid prodigiously over the bulwark, drenching themselves famously with the oil as they did so. "All the oyl out of the hold!" Frost bellowed. He paused long enough to glance toward the nau. Two cable lengths away.

"Mister Dance, require the helm to point up as much as our ship can bear! Mister O'Buck . . ." Frost's command was choked short as another wave smothered the main deck. As soon as that wave had raced away, another barrel of olive oil swayed up from the hold.

"Mister O'Buck!" Frost shouted loudly enough to be heard over the storm: "Stream a drogue, the heaviest cable you can rig, over the larboard stern quarter, veer out as much scope as you can. We must bring the bows more into the wind, the fore stays'l cannot do it alone. Prepare a lighter line with a small puncheon at the end. We shall float it down to Struan."

Ming Tsun's halberd cleaved downward, twice, battering in the head of another barrel. Caleb Mansfield and John Nason lifted the barrel and poured the oil over the bulwark. In the cat's lee the oil was spreading out in a vast greenish-golden sheen that lay ever so thinly upon the sea. Wherever the oil spread, the waves licked up beneath the oil in sullen tongues that could not pierce the oil's thin film. The sheen had spread almost as far as the nau, on whose quarterdeck Frost could just make out Struan Ferguson and Hannibal Bowditch. Frost thought fleetingly of Ishmael Hymsinger caring for the wounded seamen in the cat's lazarette. There the agony of confinement, surrounded by the sounds of the hull's working, would add another dimension of horror. Another barrel of oil was flung over the starboard side.

John Nason, at Frost's elbow, paused in the pouring of a barrel's contents, staring in wonder at the ever increasing skim of olive oil that had already spread halfway to the Portuguese nau and was subduing the angry waters over which the oil lay. "Thus saith the Lord, which maketh a way in the sea, and a path in the mighty waters!"

"Isaiah forty-three, verse sixteen," Frost snapped, his face barely a foot from Nason's face in order to be heard, "but the Great Jehovah would be vastly more pleased if you could get this oyl overside more handily, Mister Nason!"

"Aye, sir!" John Nason tipped the barrel until it was wrenched from his hands by another wave creaming over the waist. The dripping hatch cover was tipped off its coaming as quickly as the wave had passed. Another barrel came up, lifted as enthusiastically as the first.

"How many barrels of the oyl are left?" Frost shouted loudly enough to be heard by Caleb Mansfield. Caleb repeated the query to the men in the hold, and after a moment held up four fingers. Four barrels! Frost could use half a hundred more, but what he had would have to suffice.

Daniel O'Buck, cradling a fifty gill spirits carboy of heavy blown green glass that had once held best Barbados dark golden rum, with the carboy attached to a light forty fathom line, pulled himself up by lifelines to where Frost and John Nason were poised to pour another barrel of olive oil over the starboard bulwark. "Drogue off the larboard stern quarter has been veered, Captain. Your brother-in-law, the good Marcus Whipple, did the same once in a hurricane north of Jamaica. He told me later he had the idea off you."

Frost clapped onto the starboard main shrouds with both hands at the dreaded cry "She comes!" Though, por Dios and the Great Buddha, this time the wave did not dwell aboard the cat quite as long as its predecessors. Did the cat shake off the wave quicker, or was it just Frost's imagination? If not his imagination, was the storm diminishing? A quick glance to the north quickly disabused Frost of that notion.

"Daniel, see to the unlashing of the crossjack and the two spare fore yard spars. Cast not off the last wraps until we have a line aboard the nau. John Nason, pay out this small line with its puncheon towards the nau. Struan will ken our intent."

Daniel O'Buck shrugged the coil of line from his shoulder onto John Nason, then pulled himself as quickly as he could along the lifelines toward the fore deck. John Nason heaved the carboy as far as he could and paid out the line hand-over-hand, the set of the wind and current taking out the line quickly.

"This be the last barr'l, Capt'n!" Caleb Mansfield shouted into Frost's ear.

"Clap on that hatch cover, Caleb. I'll wager our cat has more than fifty tons of water swilling in her guts from that hatch way alone."

"Which is, that I should cut alow 'n' get my lads on them pumps. Better'n squattin' round a cold stove and wonderin' what's the racket up here."

"Appreciated, appreciated deeply, Caleb," Frost said. Caleb's couriers du bois were not sailors and were subject only to Caleb's orders. But they would jump when Caleb ordered, and their fresh strength on the pumps would be welcome indeed. The film of olive oil had spread as far as the nau and was beginning to flow around it. The ocean's surface between the two vessels still convulsed like a sack of reptiles, but no spume blew from the wave crests, and the sullen troughs were noticeably more shallow and further apart than the troughs that had not been ensnared by the olive oil.

The carboy in its jacket of woven wicker appeared on the top of a wave, hardly more than fifty yards from the nau. On the decks of the nau a seaman with a light grapnel was braced against the nau's weather bulwark, waiting for the carboy to float a few yards further.

The fore staysail blew out with a report like a cannon. Immediately the cat's bows twisted around to larboard, the wind, screaming out of the north, now getting a purchase on the starboard fore quarter, abruptly displacing the cat's southerly drift and pivoting the ship around the fulcrum of her stern.

Immediately the angle of the cat's drift changed from directly downwind toward the nau to a right angle that was opening into an obtuse angle away from the nau. The seaman with the grapnel cast it desperately, but the grapnel fell ten yards short.

"Nathaniel!" Frost shouted, looking quickly around for the lad and finding him wedged against the tube of the number six cannon: "Fetch George Three." The sailor aboard the nau, aided by another, hauled in the grapnel; the carboy continued to float downwind, but it no longer floated toward the nau. A quick trigonometric calculation told Frost that his vessel would pass within fifty yards of the nau's stern; too far by at least twenty yards for a grapnel to engage the carboy.

A wet, very wet nose, evident even through his sopping breeches, pushed against Frost's thigh; he knelt on the heaving main deck to take George's massive head in both hands and ruffle the dog's ears. The Newfoundland was as thoroughly soaked through as any man on the main deck, but he barked happily, long tail plying around him like a cutlass, and bowled against Frost, knocking him to the deck. Frost scrambled to his feet immediately. George reared up, forepaws playfully seeking Frost's chest. Frost turned aside quickly, so that the Newfoundland's forelegs came to rest on the starboard waist bulwark. Frost ruffled the dog's ears again, then pointed toward the nau. "Fetch me yonder barky," he commanded, and the dog began to scramble over the bulwark.

"A second, George," Frost said, both hands holding the dog's collar. "John! Cut loose the carboy, and pass the line through George's collar." The command was carried out quickly; the freed end of the light line was bent through George's collar and secured with a bowline. "Fetch me yonder barky, George!" Frost shouted, flinging an arm toward the nau some eighty yards distant.

George scrambled over the lee bulwark, launched himself with a mighty splash into the turbulent sea, sullen beneath the gossamer film of olive oil, and struck out confidently toward the nau, powerful forepaws churning. No great amount of time was left by Frost's calculation; the nau was slightly closer —seventy yards away—but the angle between the vessels had become more acute.

George swam up one great slope of water, heaving upward fifteen feet beneath its oily shroud, the upthrust wave rising so high that it blotted out sight of the nau, and disappeared down the other side. The distance between the two vessels remained seventy yards. George was lifted into sight by the crest of another wave, precisely at the same time that the discarded carboy rose into view one wave crest over from the big Newfoundland dog. Without hesitation, George altered course toward the carboy, and away from the nau.

"No! George! No!" John Nason shouted, instinctively tugging on the line. The dog, confounded, turned once again toward the nau, then, as the carboy curtsied at the crest of an oily wave, toward the carboy again.

Frost quickly laid a hand on Nason's shoulder: "Not another tug, John, you'll confuse the poor fellow even more." Inwardly Frost raged that he had not ordered the carboy brought aboard. He should have foreseen this. Both the cat and the nau lifted to the tops of their respective wave crests and Frost saw men lining the nau's weather bulwark, waving, whistling, trying to cajole George to turn toward them. But George was fixed upon the carboy, so much nearer in size to the chip log he had retrieved several times before.

Another heavy splash startled Frost: had something carried away? Then the hoarse, anxious voice: "She comes!" Frost wrapped both hands around the shroud seizing of the main backstay, bowed his shoulders, and held on with all his might, glancing to the north quickly to see if the wave would be coming over the starboard or larboard forward quarter now that the staysail no longer held the cat's bows at some slight angle across the wind.

The coming wave was a great deadly rogue, bearing directly toward the bows; Frost could feel the deck begin to lift as the bows rose to meet the rogue, though not nearly quickly enough; the bowsprit buried itself in the seething boil of water. In the half-second before the immensity of the rogue engulfed him, Frost saw a smooth black arm stroking up the heaving breast of an oily wave fifteen yards away: Darius!

Then the mass of the rogue wave overpowered him, bending Frost backwards over a cannon, the wave's terrible weight relentlessly squeezing the breath from his lungs, the urge to cry out, surrender himself to the suffocation of the blanketing water, anything to end the agony of the compression of ton upon ton of water trying to force its way into his mouth, his nose, his eyes. Then Frost's aching eyes, staring all the while upward through the greenish tumult, sensed rather than saw the tumescence diminish, then foam and spume instead of water, until, incredibly, the masking water fell away from his face and he could breathe again.

Frost, his right hand, numbed, wrapped in a death-grip around the shroud seizing of the main backstay, levered himself erect even before his feet were clear of the receding rogue wave—where was that fool lad? Had the oil slick been over-ridden by the rogue and borne Darius down? No! Darius lived! Already he was halfway to the Portuguese nau, having caught up to George and turned him away from the carboy toward the nau, both Darius and George swimming toward the nau with all their strength, rising on the sullen crest of an oil-skimmed wave, then disappearing immediately out of sight as they plunged down the off-slope into the trough.

A rope under the weight of a monkey's fist snaked out from the nau, fell five feet short of Darius' beseeching arm, was withdrawn, thrown again, falling this time across Darius' shoulders, and Darius grasped the line while George seized the monkey's fist in his mouth.

"Mister O'Buck!" Frost shouted; rather, he attempted to shout, his lungs so deprived of breath that his voice was initially only a whisper. Frost sucked in a great, grateful draught of salty air, enough for a satisfactory roar: "Mister O'Buck! Secure a stout line to the messenger, a becket bend should suffice! Stand ready to send it over, and once well on the nau secure the spars to it!"

Darius and George were against the nau's hull and willing, eager arms were straining down to pluck them from the sea. Someone, yes, it was Struan Ferguson, whipped the messenger line from around Darius' arms and began double-hauling it. The stout cable seized to the messenger with a becket bend slithered over the bulwark like a serpent. The two vessels were parallel to each other, fifty yards apart; the cat, with the far greater windage of her standing rigging, began to slip past the nau.

The cable was taut between the two vessels, so the first fore yard spar was heaved overside into the sea, to be drawn quickly toward the nau. Then the crossjack spar was secured to the cable, followed by the second fore yard spar. There was a commotion on the nau, and as a pregnant wave lifted the cat Frost saw Darius plunge over the nau's side, followed immediately by George Three.

"What foolishness this?" Frost shouted. "Darius should not attempt to return in such hellish seas—Mister O'Buck, let out more scope to that line—Darius is below the line and cannot bear up—he must grasp it." The line bellied and skittered across the oily sea, one fragile strand of spider's silk just beyond Darius' reach. From the corner of his eye Frost saw the bitter end of the line reach O'Buck's hands. "More line, more line!" Frost demanded. "Bend on more line, you men, a mate's life depends on it—two mates' lives."

The line was bellying, whipped by the fierce wind from the north, but not nearly enough to reach down to Darius and George. Somehow the cat had to veer across the wind—Frost grasped Ming Tsun's arm, no time for signing now: "Ming Tsun! Aft with your halberd and cut away the drogue!" Daniel O'Buck had frantically bent on another line and was heaving it out in great coils, but the distance between the line and Darius and George was widening.

"If ever I get that young fool back on this deck, I'll have the hide off him!" Frost swore, then felt the cat lurch slightly as the long, heavy drogue was cut away. Losing that steadying influence to larboard, the cat momentarily pivoted to starboard, across the wind, and then the wind caught the unfettered cat and pushed her back to larboard, away from the nau.

But the momentary veering to starboard had put just enough belly into the line for George to seize it in his powerful jaws, and Darius had thrown his arms around the Newfoundland's giant neck. "Steady!" Frost commanded Daniel O'Buck and John Nason, who were tailing onto the line with a right will. "Recover the line not too fast or you may snatch it from the dog's mouth . . ." Frost saw that the other end of the line had been cast loose from the nau, and he caught a fleeting glimpse of Struan Ferguson on the nau's quarterdeck, hand uplifted . . . But the nau was no longer Frost's concern; he had done all he could to aid the nau, and, Insh'allah, either Struan would bring his vessel through, or he would not. The young man Darius and the dog in the sullen, churning, oily waters were his only concerns now.

"She comes!" someone shouted, and Frost threw himself forward on the deck to tail onto the line behind O'Buck and Nason, lest they lose it in the tumultuous sea that burst over the bows and rolled the cat upward like some inconsequential fishing net float. But after the wave had burst over them and spent its fury, Frost saw George and Darius sledding down the crest of a wave toward them, and he pulled as fiercely as Daniel O'Buck, John Nason, and Ming Tsun, who had appeared to add his massive, silent strength to the task of fishing in youth and dog.

And then George, with Darius clinging tenaciously to the dog's neck, was alongside the cat, a wave sending them crashing into the strakes below the main wale. A crewman, a freedman purchased from Louis Bennington who was entered on the cat's muster as Tempel Bennington but known to all the cat's company as Colossus because of his huge size, belayed by a mate, reached out and with extraordinary, desperate strength seized Darius by his armpits as the cat sank in a trough and with a great heave somehow brought Darius and George flying over the bulwark onto the relative safety of the cat's deck.

Frost was at Darius' side, looking anxiously at the lad, eyes closed, chest still, not breathing, a drawn, deathly pallor, even as George feebly pushed under his left arm and began to lap his face with a salty tongue. "Daniel! John! Drape him over a cannon, quickly! Chaff his back! His limbs!" Frost rubbed his hand in gratitude into the oil-soaked fur of the big Newfoundland dog and felt a helplessness he had not known for a long time, not since he had looked into the face of his encoffined brother, Joseph, as Daniel O'Buck and John Nason stretched Darius over the breech of the nearest cannon.

Then Ming Tsun and Nathaniel Dance were kneeling beside Darius, covering him with thick Turkish towels, though already thoroughly soaked with rain and sea water, yet retaining some warmth, Nathaniel Dance massaging Darius' back and ribs while Ming Tsun probed the lad's mouth with his fingers, unlocking Darius' clenched jaws to release a torrent of olive oil–diluted sea water. Darius trembled and uttered a great moan.

"He breathes!" Nathaniel exulted.

"Yes, he breathes," Frost said to himself: "Allahuakbar." Then aloud: "Lay below with Mister Langdon to my cabin. Ming Tsun! Brew a syrup of horehound—chaff Darius with dry Turkish towels and get him between sheets and all blankets in my cot ever as quick you can—and chaff George in turn, for he is as near gone as Darius. Hurry, you men!"

And then Darius and George were borne from the deck, and Frost could spare a glance to the northward, where the nau was but a dark blur on a hazy, rain-strewn horizon. Then he wearily pulled himself along the life lines to the quarter-deck, where he resumed his battle against the hurricane to keep his frail vessel and all within her alive, ever mindful that all that separated his crew from a cold, watery rendezvous with eternity, Deo Gratias, was two inches of oak planking—stout Scottish oak, augmented with best seasoned oak from his cousin John Langdon's yard, to be sure, but nevertheless only two inches of well-caulked seasoned oak's thickness sealing out the sea. And, as Frost so well knew, it was mightily frail and delicate when compared to the awesome forces jousting around the cat.

## ⚜ XVIII ⚜

"⚜ ⚜ ⚜ ⚜ ⚜ ECK THERE!"

⚜　D　⚜　　"DECK, AYE?" DANIEL O'BUCK, NOW
⚜　　 ⚜ BOSUN, BUT ACTING THIRD MATE AS
⚜ ⚜ ⚜ ⚜ ⚜ WELL AS OFFICER OF THE DECK, RE-
sponded. As happy and contented as he felt the situation warranted, Geoffrey Frost, dressed in an old pair of duck breeches,
green singlet and Indian moccasins while his sodden wardrobe
was drying, like all the crew's, on a bewildering cat's cradle of
lines arranged in tiers and angles all the way to the main top,
paused in his pacing on the weather side of his quarterdeck to
glance expectantly aloft at the lookout posted in the main topmast crosstrees.

Frost was grateful and happy because his vessel had weathered the hurricane two days past without sustaining major
damages, though myriad small ones had been inflicted. The
cat was as close hauled on a starboard tack as all plain sail could
bear, making good a course of north, northwest into a warm
wind from the northeast smudged by a light tinge of dust
blown out of Africa by the awesome and immense ferocity of
the hurricane the cat had weathered.

The last toss of the log had shown a steady seven knots,
and George Three, pacing contentedly at Frost's heels, had
exhibited not the slightest interest in retrieving the chip. In
the relative respite following the cat's running out of the hurricane's reach, Frost had been trying to think of an appropriate name for his vessel; he could not simply continue to refer

to the vessel as if it had no soul. Soul this vessel had, and in plenty.

On this fair morning the majority of his crew not on watch or mending tackle was gathered around the mainmast, where Cricket Dalrymple, the run British seaman with the "R" deeply branded into his cheek, lay full-length on his back on a platform fashioned from a door and two trestles. The freshly shaved Dalrymple was not strapped down to the table, and although limp as rumbowline canvas was very much wide-awake and large-eyed. Ming Tsun was slowly rotating between his palms a healing needle inserted deeply into the bridge of Dalrymple's nose and was pressing downward slightly. The healing needle was one of five needles placed at seeming random around Dalrymple's head and neck. Darius, standing at the head of the table, was holding Dalrymple's head immobile between both his hands while Hymsinger carefully rasped away the flesh upon which the "R" had been branded with a small square of rough-tanned sharkskin. There was remarkably little blood flowing from the abraded flesh, though every now and again Hymsinger paused to wipe the cheek with a sponge soaked in salt water.

"Deck. Looks to be wreckage low in the water, one point off the starboard bow."

Daniel O'Buck cupped his hands into a speaking trumpet: "How far do you make the wreckage?"

"Deck there, little more than a quarter of a league."

Daniel O'Buck glanced at Frost, his mouth forming the word "Struan?"

"Alter course for the wreckage if you please, Mister O'Buck. It is meet that we should survey it." Then Frost spoke to his heart of hearts: "Do not let it be flotsam from the nau's sinking."

Daniel O'Buck's voice of command, which required no amplification, summoned the watch standers to trim sails. The fore course and fore topgallant yards were duly swung round by their brace tackles with an enthusiasm and economy of motion that pleased Frost no end; the cat pointed up handsomely, then, as the redirected wind sent a shiver through the battens of the cat's fore sails, minced off to starboard exactly one point.

No sound of complaint came from Cricket Dalrymple.

Frost began his solemn processional down the starboard companionway to the waist, the men gathered around the mainmast respectfully stepping out of his way. Ishmael Hymsinger laid aside the small square of rough sharkskin, sponged away the blood on Dalrymple's cheek, and peered critically at his work. Hymsinger nodded his satisfaction, reached into a worn deerskin pouch laying on the makeshift operating platform, and pulled out a spin of spiders' web. Hymsinger shaped the spin into a plaster sufficiently large to cover the deep abrasion and daubed it on Dalrymple's cheek, coagulating the seep of blood. Hymsinger placed a piece of gun flannel atop the spin of spider's web, and Ming Tsun began slowly withdrawing the healing needles that had anesthetized Dalrymple, though leaving him fully conscious and truly amazed at all that was happening to him, though no more amazed that the lookers-on.

Frost made his way toward Colossus Bennington, who was carefully measuring the storm-hammered remnants of rudder from the gig stowed on the booms with the view of fashioning a replacement. "I'm grateful to have a carpenter's mate as strong as you, Colossus Bennington," Frost said, stopping before the man.

Colossus laughed. "Can't keep no muscle on these bones jest helpin' Mister Chips, Capt'n. Now me, I needs the labor of workin' the big cannons to keep up my strength."

"I trust you've had enough exercise in that regard of late?" Frost asked.

"Always got the place for more, Capt'n," Colossus laughed, and in salute touched his brow with the carpenter's pencil held in his right hand, "'n' a heap easier than workin' Masta Bennington's grist mill." Then he leaned close to Frost and whispered, "Thankee, Capt'n, for bringin' the boy back to the gentlemens."

Frost picked up the drawknife from the canvas sack of carpenter's tools at Colossus' feet and drew a tentative thumb down its edge. "A craftsman is known by the quality of his tools, Tempel Bennington. There is not a trace of rust on this blade, and I've never felt a sharper drawknife."

Colossus Bennington threw back his head and laughed delightedly. "Gotta keep edges sharp, Capt'n. Dull edges, now they'll cut you, cut you bad."

"A fact not appreciated by most," Frost said, moving on to complete his round of the ship, but not before Colossus had managed to slip George Three a small morsel from his pocket. Colossus' delighted laughter followed Frost as he paced sedately along the starboard side of his vessel, reached the fore deck and turned between the foremast and the cat's belfry, carefully avoiding two sail makers squatting on the deck, who were stitching a spritsail of light duck, and continuing down the larboard side.

After the hurricane had blown itself out—Frost had found the cat's latitude in warm waters far to the south of the Açores—Darius had regained his strength and Frost had quietly directed Darius' berth to be shifted to the space in the gun room he had shared with the two other ship's gentlemen, Nathaniel Dance and Hannibal Bowditch, though young Bowditch was with Struan Ferguson, wherever Struan was. "He was responsible for Slocum's death," Frost mused to himself. "He realizes that, and through his efforts on behalf of the nau and its host, he has atoned." So he had restored Darius to the status of a young ship's gentleman. It was the bidding of the sea. Life ended. Life went on. Joss. Insh'allah. Jesus, Joseph and Mary.

"Deck there!"

"Deck aye!" Daniel O'Buck thundered.

"Deck—for God's life, it seems not to be wreckage but a chicken coop . . ."

"A chicken coop!" Frost heard Daniel O'Buck bellow. "God rot your lights . . ."

"Deck! There be two hands clingin' to that chicken coop!"

Frost was halfway down the larboard side of the cat. He cupped his hands to shout: "Mister O'Buck! Are we running them down fair, or should we launch a boat!"

"I reckon we'll fetch them handsomely on this tack, Captain, though we might reduce sail to avoid running past them," Daniel O'Buck cried.

"Make it so, Mister O'Buck," Frost replied in a quieter voice that still carried to the quarterdeck. Daniel O'Buck shouted another volley of orders, and hands raced past Frost to brail up the courses. Frost finished his stroll down the larboard side of the cat and returned to his quarterdeck, George Three still at heel, to look expectantly at the gently undulating seas directly off the bowsprit.

"Deck!" from the lookout.

"Deck aye!" Daniel O'Buck roared so loudly that Frost winced.

"A hen coop, by God . . ."

"Mister O'Buck," Frost broke in sternly, "I'm sure you agree that the Deity's name should be invoked only on the most solemn of occasions. I've marked you just now for using the Deity lightly, and the lookout has blasphemed twice."

"Aye, Captain," Daniel O'Buck said miserably, swallowing heavily.

The lookout, Frost's quiet words having come up to him quite clearly, shouted, "A hen coop, by the Dear, less than two cables dead ahead the bowsprit . . ."

"Clew up, clew up!" Daniel O'Buck roared, heartily glad for the diversion, "Prepare to back the main topsail!"

Frost saw the flotsam now as a wave crest bobbed something as insubstantial as a clump of sargasso weed to its top. The cat lost way perceptibly, and Frost felt again the keen thrill of satisfaction at the expert handling of the cat. He had a right crew of seamen, he told himself, not a bumbling crowd of lubbers. So masterfully had Daniel O'Buck handled the cat that her bows shouldered aside one final burst of spray as her way paid off to a full stop fifty feet from the pitiful frame of a hencoop, to which two apparently lifeless human forms were desperately attached, though not so securely as barnacles to a hull.

"A swimmer overside, quickly!" Daniel O'Buck shouted, hoping that Frost would have forgotten his blasphemy and considerably ameliorating his language. "A line there! Swim a line to those poor unfortunates! By the Dear!"

The man who leaped overside to swim out a line was not a seaman but Stephen Duncan, one of Caleb's wood-cruisers, and probably a better swimmer than any of the cat's company, Frost thought, barring Darius.

Men among the crew lining the starboard bulwark were shouting advice and encouragement: "Don't get too close to 'em, they may grab ye panic like and pull ye under—tie off the line to the coop and we'll draw 'em in—mind ye watch yer toes again 'em sharks, sharks be populous in these parts, don't ye ken?"

"Toes!" Another seaman along the bulwark remonstrated: "Sharks don't take no toes, they take legs, whole legs, up to the privates—a little faster there, mate, there appears to be a fin chargin' up ahind ye."

Duncan duly made the line fast to a slat in the hencoop and struck out mightily for the waist entry, while some of the crew walked the line aft to the entry. A half-dozen seamen, suspended by their mates, were already leaning over the entry to wrest from a fair, placid sea two men gone blue cold who were a few breaths away from surrendering their tenuous grasps upon the frail slats of a hencoop that was dangerously near disintegration.

"Gar! Look at 'em nobs," one crewman exclaimed. "They be stark jay bird nakid!"

"As nakid as the moment their mothers breached 'em," his mate agreed, " 'n' blue as jay birds."

"Don't favor none of the men we put into the Portugee," another seaman said, a hint of relief in his voice.

Frost looked around for his deck runner, Nathaniel Dance, then spied and summoned him. "Mister Dance, lay below and fetch those towels which did yeoman service in warming Darius and George; we have need of them again." Frost saw that Ishmael Hymsinger was tying off the ends of a light bandage swathing Cricket Dalrymple's cheek and was quite prepared to deal with this new medical emergency. Hymsinger nodded pleasantly at Frost. "Much better to do work such as this in the open air and the sun for proper light than in the lazarette, Captain Frost."

The two quite bedraggled men were passed hand-over-hand up the waist entry and laid on the deck near the mainmast.

"Gar, but he ain't no Christian," someone said, indicating the pale brown features of one of the rescued men.

"Nary seed the like in Newburyport," another seaman chimed in, "but plain he ain't no guineaman."

Ishmael Hymsinger, widely respected by all aboard the cat, rated as surgeon's mate by aptitude, training and temperament, reached the two recumbent forms and knelt to take one pulse, then another. Ming Tsun and Nathaniel Dance arrived with their arms laden with Turkish towels. Then Hymsinger listened in turn to the men's chests. One man lifted a hand feebly toward his mouth. "These men require sweet water," Hymsinger said. The ex-*Jaguar* nicknamed Spider already was standing by with a pannikin brimming fresh from the scuttlebutt.

Hymsinger took a towel from Ming Tsun, tipped a portion into the pannikin, and thrust the moist towel into the nearer mouth. He did the same for the second man.

"Hammocks," Frost commanded, not addressing any of his hands in particular, knowing they would decide among themselves who best to respond. "Hammocks rigged on deck, with shades against the sun."

Ming Tsun pulled the towel forcefully from the mouth of one man who had been sucking upon it with true greed; he signed: "Cook may have some broth or meat stock warm in the galley . . ."

The Caucasian struggled to sit up: "Captain Cook," he mumbled thickly.

"Mister Dance," Frost said crisply, "you know better than anyone which pot Cook Barnes favors for his simmers . . ."

But Nathaniel Dance was already charging away, hunched low, bowling his way through the crowd of seamen. The way he cleared was immediately occupied from the opposite direction by two men hustling forward with hammock rolls.

Geoffrey Frost pointed to the area he had selected for the hammocks to be rigged. "Lads, after you secure the hammocks so, fetch a square of light duck to bend a shade."

The two men were quickly turned into the hammocks. Frost nodded in satisfaction and glanced overside, seeing the forlorn hencoop drifting away and now fretting at the time to be made good on a course for Angra in the Açores: "Mister O'Buck, I would thank you to clew out to all plain sail and return to our previous course . . ."

Frost lowered his voice and looked straight at Daniel O'Buck: "Assuming you can order such done without blaspheming any particular deity, Daniel." Frost winked, and O'Buck, knowing that his captain had not forgotten, knew also that Frost would not make an issue of his language again, simply because O'Buck would never give Geoffrey Frost an opportunity to hear him take the Lord's name in vain ever again.

Seeing that both Ming Tsun and Nathaniel Dance were vigorously toweling the two men after they had been turned into the hammocks, Frost's curiosity over the identities of the men he had fished from the ocean caused him to promenade several more times around the compass of his vessel. He fetched up on the starboard side of the cat after a very deliberate, slowly paced ten minutes. In truth, Frost could as easily have accosted the two men from the larboard side, but his measured pace around his deck permitted him the opportunity to survey the men covertly.

Ishmael Hymsinger was engaged in spooning soup into the mouth of the tan-complexioned man Frost judged to be from the Antipodes as Frost stopped his deliberate pacing on the starboard side in line with the swung hammocks.

"Your patients, as is only to be expected, are thriving under your ministrations," he said to the surgeon's mate.

Ming Tsun had been too preoccupied toweling the two men to note Frost's presence, but hearing Frost, he scrambled to his feet and signed, "They are both taking nourishment. I fancy this man . . ." Ming Tsun signed toward the Caucasian, "can satisfy you as to his origins. The other man . . ." Ming Tsun shrugged, "has not the mastery of any language that I have ever heard."

Frost signed: "I have oft remarked that the majority of New Englanders I've shipped as crew have a vocabulary of some one thousand words and understand only the three simple tenses. Their elocution likewise leaves much to be desired." Frost gestured toward the Caucasian, signing and speaking at the same time: "And who may this personage be?"

The man responded by swaying himself out of his hammock as quickly as he could, though in his debilitated state it took him some moments. Frost was glad to see that in the ten minutes he had taken to circumnavigate his vessel, the two men had in some fashion been suitably clothed from the crew's eleemosynary corporation, singlets and trousers but no shoes. Frost's attention was drawn to the man's feet. A pig was tattooed across the arch of the man's right foot, and a chicken was tattooed across the arch of the man's left foot.

"I see you ascribe to the ancient and apt tenets of the sea," Frost said, as the man drew himself up into some semblance of military attention. "It is said that no one with the figure of a pig or a chicken drawn upon him will ever be suffered to drown, since pigs and chickens would always find something that would keep them afloat."

The man had brought himself to full height, and he essayed a stiff, formal salute: "Sir, Corporal Ledyard of the Royal Marines. Out of the complement of His Majesty's sloop-of-war *Resolution*, who despite the pig and rooster on his feet was nigh onto departing this life save by yere intervention inspired by the Divine."

"Pray sit upon your hammock," Frost said, keenly aware of the number of cat's crewmen who were finding duties requiring their presence close to the mainmast. "And if you may tell me how it was you came to be afloat on the bosom of the sea with only a hencoop for succor, I would be in your debt."

The man promptly and gratefully sat down on his hammock. "Thank'e, sir, my serjent alus insists me standing when officers be present, but I'm quite beside myself, ye know."

"Certainly, and who is your companion, Corporal Ledyard?" Frost asked.

"Name of Omai, sir, passenger for the Society Islands. Captain Cook fetched him from those islands his last voyage, and now he's seed London he's to be borne back to his people with honors from King George. He don't speak none of our language, got a translator on *Resolution*, he has. We wus swept overside in a thumpin' great gale two days past."

"This Omai is some personage among his people, I take it," Frost said.

"Indeed, sir, he be a prince among his people . . ."

"And I am correct in having heard on prior occasion the name of Captain Cook? Would that perhaps be Captain James Cook of the British Navy, a bantam of a man but an assured air of authority about him?"

Ledyard looked up, pleased: "Yes sir, the very same Captain James Cook, though I don't know how he would apprehend the name 'bantam.' The fo'c'sl peoples alus referred to him as resemblin' a pigeon waddlin' along with his chest pushed out. All the same, my Captain Cook has an air of authority akin to yere own. Know ye of Captain Cook?"

"If we're speaking of the same man," Frost said, glancing up at the set of his top sails to judge how the cat was faring on this tack, "he commanded the *Endeavour*, which was in graving dock at Batavia when I called there in November of '70."

"Yes sir, Captain Cook be the same as had the *Endeavour* in her voyage of discoverin'."

"As I recall," Frost said, somewhat testily, "he populated half the cemetery at Batavia with his dead, though Batavia has always been a pestilential and unhealthy place, and I count it not his fault that half his crew came down with the bloody flux. I touched there only to escape a typhoon, and I made your captain's acquaintance."

Frost gestured toward the other hammock, where the Polynesian was sipping broth from a spoon held to his mouth by Ming Tsun. "So you return this man to his own people. Well intended, for no man should be removed from his own kin unless with his approval. And you, Ledyard," Frost said sharply, changing the subject, "from whence in Connecticut come you?"

Ledyard sat upright on the hammock in as close to an attitude of dignified military attention as he possibly could while remaining seated. "How think ye, sir, that I be from a colony?"

"The Ledyards of New London and Groton are well known to me as right seafarers. I've shipped several with me on voyages to China. Without exception all have been right seamen, and you have their cast of eye."

Ledyard flushed and avoided Frost's steady gaze. "Aye," he said finally, "I hail from Groton. But I be a Corporal of Marines aboard his Britannic Majesty's vessel *Resolution*."

"A Corporal of Marines!" one of the lookers-on called derisively, "A nutmegger born, servin' in the British Navy . . ." The seaman broke off and shrank back into the crowd as Frost's gaze traveled their half-circle.

"I recall that Mister Cook had an American named Gore with him as third lieutenant on *Endeavour*. You are aboard an American vessel now, Ledyard," Frost said, "and you would be welcome in our company."

Ledyard shook his head: "Mister John Gore is on *Resolution* now as first lieutenant, but no, sir, ain't that I ain't more a rebel myself than King George would warrant, but I took his shillin' and signed with Mister Cook for this voyage. So I can't go back on my word."

"Well said," Frost agreed. "But you'll warrant I'll have quite a task reuniting the two of you with Mister Cook's *Resolution*."

"Reckon that be true," Ledyard said soberly. "It be a big ocean, right enough."

"An original thought," Frost observed dryly. "And you are

certain you and the Society Islander were in the water for two days?"

Ledyard scratched his scraggly beard reflectively. "Since afore first light this day before," he said finally. "It was a prodigious gale. I was in one round house, Omai in the other. He came out just in time for catchin' a heavy sea over the bows. I grabbed Omai when he started over, and then the hencoop atop the manger, but it broke its fastenin'. Somehow we held on to it."

Out of the corner of his eye Frost saw a slow, negative shake of Omai's head, and a forefinger lifted in remonstrance, then the pantomime of an egg being lifted from a nest. "And fortunately in warm water, though you were nigh freezing withall," he said, winking at the Polynesian. "What was your course?"

"I be a Marine, sir," Ledyard replied, shaking his head. "Bound for the Cape was all I know."

"Rest now," Frost said and turned away, biting his lower lip as he studied how best to write this equation. "Mister O'Buck," he said quietly, but with sufficient authority for Daniel O'Buck to hear him all the way to the quarterdeck. "Please prepare to bring us about on a southerly course."

"Aye, sir!" Daniel O'Buck roared. "Hands to trim the yards! Haul taut the driver!" Frost paced back to his quarterdeck, watching the efficiency with which his crew trimmed the yards as close as ever the yards could be trimmed to the axis of the hull. "Ready about!" shouted Daniel O'Buck, and the helmsman spun the wheel as far toward starboard as possible.

"Helm's hard a-lee, sir!" the helmsman shouted. Other sail trimmers let go the jib and staysail sheets as the driver, augmenting the rudder, brought the cat directly into the eye of the wind. The sails shivered, and lines without tension on them flapped wildly. The cat's bows passed through the wind's eye, and the port jib and staysail sheets were hauled taut by other sail trimmers. The fore course, fore topsail and fore topgallant thrashed against the foremast as they were backwinded, acting as levers to turn the cat's bows further onto a downwind course.

"Mainsail haul!" Daniel O'Buck shouted, and hands not otherwise employed in sail trimming seized lee braces of main and mizzen yards and brought the yards around through sixty degrees of arc, offering the sails at a reversed angle to the wind, which promptly filled with reports like loud musket shots.

With the wind almost directly from behind her now, the cat leaped forward. Frost sought for a comparison: as agilely as her original namesake. Frost lowered his chin in reflection. This fine vessel of his had been too long without a proper name. Frost shrugged as he regained his quarterdeck. He would give that thought later.

"Very nicely turned out, Mister O'Buck." Frost had Jonathan's watch in hand: "I credit the maneuver took one minute, thirty-six seconds, which shall be the standard for a course change for the rest of this cruize. And done without any necessity of recourse to profanity, as I'm sure you have marked. I believe a course holding her directly before the wind will do handsomely for the moment. I'd like her to run southerly as fast as ever she can."

Since before first light of the previous day, Frost mused. Mister Cook and his *Resolution* had some thirty to thirty-five hours' advantage, and that translated into two hundred to two hundred and fifty sea miles' advantage—as much as forty thousands of square miles of ocean. "Mister Langdon, please step down to my cabin and fetch my sextant."

Frost went through the ritual of the noon sight that he had performed thousands of times before, taking especial pains for the most accurate reading possible. He called out the times and figures to Darius, who wrote them on a slate in large, cumbersome numerals, as did Nathaniel Dance, whose hand was equally large and cumbersome. But it was creditable, very creditable for two lads whose formal education was scarce three months along. Frost reflected on the names of his men who could be taught navigation. With Struan Ferguson and Hannibal Bowditch embarked on the Portuguese nau—and no telling where that poor vessel was since their separation in the hurricane—there was no one aboard the cat with the exception of Ming Tsun, the invaluable, irreplaceable Ming Tsun, who could cipher celestial navigation and plot a course.

Of course, Roderick Rawbone possessed a basic knowledge of trigonometry, so he should be taught the fundamentals of navigation. All the more reason to bring Darius' and Nathaniel's studies along as quickly as possible.

"Thank you, gentlemen," Frost said formally. "Please take your slates to my cabin, where we shall work our position." He turned to Daniel O'Buck: "While this fine weather holds, Mister O'Buck, I would appreciate carrying all stays'ls and studs'ls you consider our cat can tolerate." There was that name again. The cat deserved a proper name. No matter. Frost needed to fix the cat's position to within one minute, or one nautical mile of arc. He handed his sextant to Darius, who reverently placed it in its wooden case.

Forty thousands of square miles of ocean. Perhaps he should give up this mad chase before it was fair begun and enlist Ledyard and the Polynesian into his crew—every sea mile of southing was a mile he would have to beat back to gain the Açores and the Portuguese nau freighting Struan Ferguson, Hannibal Bowditch, and thirty men of his complement. Had Ledyard been alone on the waterlogged chicken coop, Frost would not have thought twice about the matter. But the Polynesian, Omai, changed the equation considerably. The man was being returned to his homeland and family, a most noteworthy undertaking and one that brought honor to Mister James Cook. And, dare he admit it, to himself: the mathematical and navigational problems involved appealed to Frost.

Frost worked the reductions at his desk with Darius and Nathaniel watching, mystified, over his shoulders. He laughed abruptly when he had the last figure of longitude. Frost was no stranger to these waters. "You see here a most peculiar result, gentlemen," Frost said. "Our latitude is exactly twenty-eight degrees, forty-five minutes north. Our longitude is exactly twenty-eight degrees, forty-five minutes west. It is not often that such a concatenation occurs. The Canary Islands are six hundred miles to our east, while the Açores are five hundred miles to our north. We would fetch the Açores in three days were we not in pursuit of a collier."

"A collier, sir?" Darius asked.

"The term should be new to you, Mister Langdon, though likely Mister Dance has heard it. A collier is a vessel built quite sturdily to transport coal in the British coastal trade. Stout hull and equivalent rig. If necessary, a collier can be beached without upset. The vessel, *Endeavour* was her name, that this Mister Cook had in the Dutch Indies, though officially a barque, was a Whitby-built collier. I mind that he would replace a vessel for exploration with one of a similar nature."

"I have heard such vessels called 'coal cats' by *Jaguar* men," Nathaniel Dance said. Then as the thought struck him, he laughed delightedly. "We are a jungle cat chasin' a coal cat . . ." He stifled his laugh at Frost's sharp glance. Frost turned quickly to Darius, who, having already stifled his grin, was staring straight ahead, chin tucked tightly into his collar.

Frost chuckled. "A well-turned phrase, Mister Dance. And I call upon both of you gentlemen to reflect upon a proper name for this cat of ours. Now, pray, how do you suggest our jungle cat take up the pursuit of this 'coal cat,' as you call it, across this scentless, trackless ocean?"

"I haven't a clew, sir," Nathaniel said meekly.

"Take seats, gentlemen," Frost invited, and as the two youths seated themselves awkwardly on either side of him, Frost pulled a large scrap of paper from a folio—no, not that scrap: one side bore evidence of Ming Tsun's neat, cryptic and indecipherable writing. Frost replaced that paper in Ming Tsun's folio and drew out another scrap. Opening the lid of his ink well and dipping in a herring gull's feather whittled into a pen's nub, he quickly sketched in lines of longitude and latitude the rough positions of the Açores to the north, the Canary Islands to the east, and to the south the Cape Verde Islands.

"It is highly unlikely that Mister Cook will run between the coast of Africa and the Cape Verde Islands this season of year.

The prospect of hurricanes such as he barely missed, though gale enough to sweep two men off his deck, will likely cause him to stand well out to sea. Here . . ." Frost sketched in several lines running southwesterly, "is the Canary Current, a large river running in the ocean. I surmise our Mister Cook will shape his course southwest by south to wear the Cape Verdes by a dozen leagues or so, then alter course to fetch Ascension Island, then bear for Saint Helena."

"And where shall we meet Mister Cook, sir?" Darius queried.

"North of the Cape Verde Islands," Frost said, "offshore of Saint Anthony's Island."

"How far until we fetch the Cape Verdes, sir, and have you sailed these waters before, sir?" Darius asked.

"Yes to the second question," Frost said simply, "when I was master's mate and navigator of a John Company tea wagon." Which was true enough. Geoffrey Frost had succeeded to the master's billet of a John Company tea wagon before he could shave or his voice had broken, due entirely to the plague-borne death that had decimated half the Indiaman's crew. But Frost did not want to mention his one unsuspecting, gut-wrenching foray into the Guinea trade, or the interminable weeks he had spent on the Cape Verde Island of São Vicente and its Porto Grande after he had cut himself loose from the bowsprit of the hell ship with the incongruous, ill-suited name *Bride of Derry*. "As to the first question, with a fair wind directly astern, I estimate we can cover the seven hundred sea miles to Saint Anthony's Island in three days, so long as these trade winds hold and we can proceed southerly wing and wing."

"Sir," Darius asked, "can you be sure Mister Cook has continued his journey and is not yet north of our path, searching for the men overside?"

"Yes, Darius," Frost said gently. "I'm certain Mister Cook has continued his voyage. He may have put about and run back along his course once he became aware two of his complement were missing. But unless a man is observed overside, the assumption must always be that the man has drowned, and the ship must be about her business. It is the decision I would make in similar circumstance."

"I begin to perceive what I have heard the men in the fo'c'sl say is the truth," Darius responded, slumping backward in his chair. "The sea is a vicious master."

"Not really, Mister Langdon," Frost said formally, recovering the ink well and folding the paper he had used to illustrate the positions of the various island groups and the ocean's currents. He could hear Ming Tsun bustling about preparing his lunch. Several flying fish had come aboard the evening before, and chunks of fish grilled in sesame oil over a small brazier Ming Tsun had rigged in the pantry, and rice, would be his lunch. Frost fairly salivated at the thought. "The sea neither cares nor is uncaring. You cannot say even that the sea is neutral. The sea simply *is* in all its various moods, unfeeling, taking no notice of petty and insignificant man. The sea had existed long before we mortals dared venture onto its roads. The sea will *be* long after pitiful man has disappeared from this globe as the result of his despoliations of God and Nature."

"We shall think on it, sir," Nathaniel Dance said, a signal for Darius and him to withdraw, for they, too, were aware of Ming Tsun's preparations for Frost's lunch.

"Mind you do," Frost said, "and now that our shipboard life has some semblance of normality, I expect improvement in your cyphers. I'm sure Mister O'Buck won't mind your presence on the quarterdeck—the squeak of chalk on slate can hardly be a distraction—but if you look in on Ming Tsun before going on deck, you'll likely find he has a plate of food for the both of you."

And Ming Tsun indeed had a plate of food each for the lads to ease their way from Frost's cabin. Frost, inhaling the intoxicating aroma of the grilled fish, moved away from his desk while Ming Tsun laid the service. He used the time to rummage around in the small chest where he kept his personal papers to locate his file of sailing rutters for the bulge of Africa. Frost had not thought to find himself so far south and east on this cruise, and the rutters he sought were in the very bottom of the chest. Frost opened the file and placed the papers it enclosed on his desk, perusing them as he began to eat.

Frost ate slowly, savoring the grilled fish, fresh carrots, and sauce Ming Tsun had prepared for the rice. He unfolded the piece of paper he had used to illustrate the positions of the various island groups for the benefit of Nathaniel and Darius and began to make notes. Arranging for a meeting with Mister James Cook, given the thirty-six hours and more since his vessel had shed itself of two of its complement and departed these waters, would present a problem but not an insuperable one. Of that Geoffrey Frost was certain.

His rutters recorded Frost's observations on prevailing winds, sea conditions, currents, and water temperatures for the routes he had sailed. Frost knew of, and marveled at, Cook's accomplishments in circumnavigating the globe. That Cook was a remarkable seaman there was no doubt, but Frost had likewise been at sea the greater portion of his life, and he reckoned he need defer to no man when it came to long-range navigation.

Ming Tsun cleared away the luncheon dishes almost unnoticed and brought a large mug of hot tea well sweetened with honey. Frost signed his thanks to his old friend and turned back to the equation he was writing. His rutters had given him a fair estimation of the southerly track Cook would attempt to make good. The problem Frost sought to solve was whether to try to catch up to Cook by following his track at a faster speed or forging directly ahead to a point by which Cook must pass. An entry in his rutters gave Frost the final piece of information he needed. He made a careful tic on the scrap of paper now covered with his calculations, drank the last of the tea, long grown cold, and rose to go on deck.

## ◆ X I X ◆

"⚙⚙⚙⚙⚙ ECK THERE!" THE LOOKOUT CRIED.
⚙ D ⚙ "DECK, AYE!" GEOFFREY FROST AN-
⚙ ⚙ SWERED MILDLY, BUT LOUD ENOUGH TO
⚙⚙⚙⚙⚙ BE HEARD BY THE LOOKOUT PERCHED
in the main topmast crosstrees.

"Deck. I mark a single sail runnin' down on us from the north. Tops'ls just comin' on."

"Very well," Frost replied shortly. The cat was lying to, bows into the wind, fifteen leagues south-southwest off São Tiago, the westernmost island of the Arquipélago de Cabo Verde. To the immediate west, some fifteen leagues away, rose the faint blue outline of the mount that was the active volcano of Pico on Fogo Island, towering over nine thousand feet above the ocean's surface, its clouds a faint smudge on the southeastern horizon. Three hundred cable lengths directly off the larboard beam a pod of sperm whales, stroking leisurely north, spouted their wondrous great towers of vaporous expelled breath. Frost had been absorbed in the study of a Greyheaded Albatross, one of the great mollymawks, wheeling and pirouetting in languid chandelles some hundred yards off the cat's stern. The solitary voyager of the great southern ocean had come close enough for Frost to identify it positively by its grey head, black bill and yellow stripes. It was a bit north of the large bird's normal range between Saint Helena and the latitudes south of Cabo Boa Esperança, at the southern tip of the hulking African continent. The albatross embodied the essence of freedom from all problems arising from the land.

Reluctantly, Frost tore himself away from the study of the majestic bird. "Mister Dance," he commanded, seeing the youngster lounging against the waist lee bulwark, "carry aloft a glass and advise what you discern. I believe you have seen one or more Whitby colliers during your naval career. You should be able to advise if the approaching vessel bears any resemblance to a collier once she is hull up."

"Aye, sir!" Nathaniel Dance shouted, bouncing up to the quarterdeck to take a telescope from its beckets next to the binnacle. A moment later he was happily scampering up the lee mainmast shrouds, so fast that his feet and hands were almost blurred.

"Mister Rawbone," Frost commanded his master gunner, "please favor me by ensuring all cannons are shotted, ready to be run out in a trice, crews standing by, matches alight. But gun ports shall remain closed, and the crews may lounge below the bulwarks."

"Aye, sir," Roderick Rawbone responded, going about the formalities of ensuring all the cat's cannons were loaded, gun port lid halyards a-trip, ready for the crews to tail onto the tackles that would thrust their eighteen hundred pounds of iron forward through the cat's pierced sides. Geoffrey Frost had exercised the gun crews at sunrise every morning for the past three days, and as Frost and Rawbone well knew, the charges in each cannon had been laid fresh less than thirty hours earlier. Rawbone had taken particular care to ensure all lead aprons had been carefully affixed to cover and protect touchholes before the cannons had been secured. Now he was as carefully checking all cannons to ensure the aprons had been removed and carefully stowed.

The cat was drifting slowly backwards through the light morning chop due to the push of the Canary Current. From his quarterdeck Frost caught his first glimpse of the topsails of the vessel bearing down on the cat from the north.

"Deck!" Nathaniel Dance shrilled.

"Deck, aye," Frost responded.

"She is ship-rigged, I can vouch. In a few minutes she'll be hull up," Nathaniel called.

Since that intelligence required no response from Frost, he began pacing the weather side of his quarterdeck in his slow, methodical fashion. Five minutes later, Nathaniel called, "Deck!"

"Deck, aye," Frost said, stopping his pacing to look upward.

"She be a collier, Captain Frost, even bow on I twig her as a collier," Nathaniel Dance shouted in great excitement.

"Very good." Frost turned to Daniel O'Buck. "Mister O'Buck, please shake out the fore tops'l and fore topgallant, main tops'l and main topgallant, jibs'l and fore stays'l. Bear up north, northeast to close with the ship coming down on us." With that, Frost went below to his cabin, where Ming Tsun had laid out his best brandy-colored tai-pan's coat, white breeches and stockings, and his best tricorne—which was to say, his only tricorne, and which happened to have a bullet hole through it, though thankfully hard to discern. But first he enjoyed the unutterable luxury of a sponge bath and a shave in divinely seductive hot water, freshly washed and clubbed hair, and brushed teeth, before dressing to meet Captain James Cook.

By the time Frost had dressed and returned to his quarter-deck, the cat and the northerly vessel had closed sufficiently for Frost to identify clearly the British ensign flying from the jack-staff standing up on the other vessel's bowsprit without benefit of a glass. The approaching vessel was a collier, right enough, an apple-cheeked, weatherly hull, comfortable in a seaway, stout and good-looking, with ample depth of hold to accommodate a large cargo of coal.

Jack Lacey, who held the deck, proffered a telescope to Frost, and he took it, moving to the weather side of his quarterdeck and extending and focusing the telescope on the collier. Frost made the vessel to be a little over one hundred feet in length, and he reckoned her burthen to be roughly equal to his cat. The vessels were now one sea mile apart, and glancing at the bows of the collier, calculating their respective speeds and closure angles, elementary geometry told Frost they would converge within hailing distance in slightly more than ten minutes. Already his nostrils twitched to the strong aroma of barnyard smells given off by the livestock aboard the collier coming down on the wind.

"Mister Lacey, please run a flag halyard to the weather main tops'l yard. Reeve it through the studs'l boom, then fetch it down smartly. Raise our rattlesnake flag to the peak, allow it to fly free for one minute, then lower and bend on this bed sheet." Frost did not look at the flag, which had a large strip torn from it, for the flag bore splotches of Slocum Plaisted's blood. He gestured to a neatly folded sheet that Ming Tsun had brought on deck. "I hope a white flag will convince yonder captain that I wish a gam only."

"Aye, sir," Jack Lacey said quietly, as the flag halyard was quickly reeved, nodding to the relief quartermaster to bend on and run up the rattlesnake flag when the ensign halyard was rigged. "She be pierced for eight guns a side," Lacey said, as a prudent reminder to his captain.

"Just so, Mister Lacey, but her main deck is a menagerie and heaped so with stores that I doubt her crew can have clawed down to a gun even if they started such task when her lookout first reported our sail."

The tattered rattlesnake flag ruffled in the warm, fitful breeze for the prescribed one minute before promptly being hauled down, to be replaced by the white bed sheet. "Mister Dance," Frost called to Nathaniel Dance, who, along with Darius, was standing by as a runner. "Please desire our guests to join me on the quarterdeck at their leisure."

Knowing full well that "at their leisure" meant immediately, Nathaniel knuckled his forehead and ran down onto the main deck, having already divined his captain's wishes and having kept Corporal Ledyard and Omai constantly in sight since they had come among a knot of seamen gawking at the approaching collier from positions near the starboard cathead. Ishmael Hymsinger had been entertaining Ledyard and Omai with his

Indian flute, and both men sat on the deck, transfixed, as Hymsinger played through his repertoire.

"She's raising a white flag to her ensign staff, sir," Jack Lacey reported.

Frost nodded as he lowered his telescope: "Most likely her captain's laundry, same as ours. Mister Rawbone," Frost saw a man on a gun crew craning his neck to peer over the bulwark, "remind your matrosses to remain well out of sight." Frost did not expect treachery from a collier on a voyage of exploration, but he had to be prepared for it all the same.

Ledyard and Omai, both smiling broadly, came up the companionway and Frost pointed them toward the weather rail. "Please stand so your mates aboard *Resolution* may identify you, Corporal."

"Aye, sir, she's the old *Resolution*, right enough," Corporal John Ledyard of the Royal Marines, once of New London, Connecticut, said enthusiastically. "That be Captain Cook starin' at us through his spy glass."

"Mister Lacey, we shall come about on a broad reach to the south, southwest; topmen aloft to furl the main and fore topgallants. Back the main tops'l to take off way, and let the collier sail down to us. Please to show the British Navy how expertly we simple colonials can handle our vessel."

The ex-collier, now ship-rigged as a sloop-o-war named *Resolution*, was half a sea mile ahead as the cat's helmsmen, at Jack Lacey's order, put the wheel hard a-lee to larboard, forcing the cat's bows off the wind, turning smartly to the new course named by Lacey. Topmen flew aloft to hand and furl with a furious, determined efficiency as blocks sang, yards racked around, sheets slatted, and sails thrashed as they spilled the wind from one side, swung, and took the wind from another angle.

Frost crossed to the larboard side of his quarterdeck to watch *Resolution* bear down on him. "Now is the time for your treachery," Frost said to himself, stiffening his shoulders. "Your starboard cannons can bear on my stern and you can rake me before I can gybe around." He waited for the broadside, anxiously studying the starboard bulwarks of the *Resolution* for the tell-tale wisp of blue smoke from a smoldering match. The broadside did not come, and Frost permitted his shoulders to relax slightly.

*Resolution* was rapidly closing the distance between the two vessels; close enough now that Frost could identify the man on *Resolution*'s quarterdeck staring fixedly at him through a telescope. No doubt about it, though he had spoken to the man, a fellow ship's captain, only three times and never for more than five minutes at any one meeting while in Batavia six years before: there was no mistaking the haughty thrust of James Cook's jaw or his aquiline nose.

But they were not the jaw and nose of an aristocrat. Frost had several times heard the tale of the pre-eminent master and navigator of the age. Mate of a Whitby collier, without family, friends or influence, who had enlisted voluntarily in the Royal Navy in 1755, when Frost was a mere five years old, and through dint of quiet professional abilities and a thorough knowledge of navigation had been selected by the Sea Lords to command the homely collier launched as the *Earl of Pembroke*, then re-named *Endeavour* when purchased as a king's ship. The *Endeavour*, under the auspices of the Royal Society, sailed off to the Great South Sea to observe the transit of the planet Venus.

Frost had examined the *Endeavour* while she was in the dockyard at Batavia and had talked to several crewmen who described their tribulations on the reefs lying to the north of New Holland. So workworn had the *Endeavour* seemed in the dockyard that Frost had been amazed the vessel had managed to fetch Batavia. *Endeavour* could not have done so without a commander who knew both ship and crew well, both of which obeyed him without question.

But what of that haughty thrust of jaw, the stamp of command broad on Cook's brow. No patrician, this Cook, certainly nothing in common with Hugh Stuart, who had commanded His Majesty's sloop-o-war *Jaguar*. Frost wondered if this was how his men regarded him, the same thrust of jaw, the unquestioning assumption that his commands would be obeyed—he shook his head to clear it of everything but the angles of approach and speeds he was mentally calculating.

Then the two vessels were within hailing distance. "What ship?" James Cook, post captain in command of the King's ship *Resolution*, on his third voyage of discovery, demanded through his speaking trumpet.

Frost ignored the hail and brought his own speaking trumpet to his mouth. "Good morning, Captain James Cook of the Royal Navy vessel *Resolution*," he shouted lightheartedly, "I am returning two of your crew who departed without your leave or benison."

"I see them," Cook replied testily. *Resolution* coasted to within fifty yards of the cat, *Resolution*'s sail trimmers whipping off canvas at the command of a dour-looking master who kept his back to Frost. Frost frowned and searched his memory, for Ledyard had told him the name of the master. Ah, he had the name now, Bligh, William Bligh, standing next to a man in a lieutenant's uniform whom Frost vaguely recognized: John Gore, another American serving with the Royal Navy. Frost could hear the plaintive low of cattle, the even more plaintive bleating of sheep, and the crowing of a cock. The rich barnyard smell wafting across the interval between the two ships was not unpleasant. Frost knew that the *Resolution*'s crew would be long habituated to the smell, so much so that they had absorbed it into memory and ceased to recognize it. Doubtlessly the aroma of the barnyard aroused nostalgia among those farmers in his own crew.

"How came you by them?"

"Fortune, or the Deity, as you wish, brought the chicken coop to which they were clinging, more dead than alive, within sight of this vessel, sir, and they were thus preserved to join you again."

"They were lost overside six days ago," Cook said, disbelief large in his voice.

"I am anxious to return them to you so we can both resume our careers," Frost replied. "Will you swing out a launch, or shall I?" Frost, having seen the condition of *Resolution*'s decks, had already passed the order for his gig to be clipped to the lifting tackle.

There was an embarrassed pause, as Frost knew there would be, and then Cook shouted into his speaking trumpet: "I would be obliged if you would be kind enough to sway over a launch, as I am ill prepared to do so."

"Happily," Frost shouted. "I trust you still favor sauerkraut as a scorbutic. Would you relish a tub of my New England–prepared sauerkraut? It be made in wooden tubs, not those clay and lead-fired pots favored by the Hanoverians, which give the cabbage a particularly unhealthy flavor."

"Indeed, sir! Its excellence as anti-scurvical is unchallenged; I've shipped as much sauerkraut as bully beef." Cook bristled, his disdain obvious across the gap between the two vessels, which now measured less than forty yards: "Cabbage stewed in lead glazed pots is much favored by our sovereign. What is a specific for our sovereign is certainly a specific for the crews of the sovereign's naval vessels."

"Perhaps so," Frost shot back cheerfully, "but I've remarked how, on long passages, the sauerkraut fermented in clay pots brings on a lethargy, while the sauerkraut fermented in wooden tubs maintains its excellence as an anti-scorbutus." He paused significantly: "And I've never had to flog a man to get him to eat it."

Cook abruptly changed the subject: "How many sick do you have?"

"None," Frost replied, quite truthfully.

"Good! The great thing in all naval service is health, and you will agree with me that it is easier for an officer to keep men healthy than for a physician to cure them."

Frost's gig splashed into the water, with Daniel O'Buck jumping to the stern sheets to fit the tiller. Colossus Bennington and a member of his gun crew, another freedman named Pompey, tumbled into the gig to seize oars, while a rejuvenated Omai and Ledyard, following a flurry of handshakes and back poundings from their temporary messmates and well-wishers, carefully made their way down the rungs. Ishmael

Hymsinger pushed his way through the mob and leaned down to hand something to Omai. His Indian flute. Frost recognized the bright jewel of a ladybug clinging to the flute's barrel. Omai saw the ladybug as well and reverently and protectively cupped a hand over it. Could this be the one ladybug aboard the cat? No. The cat was singularly gifted with luck. There had to be more than one ladybug aboard, so there was luck to spare. Omai smiled his thanks to Ishmael Hymsinger and acknowledged his gratitude to Frost with a profound bow.

"I mark you now," Cook shouted, "in Batavia six years ago, you were out of a John ship from China back to England."

"Yes," Frost replied, not bothering to correct Cook. It had not been a vessel of the Honorable East India Company, but his own dear *Salmon*. "Geoffrey Frost, of Portsmouth, in New Hampshire, at your service, Captain Cook."

"You have been of inestimable service to me, Captain Frost, in returning these men to my company. Still, I can scarce credit it. Six days and over two hundred leagues ago. Yet you spring from the ocean in my very path with two I had long given up for lost." The gig, lustily rowed by Colossus and Pompey, veered alongside the starboard entry of *Resolution*, the rowers clinging tightly to lines thrown down to them while Omai and Corporal Ledyard clambered up the slippery wood cleats. The crew of *Resolution*, crowded at the entry and perched in the ratlines, raised a loud spontaneous cheer, and then another, even louder. The crew of the cat responded in kind and waved hats and kerchiefs. George tore around the main deck in an exuberance of phrensy, barking joyously and bowling over several men. One of Caleb's woods-cruisers had seized the bell's clapper and was ringing it enthusiastically. Then the two men were aboard *Resolution* and absorbed into the throng of their welcoming mates. The gig pushed away and pulled for the cat.

"I humbly thank you, sir, in the name of our mutual God, for returning people of my ship whom I had given up for lost," Cook shouted into his speaking trumpet. "It was nobly done. I treasure both men's lives equally, but failure to return the

Prince Omai would have been a bitter blow to his family in Tahiti. You'll acknowledge, however, that having rebelled against your right lawful and generous sovereign, I cannot wish you success in your endeavors, save pray you come to your senses and petition return to the grace of your sovereign, a petition which you shall find quickly and honestly answered. I can, in good conscience, though, give you an accurate position mark."

"Fare you well, Mister Cook," Frost shouted back. "I regret extremely the necessities that brought my countrymen to rebellion." He lifted his hand in farewell. "Hopefully the position you are keeping indicates west twenty-five degrees and nineteen minutes, north fifteen degrees and forty-five minutes. Again, sir, fare you well in the Southern Ocean—and Godspeed."

Cook's expression could not disguise his surprise: "Indeed, sir, that compares favorably with my computations. But I ask again, what ship? Particularly, what copper-bottomed ship, which is strictly a convention of the Royal Navy?" Frost only waved and turned away to confront the earnest faces of Darius Langdon and Nathaniel Dance.

"Please, sir," both youths said in unison, "we have a name for our cat—please let us tell it."

Frost hesitated, then smiled: "Very well, but be quick with it." He glanced to his left; topmen on *Resolution* were already loosening and unhanding canvas.

Both boys smiled their delight and immediately jumped into the larboard mizzen shrouds. "Omai, Corporal Ledyard, Captain Cook, sirs!" they shrilled.

James Cook turned away from a discussion with *Resolution*'s master and first lieutenant. Cook started to raise his speaking trumpet to his mouth.

"Sirs! We be *Audacity*, private man-o-war out of Portsmouth, in New Hampshire!" Darius and Nathaniel shouted as loudly as they could at the tops of their young voices.

"Godspeed to you, then, *Audacity*!" James Cook shouted into his speaking trumpet and lifted his hand in farewell. Both boys, legs tucked securely in ratlines, waved delightedly with both hands, long after Cook had turned away.

"A good name," Frost thought to himself. "The lads doubtlessly have shopped the name around with others, so shall it be." He quietly suggested to Jack Lacey the necessary commands that would bring the private New Hampshire chartered man-o-war *Audacity* back into the wind for the long slog upwind to the Açores. *Resolution* was unfurling all plain sail and, yes, setting studding sails and staysails.

Then from across the water separating *Resolution* and *Audacity* came the boom of a single cannon. Startled, Frost sought frantically for the splash of shot, anxiously surveying the gun crews on his main deck—where did slow match still smolder, which cannons were ready to fire? By the Great Buddha, what treachery—then he broke off, aware that the gun had been a salute. Three minutes later the gun boomed again. Frost smiled, it had taken Cook long enough to clear even one cannon. "Is he recognizing our colors?" he asked himself, looking upward toward the tattered and ripped rattlesnake flag that Jack Lacey had again raised to the weather main topsail yard.

*Audacity* lay over on a starboard tack and a long reach to fetch the Açores, and the distance between the two vessels rapidly increased. *Resolution*'s cannon boomed every two minutes or so; as a salute there was no need to load shot, so the firing, even with a crew as green as Cook had to have, could manage to thrust home and fire a charge of powder every two minutes. All of *Audacity*'s sails were drawing now, yards properly trimmed to catch the wind from the north, pointing as high into the wind as she could. Well over half a league separated the two vessels, and now the distance was too great to hear a single gun.

Geoffrey Frost paced to the stern of his vessel, looking south toward the rapidly disappearing sails of Cook's *Resolution*. A cold, wet nose—George Three—thrust into his left palm. Frost patted the Newfoundland's head absently. He thought he had counted nine cannon reports, but the distance between *Resolution* and *Audacity* was now so great that he could not be sure.

"It would be foreign to the man's character to do so," Frost thought to himself, as he ran his fingers through George's fur. "Probably seeing us off with a promise that next time he'll greet us with shot and langrage." But all the same, he was obscurely pleased. He signaled O'Buck to dip the rattlesnake ensign and resolved to note the salute in *Audacity*'s log.

# HISTORICAL NOTE

It is frequently forgotten that the War for American Independence was a naval war. The Royal Navy was essential for the transporting and provisioning of all British forces in North America, as well as providing all communications between its military commanders and the government in London. The North American Station never received the warships necessary for an effective blockade of American ports, but the Royal Navy's supremacy at sea during the years 1775–1783 was never seriously in dispute, even after Bourbon France and Spain declared war against Britain in 1778. From the rebels' perspective, a few captains, such as Barry, Manley, McNeill, Tucker and of course the redoubtable J. P. Jones, won impressive tactical victories, but the Continental Navy never possessed sufficient warships or enough daring commanders to influence the war's outcome. The Continental Navy was unable to recruit sufficient able-bodied seamen—most eligible seamen, seventy thousand of them, preferred the greater financial rewards of serving in privateers.

The Continental Congress, the states, and an occasional American agent overseas issued over 2,000 commissions or letters of marque to private men-of-war. American privateers took as prizes more than 2,500 British vessels. While never threatening Britain's naval superiority, the privateers' depredations of commerce (greatly increasing war insurance rates), disruptions of communications, and vital supplying of the Continental Army with provisions, arms and munitions—exactly as Geoffrey Frost foresaw—were indispensable to American Independence.

Because of the Royal Navy's brutal recruiting and disciplinary methods, Frost held a rather low opinion of the service's officers and was not surprised by Lieutenant St. John Lithgow's cavalier violation of his parole. But the honesty and courage of HM *Lark*'s Captain Richard Smith, coupled with what he learned about Hugh Stuart, master and commander of HM *Jaguar*, from Nathaniel Dance, caused Frost to reassess his opinion about the decency of many Royal Navy officers.

Another American who shared Frost's high opinion of Richard Smith was Ethan Allen, celebrated (Benedict Arnold's assistance conveniently forgotten) as the conqueror of Fort Ticonderoga, who as a result of a woefully inept attack on Montreal was aboard HM *Lark* as a prisoner for several weeks. Early in the rebellion, Allen was probably the best-known

American prisoner hustled off to England, a circumstance given voice in the long train of abuses and usurpations enumerated in our Declaration of Independence: "For transporting us beyond seas to be tried for pretended offences . . ." A humane Smith treated Allen with dignity, giving him the freedom of the ship and even inviting Allen to join in the poor fare his table could muster. When other American prisoners conspired to take over the *Lark*, killing or disposing of Smith and his officers—and seizing the £30,000 (some reports indicated the actual sum was £100,000) payroll *Lark* conveyed—Allen would have no part of the plot. He even vowed to protect Smith's life at the expense of his own!

The outcome of wars frequently turn on seemingly inconsequential, unheralded and perhaps illogical events. The rifle so brilliantly conceived by Struan Ferguson's cousin Patrick, a British Army officer, could easily have been the thumb on the scale. However, the first full complement of 100 rifles capable of being reloaded with far greater rapidity and affording accurate and sustained rates of fire far in excess of any firearm of the period did not reach North America until May of 1777.

Legend has it that prior to the 11 September 1777 Battle of the Brandywine, Ferguson glimpsed Washington over the sights of his rifle but refused to shoot because his personal code of honor forbade shooting an unarmed opponent whose back was turned. The account is apocryphal, but it indisputable that Washington and Ferguson were both on the Brandywine battlefield. Washington's early death would have been such a staggering blow to American arms that its consequences are impossible to calculate at this remove of two and a quarter centuries.

Would a small corps of British Army sharpshooters effectively trained in the employment of this fearsome arm have wrought a different outcome in our efforts to establish a republican form of government? Would the introduction of Ferguson rifles and a change in British Army tactics a year earlier have made a difference? Thankfully, those events were forestalled by Frost's July 1776 interception of the East Indiamen freighting such deadly cargo.

And then there was James Cook, who departed Plymouth, England, on 12 July 1776 in command of HM *Resolution* on his third voyage of discovery. Cook was the most formidable navigator of the age, but by deducing the winds and currents—as well as Cook's sailing strategy—Frost's interception of the *Resolution* off the Cape Verde Islands in early September 1776 demonstrated his seamanship was every bit the equal of Cook's.

Frost always considered Corporal John Ledyard, from a prominent family that gave its name to a southern Connecticut town and who printed an account of some improbable tales about his service with Cook following Cook's death in the Sandwich Islands, as an embroiderer of the truth. Frost believed, based upon Omai's pantomime, that it was Ledyard who had been swept off the decks of *Resolution* by the hurricane and Omai who had gone overboard to rescue him. Certainly Corporal Ledyard's account made no mention of his harrowing two days afloat on a hencoop.